HEAVEN'S
NEEDLE

HEAVEN'S NEEDLE

A Novel of Ithelas

LIANE MERCIEL

POCKET STAR BOOKS

New York   London   Toronto   Sydney

Pocket Star Books
A Division of Simon & Schuster, Inc.
1230 Avenue of the Americas
New York, NY 10020

First Pocket Star Books paperback edition May 2011

POCKET STAR BOOKS and colophon are registered trademarks of Simon & Schuster, Inc.

For information about special discounts for bulk purchases, please contact Simon & Schuster Special Sales at 1-866-506-1949 or business@simonandschuster.com.

The Simon & Schuster Speakers Bureau can bring authors to your live event. For more information or to book an event contact the Simon & Schuster Speakers Bureau at 1-866-248-3049 or visit our website at www.simonspeakers.com.

Manufactured in the United States of America

10   9   8   7   6   5   4   3   2   1

Library of Congress Cataloging-in-Publication Data is available.

ISBN 978-1-4391-5913-2
ISBN 978-1-4391-7069-4 (ebook)

This one's for Nathan, who first told me how to fix it, and Peter, who walked the dog while I did the fixing.

PROLOGUE

SUMMER 1217

The stench of river mud was suffocating. River mud and coal smoke: the twin perfumes of Carden Vale. Corban clapped his sleeve over his nose and breathed shallowly through his mouth as he edged away from the waterside and down a crooked alley, following close on his guide's heels. The cloth did little to filter the smell, but that wasn't the point; the purpose of the gesture was not to relieve Corban's nose, but to hide his face. Few knew him here, but there was no call to be careless.

Centuries past, this had been a proud town. The Baozites who'd built the fortress overshadowing Carden Vale had needed a river port to service the barges that carried grain from the farmlands and brought back coal and iron from the mountains. They had designed one unrivaled in its age. Under Ang'duradh's rule, caravans had climbed the high passes and braved the terrors of Spearbridge to buy rare herbs and furs from Carden Vale. Gull-prowed ships and flat-bottomed barges had crowded the sleek white wharves.

That grandeur was long gone. The fortress stood empty, its cavernous halls filled with dust and silence. The port below it had shrunk to a handful of creaking barges that lumbered through the silt-clogged wharves like dying beasts. Mud piled up between the piers, reeking of the town's refuse.

He should have sewn a satchet in his sleeve. The stench was worst at this time of year, after a long summer's stew, and there was no relief in sight. If Gethel had truly done as he'd promised, there would be worse smells before the day's work was done.

The stooped man in front of him seemed oblivious to the filthy-smelling streets. The hem of his robe dragged through a puddle of mud and drunkard's vomit, but he never glanced down. It took more than merely human foul-nesses to disturb Gethel these days. The man didn't look well, and it had Corban worried. Human eyes shouldn't stare so blindly; human voices shouldn't sound so dull. Mountain air would do him a world of good, or perhaps a trip east to take the waters at Dragonsblood Spring. A leave to rest.

But not until the work was done. Not until then.

"How much farther?" Corban muttered as Gethel led him down yet another stinking alley. He thought his eyes might actually be watering. A fat, evil-looking rat stared at him from the shadows, its whiskers twitching, and then scurried into the cracked daub at the base of a nearby wall.

"Only in here." Gethel stooped by the door of the house where the rat had gone. No lock or bar secured its weather-warped planks.

Spreading his hands across the dry gray wood, Gethel pushed inward, mumbling slurred syllables that Corban supposed were meant to sound like magic. A blue spark jumped from his fingertips and sizzled as it struck the wood. It might have been impressive if Corban hadn't spotted the man pinching smokepowder from a sleeve pouch as he bent to the door.

Gethel had no real magic. None of the self-proclaimed wizards of the Fourfold House did. What they had were tricks and illusions: smokepowder, sleight of hand, a bit of alchemy. Real magic, of the sort that Celestia's Blessed or the Thorns of Ang'arta commanded, was far beyond such pretenders.

But even a pretender could stumble upon power, and might be mad enough to seize it when a sensible man would have stepped back. Gethel, blinded by his belief that magic could be mastered without bowing to the gods, didn't have the wisdom to be wary. He had no idea what he'd found.

Corban had no such delusions. *He* knew what it was. In part, at least. And he knew, too, that there was no reason to share the truth with Gethel. Let the man believe what he wanted. It kept him working.

Gathering his cloak, Corban bowed his head to the low-hanging lintel and followed Gethel into the darkness beyond. A stink of stale urine intensified and then receded as he passed the threshold. There were no windows. Once the door closed behind him, Corban could see nothing but the lines of its planks against weak gray light. He could hear Gethel ahead, moving with the ease of a cat in the dark, and faint whimpers from somewhere past that, but he could see neither man nor moaner.

"Give me a light," Corban rasped, and then stopped, surprised by the tension he heard in his own voice. He wasn't *afraid*. Not of poor half-mad Gethel, the failed wizard who couldn't pinch smokepowder without getting caught. Not of him.

But of what he had found, what he had made . . . that, if Gethel had truly managed to awaken its power, was something a wiseman would not want to stumble upon in the dark.

Another spark jumped in the gloom. This time it landed on the wick of a misshapen candle in a stained clay dish. A rancid smell drifted from the candle as it burned, reminiscent of soured lard. Corban wrinkled his nose. That wasn't bad tallow; that was a dead man's candle, rendered from the fat of a hanged criminal. Idiots playing at necromancy used them, claiming that their light revealed truths hidden from the sun.

"Are you ready?" Gethel asked, lifting the candle. Under its smoky glow he seemed more demon than human. Gethel had never been plump, but the wizard had become positively cadaverous since the last time Corban had seen him. His skin sagged loose over bone; shadows seamed his face, and his eyes shone unnaturally bright in their sockets. Most of his hair had fallen out, and what was left straggled to his shoulders in colorless clumps. He looked like a walking corpse—and yet in this place, by the light of that candle, there was a coiled vitality to him that made Corban almost afraid.

Obsession. That was the look Gethel had: of a man in the throes of obsession, readying to return to the mistress who had consumed his soul.

"I'm ready," Corban said, clearing the tightness from his throat.

"This way." The candle bobbed in his hand as the gaunt man led him to the back of the hovel. There were two rooms inside, the second smaller than the first and separated from it by a curtain of stained sackcloth. The floor ended abruptly at that curtain; Corban stumbled as his foot tried to find purchase on air. Gethel had excavated the second room so that its floor was a full arm's length lower than the hard-packed dirt on the other side. Moisture seeped down, leaving wet scars in the walls.

"I needed to keep the smoke from escaping," Gethel said, evidently as explanation, although he never glanced back.

Corban looked up. There was no smoke hole, no chimney. No hearth, either, in the glimpses of wall that the candle gave him. "Smoke rises."

"Blackfire smoke sinks." And, indeed, it seemed that a gritty black glitter clung to the dirt, like a residue of sea foam left on the strand. Corban had little time to puzzle over that, though, for Gethel had reached the hovel's far corner and his light fell on the face of a whimpering man who crouched there.

The man was a beggar. That much was plain from his tattered breeches and sparse, grimy beard. Even under candlelight, his nose was red and webbed with broken veins. A drunk, and likely feebleminded; there was no sense to his moanings, and he clutched his head in trembling hands, as if trying to hold his thoughts together. His face seemed vaguely familiar, but Corban could not place it. Likely he just resembled some other beggar; poverty crushed all of them into the same miserable mold.

Corban's lip curled in disdain. "*This* is your great success? You told me you'd unlocked the secrets of blackfire, found a way to harness its power at last—and you show me a wretched old drunk?"

"What? Oh. No." Gethel set his candle down on a nearby crate and fished through its straw, heedless of how easily it might catch fire. "I've done as I promised. Belbas here is simply going to help me prove it."

"Belbas? *Apprentice* Belbas? Your sworn servant?"

The beggar groaned weakly, as if Corban's words stirred some fragment of memory from the dark mire of his thoughts, but if that truly was his name, he did not answer to it. Gethel shrugged without lifting his head from the crate. "Oaths mean so little in this day and age. He was going to betray me. But now . . . now he will be a help. Yes."

"What have you done?" Corban breathed. He'd met Gethel's apprentice only a few times, but he knew the boy was bound to secrecy in exchange for being taught the master's magic. The details of the Fourfold House's workings were fuzzy to Corban, who had never set foot in that eccentric world and had no reason to learn its rules. The wizards hadn't any power beyond rites and oaths and other mystical trappings meant to fool the gullible into believing that they had secrets worth protecting. But the members of the Fourfold House believed their own foolishness wholeheartedly, and Corban could not shake the feeling that he stood witness to a betrayal greater than he could comprehend.

Perhaps he imagined things. Belbas had been a young man, while the wretch before him was old enough to be his grandfather. Inconceivable that they could be one and the same. Yet as Corban looked harder, he could see the remains of that proud youth in the beggar's dissipation. The flesh was sagging or swollen, the mind broken behind those unseeing eyes, but the bones were the same.

Puckered gaps ran down the boy's neck where his ceremonial tattoos had been carved out. His wounded flesh was pale and bloodless as chopped salt pork; the man who wore them might already have been so much meat, though he still drew breath.

Impossible. But there it was, sprawled before his feet.

Gethel straightened from the crate, holding a small crossbow and a pair of quarrels. The weapon glistened with packing grease; flecks of straw clung to the oiled wood and metal. Gethel loaded the weapon and hooked the strap around his foot, grunting as he tugged the crossbow upward. The trigger fell into place with a click, and Gethel offered the spare quarrel to Corban as he mopped the sheen from his brow.

Though the crossbow seemed smaller and lighter than most of its type—at least in Corban's inexpert judgment— the quarrel was heavy and oddly balanced. Its head was swollen big as a cherry; he couldn't see how it was meant to fly. Although the quarrel ended in a sharp iron point, the rest of its tip was filigreed like jewelry. A pebble of gritty black sand glittered between the metal strands. *Blackfire.*

Corban held a fortune between two fingers . . . if the crazed charlatan was right. He reined in his rising excitement. He hadn't seen it work.

"As I promised," Gethel said. "You hold the proof in your hands."

"It seems an ungainly design." Corban turned the quarrel over and handed it back. He wiped the packing grease off on his cloak. "Does it fly? It surely can't bite very deep when it hits."

"It has no need to strike deep. It suffices to draw blood; the magic does the rest. Watch." Gethel took the candle's dish from the crate and set it down beside his strangely aged apprentice. A hunched creature scuttled away as the light approached: the rat from the alley. Belbas' hand was peppered with raw pink spots where it had gnawed at his unbleeding flesh. Yet the apprentice had never pulled back, never flinched; he seemed as insensible to that as he was to the rest of the world.

Gethel retreated from the candle, beckoning Corban to join him. He pulled back the sackcloth curtain and hoisted himself onto higher ground. "Best to be out of the smoke."

"Why?" Corban asked, following. "What happens?"

"Madness." Gethel leveled the crossbow across the room, sighting it toward the candle and then up. His hands were steadier than Corban would have believed possible; the weight of the weapon didn't seem to strain his bony arms at all.

There was no light beside them, and Corban couldn't see the gaunt man's expression. The end of the crossbow stood against the distant candle, though, and he saw where it aimed.

He folded his arms and said nothing. It wasn't his place. If the boy thought to betray their work, then this was for the best. And if not . . . it was still safer to be sure. Corban had invested far too much to risk a word breathed into the wrong ear.

Besides, he was curious.

The crossbow twanged. Its bolt took Belbas in the gut. The boy made no attempt to avoid it, and didn't cry as he was struck. He only sighed, almost gently, and folded forward with his chin slumped to his chest. As Corban had expected, the quarrel's clumsy design kept it from piercing deeply. Even at this short range, it hadn't sunk more than half its length into Belbas' stomach.

"Is that all?"

Gethel held up a finger. "Wait."

Perplexed, Corban looked back at the apprentice. Belbas drew two breaths, the second weaker than the first, as a dark wet stain spread through his rags.

On the third breath he exploded.

Fragments of gristle and bone spattered the walls as his

rib cage tore itself apart. Hot blood, speckled with stinging grit, sprayed across Corban's face; he squeezed his eyes shut so it wouldn't blind him. When he opened them again, the wreckage of Belbas' corpse was thrown back in the corner, shrouded by foul-looking black smoke. Gore streaked the walls and dripped from the curtain, yet somehow the candle burned in its dish with barely a flicker to its flame. Its light was murky, but there was no doubting its steadiness amidst the devastation of what had once been a man.

Corban stared at the wreckage in disbelief. The possibilities dazed him more than the blast had. The *force* of it . . . no armor could withstand that. No man could survive it. And that had been a pebble no larger than his thumbnail. What might a larger chunk do?

What would a king pay to possess it? Gold? Land? Was there *any* limit to what he might ask? This was, at last, a weapon that ordinary rulers could use to hold back the Thorns of Ang'arta. Magic at their fingertips, with no need to rely on Blessed . . . and then, as others saw its power and were frightened, they, too, would come to him to beg their own arsenals. At any price.

He'd never dared dream, when he'd first found Gethel laboring in obscurity and had given the man a handful of silver to pursue his obsessions, that the prize would be so rich. Never. But now, it seemed, the world might lie open before him.

If he played his hand well.

"Blackfire stone wreaks great destruction upon our mortal flesh, yet it scarcely seems to touch anything else," Gethel murmured, sounding almost mournful. He hopped down from the earthen bank and waded into the smoke that pooled around the body. "Its properties are . . . peculiar. I have hardly begun cataloging them."

"I thought you said the smoke was to be avoided."

"It is," Gethel said, but he offered no further explanation. He stooped into the haze to retrieve the candle. Corban imagined that the smoke drifted up to greet the gaunt man as he knelt; he fancied that tendrils of it curled into Gethel's colorless hair, like the fingers of a lady drawing her lover down for a kiss.

A whiff of the smoke drifted toward him. It stank of sulfur and carrion, of dead things rotting in dark places. And yet . . . there was something almost recognizable within it, something that called to an old, dim memory. He breathed deeper, trying to place it, reaching for remembrance. It seemed important, somehow—but it was gone.

Corban shook his head and wiped the blood from his face, taking care to use the inside of his cloak so it wouldn't show when he walked away. The reality of what he had seen was astonishing enough. No need to complicate it with figments of fancy.

"How many of these quarrels can you make?"

"The miners have struck a rich lode. There's no telling how much they might bring out. But my shapers . . . my shapers have become quite exhausted. If I had more of them, I should be able to work faster." Smoke swirled around Gethel's robes as he came back to the edge of the room. Corban stepped back, holding his breath.

He had nothing to fear from it, though. The smoke was the smell of triumph, of wealth coming to him after a lifetime's waiting.

Corban let it fill his lungs. "What are their limitations?"

"The shapers'?"

"The quarrels'."

Gethel shrugged, setting his candle on the higher ground before clambering up to join it. Smoke roiled and fell from his clothing like water sliding off a swimmer's back. "I cannot yet say. The work is still very new; what you have seen today is only an early attempt. It wants perfecting. But it will be devastating when we are done. You have seen the power that lies within a tiny pebble. We have much more. Wet it with blood, and the fury of blackfire stone knows no limits."

"I'm glad to hear it. What do you need for shapers?"

"Small hands. Small hands are better for making the pebbles and placing them so deftly." Gethel tapped the unused quarrel's filigree tip. "Big hands cannot do such delicate work."

"You'll have them. What else?"

"Time. Only time."

"Time." Corban sucked the word through his teeth, along with a black skein of smoke. It wasn't rank at all, really. It was perfectly sweet. "Give me what you have, and I will get you time."

1

Night was falling under Heaven's Needle.

Bitharn rested her elbows on the windowsill and watched the world darken below. She stood near the pinnacle of the crystalline tower. Far beneath her, to the south, she could see the green hills and high walls of Cailan, and past that the rippling gleam of the sea. Above her was nothing but glass and sky.

The tower was a thing of beauty, rising from deep rose and violet at its base to swirl upward through honey and amber, lightening steadily until it reached the white brilliance of pure sunlight at its tip. Save for the sunburst that crowned it, Heaven's Needle was perfectly smooth, translucent as cloudlight through water. No human hands had built such glory; Celestia's Blessed had called it into being with their spells, weaving magic strong enough to turn sunlight to stone. The tower was older than Cailan, older than the kingdom of Calantyr, but younger by far than its purpose.

Heaven's Needle was a prison.

Not, of course, for ordinary prisoners. There were no thieves or murderers in the tower; the dungeons of Whitestone sufficed for those. Heaven's Needle was reserved for enemies of the faith, those too dangerous to be held by chains, too risky for the executioner's block. A few were souls that the Blessed thought not wholly beyond salvation, but most prisoners in the tower were there because they held secrets the Celestians needed, because they were politically sensitive, or—most rarely—because their bodies were such vessels of corrupt power that killing them would release the foulness held trapped in their flesh.

Bitharn hoped that the man she needed was one of the first group. She didn't want to think about what might happen if he were one of the last.

A candle burned on the sill before her, smelling of sweet spices: cinnamon and cloves, angel's kiss and nutmeg. As twilight claimed the towns and villages, she saw tiny buds of light blossom across the earth, echoing the faraway glow of her candle. For a short while they shimmered in the dusk, like will-o'-the-wisps glimpsed in blue fog, and then the night came in earnest and Bitharn could see nothing in the shadowed glass except the reflection of her own candle's flame, floating anchorless in the dark.

Across the room Versiel was watching her, though he made some pretense of reading the book in his lap. Concern creased his careworn face. Versiel had never looked young, even when he'd been a fuzz-cheeked boy of sixteen, and life had written a palimpsest of worry on his brow in the decade and a half since.

He'd have more lines before dawn.

Bitharn regretted that, but there was no way around it. *One of mine for one of yours,* the Spider had said, and Bitharn had taken that bargain.

The memory of that meeting was branded on her soul. It was a moonless night, far colder than this one, with the dregs of winter brittle in the air. She'd spent months scouring the underbellies of every city from Craghail to Cailan to find someone who could take her words to the Spider. Then she'd waited, terrified, to see what answer might come.

It was a summons. To Aluvair, city of towers, capital of Calantyr. Her homeland, as much as she'd ever had one. Long past midnight Bitharn sat alone on a marble bench outside the Temple of Silences, watching moonlight dance across the frost on the reflecting pool and trying to keep her legs from freezing on the chill stone. She'd begun to think the Spider wouldn't come at all. Then, between one breath and the next, the woman was *there,* wrapped in a fur softer and blacker than the starless sky. She'd stepped out of shadow without a sound, and her eyes had been infinitely dark, infinitely cold. The memory still made Bitharn shiver.

"One of mine for one of yours," the Spider said. "You have one of my students in Heaven's Needle. Bring him to Carden Vale on the second full moon after Greenseed, and you will have your knight returned."

"Unhurt." It was the only word Bitharn had been able to force past her frozen lips.

The corners of the Spider's lips curled very slightly at that. "Of course."

Three times the moon had circled and fallen since that midnight meeting. A little less than a month was left . . . but tonight she stood in Heaven's Needle, and before dawn she'd have the Thornlord free.

"Are you well?"

"Of course," Bitharn answered, forcing a smile as she

turned from the window. She willed her face not to betray her, even as the concern in Versiel's question cut to the bone. He was one of her oldest friends.

But he was also Keeper of the Keys for Heaven's Needle, and tonight one of those things had to outweigh the other. Bitharn had made her choice before she'd come. Love locked her on this path, even if she didn't dare utter that word. If the only way to secure Kelland's freedom was by betraying her friends, her beliefs, and the faith that had raised her since she was an orphaned cloister child wailing on the temple steps . . . then her only question was how to do it well.

That much, she thought she knew.

"Are you certain you wish to do this?" Versiel asked, fidgeting with the ring of keys on his belt. "Kelland was a good man, one of our best, but—"

"*Is.* He isn't dead."

He hesitated, then shrugged too quickly. "Is. Still. What do you hope to learn from the Thornlord? We captured him before Kelland was taken; how could he know anything about the Thorns' plans? And even if, by some strange grace of the goddess, he did . . . what good would it do to hear that Kelland's being tortured in Ang'arta?"

"None," Bitharn admitted. "But I have to know that. I have to ask."

"We aren't supposed to let anyone up there. Especially not armed," he added with a significant glance at the yew bow that crossed her back and the long knife at her belt. Half a dozen smaller knives, balanced for throwing, were secreted about her person. Both of them knew that Bitharn had seldom gone unarmed before Kelland was captured, and never afterward.

"Well, it's a good thing I'm not *anyone*, isn't it?" she

said, raising her eyebrows with feigned asperity. "I only want to ask him a few questions, Versiel. Please. Kelland was your friend as much as mine, and if there's anything this prisoner can tell us that might help—"

"I just don't want to see you hurt. Thorns delight in twisting words, you know that. Anything he tells you will be half true at best, and he's like to tell you awful things just to cause you pain."

"Not knowing is worse."

He sighed and separated a slim golden key from the ring, holding it out without looking. "Be quick. My sanity will return at any moment."

"Thank you," she whispered, pressing the cold metal into her palm. "Where is he?"

"The Seventh Ring. Northeast cell."

"Anyone else up there? Anyone who might hear?"

"Only the other prisoners." Versiel hesitated again as she took the key, and clasped his other hand over hers. "You don't have to do this."

"I do." Bitharn pulled away. She went back to the candle on the windowsill, bowing her head over the flame as if gathering her resolve. Dropping her hand to the dagger belted at her hip, Bitharn picked at the silver wirework and pearls that adorned the hilt. As a girl she'd been a fidgeter, and she hoped Versiel thought she'd kept the habit. *Bright Lady, let him think I'm only nervous about confronting the Thorn.* If he guessed her true purpose, she was lost.

Two of the pearls came loose in her fingers. Immediately Bitharn flattened her hand to trap them and pretended to fidget with her necklace instead. Shielding the small movement with her body, she dropped one of the pearls into the well of molten wax around the candle's flame.

As the pearl sank into the hot wax it became translucent

and collapsed into liquid. The "pearl" was a ball of *irhare* sap, rolled in tailor's chalk and cooled to temporary hardness, then affixed to her knife with a drop of pine gum. An apothecary in a dusty shop tucked into a shabby corner of Cailan had made it for her. Bitharn suspected the harelipped young man did most of his trade with assassins, but she hadn't asked, any more than he had asked why she wanted a dram of *irhare* sap disguised as pearls.

In moments the sap would boil off under the flame, releasing a powerful soporific into the air. The candle's scent would disguise its odor. If all went well, Versiel wouldn't suspect a thing until it was too late.

Bitharn paced around the room, fidgeting with her dagger, until she'd made a circuit of the candles and dropped a poisoned pearl into each one. Then she paused by the doorway, drew a breath to steel her nerves, and waved farewell to the friend she'd just begun to drug.

"Wish me luck," she said, and slipped out.

The tower stairs were cool and silent. There were no torches; the glass walls of Heaven's Needle radiated their own golden glow, an echo of sunlight from the day past. Bitharn's footfalls resonated hollowly around her as she went up the spiral stairs. With each step the aura of holiness in the air grew stronger. She was not Blessed, and had no magic of her own, but even she could feel the tingling presence of the divine as she neared the tower's peak. It filled her with both glory and dread, and she wondered whether Celestia would smite her for what was in her soul. Surely, *surely*, the Bright Lady had to know her intentions.

No smiting came. After three turns around the tower, Bitharn reached the rune-enscribed arch that led to the Seventh Ring. Like all the entrances in the tower's high reaches, this one had no door. Instead its finely carved marble held a curtain of gossamer light, shimmering through a thousand shifting shades of gold and white.

If an enemy of the faith tried to pass through that gate, the fires of the sun would boil the blood in his veins and char his bones to crumbling sticks of ash. Should the prisoners on the other side ever manage to escape their cells, they would get no farther than that delicate web of light—unless they intended to flee this life altogether.

Only a soul anointed to the sun could pass through Celestia's portals safely. And only such a one could ensure safe passage for sinners, and then only for good cause. The unworthy came to swift and fiery ends.

Bitharn drew up the chain that held her sun medallion, pulling the emblem out of her shirt and laying it across her breast. The pendant felt impossibly heavy for such a tiny piece of gold; it weighed on her chest like a millstone. She laced her fingers behind her back to hide their trembling, though there was no one but herself to see it.

She stood squarely before the arch as she had been taught, less than an arm's length from the light. This close she could feel its heat and see it rippling before her like the air over a baker's oven in midwinter.

Swallowing around the dryness in her throat, Bitharn lifted her chin and recited the words for passage. "Celestia, Bright Lady, grant me your blessing that I might walk through fire and into the light of your truth." And then, softly, she added her own: "Please. I know what I do here is wrong—but it is a small wrong, for a greater right, and I know that you must see it. Please, bright goddess, if you have any love for your mortal children, let me pass through and bring Kelland back."

She stepped into the portal, eyes open.

It felt like something from a dream, like falling from

an infinite height without any sense of being trapped in a body. Like being a sunray, surrounded by warmth and light, woven into it and inseparable from it. There was heat all around her, but it seemed to be part of her own flesh and it did not burn.

Then she was through, and back in the world she knew. It seemed impossibly cold and dim. She stood inside the Seventh Ring, the sun portal a shimmer of gold at her back. The cells opened around her like the glass petals of a jeweler's flower, the tower stairs coiled at their core.

A compass rose was traced in gilt on the floor. Bitharn followed its rays to the northeast cell. Its bars, like those of all the cells on this level, spiraled out from the center in a sunburst. The bars appeared to be made of glass, and were transparent but for a slim strand of gold in the center of each one. The thickest was no wider than her wrist. Bitharn couldn't see how they could imprison a child, but as she approached, she felt a low thrum vibrate through the bars and saw a tall figure rise from the cell's depths to meet her.

Malentir. The Spider's student. Bitharn had never laid eyes on the man, but she knew his name and his crimes. Two of Celestia's dedicants, and one of the Blessed, had died to capture him in a tiny village north of Aluvair last fall. It had been a brutal battle, cruelly fought and hard won. Thorns were hard to kill, and harder to capture. Malentir was the only one the Celestians had ever taken alive.

And she was going to set him free.

"A visitor," he said as he came to the bars. His voice was cultivated, melodious; it carried a soft eastern accent. "To what do I owe the pleasure?"

Bitharn studied him carefully before answering. Captivity had not been kind to the Thornlord. He was handsome, in a fey, cruel fashion, but after half a year in the tower his features were haggard and wan. Dark circles shadowed his eyes, and his robes were threadbare at sleeve and hem. A collar of glass, clear as the bars, with the same thread of gold at its center, ringed his throat. That collar crippled his magic; it kept him safe, kept him harmless. Yet he carried himself with such hauteur that he might have been a king, and she a supplicant before his throne.

She gritted her teeth. "My name is Bitharn. I'm here to take you out."

"Ah." He gave her a faint, condescending smile, as if she'd announced that she'd come to clean the chamber pot, and adjusted one tattered sleeve. The cloth was slashed with ivory and black, matching his varicolored hair. She caught a glimpse of pale, pocked scars ringing his wrist. "By whose authority, might I inquire? Ordinarily there are more guards in my escort, you see. I should hate to think that my hosts had stopped caring."

"No one's. This is an escape."

"An escape," he repeated, and Bitharn thought she saw something flash in the Thornlord's cool black eyes.

"That's what I said. Are you coming?"

"That depends. What is your plan? I have not much interest in being recaptured. There are quite a few sun-blinded fanatics who would prefer to see me dead rather than imprisoned, and I have even less interest in giving them a chance to correct that."

"The Keeper's been drugged. He has spare clothes in his quarters. We'll dress you as a solaros, you'll pull the hood low, and we'll leave while it's dark enough to keep you hidden. The guards outside the tower know me; they won't ask too many questions. They changed after sunset prayers, so the ones who saw me go in won't know that

I came alone. I have horses waiting at an inn not half a league away."

He cocked his head to one side, considering. Then he shook it. "No."

Bitharn felt as if she had been punched. "What?"

"Oh, it's a pretty story. It might even be true. But I am not inclined to gamble my life on uncertainties, and I have no assurance that what waits for me outside is a horse rather than an arrow. Escaping prisoners do tend to end badly . . . and predictably. No, I believe I'll stay."

"If you knew what I'd done to come here—"

"We all have our sins." Something about the way she said it must have given him pause, though, for the Thornlord did not return to his bed. "What made you commit yours?"

He didn't deserve the truth, and yet she couldn't think of a lie. "You are to be exchanged."

"For whom?"

Bitharn didn't reply, but all the answer he needed was in the jut of her jaw.

"Ah," he murmured, "I begin to understand. They have someone dear to you. A sibling? A friend? A lover, perhaps? Oh, keep your secrets if you like. It doesn't matter. There's been a trade arranged."

"There has."

"By whom?"

"The Spider herself. Avele diar Aurellyn."

"And to think I feared I'd been forgotten." Malentir closed his hands around the crystalline bars. Their glow lit his pale fingers so intensely she could see the shapes of his bones through his flesh. His black eyes were bright, now, and the shaggy dishevelment of his ivory-and-black hair gave him the look of some caged wild beast. "Where is the exchange to be made?"

"Carden Vale. Do you believe me now?"

"No. But I will let you prove yourself. Free me, and I will take us there. If you aren't planning treachery, you should be glad to save the ride. The roads are cold and hard this close to winter. If you had other plans . . . well, I'm afraid you'll have to learn to live with disappointment."

"I will not have you casting spells." Bitharn drew a sun sign across her chest. She knew the price of the Thorns' magic: blood and death. They worshipped Kliasta, the Pale Maiden, whose province was pain. The stronger the spell, the greater the agony needed to fuel it. Bitharn could guess that a spell powerful enough to carry them to Carden Vale would require tremendous pain. Perhaps a death.

"Then you will not have me at all. Spare me the outrage, please. The men around us are wretches and murderers, every one. They are destined to die in these cages. A life like that is a small price, hardly worth considering . . . and, even if we left on horseback, you would have to bloody that pretty little blade at your belt."

"What do you mean?"

"Did you think these cells had some enchantment that quiets sound?" Malentir nodded toward the next cell's entrance, not three paces away. "The east cell is empty. But the north one is not, and I am sure Parnas has been listening with great interest to things that do not concern him. Things that he will likely blubber out as soon as someone comes asking. Isn't that so, Parnas?"

Bitharn hardly heard the prisoner's answering moan through the rush of blood in her ears. The heat of mingled fury and embarrassment burned in her cheeks. She'd been foolish as a wine-sotted girl, letting the Thorn bait her into betraying herself.

"No," a man whined from that cell. "I won't tell anyone."

Bitharn ignored that voice. She didn't turn to see the face; she didn't want to think of the pleading as coming from a person. It was easier to think of him as a nameless crime. Her eyes stayed on the Thorn, and on his tiny, taunting smirk. "What did he do?"

"Besides listen?"

Bitharn didn't answer that. She simply stared at him, crushing the key in her hand until its metal teeth bit hard into her palm.

At length Malentir sighed and shrugged with an elaborately affected casualness. "He dabbled in bloodmagic. Poorly. I don't know what half-forgotten god he claimed to worship; he wouldn't say. I do know he was never one of my Lady's servants. She does not touch such feeble tools."

"Why is he here?"

"Prominent relatives, he tells me. Something about a brother with a castle."

Bitharn nodded. She knew who was in that cell now. It had been a great scandal in Cailan some years back: Lord Corsavin's younger brother unmasked as a murderer and dabbler in bloodmagic. The revelation had nearly cost the family its title; all that saved them was Lord Corsavin's hasty, secret pilgrimage to King Uthanyr's court in Aluvair to beg royal mercy. Even so, Parnassor Corsavin had quietly vanished before he could bring any further shame to their house. She hadn't heard that Parnassor had been sent to waste away his remaining years in Heaven's Needle, but it was hardly a surprise.

"I've heard he killed children," she said, unlocking the Thorn's door. She willed away her trepidation and went in, coming close enough to take hold of Malentir's collar. The glass was warm against his skin; his hair brushed across her fingers. He smelled of amber and bitter almond, beautiful and poisonous.

"We all have," he said, and she felt the vibration of his laughter through the glass. "Do you trust me to take you to Carden Vale, then?"

By way of answer, Bitharn snapped the collar. She stepped away quickly, dropping the curved shards. "Not for my own sake. But the Spider expects you to be there before the moon turns, and me with you. I don't imagine you're eager to disappoint her."

"Indeed not," Malentir murmured, following her out of his prison. He went to the north cell, gazing through the translucent bars. His back was turned to Bitharn, and she could not see his expression, but whatever it was drew more whimpers from the man inside. "Do you have a key?"

"No."

"Do you have a knife?"

Wordlessly she unsheathed her dagger and offered it to him. He took it and closed his hand around the blade, exhaling a sigh as blood ran through his fingers. Then he let go of the knife and pressed his maimed hand against the lock of Parnas' door. The glass shattered with a high, musical tinkling, and Parnas moaned. Bitharn heard the man's nails scrabbling as he pushed himself backward along the floor.

She looked away, and wished she could avert her ears as easily as her eyes.

Sometime later the screams died. Awhile after that, Malentir returned. He'd wiped most of the blood from his hands, but red crescents still showed under his nails. A trickle of crimson snaked across the floor of Parnas' cell.

"Are you ready?" he asked, handing back the dagger. It was wet with blood on blade and hilt; Bitharn took the knife between two fingers, glanced at it distastefully, and dropped it on the ground.

"Now that I've been overpowered and kidnapped by an escaped murderer of a Thorn, yes," she answered sweetly, and took a fleeting pleasure in his surprise. The evidence was damning: a broken collar, a magically shattered door, and a prisoner slain by her obviously stolen knife. The last traces of the poison she'd used on Versiel would melt away by morning, so his drug-induced dreams could be blamed on the Thorn's magic too.

Even through her anger, Bitharn felt a hard glint of satisfaction. She could trap him right back.

The satisfaction didn't last long, though. "Come," Malentir said, beckoning her to follow him into the dead man's cell.

Bitharn balked. "Why?"

"We must have shadows to leave this place. This tower was made to let light flood in from all sides. Your cloak might cover our heads, but the light would still come from beneath. I need full darkness for my spell. Parnas will help us."

She went in reluctantly. The smell of blood hung sweet and foul in the air, and with it the nauseating stench of bile. Parnas lay sprawled on the glass floor, his bowels tangled about his legs. A coil of intestine was clenched in his teeth: the Thornlord had gagged the man with his own guts. Bitharn inhaled sharply and looked away, but the obscenity of the death was seared into her sight. She had allowed it to happen, and she bore her share of the guilt.

"He was a wretch," Malentir said, watching her. "A murderer and a coward. A waste of life."

"That doesn't matter."

"Doesn't it? I think it makes all the difference in the world. Or should." He stepped onto the body, keeping his balance effortlessly as Parnas' torso rolled under his weight. The Thornlord offered a hand to help her up beside him.

Bitharn pushed it aside. She used the wall instead, doing her best to block out the disconcerting softness of the corpse underfoot.

It wasn't the first corpse she had stepped on. She clung to that thought, trying to find some kind of solace in it. But the others had been strangers on battlefields, dead by no fault of hers. Nothing like this. This . . . this . . . she failed for a word, something that might begin to capture the enormity of it, and found herself settling on the same unwanted answer: obscenity.

Her work. The Spider's price. She closed her eyes to hold back angry tears.

Malentir was chanting. His words were in no human tongue; they flickered at the edge of understanding and conjured phantoms in the corners of the mind. The Thornlord's prayer was almost an echo of the ones she knew so well, but where Celestia's invocations were proud and solemn, those to Kliasta were soft and sadistic. The torturer's caress, the kiss of hot iron—those were the visions his prayer evoked, and they came with a purring pleasure that made her stomach twist.

Cloth brushed across her shoulders. Shadows blotted out the tower's glow. The scent of amber and almond wrapped around her again with the sweep of the Thornlord's cloak; Bitharn tensed and kept her eyes shut. She'd stood so close to only one man before.

Please, Bright Lady, Bitharn prayed as Malentir finished his invocation and the darkness drew down, *let me be doing the right thing.*

2

Time lost its meaning in the dungeons of Ang'arta. Neither day nor night touched those grim, circled halls, dug deep into the granite beneath the fortress. There was only torchlight, the smoky glow of the torturers' fires, and the screams from the breaking pits. Kelland could not say how long he'd lain in his cell listening to that endless wail. It might have been months; it might have been years. He had no way to tell. He had nothing save the firelight and the screams.

Worm had put out his eardrums to end that screaming. It had taken him ages to sharpen some dead prisoner's finger bone to a point, clenching it in his teeth and scraping it against the stone of his cell. Then he had wedged it into a crevice and rammed his ears onto it, one side after the other, to buy himself silence with pain.

He died not long after. Kelland had never learned what his true name was or how he had come to the dungeons. He was only a pale, mutilated face in the cell opposite. The torturers of Ang'arta had taken his arms and his legs, his eyes and his tongue. They left him blind and voiceless, a worm that had been born a man.

The soldiers came when the body started stinking. They took Worm's corpse to feed the *ghaole* or the greenhounds or some other creature of the Thorns', and a new prisoner filled his cell. Kelland did not know his name either.

"Don't Speak," someone had scratched into the stone near the cell's mouth. The warning was well founded. There was no talking in Ang'arta's cells. Any attempt to speak, or to tap a message through the walls to the man in the next hole, led to a swift and brutal beating. Not for the one who'd spoken—Kelland would have accepted that penalty without complaint—but for the one he'd been trying to reach. That kept them quiet, mostly. There were a few who didn't care, or were glad to inflict suffering on others to relieve their own misery, but most of those were soon taken from the solitary cells. They went down to the breaking pits, to suffer the soldiers' casual abuse and fight their fellows tooth and nail for scraps of food, drops of water.

If they were lucky and cruel, they would survive to take their place among the Iron Lord's reavers. If not, they joined Worm in a *ghaole*'s belly.

Kelland wondered how long it would be until he fed the *ghaole* himself. It was hard to imagine, sometimes, that there had ever been anything more in his life than this.

There had been, once. He remembered fighting in a winter wood, his sword bare in his hand and his goddess' power bright as sunfire in his soul. He remembered the Thornlady and her pack of dead-eyed *ghaole*, and the touch of her magic like rust creeping through the iron of his resolve. He remembered the moment of doubt that had shattered him—and now, as he lay imprisoned in the stronghold of his enemies, surrounded by the stink of sweat and blood and shit, that doubt consumed him.

He had no magic here. His cell was carved from the bowels of the earth, sunk in stone and barricaded by iron so that the sun could not reach him. Without sunlight he was powerless. Kelland needed the sun as surely as the Thorns needed pain, for one was the manifestation of his goddess as the other was of theirs, and without that touch of the divine he was nothing but flesh and blood and breath. Only mortal.

Death was never far away. Fever took its share of souls; putrefying wounds and ill-use claimed others. Some prisoners simply lost their will to live, becoming hollow-eyed ghosts that sat mutely until their bodies followed their spirits across the Last Bridge. Stripped of his goddess' presence, cold and friendless in the dark, Kelland sometimes felt himself sliding toward that final, absolute despair.

It was the memory of Bitharn that pulled him back from the abyss. He remembered her in flashes and fragments, as if some instinct warned that it would hurt too deeply to remember her in full. If he dwelled too long on what was lost, it would break him.

Instead he allowed himself moments: the sun catching gold in her hair; the quick warmth of her hand on his arm; the silhouette of her sitting watch by the fire, tireless and vigilant. Her bravery and her cleverness and the intensity that sharpened her eyes—sometimes gray, sometimes hazel flecked with motes of greening gold, depending on the light—in the fraction of a heartbeat between drawing back an arrow and loosing it. She had the same intensity whether she was shooting at a straw-filled dummy or a charging boar. And sometimes, too, when she looked at him. When she kissed him.

That thought was dangerous as a live coal, and just as likely to burn. Kelland always pulled away from it, and always came back to it, unable to let go of the gift and burden of truth.

Bitharn had loved him. She had never said so, but he had known all the same. A blind man would have seen it. And he had loved her in turn—loved her, and desired her, despite his Blessed oath of chastity.

He had never touched her. But he had *wanted* to . . . and that wanting had been his undoing. A mistake, not seeing the truth within his own soul. Desire had weakened his will and undermined the faith that was the wellspring of his power. The Thornlady saw it before Kelland did. Without faith, he had no magic; without magic, he was defenseless against the Thorns. Unable to choose between his lady and his goddess, he lost both.

He didn't know what had happened to Bitharn after he was taken. Perhaps she had been captured too; perhaps she'd stayed safe, as he hoped. Kelland didn't know. But the thought of her trapped in Ang'arta was bleaker than the absence of sunlight, and so he tried to put her out of his mind. Instead he slept, seeking refuge in dreamlessness from the nightmare that awaited when he woke.

A pounding on the cell bars roused him from uneasy sleep. Not a nightmare, this time. It was a man who waited for him, one of Baoz's hard-faced reavers, clad in boiled leather with a red fist on his chest. A wide, cruel scar striped his face from cheek to chin; his teeth were blackened splinters where it passed across his mouth. He unlocked the door with a jangling iron key ring and lifted his tarred torch. Its flame, painfully bright after so long in the dark, stung tears into Kelland's eyes.

"Celestian. You are to come with me."

Kelland crawled to his knees and, with a great effort, out of his cell. He could hear drums booming down the hall. Their hammering was no louder than the thundering of blood in his ears. He swayed on his feet and caught himself against the wall before he fell. Scar Face watched, pitiless.

He mastered himself and stood. *I am a Knight of the Sun. I will not be weak.* It was pride, foolish pride, but what else did he have? The Baozites respected one thing and one thing only: strength. Kelland willed away the trembling in his knees and the hollowness in his stomach. They had fed him nothing but cups of watery gruel, one a day for however many days he'd spent locked in this hole, and standing left him light-headed. But he made himself let go of the wall and forced his spine straight as a swordblade, drawing on will when his body threatened to fail.

"Why? Where are we going?" His voice was a rusty croak, hardly recognizable as his own. He hadn't spoken in so long.

Scar Face spat on the floor. "The Spider wants to see you."

Without another word the soldier strode down the hall. Kelland was hard-pressed to keep up, and the whirl of his thoughts didn't help.

For centuries Ang'arta had been a blight on the surrounding kingdoms. The reavers of the Iron Fortress worshipped war; they trained for it from childhood, and as youths were plunged into the pits to be reborn as warriors. Their discipline was as legendary as their cruelty, and they were the finest soldiers in the world.

Yet they were, and for centuries had been, also the weakest in magic. Baoz gifted his favored warriors with divine power—strength and endurance beyond that of ordinary men, swift healing, bloodmadness in battle. But he did not give them spells. Only his red-robed priestesses with their iron horns and crimson smiles commanded true magic, and the last of those had died three hundred years ago.

And so, over the years, an uneasy equilibrium took hold. Few kingdoms had ever been able to field armies that could match Ang'arta's, but the Knights of the Sun stood ready to lend their spells where steel might fail. Because of them, the ironlords had been held back from conquering Calantyr in its fragile youth or devouring the crumbling ruins of Rhaelyand before new kingdoms rose out of the empire's ashes.

It was not an easy balance or a bloodless one, but it held.

Eight years ago, that had changed. Eight years ago, Aedhras the Golden, then an ordinary soldier, returned from his sojourn to the east with the Spider as his wife. Soon after that, the Baozites had magic. *True* magic. It was not their god's, but it was theirs to command, and that was the Spider's doing.

Kelland had never seen Avele diar Aurellyn, the Lord Commander's wife and the leader of the Thorns in this part of the world. Few had. Rumor had it that she spent her days spinning webs high in the Tower of Thorns, and sent her maimed disciples out to do her will rather than risk herself. She was said to be beautiful, ruthless, and cunning as a fiend.

He followed Scar Face up a long crawl of stairs, passing soldiers who chuckled to their companions and jeered at him as they shoved by. Kelland tried to make himself deaf to their words, but he couldn't ignore them completely. They knew who he was: his dark brown skin and the white shells braided in his hair made him as unique in their world as he'd been at the Dome of the Sun. The Burnt Knight, champion of the Celestians, had become a prisoner paraded for their amusement. Anger and shame twisted around each other, hot in his heart, but he kept his face still as stone.

One of the Baozites drove an elbow into the knight's ribs as he passed. Kelland tried to pivot and thrust an arm out to catch himself, but he was too slow, too weak after so long in the cell. The side of his head cracked against the wall. Pain blinded him; he felt blood running down his cheek. He stumbled to a knee on the steps, defenseless.

Scar Face stepped between them. He swung his torch at Kelland's attacker as if fending off a wolf. "Enough. The Spider wants to see him, and she doesn't want to see him with half his face a pulp."

"Not pretty enough for her bed that way?" the Baozite sneered, but he backed away.

"She just likes to do it herself," one of his companions said, to laughter, and they left.

After they had gone Kelland pushed himself back up against the wall. There was a wet smear on the stone where he had struck it. He held a sleeve to his temple, trying to quell the throbbing in his head. Scar Face watched, impassive, and made no move to help. But he set a slower pace until they reached the top of the stairs, and he kept himself between Kelland and the Baozites on the steps.

"Thank you," Kelland mumbled as they came to the landing.

Scar Face gave him an unreadable look. The shiny welt of his scar flexed as his jaw worked. "She wants you, so she'll have you," he said, "and I'm not sure you should be thanking me for that."

Kelland nodded, and regretted it as the torchflame

swam in his vision. For the rest of the way he simply followed the soldier, concentrating on the monumental task of putting one foot before the other. After an eternity of steep gray steps. Scar Face unlocked a massive wooden door and took him down another hall.

The air was cleaner up here. Kelland noticed the change even through his daze. The dungeons stank of excrement and misery; the common halls were thick with the smells of old rushes and unwashed bodies and sour ale. This hall was quieter by far, and the air carried only a whiff of woodsmoke and sweet pine.

The first door they reached was barred by an oak beam, thicker than Kelland's arm and mounted in iron brackets. Spidery marks, inlaid with some lusterless gray metal, were carved along its length. Scar Face lifted the beam, grunting at its weight, and let its butt end slide to the floor. He pulled the door open and propped it with a boot. "You'll wait here."

"Another cell?"

"A guest room."

"Your lady's hospitality warms my heart." Still, he was too weak to fight, and there was no reason to lose his dignity over such a petty struggle. Kelland went in.

The door closed behind him. He heard the scrape of wood on stone, the soldier's muffled curses, and the dual thud, one side after the other, as Scar Face wrestled the beam back into its brackets. But these noises barely registered, for in the room was a pure gift of hope.

It was clean. That in itself was a gift. There was a bed with fresh linens, a platter with cheese and dried plums and new bread. Beside it was a washing bowl with brush, mirror, and razor. The luxury—the *cleanliness*—of it was unimaginable, but all those things paled beside the greatest blessing of all.

Windows. Tiny, high, and barred, but open to the sky.

It was almost dawn. He could see the first tendrils of it beginning to soften the deep blue of the fading night. In an hour, perhaps less, the sun would rise and morning would break and he, who had been so long immured in the dark, might feel his goddess' radiance on his face again.

Kelland bowed at the waist to the dawn. He raised his arms to his chest as he came up, then over his head and back down in the ancient forms. His muscles protested at the stretching—it had been too long since he had observed the full dawn prayer—but the grace of the movements was not lost to him. He had not been broken. He could still pray.

The Sun Knight bowed again, continuing the measured sequence, and wept silently in gratitude as his Lady's light filled his soul.

"I TRUST YOU ARE WELL RESTED."

Kelland opened his eyes. There had been no sound to signal the Spider's arrival; he had not heard the bar lift, nor the door open. It was possible she did not need to lift bars or open doors to move about the fortress. The Thorns could pass directly from shadow to shadow, flitting through darkness and avoiding the light.

If she had hoped to surprise him, though, she would have to be disappointed. Kelland hadn't been sleeping. He had been in light meditation, renewing his atrophied muscles with the blessings of his faith. Months in that tiny hole had crippled him . . . but one short day after being allowed sunlight, Kelland was almost fully restored. Awake, and immersed in prayer, he had felt her approach like a shadow falling across his soul: the presence of her goddess against his.

The Spider sat in a high-backed chair near the door. She was not what he had expected, but no one could have been.

Avele diar Aurellyn was thin, small breasted, and finely boned, with the pale golden complexion and slightly tilted eyes of her homeland. She was as beautiful as the stories said, though it was a coolly elegant beauty, no more welcoming than a frost-laced mountain pool. Jewels sparkled on her fingers and in the silver lattice of her necklace, bright over a high-necked dress of black velvet. Unlike every other Thorn he had seen, she was not visibly maimed.

"As well as any man can be in his enemies' den," Kelland said, swinging his feet to the floor. Several paces separated him from the Spider, but the intimacy of this audience still set his teeth on edge. He took refuge in formality, using brittle courtesy to create distance and sanctuary.

A smile touched her lips. "I am not your enemy, sir knight."

"No? Then I must apologize. No doubt when your minions captured me and locked me in that pit, they did so out of dearest friendship."

"I do not dispute that things were done in the past. Put them aside. You have more urgent concerns, as do I. Why do you suppose you were brought up here?"

Kelland had been wondering that himself, but he pressed his lips together, mute.

The Spider had been admiring her rings. At his silence she glanced up, then laughed aloud. Her laughter was warm and low, and deeply discomfiting.

"Not for that," she said. "I can only imagine what the soldiers must have said—but I hope it will not insult your pride to say that, however charming you might be, there is nothing in you to tempt me away from my lord."

"What, then?"

"You want to be free, yes? That is what I am offering you: liberty."

Freedom. Clean air, sweet water, the ability to walk wherever he wanted, as long and as far as he wanted, without the screams of the breaking pits echoing in his ears. The freedom to read a book, tucked away in a sunlit corner of the Dome's library, or to eat meals—to taste real *food*—of his own choosing.

The freedom to find Bitharn. To rejoin her, if the Bright Lady smiled on his search.

And then?

He didn't know. Dangerous even to let his thoughts stray in that direction . . . but he would have the freedom to make that choice too.

The idea dizzied him. After an eternity in Ang'arta's dungeons, freedom was not just a word. It was bigger than that, and smaller. It was hot bread and cool wind and the shared joy of prayer in a cathedral, smoky incense swirling to the eaves. It was, if he was lucky, a smile and a touch he'd missed for too long. "But with a price."

"Of course," the Spider agreed serenely. "There is always a price. That hardly bears noting."

"What is yours?"

"What do you remember of Duradh Mal? Surely it must have been mentioned when you were in training at the Dome of the Sun."

It had, although Kelland remembered its history only vaguely. Six hundred years ago, Ang'arta had not been the only seat of Baozite power in the west. The fortress of Ang'duradh, nestled among the peaks of the Irontooth Mountains, was its twin and rival. Had the two strongholds been closer to each other, they might have fought the other more viciously than any outside foe; their god rewarded strength, and there was no worthier foe than his other dedicants.

But Ang'duradh had not been conquered by its western sibling. No one knew what had befallen it. The last known visitors to the fortress were a small band of pilgrims seeking refuge from an early snowstorm. The Baozites let them in for a handful of silver, as was their custom. After that, they closed their gates . . . and no more was known.

The Irontooths' passes froze in autumn and thawed in spring; months passed while the fortress lay locked behind walls of snow. That spring, a few desperate travelers knocked on the Baozites' doors for shelter, only to find silence at their gates and rotting corpses behind their walls. Not a single soldier survived. The mystery of their deaths had never been answered.

The ruins were named Duradh Mal: Duradh's Doom. They were reputed to be cursed, or haunted. Wise men and fools alike avoided that place. Since then old kingdoms had fallen, new kingdoms had risen, and six hundred years later, Duradh Mal was still no concern of his.

Kelland shrugged. "A long time ago, a Baozite fortress fell. No one knows why."

"And the town of Carden Vale sits below its ruins."

"What of it?"

"A curious coincidence. No more. For now." She laced her jeweled fingers together and rested them on her knee. "There is one other thing I wish to discuss with you before I go. Faith."

"I doubt we share much in that regard, lady."

"More than you might think. You serve your goddess faithfully, as I do mine. Without that devotion to guide it, your life would have no purpose. Yet you are tempted by love, as I was, and you do not know how to reconcile the two. Do you deny it?"

Behind his calm facade Kelland's temper began to burn. He reined it back firmly. It was no surprise that the Spider knew of his weakness; it was, after all, how her disciple had caught him in the woods. He'd let them manipulate him once. It would not happen again. "No."

"Good. Then I will tell you, and perhaps you will listen. Now, or when you are ready. I cannot, of course, force you to believe what is true." Her smile took a wry twist. "But you are crippled until you do. A divided heart is no proper vessel for the gods' power. So.

"We spend our lives in service to our gods, and yet we know so little of what they require. Oh, we know the simplest rules. Sunlight. Pain. But beyond that? Laws and oaths are handed down through the ages, and some of them truly must be observed, while others . . . others, I think, were invented by mortal men to enhance their own prestige, when the gods care nothing either way. And sometimes the intention is all that matters.

"If I tell a lie, *knowingly*, my magic fails. Honesty is required of us. It is not difficult to understand why: the truth cuts deeper than any lie, and if everyone knows that the Thorns are truthbound, no one can salve his suffering by pretending otherwise. What we say must be true. That is a holy order. But if I say something that is not true, while believing it to be so, nothing happens. Perfection is not required. Intentions matter."

"Your point?"

"Is very simple. Your oath of chastity is one where intentions make the difference. If the act is not a choice, there is no sin. Celestia does not withdraw her blessings if her servants are raped . . . to the chagrin of some of my lord's soldiers, who had hoped we might have found an easy solution there. And if the act is an expression of love, rather than baser desires, there is no impurity of the soul and, again, no loss of your Bright Lady's blessing."

"Bysshelios believed that," Kelland said grimly. The Bysshelline Heresy had nearly torn the Celestian faith in two before it was stamped out. The infighting had ended less than a century ago, and the rifts were not yet healed. Some of the villages in the remote reaches of the Cathil-carns still clung to Bysshelline beliefs.

"He was right."

"He was a heretic."

"Heresies seldom survive, much less spread, without some truth at their core."

Kelland shook his head. The cowrie shells braided into his hair clinked. "Pretty promises from a treacherous tongue. You will forgive me, lady, if I choose to believe the High Solaros over you when it comes to the strictures of my faith."

"As you like," the Spider murmured. "I cannot force you to believe. But I hope you will come to accept the truth soon, as you are useless until you do."

"I'm sorry to disappoint you."

"It is not me you disappoint. It is your faith that needs you, not I. They are the ones in danger." She bowed her head politely as she rose to depart. "But now it is near sunset, and I will take my leave. I should not wish to interfere with your prayers."

3

*T*hirteen.

Sweat dripped into Asharre's eyes as she pulled her chin up over her knotted fists and the iron bar between them. She blinked it away, ignoring the sting, and lowered herself with deliberate slowness. Her arms burned, her jaw was clenched so tight it ached, and her feet were going numb from the weights around her ankles, but she wasn't ready to stop. Another set. Another after that, if exhaustion failed to claim her.

She reached the full extension of her arms. Her toes would touch the ground if she let her legs straighten. She didn't. Instead Asharre tensed her wrists and pulled herself up again, forcing herself through the burn until her chin came over the bar once more.

Fourteen.

As many as it took to reach oblivion.

"Asharre. Asharre!"

She ignored the call. The voice was a gnat trying to disrupt her concentration. There was nothing worth coming down from the bar. There hadn't been since Oralia died. Everyone at the Dome of the Sun knew that, and left her to her misery.

Fifteen.

"Asharre!"

Everyone except this gnat, evidently.

Asharre shook the sweat off her face and tilted her chin so that she could see the speaker. He was a young man, conventionally handsome, with strong shoulders and a square jaw beneath a fall of red-gold hair. Not Blessed; he wasn't wearing a Sun Knight's white tabard or an Illuminer's yellow robes. No doubt he cut quite a swath among the ladies of Cailan, then. What was his name? Heras—no, Heradion, that was it.

"What?" she snapped, keeping her arms flexed and herself suspended in the air. She could still work toward exhaustion, even if she had to waste time talking on the way.

"The High Solaros wants to see you." The youth was out of breath; he must have run to get her. Of course he had. Thierras d'Amalthier, Anointed of Celestia, stood highest among the goddess' servants in Ithelas. His voice spoke for the entire faith. Kings quailed before his displeasure; the Emperor of Ardashir sent gifts of spices and carved ivory to curry his favor. No one kept the High Solaros waiting.

Asharre didn't straighten her arms. "Why?"

"I don't know." The boy was not good at hiding his anxiety. "But you must come at once."

She grunted and went back to ignoring him. Only after completing her count of twenty did Asharre lower herself to the ground. She stripped the weights off her ankles and stretched through a modified version of the dawn prayer to keep her limbs from tightening, then mopped her brow with a towel from a nearby bench. "Well, let's go."

Heradion stared at her sleeveless, sweat-soaked tunic and loose cotton breeches. After an impressively short pause he mustered the courage to ask: "Do you need a moment to ready yourself?"

"No. He wanted me to come at once." And Thierras d'Amalthier did not deserve that much respect from her. He was one of the reasons her sister was dead.

It was a credit to his good sense that Heradion did not protest again. He closed his mouth and took the lead, setting a swift pace through the chalk-dusted gymnasium and the baths beyond. Bathers crowded the communal pools of hot and cold water, soaking in the lassitude that came after hard exercise. Their conversations dwindled to uncomfortable silences as the pair passed. Asharre could feel their stares, curious and pitying, on her back. As tall as Heradion was, she stood a head taller, and her arms were thicker muscled to boot. There were no women like her in the summerlands. Southerners never knew what to make of *sigrir*.

She walked faster. Past the honey-veined marble arches that led to the baths, through the summer gardens that Oralia had loved and Asharre now avoided. The gardens lay dormant after a long winter; the rosebushes were gnarled brown sticks, the fountains dry. A thread of perfume from some early-blooming flower caught her, and she quickened her step to escape it.

The Dome of the Sun rose up before them. Its namesake dome glowed with the warm light of late afternoon; its ornate rose windows sparkled like gems. To the north, the spire of Heaven's Needle gleamed pink and gold against the clouds. The smaller buildings that serviced the temple's daily needs ringed the base of the hill where the Dome stood, so that none of them would touch it with shadow.

For Heaven's Needle, that was not a concern; the glass tower cast only a ribbon of softer light, clear as water, and never dimmed the earth at all.

Heradion led her through the budding trees and broad avenues to the Sanctuary of the High Solaros. The guards at the door were not ones she knew, but she saw recognition flash across their faces as she approached. They were too professional to let the pity show, though. Asharre was grateful for that.

Inside there were more guards, and long, hushed halls lined with rich Ardasi carpets over saffron marble polished until it shone. Maps and books in gilt-edged cases covered the walls. Scrolls from a hundred dead kingdoms, sheathed in ivory and bronze, rested in niches between them. Celestia represented the metaphorical light of knowledge as well as its more literal forms, and her temples drew scholars from sun-scorched Nebaioth to the White Seas. The High Solaros' private library was the envy of emperors.

In spite of herself Asharre was awed by the Sanctuary's grandeur, though she had seen it before and felt no particular reverence for the man at its center. Celestia had been Oralia's goddess, not hers, and while Asharre was not so foolish as to deny the Bright Lady's power in Ithelas, neither was she inclined to bow her own head in prayer. The goddess had failed them in their time of need. Asharre owed her nothing.

But she was conscious of the cooling sweat that matted her hair and made her clothes cling, and she half-wished she'd taken Heradion's hint.

Too late for that. Heradion bowed formally to the last set of guards and recited the first half of the holy verse that served as the day's passphrase. Even when guards could see their visitors' faces, they required passphrases for entry: it was a safeguard against assassins who could wear the faces of the dead, or Thorns who seized people's bodies and used them like puppets.

The guards returned his bow and the verse's second part. Something about seasons of the soul; Asharre listened with half an ear. The doors to the High Solaros' private quarters swung open between them. She stepped through.

"The High Solaros will meet you in his study. Do you know where it is?" Heradion asked.

"I've been a few times." More than a few. It seemed that they'd been summoned whenever Thierras needed a healer to ride circuit on dangerous roads. At the time Asharre had been pleased that her sister's talents were so well recognized by her temple, and proud to protect her in the course of her duties. Now those honors were bitter as ashes, and the thought of them brought only emptiness wrapped around a kernel of rage.

"Then I'll wait here for you," the boy said, taking a blue-bound book from its shelf and settling onto a chair. "Good luck."

That earned a snort. She wasn't the one who would need it.

Thierras was, as advised, in his study. It was a bright and airy space, with quatrefoil windows overlooking the south gardens. Red and gold glass in the mullions threw sparks of color across the parquetry floor. The High Solaros was reading at his desk when Asharre came in without knocking, but he rose and inclined his head courteously. "Asharre. *Sigrir.* Light's blessing upon you."

She didn't return the greeting or the courtesy. They were alone, so there was no one to be shocked by her rudeness, but she wouldn't have bothered feigning politeness if they'd been in front of the Midsummer dawn service at the Dome of the Sun. No doubt Thierras knew that, and had chosen to see her privately because of it. "Some boy said you wanted to see me."

"I did. I have a task I hoped you might consider."

"You don't give me tasks. You gave Oralia tasks. I went with her."

"I am aware. I would not presume to order you. This is only . . . a request. A favor, if you will." Thierras sat again, steepling his hands on the desk. The years had put a slight stoop in his shoulders, and his sandy hair was thinner and grayer than it had been when Asharre came to Cailan, but these things only added to his self-possessed dignity. His voice alone—patient, infinitely reasonable—could have calmed a battlefield.

It had no effect on her. "Why should I do you a favor? You've done me none."

Thierras sighed. "Asharre. I share your grief. I will not trivialize it by asking you to simply move past it. Oralia was a bright soul, and her memory is not easily laid aside. But the needs of the living do not stop for our sorrows, and your talents are too valuable to let rust. You know this as well as I do."

Asharre didn't answer. She'd kept in training, but only because it had been hammered into her so deeply that stopping would have been harder than maintaining the routine. It helped, a little, to work herself into exhaustion; then she didn't have to think, didn't have to remember. It held the memory of loss at bay. But she trained because it was a habit, not because she had any use for those skills. She stayed at the Dome, likewise, because it was habit, and because nothing had come to dislodge her from the simple inertia of grief.

There was no place for her in the world. Not really. Not that she cared to find. The Celestians made space for her, letting her walk among the ghosts she hated but couldn't let go. Leaving them—and she wasn't sure which "them" she meant—would mean accepting herself as a solitary entity, and trying to make her way in the world that way, when all her life she'd been defined by her duties to another.

She wasn't sure she wanted that. She wasn't sure she wanted a new charge either. Why, when she'd failed her last so badly?

The High Solaros was undeterred by her silence. "You are *sigrir*," he reminded her, as if she could have forgotten. His gaze lighted briefly on the blackened sigils that scarred her face from brow to chin in two vertical lines. "I know what that cost you."

"You know nothing of *sigrir*."

"I don't know *much*, it's true. But you might credit me with a little more than 'nothing.' I've read Gaodhar. Attentively."

"He was a summerlander."

"He was a scholar, and he married into the Skarlar. Your clan."

Asharre scowled, crossing her arms. "Giant's Spear Skarlar, not Frosthold, and that before my grandfather's day."

"Have the *sigrir* changed so much?"

When she did not answer, Thierras sighed again and pressed on. "The point, if you will allow me one, is that I know it takes enormous dedication to become *sigrir*, and still more to bring a child safely from the White Seas to Cailan, particularly when you were a child yourself. It is a sin to waste such skill. You've had the winter to grieve. You may have the rest of your life to grieve, if you like, but I will not let you sit here idly while you do it."

"My ward is dead." Her *sister*. The last of her family in this world.

"There are others who need protection."

She did not unfold her arms. But she asked: "Who?"

"I received a letter last week. The solaros in Carden Vale wishes to retire. He is an old man, and in poor health; it is past time I let him lay down his burdens. The town will need a new solaros. I've decided to assign two young Blessed to the post. Falcien and Evenna are ready for their *annovair.*"

Asharre nodded. Oralia had been given a similar assignment after completing her training in Cailan. The Celestians believed that it was important for one blessed with the goddess' power to serve a year or two as an ordinary solaros, learning the rhythms of village life and developing an understanding of the people they were meant to serve. The Knights of the Sun did not always serve the *annovair*—their gifts were often needed too urgently elsewhere—but all the Illuminers did, teaching and tending the commonfolk and learning from them in turn. The *annovair* strengthened the bond between the faith and the people. For most, it was a happy memory. Oralia had delighted in hers.

Was that why he wanted her to take this assignment? For the memory of her sister's happiness? Asharre narrowed her eyes, wondering, but Thierras' face revealed nothing.

"The mountain roads are wild and infested with bandits," he continued. "I don't anticipate serious trouble, but I would like my Blessed to reach Carden Vale safely. Heradion will escort them, but he is young himself. I'd feel more confident if you went as well. Would you be willing to accompany them?"

Asharre did not answer quickly. She had grown tired of her ghosts, yes, but traveling with newly sworn Illuminers might reawaken them as easily as it put them to rest.

What was the harm, though? It would not be an especially long journey, or a hard one. She could always leave if she wanted; she was not beholden to Thierras or his goddess. And there was nothing to hold her here. "I'll go."

"Thank you," said the High Solaros.

Heradion was waiting by the great doors when she left the study. He followed her out wordlessly, warned into silence by the look on her face. Outside the Dome Asharre hesitated, unsure whether she wanted to go back to the gymnasium or into Cailan. The city was not hers, would never be *home,* but it was familiar and, at the moment, she wanted to be away from Celestians.

"I knew her," Heradion said, unexpectedly, as Asharre stood undecided on the street. The dying sunlight caught his hair, brightening it almost to the fiery copper of Oralia's. "Your sister. Not very well, but we met a few times. She was years ahead of me, but the Burnt Knight was my *hadriel* and they were friends. It was a blessing to have known her."

That was more than she wanted to hear. "I need a drink," Asharre muttered.

"I know just the place."

THE WHITE HOUND, SHE HAD TO admit, was a good choice. Located near the city's north-facing Sun Gate, it was far enough from the main road to avoid travelers' dust and clamor, but close enough to draw their custom. The inn was two stories of whitewashed stone topped by glazed blue tile. Its window boxes were bare but for frosted dirt, but later in the year they would hold fragrant basil and mint.

Asharre had stopped in a few times, but, as Blessed were

forbidden wine or beer and she disliked being parted from her sister, it had been a year or more since she'd darkened its doorstep. "How did you know this place?" she asked as they approached.

Heradion shrugged. He was not as young as she'd initially guessed. Closer to twenty than fifteen, if not a little older. "Rich friends."

She wasn't in the mood to deal with a crowd. "Will they be here?"

"Doubtful. We only come here to play cards, and it's not Godsday."

Asharre snorted. "You play cards on Godsday?"

"Best time to do it. All the pious people are at services, so there's no one to look down their noses at you. I'm not Blessed; I'm allowed my sins. And I must say, right now, a tall mug of Tarrybuck brown sounds like a good one."

"Agreed."

Only half the common room was full. This early in the year, few merchants were on the road, and farmers were busy turning the fields before spring planting. They had their choice of tables, so Asharre picked one that commanded a view of the door and set her chair's back to the wall. It was a little chill so far from the fire, but the hearth was crowded and she had a good cloak. She tossed a silver shield to the nearest serving maid. Even at the White Hound's prices, that would keep them in ale for the night.

"Not the friendly sort, are you?" Heradion commented as he took the chair opposite. "Seems like the only way you could get a table farther from the crowd is if you carried it outside."

"I'm not in the mood for company."

"I hope that doesn't last. I don't love the sound of my

own voice *quite* enough to want to listen to it all the way up to Carden Vale and back."

"I could gag you, if that would help."

"Ah, the lady has a sense of humor! I'd begun to wonder."

So had she. There'd been little room for laughter in her life before Oralia died, and none after. She had almost forgotten what it was like. The simple pleasure of a good ale shared with friends was not one Asharre had often enjoyed; she had no gift for words, much less the aimless chatter that summerlanders seemed to love. But Heradion had an easy manner, and a stock of stories from growing up with three troublemaking brothers on a farm, and he did not seem to mind that she said little herself. She drank and listened, and once in a while she laughed.

Finally, Heradion pushed his empty cup aside. "Enough about me. Will you tell me a little of yourself?"

Asharre shrugged, gazing into the last of the ale sloshing about in her chipped mug. She wasn't drunk, but three tankards of Tarrybuck brown and the evening's conversation had left her with a pleasant muzziness. "What do you want to know?"

"What do you want to tell? I don't mean to pry. It's just that if we're to travel together, it would be nice to know something about my companion. Beyond your formidable skills with a sword, of course."

"Not that formidable."

"You're too modest. I've seen you in the yard. If I had a third of your talent, I'd hie myself off to Craghail and fight a Swordsday melee. Win myself a princess, a fortune, and the right to bore my listeners senseless with bragging until I was a graybeard." He grinned. "Well, I have the last already, but it'd be a good deal more impressive if I'd *won* something first."

"They don't give away princesses anymore."

"No? I suppose it's back to hard work and humility then. Curses."

She grunted and finished her drink in silence. Then Heradion suggested: "Tell me about your scars. What do they mean?"

Her first instinct was to refuse. The marks of a *sigrir* were not something to be discussed with summerlanders. She had never done so before. It was a fair request, though, and he was right: if she was to travel with these people, they should know something about her.

Asharre traced her scars with a fingertip. "That I have bad luck."

"All scars mean that. Take this one here"—Heradion touched a crooked white line across the back of his wrist—"*that* was a spot of bad luck, thinking Merilee's brother was joking when he said he'd cut my nose off if I tried to kiss her. Fortunately for me he was drunk and his aim was bad. I suspect your story's more interesting than that."

She managed half a smile. "I had a different sort of bad luck. My mother had no brothers. She bore four daughters, but only one son. He died of fever when I was eight. My father was killed in a raid when I was twelve. After that . . . after that there was not much choice, really. Among the White Seas clans, women have little privilege. They cannot defend the family's honor in feud, cannot hold property . . . cannot do many things. Someone had to negotiate my sister's marriages, and there were no men left in the family. So I became *sigrir*."

"Siegrar?"

She corrected his pronunciation, emphasizing the second syllable. "*Sigrir*. You have no word like it. 'Honorable virgin' might come close. Among the tribes it is an ancient custom, although one that is fading. I cut my hair, swore never to marry, and took the brand; then I was allowed the rights of a man. I was thirteen."

"That's why you have those scars?"

"That is why I have this one." She touched the center sigil etched on her left cheek, just below the eye. The ridges were old and familiar under her finger; she had worn the mark for more than twenty years.

"What about the rest of them?"

"Those came later." Asharre's mug had gone empty. She leaned back in her chair. The happiness seemed to have drained out of the evening; a great weariness had settled in its stead. "Most *sigrir* take only the first oath. The clans do not feud as they once did. It is not necessary for most girls to fight, only to handle property and find good husbands for their sisters."

"What was different for you?"

"Oralia . . . the youngest of my sisters was Blessed. By Celestia." The smoke was stinging her eyes. Asharre rubbed it away irritably. "The Frosthold Skarlar live in the true north, close on the shores of the White Sea. We keep to the old ways. Split Pines Skarlar do not even have *sigrir* anymore; they have taken to summerlander customs, and are barely worthy of their clan name. In the true north it is different. We still have wildbloods and white ragers.

"There is—there has always been a great enmity between wildbloods and the servants of your goddess. The wildbloods believe that there are only a few souls in the clan strong enough to join them. When such a child is called to Celestia as Blessed instead, that is a theft from our faith: a strong soul, one that should have belonged to the old spirits, leaves our people for a foreign temple—and, to the wildbloods' way of thinking, is turned against them.

For this reason they hate Celestians. I remember once, when I was very young, they took a solaros in a raid against a summerlander village. The warriors brought him back with them to die in the snow, far away from his goddess. All the children were called to watch."

It had been the first death she'd seen, and it remained one of the ugliest. They had broken his teeth and smashed his face into a slimy red pulp. Unable to scream, the priest had moaned instead: a hideous whistling sound that lasted long into the dark and echoed in her nightmares. In the morning he was silent, and the meat of his face was black with mosquitoes.

An old memory. She put it away, as she had done a thousand times before. Heradion was still watching her, waiting for the end of the tale.

"If she had stayed there—if what she was became known—Oralia would have ended like that priest. She had to go south. But I knew that it would not be easy, that many might try to stop us. So I learned to fight." Her fingers traced three more sigils in a line down her right cheek. "Sword, spear, axe. This one, for reading the stars and the waters as dragonship guides do. This one, for tracking and trapping prey in the snow. So that we would not get lost on our way south, you understand, or starve as we traveled. For every man's secret I wanted to learn, there was another scar to take.

"I might have had more, but by then Oralia was losing control of her power. There was no one to train what she was. So we left. In time we came here, and she was able to become what her goddess wanted her to be."

"That is an extraordinary sacrifice," Heradion said quietly.

"It was a long time ago." She shrugged. The preparation was the easy part; it was the journey that had been hard.

And she'd failed in the end anyway. "I was sworn as *sigrir* already. There was no reason not to use the privileges of the oath, and no sacrifice in it."

"Some might disagree. All the same, it will be an honor to travel beside you. Although, I hope, we won't have anything half that dramatic on the way to Carden Vale. A couple of cowardly bandits with sticks for swords might do. Maybe an old toothless dog."

"No taste for adventure?"

"Adventure's the story you make up after the fact. You just get us there nice and boring, if you please. I'll embroider on enough 'adventures' to make Rwen the Dragonslayer blush . . . once we're all safe back home."

4

It was raining when Corban returned to Cailan: a late-summer downpour that washed over the streets and whipped the Windhurst River into a gray churn. The dockhands cursed the storm for making their work more difficult, but Corban was glad for it. As long as the rain went on, there would be fewer people in the streets, and fewer curious eyes to see where he took his blackfire crates.

There were a few porters waiting by the wharves, their heads bowed against the weather. Corban flipped a silver shield to a big fellow whose eyes were dull under his dripping hood. It was a generous payment, just shy of extravagance, and it caught the porter's attention at once.

"Greensmoke Alley," Corban told him, naming the crime-ridden warren where the city's alchemists and apothecaries plied their trade. It was a dismal neighborhood. Few who could afford to live elsewhere wanted to stay near the odd sounds and odder smells that accompanied the alchemists' work, and dark rumors abounded about kidnappers who stole people off the street to sell for necromancers' experiments. Ridiculous as such stories were, they terrified the gullible.

The porter either didn't believe such things or was willing to brave them for the silver. He grunted in acknowledgment and hefted two of the blackfire crates waiting on the pier. Corban carried the third himself, cradling it close to his chest as he splashed through the crooked streets toward the safe house he'd chosen.

Two blocks from the safe house he stopped. A sign showing a bearded hydra swung outside the shuttered windows of the nearest shop. Corban lowered his crate onto the cobblestones by its door. "This will do. Take care with the boxes. Smokepowder can be dangerous to an ungentle hand."

The porter's eyes widened, but he nodded and set down the crates with exaggerated care. Once the boxes were out of his hands, he backed away as if he half-expected them to chase after him, and he asked no further questions before making a hasty retreat around the corner.

Corban chuckled, as amused by his own cleverness as by the porter's fear. The smokepowder story explained why he'd paid the porter a full silver shield—it was the least a man could expect for lugging around a box that would reduce him to red vapor and boneshards if he dropped it— and if the porter's nose was sharp enough to pick up the blackfire stone's scent of sulfur, the story would explain that away too.

When the porter was well out of sight, he adjusted his grip on the first crate and hurried past the shop into a twisting alley. The rainwater that skipped down its cobblestones wore a scarf of acrid orange foam—a gift from the neighboring alchemists, whose runoff funneled down this alley to the sea—while the stones themselves were pitted and oddly soft, eaten away by years of such corrosive floods.

His safe house was here, down a poor street in a poor neighborhood where people were in the habit of ignoring strange doings. Ten or twelve years ago it had belonged to an apothecary, but the man had been hanged for dealing in poisons. After his execution, the Royal Justice had posted a ban on his shop and ordered that it be torn down.

It was never done. The shop sat at the end of a mazy warren confusing even to the denizens of Greensmoke Alley. Its destruction promised to be an unpleasant, unprofitable job. Amid the press of more urgent matters, it was easily forgotten—by the Royal Justice, if not by the people who had to live in Greensmoke Alley.

Over the years, the apothecary's hovel took on an ominous cast in the collective imagination. Eye-watering smells wafted out of its alley on rainy nights. Fish pulled from the waters nearby sometimes came up scaleless and slimy, their deformed fins grabbing at the air like soft pink hands. Rumors about the curse on the house, and what the apothecary had *really* been doing behind those blind, crooked windows, proliferated with each new sighting. Soon people avoided its alley altogether, turning away out of habit, almost instinct.

Corban had seen the opportunity at once. And seized it.

No one would trouble him here. He could leave his blackfire quarrels safely hidden in the apothecary's cellar—the man had been a smuggler as well as a poisoner, and had dug out a secret sea access under his shop—and no one would think to look for them, or connect Corban to the quarrels if they did.

He didn't expect that to be a worry. No one had visited the shop in a dog's age. Bird droppings crusted the stoop in speckled white. A sun-bleached ribbon, showing a weary remnant of pinkish red at one end, flapped on a scabby-barked tree outside: the last legacy of the posted ban. The door, lifted off its hinges by would-be thieves, leaned against a crooked square of darkness.

Corban moved the door out of the way, slipping it to the side until it was no longer in danger of breaking the soggy piles of bird droppings. It didn't really matter, of course. Rain would cover some of the disturbance, and the birds themselves would soon cover the rest, but Corban wasn't a man who liked to take chances. He wanted to leave as few traces of his visit as possible.

He ducked as he carried the first blackfire crate inside. The sagging ceiling didn't offer much room, and the hovel was impossibly crowded. Mummified herbs hung from hooks in the rafters. Their leaves were wrinkled gray and flecked with dead white mold. Fungus pocked their knotted roots. Most likely it was harmless . . . but that was another chance Corban wasn't inclined to take. He kept his head low and measured his breaths as he passed beneath them.

The herbs weren't the only things the apothecary had left behind. Amid the foliage of that dead, dangling forest, eyes glittered.

Those eyes were glass, Corban knew. Dead eyes. Harmless. The apothecary had been a taxidermist as well. Stuffed rabbits and moth-eaten foxes pranced over the warped wooden shelves, frozen in eternal frolics around bags of mildewed tea leaves and boxes of pastilles melted together by the damp.

They still unnerved him. And there were worse creatures among them: the monsters that had sent the early thieves screaming, white-faced, from the apothecary's shop. Monsters that had started legends which kept other thieves away to this day.

Bulbous jars held them immured in cloudy brine: two-headed snakes, chunks of intestine packed with ropy worms, a cleft-jawed white piglet with a single round eye in the center of its head. A puppy with six legs and no tail. Two hatchling crocodiles whose limbs, seized by some wasting disease, were bare bone wrapped in green paper skin. The crocodiles had tried to swallow each other in the jar.

The walls were lined with uneven ranks of pickled monsters—and, Corban suspected, a few stillborn babies, as malformed as any of the animals—slowly disintegrating into fluffy sediment. An unpleasant aroma, like vinegar and fermented fish, lingered over the jars.

He didn't like to look at them. Oh, he knew the beasts couldn't hurt him, couldn't even bring bad luck; he wasn't some superstitious fishwife to make sun signs at every shadow or throw salt over his doorstep if a black rooster came near. But the animals floating in those murky jars were . . . unsettling.

Useful, though. They frightened off the locals. Corban held on to that thought as he retrieved the other two black-fire crates, keeping his eyes averted from the hanged man's grotesque trophies.

A wrinkled rug lay at the back of the hovel. Under it was a trapdoor anchored by a heavy iron ring. Corban lit a candle, then grabbed the trapdoor's ring with both hands and pulled. The planks were swollen with age and moisture, but on his second try the door came open with a sucking pop. A rusted ladder, bolted to the rough brick wall, descended into the black below.

Waves lapped in those gloomy depths. The salt breath of the sea blew damp against Corban's face.

He hoisted one of the crates into a leather harness, affixed the candle to its top with a gob of cooling wax, and buckled the unwieldy burden onto his back. Offering a silent prayer to whatever god felt like listening, Corban climbed down to the apothecary's secret cellar.

It wasn't much. A dripping brick cavern, a low wooden pier, two bollards for the tying of small boats. If the apothecary had owned a smuggler's boat of his own, it had been lost before Corban broke into his house. All that remained was a frayed rope wrapped around one of the bollards, its end trailing into the water.

The cellar was enough to hold his blackfire quarrels, however, and that was all Corban needed. He didn't expect to use it for long. Once he found a buyer, he'd move the crates out quickly; he only had to hide them until the sale was struck.

At the end of the pier, Corban took a moment to mop the sweat from his neck, then unbuckled the harness and eased the blackfire crate awkwardly off his back. The other two soon joined the first. He turned to leave, breaking the candle stub off the last crate to light his way, but hesitated before stepping off the pier's barnacled wood.

Were the quarrels in good condition? They might have been jostled or broken during the long river ride back to Cailan. The rain might have seeped into their boxes. Corban didn't *think* blackfire stone melted like lump sugar if it got wet, but he also didn't know, not really. Gethel hadn't told him anything about how the quarrels might react to the damp.

Corban could hardly sell broken quarrels, nor ungainly, useless ones with their blackfire stone melted out. He had to check. Sticking the candle stub onto one of the bollards, he pried the first crate open.

A mass of bristly, tarry straw greeted him. Corban plunged his hands in, digging around in search of a quarrel. The straws stuck his fingers and scratched the backs of his hands, but he was in too much of a hurry to care. Although he knew that the quarrels had simply shaken to the bottom during their transport, he felt an irrational pinch of worry. What if something *had* happened? Would he have to go all the way back to Carden Vale for more?

No. The quarrels' filigree was undamaged; their pebbles of blackfire stone were whole. Corban opened all three crates, plucking out every bolt and laying them in neat lines on the subterranean pier. He counted them—none was missing—and then counted them twice again to make sure.

Perhaps he worried too much . . . but he didn't think so. The blackfire quarrels were precious, almost priceless. There was nothing like them in Ithelas.

Every child knew that magic belonged to the gods. Only their Blessed could wield that holy power . . . unless the god, acting through those Blessed, imbued a fragment of magic into an ordinary object, creating a *perethil.*

Perethil, unlike prayers, could be used by anyone. Devout or impious, sinner or saint, they would serve their wielders just the same. But *perethil* were rare, the stuff of legend; the Dome of the Sun held only a handful. Even if Corban had the means to find or buy one—and he doubted the Emperor of Ardashir had wealth enough for that—it wouldn't have suited his needs.

The greatest *perethil* that Celestia had ever created—the eight Sun Swords forged during the Godslayer's War— could each be wielded by only one champion at a time. All the *perethil* Corban knew about had similar limitations. By restricting their use to one person, they could keep too much of the god's magic from falling into dangerous hands. Good for their faiths, Corban supposed, but not for him. He wanted a weapon that could outfit entire companies.

The idea had come to him after the Battle of Thelyand Ford. Corban hadn't been there, but he'd heard stories from other traders who'd spoken to survivors, or claimed to. The stories were thirdhand at best, and stretched until they had barely a nodding acquaintance with the truth, but they told him three things: first, that no army without magic could hope to stand against Ang'arta; second, that Celestia's Sun Knights *could* stand against them; and third, that there were too few Sun Knights, far too few, to hold the borders against Ang'arta's next push.

Taken together, those three things meant that there was enormous wealth to be had for a man who could turn the gods' power into a weapon that ordinary soldiers could use.

Corban had investigated the possibility at once. He did so cautiously, expecting little; if the priests were right and the gods were as miserly with their magic as he himself was with his gold, then no *perethil* existed that could suit him.

But priests were wrong more often than they liked to admit, and it didn't cost much to look. Corban turned to the Fourfold House. Its wizards had spent decades searching for godless magic; if any such thing existed, he reasoned, they were the most likely to have found it. And although the wizards liked to pretend they were above such petty concerns as coin, Corban knew that every man living under the Bright Lady's sun needed gold. The Fourfold House, lacking the prestige or real magic of Celestia's faith, was starving . . . for money, and for respect.

A few coins and a little lip service, and their loyalty was his. Through the Fourfold House he found Gethel, and through Gethel he found the slender possibility of a *per-ethil* that could be used by the masses.

As soon as Corban heard the legends of Duradh Mal, he understood that the ruined fortress might hold the key to his ambitions. What but divinity could have destroyed a citadel defended by the finest soldiers Ithelas had ever seen? The same soldiers, it happened, whose fellows in faith now threatened every kingdom from Calantyr to the Sunfallen Sea.

It was more than coincidence. It was a sign. Corban had paid for Gethel and his apprentice to travel to the immense libraries in Aluvair. He'd paid for their meals and lodgings and books. He'd paid for them to go to Carden Vale, never asking what they expected to find. Corban had never been superstitious before, but he felt it would be bad luck to put his hopes into words. He'd simply sent the silver, and waited . . .

. . . and now he held the rewards of his patience in his hands.

What price to put on that?

Of course he had to set *some* price. But how much?

Corban weighed the quarrel across his palm, marveling at the power contained in its rough-worked iron and unassuming blackfire pebble. It seemed, somehow, very important to give the bolt a correct price, as if selling it cheaply would dishonor the magic it held.

His candle burned out. Corban sat by its cooling puddle, still wondering.

What was an army's magic worth?

THE SCRATCHES WERE AN ANNOYANCE.

Some of the packing grease had gotten into them, or else he'd had a bad reaction to the straw. Whatever it was, the scratches in Corban's hands were discolored and the skin around them flushed and bee stung by the time he left the apothecary's house.

Nevertheless, Corban decided to put off asking anyone about the scratches until the next day. If they troubled him in the morning, he might seek out a physician or, perhaps, venture to the Dome of the Sun to consult with one of their Blessed . . . although that would mean wasting at least a day among all the other petitioners who begged for their aid, unless he felt like paying the exorbitant price for a private consultation. It was possible, too, that an Illuminer might connect the scratches to his blackfire stone and ask questions that Corban wasn't prepared to answer.

He was reasonably confident that the blackfire quarrels couldn't be traced to any particular deity. Gethel claimed he'd "freed" the magic, severing the creator god's connection to the *perethil*. Even so, Corban doubted that the Illuminers needed to identify *which* dark god had created the blackfire quarrels to conclude that *one* of them had, and then to hang him for consorting with fell powers.

It wouldn't even matter whether he was guilty, or how good his intentions might be. They'd execute him just to preserve their monopoly on holy power. They'd do it even if it meant ceding half the Sunfallen Kingdoms to Ang'arta.

He could not, therefore, risk going to an Illuminer over something as petty as a few scratches on the backs of his hands. If it was worse the next day, perhaps.

But the next day came and went, and the scratches stayed the same. Corban chose to ignore them. They weren't getting worse, so they probably wouldn't kill him, and he had other matters on his mind.

He still hadn't set a price on the quarrels, and he was

beginning to wonder, in his heart of hearts, whether it was altogether wise to sell them at all.

What if the Celestians traced the quarrels back to him? What if his buyers didn't believe the blackfire stone could do what he claimed? What if they *did,* and chose to rob him instead of dealing fairly?

Old thoughts, old worries. Corban had considered, and dismissed, all of them long before he paid the first silver shield to send Gethel on his way. Yet somehow they loomed larger now that he had the blackfire quarrels in hand—literally. He had fallen into the habit of carrying one around with him. He liked to touch it, reassuring himself with its rough solidity whenever he began to imagine that the promise of blackfire stone couldn't possibly be real.

It was real, and it was his. And it would kill him if he dealt it wrong.

5

"Come," said Avele diar Aurellyn. "There is something I want you to see."

It was very late. The moon had vanished from Kelland's high, barred windows. Past midnight, still far from dawn. He had been sleeping.

She had not. The Thornlady's hair hung loose over her shoulders in dark brown waves, framing rather than concealing the necklace of purpling bruises that ringed her throat. Her lip was split and bleeding at the corner: someone had hit her, and hard. And yet she seemed luminous, deeply content, like a maiden in the blush of new love.

The stories said that Aedhras the Golden had been traveling through the decadence of Kai Amur when this woman had captured him and, as was the Thorns' custom, taken him to their temple for questioning. That he had slipped his chains and turned on her with all the savagery of a man who had fought his way up from the breaking pits and lived. And that she, improbably, had been so charmed by his violence that she had released him from captivity and followed him west across Ithelas and, in time, bound herself to him in marriage.

It was the strangest courtship story Kelland had ever heard. But looking at her, bruised and blissful, he could well believe it true.

He rubbed the sleep from his eyes and wrapped a robe around himself. The fortress, like any drafty castle, was chilly so early in the spring. "What?"

"A woman. One who claims to be of your faith, though you might disagree."

He got to his feet. "You have another Celestian imprisoned?"

"No. No, you remain unique in my collection."

"Who is this woman?"

"That is for you to decide once you have seen her."

"Where is she?"

"Cailan. Dress for the road. You will not be coming back."

Kelland hesitated. Travel to Cailan meant bloodmagic, and another journey through the shadows. He hated the feel of the Thorns' magic . . . but he was a prisoner, and it was foolish to think that the Spider could not force him to her will.

He dressed, trying to ignore her presence as he exchanged his robe for the clothes she had brought him. Trousers and tunic, good leather shoes, a cloak of plain warm wool. No weapons. It felt strange to wear anything other than the sun-marked white of the Blessed, and stranger still to venture back onto the road without a sword, but for the first time since his capture, Kelland felt like a person rather than a prisoner.

While he was dressing, Avele had drawn up a silver chain from her sleeve. A small glass bottle filled with dark liquid dangled from the chain. She unlatched the bottle's silver cap as she stepped close to the knight. Kelland caught the scent of blood mingled with the myrrh and frankincense of her perfume.

"What—"

She interrupted his protest before it was out. "You must be disguised before we go to the city. You are a very distinctive man, and a very famous one, and even by night you would likely be recognized. That would be inconvenient. At best, it would mean questions that I do not have time to answer; at worst, someone might try a rescue, and then I might have to kill half the city to keep you. A nuisance. Better you should let me paint your face."

"With blood?"

"With magic."

Her fingertips were feather light as she traced runes in blood across his face, whispering an invocation to her cruel goddess. The blood was warm, perhaps because it had been kept close to her body, perhaps because it was freshly drawn. Kelland stared fixedly at a point on the far wall, waiting for it to be done.

The painted sigils cooled swiftly on his face. As she finished chanting, they warmed until the marks were painfully hot, the blood boiling on his skin. Then, abruptly, the heat was gone, and the wetness with it.

He looked down. His hands, which had been a deep, rich brown all his life, were now sun browned on top and pale beneath, with the calluses and ridged, swollen knuckles of a man who'd spent his life fighting, and had done it with fists as often as swords. Astonished, Kelland went to the mirror and saw looking back at him an unfamiliar face, hard eyed and stubble chinned, and *light*. He pushed back his cloak and pulled open the neck of his tunic. Where his skin was shielded from the sun, it was almost white.

White, and branded with the emblem of a gauntleted, upraised fist.

"You've made me a Baozite," he said, and then stopped at the sound of his spell-altered voice. It was harsher and deeper than his own, a voice that had rarely spoken in joy, whose prayers would sound like curses. A Baozite voice.

The Spider shrugged, unperturbed. "He was rebellious. His life was forfeit, and his death not to be mourned. If I had not intervened, my lord husband would have killed him anyway. Instead, he serves as an example, and you have a disguise."

"How efficient."

"Yes." She emptied the last of the bottle's blood into his washing basin, then swirled the glass through the water to rinse it, replaced the cap, and tucked it back into her sleeve. "Come. The night is fading."

He bit his tongue. She was close enough that the silver foxfur on her sleeves brushed against his wrists; the scent of myrrh and frankincense clung to her hair. It was no longer alluring.

The Spider began a new chant. Softly, sibilantly, in a language that was not made for human tongues but seemed to speak to the darkest parts of his soul. The shadows gathered around them, and with the darkness came a breath of unearthly cold. Her hand closed around his wrist, and blackness engulfed him.

An uncountable time later, the soft light of the stars told him that he was back in the world of the living, back under the open sky. A cool wind carried the scent of the sea and, closer, the rankness of tidal mud and rotting fish. He could hear the lap of waves in the harbor and the creak of mooring ropes. The water was out of sight, though, and the buildings silhouetted before him were cramped and sagging, their walls scabbed with scalloped crusts of salt. To the north, above their slanting roofs, the spire of Heaven's Needle shone against the sky.

He was in Cailan. The worst part of it, but still the city that had been home, or something close to that, for almost all his life. The knowledge lifted a weight of despair from his soul. He had never really believed, until now, that the Thorns would release him.

Avele moved with perfect confidence through the warren of Cailan's dockside. Occasionally Kelland glimpsed retreating movements and half-seen figures in the alleys, but no one confronted them. No one even came into view. That puzzled him. The Spider was ludicrously out of place in her jewels and furs, and unlike himself, she was not so unusual that footpads should have recognized her and backed away from a distance. At this hour, an unarmed woman in rich clothes should have been accosted by a dozen beggars, and twice as many robbers, before she reached the first corner.

Instead the streets were silent. He saw no living souls.

"Are they so afraid of this face?" he asked as she stopped outside a swaybacked house.

"No. They think we are a hunting party."

"What?"

"Sometimes we come to the slums when we are short of bodies. One Thorn, a soldier or two. We take as many as can easily be transported and return. Ordinarily, vermin are preferred, but if someone wants to be foolish and offers himself up, who are we to refuse? Earlier it was easier. Since then, the clever ones have learned, and the stupid ones are gone."

"You come all the way to Cailan to seize victims for your sacrifices? Why?"

"I dislike killing the useful. It weakens my lord's domain. Oh, on occasion there are *veselde* who forget their places, or soldiers who become disobedient . . . but for the most part, people fulfill their duties and so strengthen my lord's rule. Why, then, should we prey on them? Better to come to Cailan and remove some of the filth from its gutters. The city should thank us."

Kelland's borrowed skin crawled. "Why are you telling me this?"

She knocked on the door, twice in close succession and a third time after a pause. "Because you asked."

From inside the house came the rasp of a bar sliding back. A girl opened the door. She was very pale, unhealthily so, and wore a modest blue dress that brushed the floor.

"Lady," the girl murmured, curtsying low. She held a candle cupped in a ceramic dish, and did not seem surprised to see them.

"Brielle. Take me to your guest."

The girl straightened and nodded. The irises of her eyes were red, Kelland saw; not the deep red of blood, but the cloudy near pink of jasper. If she had been a Thorn, it would not have been so striking—the Maimed Witches were known for much worse than red eyes—but he would have put her age at sixteen or seventeen, too young to be a Thornlady, and she was otherwise ordinary.

She led them up a rickety staircase. Spiders clung to dusty webs in the corners; mice scurried inside the walls, heard but not seen. At the top of the stairs was a room bare but for a three-legged chair in the corner and a mold-spotted hanging on one wall.

The girl put the candle dish down on the chair and

pushed the hanging aside. Behind it was a door, which she unlocked to reveal a steep staircase leading down through the wall of an adjacent building. The secret stairs smelled of dust, hot wax, and oiled metal. Old blood spotted the steps.

"Shall I come?" Brielle asked, retrieving her candle as she stepped aside.

"No, thank you," said the Spider, drawing up her robe. She lit a second candle from the girl's and speared its end into an empty dish. "Wait here. We won't be long."

Avele went down the narrow stairs. Kelland followed cautiously, trying to ignore the smell of blood and sweat. The same stench filled the dungeons beneath Ang'arta—but this was Cailan, he told himself, and surely the city guards would not turn a blind eye to such abominations in their midst.

At the end of the stairs was a curiously fashioned door barred in iron. It was tiny and set deep into the wall, and it had an ivory lock without a keyhole. The Spider shook back her sleeve and pressed a fingertip to the lock, murmuring a verse of prayer.

Soundlessly the door swung open. Kelland saw that it was at least six inches thick, though compared to the walls it seemed thin as a parchment leaf. Both walls and door were hollow. Raw wool and scraps of cork stuffed the gaps between their planks, and as the door opened, the knight understood why: to silence the screams.

A gaunt woman lay shackled on a table inside. Her hands were curled in bony claws, her temples stained with bloody tear tracks. A sweat-soaked yellow dress clung to her body. She screamed endlessly, senselessly, her voice feeble as a wind through rattling reeds. The walls were hung with hooks and knives and stranger implements of pain, but Kelland could see no injury on the woman except the rings of blood around her eyes.

He came closer. There were crystal lenses laid flat over her eyes, each one fringed with minute steel blades like the petals of some grisly flower. Though the lenses themselves were smooth, the woman blinked constantly at the weight of them resting on her eyes, and she had cut her lids to shreds upon the blades. The tiny razors were caked with clotted blood and loose eyelashes, and still she blinked against them.

Kelland looked away, disgusted. He had seen brutality in war and more of it in the Baozite fortress, had even dealt some of it himself, but the things the Thorns did—the things they called "art," and prided themselves on perfecting—turned his stomach. "Why was this done?"

On the other side of the table, the Spider stood and gazed down at her victim with a gentle smile. She stroked the woman's brow after setting her candle in an alcove overlooking the table. A line of blood followed her touch, though there was no blade in her hand. "Why? Because what Brielle lacks in wisdom—and that is no small lack— she tries to make up for in zeal. As I never told her *not* to touch our guest, it is little surprise to find her wearing eyeflowers."

He had no reply for that. "This is why you brought me?"

"It is." Avele drew her hands away and folded them behind her back, smudging her robe with crimson. "I didn't expect the eyeflowers, but they should not affect any interrogation. The woman's name is Jora. She claims to be a Celestian, though you might disagree. We caught her stealing children from the streets."

"You didn't thank her for helping to clean the gutters?" There was little humor in the question, but black humor was better than rage. Whatever game the Spider was playing, he'd need his wits to counter. Anger could only lead him into folly.

She shook her head. "Listen to her. Listen, and you will understand."

He did. At first he heard nothing. The woman had screamed herself past hoarseness. Her howls had become pantomimes, empty of sound. But as he stood there concentrating, Kelland became aware of something more: a faint, unpleasant sensation, just below the level of hearing, like the buzzing of a thousand unseen bees or the swarming of black flies over a battlefield. The vibration thrummed along his skin and under his nails, maddening as an itch that couldn't be reached.

Maol. Kelland drew back abruptly. The buzzing sensation vanished, but he still felt unclean. The taint that emanated from the ragged woman was as different from the Spider's as a song howled by dissonant throats was from one played on a master's harp . . . but just as both those sounds were "music," so he knew that what lay in both their souls was the touch of divine evil.

There was no mistaking that jangling discord. The Mad God had laid claim to this woman's soul. "She's no Celestian."

"I see your years of training were not wasted." There was an acid edge to Avele's voice. "No, she is no Celestian, but she claims she is. She *believes* she is. Ask her. If you can force any sense into her answer, that is what you will hear. *That* is what I brought you to see."

Kelland frowned. The Thorns could not lie, but what they said was not always truth, not as any reasonable soul would take it.

He set his palms on the bloodstained table, framing the

woman's head between them, and reached out to Celestia's power. Doubt flickered in him for an instant—had his failure in Tarne Crossing severed his link to the divine?—and the prayer would not come. He stopped, steadied his focus, and began the invocation again. This time the glory of his goddess' presence filled him, humbling and terrifying. Sweet as the sight of the sun had been, it was nothing compared to the return of the Bright Lady's magic. The familiar words of the prayer guided his concentration, letting him gather and shape the formless magic like sunlight through a glass.

Holy light surrounded Jora in a halo. It was a hazy blue-violet, fragile as the last gleam of twilight, and dimmer than Kelland had expected. Had his captivity made him so weak? Or was his magic still diminished by doubt? Then he saw the Spider watching him, and understood. Her power was that much greater than his; she was holding him back.

She hadn't spoken a word, though, and she made no movement. His unease grew stronger. It was *possible* to invoke magic without word or gesture, but it was not easy, and the difficulty increased monumentally with the strength of the spell. Magic, as given by the gods, was amorphous as water. Prayers created a vessel that could channel it toward a purpose. But first the spell caster had to *convey* the purpose, and few had the clarity of mind necessary to do that without words. It was like trying to hold the entirety of an epic poem in one's mind at once. Nuances of meaning slipped away; sequences tangled and tumbled around one another. Irksome, when retelling a saga; fatal, when controlling a spell.

But the Spider seemed to have no difficulty. And if her control was that strong, then she could break his prayer and return the room to night on a whim.

She did not. After a moment he looked back to the woman on the table. Jora's hair had been cropped to the skull recently. Beneath the stubble, her scalp was stark white and dotted with eight large blisters in an uneven circle. Elsewhere her skin was nut brown and wrinkled by long days spent laboring under the sun. A farmwife, maybe. Before Maol's touch had taken root in her soul.

Jora's eyes focused on his face. He couldn't tell whether she was lucid, or whether she would be responsive to his prayer. She seemed calmer, though, and it seemed to him that the holy light soothed some of the madness that roiled in the woman.

"How did you come here?" Kelland asked. He kept his voice gentle. His magic would bind her to tell the truth, or what she *thought* was the truth, but he had no idea how much the prayer would help with a mind so corroded.

Jora licked her lips. Blood from the eyeflowers had funneled around her mouth while she screamed. The dried tracks of it cracked when she answered. "On a boat. I served. I did blessed work . . . until *she* caught me." Her eyes rolled white under the bloody lenses.

"What blessed work?"

"The children. We need them. We need them. The nightmare is waking. The old death is coming." Her words were so faint that Kelland had to lean closer to hear. He tensed, wary that she might lunge up for a bite. "Only pure hearts can hold it back. Only the pure can draw fire from the stone. The scholar told us. The scholar warned us. Keep the fires burning, and the nightmare cannot take us."

"What nightmare?"

"The old dream. The old death. So long it's been waiting, whispering . . . but it is louder now. We are holding it back, with help, with pure hearts. But it eats them . . .

it eats them . . . and the longer we hold it, the stronger it gets." She nodded furiously, as far as her bonds would let her. Half-dried blood clotted at the corners of her eyes like poisoned tears. "It comes in the dark, it speaks in the dark, and the whispers never go away . . ." Real tears began trickling out under the glass, softening the knots of gore and cut lashes at the eyeflowers' edges.

None of the woman's ramblings made sense to Kelland, but he pressed on doggedly. If she let slip *something* that he could follow, it might shed some light on the rest. "How are you holding it back?"

"Prayers. Prayers and pyres. The Bright Lady has shown us the way in her flames. The fire takes them and cleanses us. The fire keeps us safe."

"If fire keeps you safe, why do you need children?"

"They are the shapers. Little hands. They bring the holy fire from the stone, stone cut from death's hollow heart. It is their blessing, their gift . . . theirs to shape, and share with us. It is the only weapon that kills the monsters. Without them we would fail."

"Where are the children?"

"Safe."

"*Where?*"

Jora's hands trembled against the table. Her wrists, raw and bleeding, shook in their restraints. A soundless word rose to her lips and died. She tried again, and the second time managed to whisper: "Shadefell. You must go. Go to them. I know what you are . . . what you can do. Protect us. Our prayers are failing . . . and they are in Shadefell."

The name meant nothing to Kelland, but he could not press her further. His prayer was exhausted. The magic slipped out of his grasp, elusive as sunlight once more.

Kelland plucked the eyeflowers away carefully. The tiny

blades pricked his fingers, but he got them free. He could give the woman that much mercy. Jora sighed and closed her eyes, or tried to. There was too much flesh missing for her lids to meet, and the red-veined whites of her eyes peeked through the gaps. The last of Kelland's dawn light danced across those bloody whites, and then the dark returned.

Avele took the candle from its alcove. "Is there anything more you wish to know?"

"What did you do with the children she captured?"

"We destroyed them, of course. They carried the Mad God's contamination; there was nothing else to be done. But we did not find them all. Some were sent back to Jora's village. Precisely how, I cannot say. Smuggled, perhaps. We found tallies for them, but no record of their transport."

Kelland gave her a hard look, but no reproval. If the children had truly carried Maol's touch, they were more dangerous than plague bearers. He would have preferred healing them, but if the Thorns had neither the means nor the will to do so, a cure by fire was better than letting them roam free.

Maol—the Four-Armed Beggar, the Mad God—was unlike any other deity in Ithelas. Like them, he could not exercise his will in the world except through his mortal servants. But the Mad God was different in that he did not seek out strong souls to champion his faith. He sought weak ones, and he corrupted and consumed them, eventually destroying any creature who fell under his sway. His Blessing leapt from host to host like a disease, and it had to be treated like one to be stopped.

Sometimes, if the contagion was caught early, its victims could be cured. Sometimes they couldn't.

Three years ago, the last time a Maolite had been active in Cailan, he'd done his god's work by kidnapping children, inducting them into the Mad God's mysteries, and releasing them to be found by their families. Even after several families were found with throats slashed in their sleep, few had been willing to test their children for the taint, knowing that their sons and daughters might spend the rest of their years in Heaven's Needle if it was found. No one wanted to believe that a child gone for a single afternoon could have been warped so badly. The carnage went on for weeks before the Celestians found and stopped the Maolite cultist, and even after that there'd been more killings as the last few children returned home.

It was ugly. But it would have been uglier if they hadn't acted swiftly.

"You must go to Carden Vale," the Spider said.

Kelland did not answer immediately. He'd felt the creeping corruption in Jora's soul. He'd heard the torment in her ramblings. Whatever her "nightmare" was, whatever the "old death" meant, he was sure that Maol lay at its heart.

It was his duty, as a Knight of the Sun, to stand against the enemies that no one else could. If that was the Spider's price for his freedom, it was no more than his oaths already bound him to. And yet . . . what she offered him was not truly freedom, was it? Only a longer leash. If he went to Carden Vale, he'd run as Ang'arta's dog.

For an instant he longed for his tiny hole in the dungeon. In the safe, stinking dark, nothing had been expected of him. It had been miserable, yes, and it was cowardly even to think such things . . . but, in a perverse way, he missed it. He'd have died there, but he would have died honorably, quietly, *simply*. Unconflicted.

Duty was cold comfort. Though he should have been grateful for the chance of glory and a last glimpse of the sun, Kelland found himself wishing that Celestia had given her Blessing to someone else. Anyone else. He'd lost his taste for glory somewhere in the dark, and his cowardice made him unworthy to stand in the light.

"Bitharn will be so disappointed," the Spider said into the silence of his hesitation.

The knight's head snapped up. "What?"

"We made a bargain, she and I. She cares for you very much. And she expects to see you in Carden Vale."

"Why?"

"Because it is your duty to be there," the Spider said, her eyes glittering with malicious mirth. "Isn't it?"

It was. Kelland looked at Jora and thought of the children, the ones tallied but never found. There was no choice. He was a Knight of the Sun. Whatever his fears about Ang'arta's plots, whatever his secret indecision between duty and desire, he was oathbound to help. That much, at least, was clear.

He looked back to the Spider. There was no harm in speaking frankly; the only other witness was the madwoman on her table, and it was unlikely that she'd live to see another morning, much less tell anyone what she had heard. "Why does it matter to you?"

"I have my own interests there, and reason to believe they are linked with yours. It would please me, and benefit us both, if we worked together in this."

"If not?"

"Then you will do what you must do, and I will do the same. Regardless, you must go." She gestured to a long, flat box lying against the far wall. The table and the feebleness of the candle's glow hid it from view; Kelland had not noticed it earlier. "My parting gift. Take it. I expect you'll need it."

It was his sword.

6

They left Cailan two weeks before Greenseed, the festival of first planting. It was early for travel, but the two young Blessed were eager to begin their *annovair*, and Asharre, once she'd made the decision to go, was eager to leave her unwanted memories behind.

The ride gave her time to take the measure of her companions. Evenna was a soft-spoken beauty who carried herself with a solemnity far beyond her seventeen years. The young Blessed had blue-black hair that she plaited and looped around her head in a healer's halo, a style among the Illuminers that dated back to Alyeta the Redeemer. Oralia had worn her hair the same way. She had moved with the same quiet grace, too, and her clothes carried the same fragrance of wormwood and wintermint, anise and aloe. Healer's herbs. The perfume of ghosts.

Asharre tended to avoid her. It was no fault of Evenna's, but it was too easy to catch the girl in the corner of her eye and forget, for an instant, that it was not Oralia riding beside her.

Falcien's company was easier to bear. The other Illuminer had the small, wiry build of an Ardasi knife fighter. His coloring was southern as well: olive skin, eyes and hair of a rich, mutable color between brown and black. His accent was pure Cailan, though, and he laughed easily with the others about things that had happened in the city when they were young. He had never been an outsider. Not like her.

Her companions gave her space. Sometimes Asharre caught them looking at her scarred face, or at the two-handed *caractan* she wore across her back, but they kept their questions to themselves. The *caractan* was thicker and heavier than the longswords favored by the Knights of the Sun. Though it had an edge and Asharre kept hers sharp, it was a weapon made to crush rather than cut. It seldom saw use outside the White Seas clans, for none but Ingvall's children had the strength or stature to wield it effectively. Still, strange as it must have been to them, neither the Blessed nor Heradion asked about her sword.

She was content to let them wonder. The ride settled her spirits, allowing her a tranquility she hadn't felt since Oralia's death. It wasn't until Heaven's Needle dwindled to a sparkling mote on the horizon that Asharre realized how much Cailan had been her sister's city. There was hardly a handspan at the Dome of the Sun that did not carry a freight of memory. Away from it, at last, she could see the world with her own eyes.

It was more beautiful than she remembered. Asharre had never been on the road without a certain wariness, if not outright fear. Her first journey had been away from their homeland, guarding her sister through hostile territory, toward the unknown. She knew when they left that they would never return. Afterward she had traveled only as Oralia's protector, and while they had seldom been in real danger after that first year, she had never let down her guard.

Now she did, a little, and looked at the world unfolding.

They rode past untilled fields blanketed by yellow straw and wrinkled, frost-kissed leaves. Ancient stone walls and dark green hedgerows separated one farmer's land from the next; gnarled apple trees and pollarded willows dotted the hills between. Mastiffs barked at them from farmhouse yards, while small, timid deer darted through the trees.

The land grew rockier and the hills steeper as they continued. Village walls changed from simple boundaries to solid fortifications of mounded earth and stakes. Then those, too, receded in the distance as the earth became too stony to support farmers. Two weeks north of Cailan, all Asharre could find to mark human habitation were thin brown goats cropping at weeds between the rocks.

The last town worthy of the name was Balnamoine. It marked the informal boundary of Calantyr; though the villages and mining towns to the north belonged to the realm on maps, in truth the king's rule ended at Balnamoine. The mountain people kept to their own ways.

That might, Asharre reflected, be why the High Solaros had sent two of his Blessed to serve their *annovair* in Carden Vale. Their presence would be a light touch of civilization, a gentler means of bringing the mountain villages into the fold than sending a company of the king's soldiers to force their allegiance.

Perhaps. The politics of northern Calantyr weren't her concern. Her only duty was seeing the Celestians safely to Carden Vale. Ahead, the Irontooths solidified from a misty band across the horizon to a towering wall. The mountains' slopes were rough and gray as battle-scarred steel, their peaks so white they vanished into the clouds.

Evenna drew them aside as they came to the gates of Balnamoine. "I have an old friend here," she told them. "An old patient, really. Nessore Bassinos. He's a merchant who does some trade with the mountain villages. I thought it might be helpful to talk to someone who knew the lay of the land, so I sent him a letter before we left Cailan. We have a standing invitation to dinner."

"How's his cook?" Falcien asked.

"Better than you," Heradion said. "If he offered us boiled boot leather and fried mud, I'd consider it a welcome respite from what you've been serving up."

Asharre shook her head, amused despite herself. "Where is his house?"

Evenna showed them. It was a large dwelling, and Nessore Bassinos had not stinted on its ornaments. Both the balustrades flanking the great doors and the doors themselves were marked with the Celestian sunburst and looked like new additions. The earth around the house was rutted by builders' wagons and trampled by their boots. Come summer, the house's gardens would cover the damage, but for now it was still raw.

A servant greeted them as they rode up. An old woman with a snow white scarf tied over her hair in a fashion that had gone out of date in Cailan generations ago, she fussed over Evenna like a mother embracing a wayward child. Asharre was glad to hand her horse's reins to the stablehand who came for them, and gladder when the old woman offered them the use of Bassinos' baths.

The merchant had not one bathhouse but two, one for the men and one for the women, that faced each other across a portico of yellow sandstone. Tiny windows near the ceiling pierced their curved walls. A garden lay behind them, and a chapel past that.

The chapel wasn't new, but several of its windows were. Their stained glass sparkled against mastic as pristine as fresh snow. Other windows were boarded over, their old glass not yet replaced. The holy sunburst in the largest of the new windows had an unusual design; its eight wavy rays were all of a size, instead of being longer at the cardinal points and shorter between, and the tip of each one was rounded like an onion's bulb. For some reason they made Asharre think of open palms reaching for something. Enlightenment, perhaps? One of the Blessed might know. She brushed the thought aside and went in for her bath.

The bathhouse was extraordinary in its luxury. It held basins of hot and cold water, three kinds of scented soap, a goldenwood brush with boar's-hair bristles, and decorative trinkets whose uses baffled her. Evenna came in as she was examining a sculpture of a dancing woman holding a bowl. Putting the tool aside, Asharre filled a bucket from the steaming basin.

As she sluiced water over her head, she caught Evenna looking sidelong at the scars that striped her ribs. That, too, was something Asharre had taught herself to ignore, but something in the younger woman's face made her pause.

Their eyes met. Evenna had the grace to blush. Asharre did not think it was because they were unclothed; a healer would be used to that, just as she was. Modesty died quickly on the battlefield.

The first words out of the girl's mouth confirmed her suspicions. "I'm sorry," Evenna said, still blushing. "It's just . . . I've never seen so many scars on a woman."

Asharre grunted. She supposed her stripes and welts, earned across a decade and a half spent fighting one thing or another, might be startling to a stranger. Over the years, her skin had become a tapestry of old hurts. "Lucky for them."

"Are they . . . did you . . . those aren't from Oralia's *annovair,* are they?"

Asharre shook her head, understanding the girl's trepidation at last. This was the first time Evenna would have been so far from home or temple, and the tales of the mountain people could be frightening to someone who did not know the truth.

"No," Asharre said. "Most of them . . . the first man who taught me how to hold a sword was Surag One-Eye. He had to teach me, had to respect my oath as *sigrir.* You understand? It was his obligation as a warrior of Frosthold. But he did not have to like it, and he didn't have to be gentle about it. Most of them weren't. For a woman to become *sigrir* to negotiate her sisters' marriages is not so strange, even today. For her to take up arms is . . . an old custom. Very old, and very rare. Even before the sun worshippers came to the north it was not a common thing. Most often, women took that oath when all the clan's warriors had been killed raiding and warring and the only men left were graybeards and boys. So for me to learn the sword . . . it was not the same as saying that Frosthold's warriors were feeble or childish, but it was not far from that, and most of the men were not pleased by it.

"Surag was different. To him it was a source of pride, not an insult, that I wanted to learn the ways of war. He was . . . tradition was very important to him, and a *sigrir* who hewed to the old ways was, in his mind, a credit to our clan's honor and fierceness. He was proud to teach me.

"He was the one who found us when Oralia and I left Frosthold." Asharre closed her eyes. More than fifteen years ago, that was, but the memory still grieved her. "When we disappeared, he tracked us. No one else did. We were not much loved in the clan. There had been rumors all winter about my sister's afflictions. Most of them . . . most of them would have been content to let us go, and would have counted themselves well rid of her strangeness. Not Surag."

"What happened?" Evenna whispered. Her bare shoulders were so white they glowed in the thin gray light; her face was almost as pale.

"He tried to stop us. Surag One-Eye was, as I said, a man to whom tradition mattered. For us to go south, to join the Blessed, was a betrayal of the clan's beliefs. He would not let us pass. I fought him. Surag was much more experienced, and still strong . . . but he was old, and blind on one side, and the cold did him no favors." Asharre had never been more frightened in her life than she was on that winter morning, her teacher's face become a stranger's and a blade bare in his hand. Terror, and desperation, had lent her ferocity. "I did not want to kill him. But whenever I flinched, he cut me again, and finally it was clear there was no choice. So: that is where I got most of these scars. He taught me one last lesson as *sigrir* that morning."

Asharre finished washing—the water had grown cold— and toweled herself dry. Evenna followed suit more slowly, looking thoughtful.

As Asharre was buckling the strap of her *caractan* back over her gray-green cloak, Evenna touched her forearm.

"I'm sorry for your scars," the young Blessed said.

"Don't be. Vanity is nothing. Scars mark what you have done."

"Yes, I suppose that's true," Evenna said uncertainly. She rallied behind a smile. "I'm grateful to have such a formidable guardian. We all are."

"You should have no need of me. You are only going to serve your *annovair*. Thi—the High Solaros would not have sent you into danger." *Or me,* she added silently. Thierras d'Amalthier knew when his tools were too brittle for a task.

They rejoined the others for dinner. It was a small meal, served only to the merchant's family and his guests, but a lavish one. Asharre sat between Heradion and Bassinos' eldest daughter, Melora, a plain-faced girl who seldom lifted her eyes from her plate. After her halting attempts to draw Asharre into conversation were met with grunts, Melora sank into a timid silence that lasted until Falcien, sitting on her left, distracted her with gossip about courtiers in Cailan. Asharre paid little heed; the pratfalls of the pompous held no interest for her. Instead she turned her attention to the food.

There was plenty of it, served on dishes inlaid with bright lines of gold and copper. The drinking glasses bore the same design: eight-rayed sunbursts, Celestia's holy sign, rendered in the same curious fashion as the ones on the chapel windows.

Asharre was not the only one who noticed them. "I don't remember you being so pious," Evenna teased, holding up her glass. She drank cold whitebriar tea, as Falcien did, and it sparkled in the candlelight. "When did you turn your house into a chapel?"

Bassinos shrugged, smiling. He was in his late middle years, broad shouldered and blunt featured, and had the easy confidence of a man who had built a good life using his own hands and wits. Though his beard was more silver than brown, his eyes kept a boyish twinkle. "Piety is profitable these days. The mountain folk are all mad for prayers and sunbursts, especially the Open-Handed Sun. Some of them won't deal with a man who doesn't pray under it. I don't mind. One chapel window looks the same as another to me, and whatever I spend on glassblowers and builders, I'll recoup three times over by this time next year. I've already snatched a dozen contracts for coal and furs from Wyssic, and the passes are still frozen. I'll have twice as many when they open."

"Why's that?" Heradion asked.

"Wyssic likes his feather bed. I can't fault him for it, at his age, but he misses too many dawn prayers. Best time to negotiate with these Vale men is right after services. Meet them at the chapel, bring them back for breakfast, and the deal's good as sworn once they see their new sun on my plates and windows." Bassinos chuckled, refilling his glass with cold whitebriar tea. In deference to the Blessed at his table, he hadn't served ale, although Balnamoine was said to have several good local brews. Asharre regretted his courtesy; she would have liked a mug to go with the chestnut-sauced quail.

"New sun?" Falcien sounded casual, but he leaned in, putting an elbow on the table. "Do you mean these sunbursts with the rounded rays?"

"Aye. You noticed? Well, of course you would. That's your business, after all." Bassinos covered a burp politely and reached for another helping of baked turnips. "The Vale traders insist on it. Past the point of decency, if you ask me. One of them smashed our town chapel's window for its 'impious' design. Do you have any idea how much that damned window *cost*? That red glass came from Aluvair! And the gilding—aaah, but no matter. It's done. Anyway, that one was a fool and a fanatic, but they're all a sight more comfortable under their new suns. Don't seem to care much for our old ones."

"A heresy?" Evenna asked. A thin line appeared between her eyebrows.

"The High Solaros never mentioned one," Heradion said. "I doubt he'd have sent us if he had any such suspicions. Most likely it's just some local fashion—maybe a bit of folklore they've woven into their prayers. Every village seems to have a few of those. Farther you get from Cailan, the more there are. But they're harmless, really, and good business for the glaziers."

"Good business for anyone who'll pray with 'em," Bassinos said. "Crass to use my faith like that, I expect, and worse to admit it to the Bright Lady's own Blessed, but I've always been honest about my sins. They're not such awful sins, are they?"

"I've heard worse," Evenna said. "As long as you aren't cheating on your tithes—"

"Never that," Bassinos said, mock aghast.

"—then I suppose we'll have to forgive you. But when did the mountain towns rediscover their faith? Was there some disaster up there? Men aren't usually swept by a sudden love for prayer unless there's been war, plague, famine . . ."

"No, nothing. I haven't been north myself in some time, but I would have heard the stories. There's been nothing like that. Well, bandits, but there've been bandits on the iron road and pirates on the Windhurst since there was a road and a river." Bassinos paused, momentarily reflective. "Not many of those either, lately, come to think of it. Usually I lose a shipment or two every season, but this past year . . . it's been quiet. Completely. Even Gerros Tulliven hasn't been raided, and he manages to hire a few highwaymen disguised as guards every year."

"There are stories," Melora said, lifting her head. Her fingers danced over the tines of her fork. "The mad wind."

"Melora, dearheart," her father said gently, "those are just stories. Our guests are worried about threats on their way to Carden Vale. The mad winds aren't likely to give them any trouble."

"Oh," the girl said, flushing pink. She dropped her head again, and Asharre thought with astonishment that she might be hiding tears.

Falcien cleared his throat. "I'd be interested in hearing about these winds. There's often a grain of truth in those old folktales—and even if there isn't, I love a good story."

Bassinos nodded, a flicker of appreciation crossing his blunt face at the Celestian's courtesy. "I suppose there's no harm in the telling. It's an old tale, but it seems to have picked up new life this past season. The way the story goes, the ghosts of Duradh Mal ride the night winds in the Irontooths. They're cursed, either for what they did in life or by how they died, depending on the teller. They can't cross the Last Bridge until they've confessed all their sins, and there's no one like a Baozite for sinning. So they roam the mountain peaks looking for travelers who'll hear their confessions . . . but the sins they've committed are so ghastly, and the suffering they endure as ghosts so awful, that anyone who listens to them goes mad. Men strip naked and wade into the snow, letting themselves freeze to death, after listening to the mad wind. Women leap from the peaks or throw themselves into the rivers. Their deaths add to the spirits' litany of sins, and so they wander on, seeking new listeners forever."

"It's a ghost story?" Asharre said, disbelieving.

"This is a land for ghosts, my lady. We've nothing else to do but tell stories to fill the winters. Anything can spawn a tale, and that's likely how this one started. Someone heard a wind that sounded like screaming and invented some meaning to fit it. Someone else found a poor frozen soul who wandered out at night and got lost. Put one with the other, and that's your story. Oddities and accidents, with a dash of ghost lore thrown in for spice. To hear it told now, the wind freezes plants in summer, turns winter snow red as blood, and drives people mad all year round. Sometimes the ghosts who ride it are said to come from Duradh Mal, sometimes from Shadefell. Whatever the teller thinks sounds best."

"Shadefell?"

Bassinos only shrugged. He scooped more turnips onto his plate, seeming faintly embarrassed. Heradion took up the tale. "That one's a ghost story too. King Aersival gave the first Lord Rosewayn the land around Duradh Mal as his fief. He'd earned it, fighting in two hard campaigns and clearing out the Long Knives from the Smokewood, but some said that the king gave the valley to Rosewayn because he wanted the man as far from the capital as possible. Rosewayn had an ugly reputation. Some of the things he did to make captured Long Knives betray their brothers . . . there were rumors that he was a secret Kliastan. It was that bad. Many historians claim King Aersival felt it would be easier to turn a blind eye to Rosewayn's excesses if the lord was in Carden Vale.

"The Celestians sealed the lower reaches of Duradh Mal and some of its high towers, but they didn't seal the central fortress, perhaps because some lord at the time wanted to lay claim to the castle. I don't know. Be that as it may, Lord Rosewayn certainly wanted it. The locals told him the place was cursed, that the Doom would claim him, too, but the old lord wouldn't hear of it. Said it was the best strategic hold in the Irontooths, which was likely true. Say what you will about Baozites, but those bastards know war.

"The Baozites couldn't keep Ang'duradh, though, and Lord Rosewayn's luck was no better. He drained his fortune trying. Few craftsmen would travel that far, or brave the curse of Duradh Mal, and those who did met bad ends. Walls collapsed, beams broke, keystones cracked over the builders' heads. Some of them wandered into the empty halls and were never seen again. Other men swore they could hear the lost ones' voices calling from the dark, crying out for help.

"When the old lord died, his sons were glad to end the folly. They left Ang'duradh to its ghosts and built a new hold in the mountains. Shadefell, they called it. From there the Rosewayns ruled for a time, no better and no worse than any other lords. But over the years, the stories started to change.

"People vanished from the roads around Carden Vale. Mostly children and virgins, according to the stories. Travelers too. Entire parties disappeared, only to be discovered as chewed bones when the snows melted. Finally word came back to the Dome. Armed with Aurandane, the Sword of the Dawn, some Knights of the Sun ventured up to Shadefell to end it. The Rosewayns greeted them as honored guests, then tried to eat them as they slept. When their hosts revealed their true faces, the Knights saw that they were monsters. They fought a desperate battle through Shadefell's halls, half the house burned down, and when the smoke cleared, they found all sorts of atrocities in the ashes. Human bones in the pantry, torture pits in the cellars, tubs of rendered corpse fat that Lady Rosewayn smoothed into her skin for eternal youth—any horror that a bard might embroider onto the tale has been claimed at one point or another."

"And these voices, too, whisper on the mad wind?" Asharre asked.

"So they say." Bassinos refilled his glass with cider. "It's only a story."

Melora was still blushing and fidgeting with her fork. Asharre was not surprised to hear Falcien take his turn at distracting her. These Blessed were gracious to a fault.

"As you've been kind enough to give us a story, and Heradion has as well, I suppose I should take my turn," he said, and told them about the Winter Lake, a few weeks' ride east of Cailan, where the water was near freezing even in midsummer. Fishermen saw ice glistening over its heart, no matter how hot the sun shone, and heard the voices of women singing over its waves at dusk. Those who listened to the songs said that they were beautiful but unsettling; those who listened too often pushed their boats to the lake's center, where they leaped eagerly into the water and drowned.

By the time he had finished, Melora was listening raptly, her timidity forgotten. "Is it true?" she breathed, eager as a child listening at her nursemaid's knee.

"It's true that the water is cold," Asharre told her. "I've been there. It's cold enough to kill a man, but I've never seen ice or heard songs. I stayed with a woman who swore her husband had been called to his death by a fairy lure . . . but gossips in the village told me he was a drunk, and just as likely to fall out of his boat as come home every day. It's a cold lake, nothing more. By the White Seas we have springs that come up scalding. If rivers run hot under the snow, why should they not run cold in the summerlands?"

"Why not, indeed," Melora agreed. She did not seem disappointed by the explanation; if anything, her dark eyes shone brighter. "Do you have any stories?"

Asharre would have preferred to keep her silence, but she saw no way to decline gracefully. She'd never felt comfortable retelling folktales—she didn't have the gift to make them come alive—so instead she told them about the travels she'd had with Oralia: the cities they'd seen, the people they'd met, the odd dishes her sister always insisted that she try. Her sister seldom took so much as a nibble herself, pleading her restrictions as a Blessed, but Asharre had long suspected that Oralia just used that excuse to make her eat sheep-gut sausages and honey-baked crickets because, as she said every time, "one of us has to pay respect to the local delicacies, and *I* can't. Enjoy!"

It was the first time she'd spoken about Oralia since reporting her death to the High Solaros. Somehow, sitting around this table in the company of friends, it didn't hurt. The memories were good ones, and as she spoke, Asharre felt the weight of her grief lighten to something almost bearable.

Evenna followed her with a story about Mesandroth Fiendlorn, the sorcerer who burned the Belled Stag. On moonless nights, the story went, a ghostly inn appeared on the ashes of the sorcerer's crime, and the dead gambled with the living for their souls.

After her telling, a quiet descended on their table. Then Melora laughed, and Heradion clapped, and the mood was broken. Bassinos poured himself a last glass of tea. The servants came to clear the dishes, and Melora showed them to their rooms.

Asharre lay awake long after. Heavy curtains covered the windows for warmth. It was black as pitch inside her room. Somewhere down the hall, a man was snoring. A dog barked at passing shadows outside.

Restlessly she got to her feet and pushed the curtain aside. The moon painted the world in silver and sparkled on the chapel's frosted roof. High above, the vaulted sky seemed a reflection of that jeweled lace. If the Belled Stag only appeared on starless nights, its ghostly gamblers would be idle tonight.

Evenna's story of the cursed inn lingered in her thoughts. It was only a story, she knew, with no more substance than the fairy songs on the Winter Lake. The shades of the dead did not dice with the living. If they came back at all, it was as a bloodmage's thralls.

Still . . . if it were true, what would she give to gamble with ghosts? What would she risk for that? To give them a message, if she won, and hope that they might carry it back across the Last Bridge when they disappeared. To say *I'm sorry* and ask *Why?*

Was that worth the chance of never coming back?

Asharre stood by the window awhile longer, gazing at the silent chapel, and then went back to bed.

7

"Someone's coming up the slope."

"Hunters?" Malentir asked.

Bitharn shaded her eyes against the sunlight. The morning was new and cold, but the sere hills shimmered with heat, making it difficult to tell if anything moved among them. She shook her head. "Maybe. They're gone now."

They were a day north of Carden Vale, at the bottom reaches of the bleak, scarred hills that the maps called Duradhar and the locals called Devils' Ridge. Once these slopes had been rich and green, fertile enough to feed the Baozite host that held the fortress above. Then Ang'duradh fell, and the same curse that killed its soldiers blighted the land around it. Wheat fields and orchards burned from their roots up, leaving barren rocks and steaming rifts where they'd stood. Six hundred years later, the earth still smoldered all through Devils' Ridge. Wraiths of pale blue smoke drifted down the hillsides, and the earth was ash gray underneath.

For centuries, Devils' Ridge had been abandoned to its smoky ghosts. That desolation was one of the reasons Malentir had chosen to come to Devils' Ridge rather than travel directly to Carden Vale. Anyone who saw him would know him for a Thorn, and in town that would end badly. Out here, there were fewer eyes to find him, and a greater chance that anyone who did could be quietly subdued. It was likely, if that happened, that he'd want to kill the witness and wear the dead man's face for a disguise. Bitharn hadn't decided what she would do about that. She hoped she'd never have to.

She looked down again. Near the last fringe of green in the valley, metal glinted amidst the budding trees. Bitharn crouched, watched, and waited. After a long moment she saw another flash, and a pair of waxwings startled into the sky.

Malentir had seen them too. "No hunter in these hills will be looking for game," he said.

"They won't be looking for us either."

"No?"

Irritably Bitharn brushed a loose strand of hair from her eyes. "How could they? No one knows we're here. We— the Blessed, I mean—can't talk to the dead the way you can. Parnas couldn't have told anyone where we went, and he's the only one who knew. Even if they did somehow learn we're here, the Blessed can't walk through shadows. It's impossible for them to have gotten to Carden Vale so quickly. Whoever's down there can't have anything to do with us. It might not even be a person. Likely it's just a stray pack mule."

"A pack mule," Malentir repeated, hardly bothering to conceal his disbelief. "No doubt."

"Stay here. I'll have a look."

"You trust me at your back? Already? I'm touched."

"I don't trust you as far as I can throw you." She gestured to his slashed ivory-and-black robes and equally striped hair. "But you stand out like a gold crown in a beggar's bowl, and I'd rather not be spotted coming down the slope. Stay here and keep low."

"That must be a fearsome mule," the Thornlord said, but he found a rock to sit on, and he stayed out of her way.

She was glad to leave him behind. The hills were steep and treacherous, and keeping quiet took all her skill. Spellblasted stones offered scant cover, but at least the smoke's swirl masked her movements. Bitharn moved carefully, testing each step before trusting her weight to it. No matter how cautious she was, loose rocks skittered away underfoot, rattling down the hillside and sometimes letting up plumes of sulfurous steam. The noise made her wince, but there was no sign that it alarmed whoever, or whatever, was approaching from below.

She didn't think it was a pack mule. She didn't think it was Celestians either, but that possibility was harder to dismiss. Her subterfuge wouldn't last more than a day or two before the Blessed's goddess-granted visions revealed the truth of what had happened in the tower. Then the High Solaros would send Sun Knights and dedicants out to recapture the Thorn, and to take her as a traitor for helping him escape. They couldn't have come to Carden Vale so quickly . . . but they *would* come, eventually.

Not a pleasant thought. But she had known what would happen before she started, and she'd done it anyway. She hoped they would understand, that they would forgive the necessary evil she'd done . . . but if they didn't, Bitharn had made her peace with that. Let them call her a traitor if it meant getting Kelland back. Nothing the Celestians did to her could be worse than what he was suffering in Ang'arta.

There would be time to pay that price later. Here and now, her only concern was staying clear of pursuit long enough to trade the Thorn for Kelland's freedom. She'd thought they were too early—it was barely past Greenseed, and the full moon was still three weeks away—but Malentir had assured her it did not matter. He said the Spider would know he was free, and would come early to claim him. Bitharn could only hope that was true.

The sun was past its peak by the time she reached the end of Devils' Ridge. Green shoots poked through the cracked rocks. Oaks grew ahead, and chestnuts showing their first spring buds. Bitharn breathed a sigh and slipped gratefully into the forest, moving more quickly through familiar terrain.

It wasn't a hunter coming up the hill. It was a boy, barefoot and in a tunic far too thin for the weather. He was fourteen, or a little younger. His left foot was badly twisted, though he stumbled on despite it. The limp made him clumsy; that was why Bitharn had been able to sneak up on him so easily. He made so much noise blundering through the forest that he would never have heard her.

Bitharn was about to call out to the boy, to offer him her cloak or ask what had driven him so urgently into the forest, when he lifted his head toward Devils' Ridge and she caught sight of his face. The call died in her throat.

His face was bloated and pale, underlaid with a violet tinge like an old bruise. Inky spatters stained the corners of his lips and dotted his cheeks in a smiling arc toward his ears. As the boy stood there, chest heaving, Bitharn saw that the purple-black spatters weren't stains. They were sores eaten through the inside of his mouth, as if he had packed his cheeks with lye and waited for it to find its own way out.

She crouched in the brush, too shocked to move, until the boy regained his breath and plunged back into the trees. He went north, heading toward the blasted ridge as swiftly as his bad leg would let him. By the time she thought to follow, there was another crashing in the forest. Someone else was coming.

A sense of *wrongness* seemed to roll through the air, sharp as the tingling before a storm. Bitharn pressed herself closer to the ground. She didn't know what was coming, but she knew with a sudden, wild desperation that she did not want to be seen. There wasn't any reason for it, and that frightened her almost as much as the terror itself did. She wasn't a child, wasn't given to jumping at imaginary dangers . . . and yet she was certain, somehow, that what came through the forest was far worse than the boy with the spotted face. Chin in the dirt, Bitharn breathed shallowly through her mouth, praying that whoever—*whatever*—it was would not find her.

The branches parted. Four men came through. They were deeply sunburnt and wore miners' clothes blackened along the seams with greasy coal dust. The incongruity of their clothes and their complexions was hardly the only oddity about them. Their heads had been shaved recently, and their scalps were white through the stubble of returning hair. Blisters dotted each man's head in the same pink constellation, four over four.

The men carried picks and shovels slung across their backs. Each wore a long bone knife, too, strapped bare bladed at his hip. The knives were smeared with something dark. Not blood; it was the wrong color for that, and too grainy. She was too far to be sure, but it looked like the blades had been rolled in tarry sand.

The sense of wrongness did not come from them. It

came from the fifth man, the one who ran at their head, the one who wore a collar hooked into his neck by steel rings punched through scar tissue. His eyes were gone. Welts of slick pink flesh filled the sockets.

As the men came to the trampled brush where the boy had paused, the eyeless one raised his head and snaked his tongue into the air. That tongue was impossibly long, impossibly wide; laid against Bitharn's forearm, it would have stretched past her fingertips. Five holes, like the finger holes of a flute, ran along its length. The lowest was big enough for a hen's egg to slip through, the last one was small as a fingertip, and all of them whistled softly as the eyeless man licked the wind.

His head turned blindly to follow whatever his tongue felt. Bitharn shivered as the eyeless man's gaze passed over her, his tongue darting quick stabs in the air. He took a step toward her and her fingers closed around the hilt of a knife, even though she knew her accuracy would be hopeless if she threw while lying on her belly in the dirt.

The eyeless man took another step, swaying from side to side. Muttering, the man holding his leash jerked him back. "*Ank'raah.* Blackfire, not blood. Find the boy."

"What's the problem?" asked another miner.

"He smells blood." The one with the leash spat. "Deer, maybe. Or a rabbit. He hasn't eaten in so long, he might even be lighting on sparrows. Not our boy, though." He flicked the leash. "*Ank'raah.* Find the boy."

The eyeless one whined, but he curled his tongue back into his mouth and sent it undulating out again, glistening with black-flecked saliva. This time he turned north, along the path that the broken-footed boy had taken, and plunged ahead as far as the leash would let him. The other men followed. In a few moments they were out of sight.

Bitharn pushed herself up and brushed the wood loam from her clothes, swallowing to get rid of the cottony taste of fear. She wasn't sure what she'd seen, but she remembered the terror on the boy's face and knew she couldn't leave him to face them alone.

The miners had no slings or bows. If she kept her distance, she'd be safe enough. In the forest, with the advantage of surprise, she could kill five men—six, if she was wrong about the boy—before they closed on her. She had no illusions about how many things might go wrong, but the odds favored her.

If they were men. If he was a boy. .

Kelland would have been able to tell her. He would have known who those people were, and what they wanted, and what the right thing to do would be. With him beside her, she wouldn't have been nearly as afraid.

But he was in the dungeons of Ang'arta, being tormented by the Thorns, and her meeting with the Spider was his only hope of freedom. The thought brought a familiar wave of despair and a swift stab of anger. How could he abandon her to carry such a weight of choice and consequence by herself?

It wasn't a choice. Duty trapped him as surely as it did her. She couldn't leave that crippled boy to his fate.

She checked her knives and her bowstring, then stalked after the hunters.

They never heard her coming. The men shoved carelessly through the brush, drowning out any sound Bitharn might have made. The eyeless one canted his head in her direction, curling his tongue out again, but the man holding his leash forced him onward with a curse. She circled around them, hurrying to reach the boy before they did.

She found him slumped against a log, sobbing for

breath. His bad leg was stretched out to the side. A huge purple canker swallowed his foot and crept halfway to his knee. She'd never seen its like on a human limb; it looked like an eruption on a birch trunk, all twisted bark and gnarled wood. Not flesh.

That sense of wrongness came from him, too, foul as the stench off a tannery . . . but Bitharn had to help him. Had to *try.* She stepped out of the trees. "What's happened to you?"

The boy looked toward her. Bitharn recoiled. The spots on his cheek had widened and deepened. Now they were black fissures in his face, their insides glistening wet and gritty. The skin between them had wrinkled and bunched, as if his face were a mask about to slide off. Only his eyes were human, and they were filled with fear.

"Are you real?" he whispered. His drooping lips distorted the words so that she could barely understand.

"I am."

"Please." Tears trickled down the wrinkles of his ruined face. "Please . . . if you are real, help me."

"How?" She wasn't Blessed; she couldn't heal him. She wasn't sure Kelland could have. The boy's affliction was obviously unnatural, and there were limits when magic ran against magic. What those were, and where they lay, Bitharn wasn't certain, but she knew there was nothing she could do to cure him.

He didn't want a cure. "A knife. An arrow. You have a bow. Give me mercy. Please. They will come for me. I was a thief . . . but take pity on me, please. I stole only because I *needed* it. Needed its taste. Have mercy."

"No," Bitharn whispered, horrified. She couldn't heal him, but someone else could. There might be a Blessed in Carden Vale or another town along the river. Malentir might help. The Thorns could heal—differently, drawing on darker powers, but their skill was well known. Some said they were the best healers in Ithelas. They had to be to keep the victims of their interrogations alive, and Malentir was powerful among them. Perhaps he could turn cankers back into flesh. "I'll find a healer."

"Please." He tried to stand and failed, dragged down by his cankered leg. "They will come."

"I'll defend you."

"You can't. You cannot save me from my sins. I wanted—I wanted the fire under the mountain. Unworthy. I touched it. I dared, I devoured . . . and I burned. The penance is mine, the price . . . but will you forgive me? Please? Oh, Bright Lady, forgive me. Forgive me. I *wanted*." He spoke to the air, sobbing, and did not look at her again.

The miners were coming. Bitharn heard them kicking leaves and breaking branches. Cursing herself for a fool and a coward, she pulled back into the bushes to hide.

She watched, though. She could not help but watch.

They fell on him, swiftly and savagely. There were no cheers, no cries. The lead miner tied the harnessed one to a tree, like a dog, and all of them went at the boy with their black-bladed knives. They cut the canker from his leg and crammed its dripping pieces into their mouths while he watched glassy eyed. They wrenched the bones from his body and made them into tools. With swift, crude cuts, they made picks and handles from the long bones of arm and leg, shovels and scrapers from the wide bones of hip and shoulder. Their other tools were bone as well. Bitharn hadn't noticed, dirty as they were.

It wasn't torture, and it wasn't butchery. Both those words captured part of it, but what she saw was wilder, more savage, than that. Bitharn felt as if she were watching an old rite, something from the ancient days when the White Seas clans drank the blood of their enemies and left their living bodies staked hand and foot to the ice for their gods.

The boy never lifted a hand to defend himself, and the miners never said a word. The only sound was the scuffing of their boots, the wet noise of knives tearing through flesh, and the whistles of the harnessed man straining toward the slaughter, his tongue sieving blood spray from the air. Very soon the boy was dead, although the cutting went on for some time after that.

Bitharn waited until they were done. Then she turned away and was quietly sick in the woods.

Darkness fell before she reached the rock on Devils' Ridge where she had left Malentir. By night, the blasted ridge was like a glimpse into Narsenghal, where the ghosts of the sinful dead were condemned to wander. The crevices between the stones were chasms of depthless black, the stones themselves a mosaic of broken silver. Moonlight glowed within the smoke, turning the rising wisps into coils of drifting light and covering the slopes in a pearly, dreamlike haze.

To her surprise, the Thornlord was waiting when she returned. Bitharn had half-expected him to leave, although she wasn't sure why. He could go whenever he wanted; she had no more control over him than if he'd been a lion on a leash of string.

Garbed in slashes of silver and shadow, Malentir seemed as alien as his surroundings. A sparrow perched on his shoulder. Its chest feathers were dark with blood. It cocked its head at Bitharn, and in its beady black eyes was a gleam of pallid light. Not moonlight. Magic.

"You were gone for some time," he said, while the bird

stared at her with dead eyes. "Was the mule so hard to subdue?"

"It wasn't a mule."

"Oh?"

"It was a boy. Something that used to be a boy, at least." Bitharn told him what she had seen. She spared no details. There was nothing about it she needed to hide, and she suspected he had witnessed the whole grim hunt through the bird's eyes anyway. The Thorns used dead things as spies, and if he was showing his so openly, he meant for her to know it.

Recounting the boy's death made her feel sick all over again. Bitharn scrubbed a sleeve across her mouth when she was done. "Could you have saved him?"

Malentir shook his head. "I wouldn't have tried. Another power had already claimed that one's soul, and that would have made it . . . dangerous. For a second deity to prevail over that claim would have required someone very strong and very skilled. My mistress might have done it. Not I. Not for some useless villager."

She quelled her irritation. "Then you know what afflicted him."

"No. I have a guess."

"What's the guess?"

"No concern of yours." Some of her frustration must have showed, for the Thornlord made a small, placating gesture. "Not yet. Not until I speak with my mistress, and know what my orders are and what I am permitted to say. It may be that I will tell you then . . . but not before."

"Such loyalty."

Malentir gave her a mocking smile, but it did not touch his eyes. "Of course. No disloyalty survives the Tower of Thorns. Our mistress reads our hearts and minds; those who do not love her never leave."

That sounded like a nightmare. "How many fail?"

He shrugged, looking away. "It is easy to love her, if she chooses you." The bird on his shoulder fluttered its wings and flew off. "Do you intend to spend the night on these rocks? I had hoped for a more comfortable camp. Or at least a less sulfurous one."

"Fine." Bitharn led him down the smoky slope, picking her way as carefully as she had the first time. There was little need for quiet—she was quite sure that the Thornlord's bird had been sent ahead as a scout, and would warn him if anyone lurked nearby—but the rocks were twice as treacherous by moonlight as they had been by day.

It was near midnight when they came to the forest. Bitharn's eyes blurred with weariness and she stumbled with every step. She hadn't pushed herself so hard since she'd ridden for help after Kelland's capture. Her back ached, her feet were stone bruised, and her hands felt like useless blocks of ice. Making a camp was beyond her, and Malentir was hopeless at woodcraft, so Bitharn wrapped a thick wool blanket around her body and buried herself in a drift of dry leaves.

Despite her exhaustion she lay awake for a while, thinking about the boy, and when she finally fell asleep she thought of him again. In her dream he had Kelland's face, and the hunter with the holes in his tongue had an eye that shone blue and bright as a winter star. She watched, helpless, as the miners sank their knives into the crippled knight. Smoke and light poured out of his wounds instead of blood. The smoke tangled around the light in dense black ropes, trying to strangle it, and the more they cut him, the darker it grew. Kelland screamed and she screamed with him, despairing. Then the knives were suddenly in her flesh, too, stabbing and tearing.

It hurt. It hurt so *badly,* sharper than dream pain should.

Bitharn woke with a gasp. The dead sparrow was perched on her shoulder. It tilted its head to one side and then the other, regarding her with empty eyes, and hopped to a branch nearby. The blood on its chest had dried to a prickly-feathered streak, but there was fresh wetness on its beak. She could feel the sting of little stabs along her neck and shoulder. Groggily, she understood.

"I was shouting," she mumbled. "Too much noise. Sorry. I'll be careful."

The bird made no answer. She sank into sleep again, strangely comforted by its dead gaze. This time there were no nightmares.

In the morning the leaves piled atop her blanket crackled with transparent frost. The sky was gray and cloudy, echoing Bitharn's mood. She longed for a cup of hot tea to banish the chill. A bowl of steaming porridge and a fire would have made it . . . not *pleasant,* but bearable. She'd had many such mornings on the road with Kelland, and had loved every one.

There'd be no fire today. They were too close to Carden Vale, and she didn't want to risk anyone finding the Thornlord. The miners still troubled her. Whoever they were, they couldn't have come from far away; they'd carried no food or traveling gear. Most likely they were from Carden Vale. If that was so, then the town held monsters. She didn't know what to make of that possibility, and Malentir offered no help.

Breakfast was a handful of cold biscuit and dried fruit washed down with water that tasted of the leather skin it had been carried in. Once they had eaten, Bitharn resumed their descent, ignoring the protests of her aching muscles. She'd been riding for too long; she had forgotten what it was to walk.

A fine rain was falling by midmorning. The drizzle washed the color from the world, surrounding them in a velvety gray gloom. Bitharn lost all sense of time in the blurred forest. She was startled when the sky began to darken, and more so when the trees thinned ahead. Past them, she could look down on Carden Vale.

It was a small town that had once been a great one. The ruins of its grandeur were still imposing. Smooth stone wharves reached out toward the river, delicate as a lady's fingers, though now they grasped a fistful of mud. A high wall curved around the south end of the valley, shielding the town from invaders. Black spears, tiny as flyspecks from this distance, marched along its parapet.

To the east and west, the Irontooth Mountains stood guard over Carden Vale. A long road crawled from the town to the ruins of Duradh Mal. The road was cracked and broken, shattered like the fortress it served, but the scar it made on the mountainside remained. Dusk hid Duradh Mal from view, but Bitharn fancied she could *feel* its presence, malignant behind its veil of shadow.

North of Carden Vale there were no defenses save a mossy palisade and an earthen wall so eroded that Bitharn could barely tell it was there. More of the palisade's wooden stakes were missing than whole. An unpaved cart road ran through the widest gap, reaching to where the mountains closed in at the valley's end. Miners' picks left pockmarks in those mountains' faces, dimly visible through the misty rain.

Within those walls, the town was a tiny, shrunken thing. Half its houses had been scavenged for stone. Perhaps two hundred stood intact, and of those, many stood on streets that the wilderness had begun to reclaim. Some of the roads were more green than gray. Saplings stretched out of empty windows, while brown threads of winter-bare ivy reached in.

"Where are we to meet her?" Malentir asked.

"By the paupers' pyre, below the dule tree, at midnight." She pointed to it outside the northern palisade: a sprawling chestnut with pale rings on its limbs where they'd been chafed by hangmen's ropes. Next to it was a wide, shallow pit stained with the ash of countless pyres. The dule tree was not far from the town's walls, but it was far enough to lie well outside their torches' reach after nightfall. "The Spider has a taste for theatrics."

"She does. But it is a sensible choice. The dule tree is easy for a stranger to find, and these mountain villagers take their hauntings seriously. Anyone who braves the dark to see us will likely take us for ghosts and flee back to their beds . . . if there is anyone still abroad here."

There was an odd hint of foreboding in Malentir's last words, Bitharn thought, but she doubted he'd elaborate if she asked, so she merely nodded. Common superstition held that rapists and murderers, denied absolution at death and so forever barred from the Bright Lady's paradise, haunted the sites of their executions. Their souls were condemned to Narsenghal, but on full-moon nights, the stories said, the veil between worlds thinned, and some of them slipped back to lure the living into taking their places in hell.

It was only a story, but she had little doubt that any villager unlucky enough to stumble upon the dule tree on *this* full-moon night would soon be meeting his gods one way or another. She hoped the people of Carden Vale were uncommonly superstitious. It might be all that kept them safe tonight.

Bitharn pulled back into the forest's cover, waiting for night to fall. As the gray sky darkened to inky blue, anxiety crept over her. What if she'd gambled everything on a lie?

What if the Thorns had killed Kelland, and meant to fulfill their bargain with a corpse or a mind-blasted shell of a man? It would satisfy the letter of their promise to return him "unhurt," but only because he'd be unable to feel anything ever again.

Old doubts, all of them, but they seemed new again as she sat shivering in the rain. Bitharn closed her eyes and tried to pray, but the words felt empty. She'd done all she could. Her prayers would be answered, or not, in hours. Repeating the words wouldn't change anything.

She opened her eyes and stared at the sky. The rain had stopped, but clouds blotted out the moon and stars. It was impossible to tell the hour.

Beside her, Malentir stirred. "She is here."

"How do you know?"

"I can feel her. We all can." There was a note of diffidence in his voice, strange in a man so arrogant. "It is a part of how she does what she does. We who share her gifts can . . . sense the strength of her blessing from afar."

Bitharn wasn't sure she understood that, but she didn't care. She wanted this over. "Best not keep her waiting."

"Yes." The Thornlord stood. He was a shadow of warmth in the night, more felt than seen. "If I do not have the opportunity to tell you later . . . thank you. For what you did in freeing me from the tower. I know you did not act for my sake, but I am not . . . unmindful of what it cost you, and not ungrateful. Whatever happens at the dule tree."

"Do you expect it to be such a disaster?" Bitharn tried to keep her tone light, and failed miserably.

"I expect nothing where my mistress is concerned." He touched the back of her hand. His fingertips were fever hot. Then he began walking down to Carden Vale, and Bitharn had no choice but to follow.

The darkness did not seem to trouble Malentir, but Bitharn tripped over unseen stones and tree roots all the way down. The more she hurried, the more she stumbled. The descent took so long she began to worry that the Spider would think she'd broken her word and leave without waiting for them to arrive. The new worry tangled up with the old ones, and by the time they reached the bottom she was shaking with fear.

Malentir caught her wrist. His touch had grown even hotter; it felt like he was burning. "Do not be afraid. She has not deceived you."

"How do you know?" she asked. He let go of her wrist, and did not answer.

A spark of magic, pale as bleached bone, burned between the branches of the dule tree. Two figures stood in its wavering radiance: a thin, dark-haired woman enveloped in a fur-trimmed robe, and a plainly dressed man, shorter and stockier than Kelland, with a soldier's physique. The spell-cast light blanched the man's hair to near white, and his skin was the same color as her own. A sword hilt poked over his shoulder. By his foot, a pile of bags held clothing, food, a shield.

There was no one else. Kelland wasn't there.

Bitharn stopped by the scorched edge of the pauper's pyre, willing her eyes to find a third man. He *had* to be there. He had to. The Thorns could not lie, everyone knew it, the Spider had *promised*—but there were only two people standing beneath the hangman's tree, and neither of them was the Burnt Knight.

She pressed her hands to her mouth, unsure if she wanted to vomit or cry. Versiel's betrayal, Malentir's escape, Parnas' murder . . . the lies and the deceptions and the griefs. Had it all been for nothing? She'd trampled her honor through mud and blood and filth, believing it would help him. How great a fool had she been?

"Bitharn?" The voice was rough, unfamiliar. She lifted her head and saw the strange man take a step toward her, his hands raised halfway as if he feared to reach for what he saw. "Bitharn, I . . . is it really you?"

She wanted to believe. She wanted so desperately to believe. Bitharn hugged her arms around her shoulders, not trusting herself to speak. "Who asks?" she managed at last.

"It's me. Kelland. I—the Spider gave me this face as a disguise. But it's me."

Her hands were shaking. Her voice was too. "Prove it."

A tremulous smile softened the stranger's hard features. "Bitharn, it's me. When I was eight years old I tried to play at swordfighting and stole Sir Maugorin's shield and dropped it on my foot. You saw how hard I was trying not to cry, so you made fun of me until I was so mad I forgot. I broke two of my toes that day. They still don't line up straight."

"I believe you," she said, and then she was crying, unable to stop it, and somehow he'd come and wrapped her in his arms. The feel of them was different and the scent of him was wrong, but the strength was what she remembered and she buried her face in his chest and she cried.

He held her close, nestling his cheek against her hair. Softly, almost inaudibly, he whispered into her ear: "Bitharn. What have you done?"

She couldn't answer. But she was suddenly aware, again, that they were not alone. Bitharn looked past his shoulder to the Thorns. The Spider was watching them, a little smile curling one corner of her mouth, and Malentir . . .

Malentir was watching *her*, and there were so many things on his face that Bitharn could not read them all.

Longing and terror, hatred and adoration. He watched the Spider with the look of an apostate priest confronted with his goddess: fearful and resentful and yet strangely vindicated, and above all else there was a twisted, tormented kind of love. The emotions were so nakedly unguarded that Bitharn shivered and turned away, looking back to the Spider . . .

Who stirred, as if belatedly aware of her student's stare, and took out a pair of silvery bracelets as she went to him. No, not bracelets. Hoops of thorned wire, twisted around and around so that the barbs bit in all directions.

"These are yours," she said, dangling the barbed bracelets from a crooked finger.

"They are," he agreed, and pushed back the sleeves from his wrists so that the white scars that ringed each one were visible. Now Bitharn understood how he had gotten all those layered cuts, and she shuddered at the understanding. "Will you replace them?"

"You should never have lost them," the Spider said. She pushed the bracelets over his hands, scratching his hands and hers so that thin lines of blood welled up from both. Once they encircled his wrists, she drew the wires tight.

"I failed."

"Yes. Your task remains unfinished."

"Will you—will you let me try again?"

"Of course," she said, and rested her fingertips along his jaw as she drew him in for a kiss. It was a long kiss, and though Malentir's striped hair fell forward to hide it, Bitharn saw that the Spider bit him before breaking away. Blood glistened dark and wet on the inside of his lips when she pulled back. The Thornlord stayed silent, breathing hard.

"I would, however, prefer that you not fail again," the

Spider murmured, stepping back across the pyre pit. Bits of charred bone cracked under her feet. "Please don't disappoint me. I had such high hopes for you."

"For all of you," she said to Bitharn, turning to the two Celestians with the same blood-reddened smile, before the darkness folded around her and she was gone.

8

"You'll want to have plenty of water," Colison told them. Behind him, two workmen wrestled another barrel onto a wagon. Their breath plumed white in the frosty morning; sweat stained their tunics despite the chill. "Food too. Fodder for your animals. Things might get a bit dicey up there in the passes."

"Snow?" Asharre asked.

"That too."

"What else is there?"

Colison stuffed his hands into their opposite sleeves and chafed his forearms. Embarrassment creased his windburnt face. "Call it . . . superstition. Not sure I could explain it any other way. Look, you trust me, don't you?"

Asharre nodded slowly. Colison was one of Bassinos' merchant-captains, tasked with guiding caravans of his merchandise from Pelos to the Irontooths in exchange for a stake in the cargo and a share of the profits. He'd been traveling the roads of Ithelas for longer than she'd been alive. There wasn't a pennyweight of fat on him, and he had more scars than most mercenaries she'd known.

Bald, browned by years under the sun, and hard as old hickory, Colison was not one to be discomfited easily. But he was plainly uncomfortable now.

Colison blew out a breath that misted and hung in the air. "Take my word for it, then. You'll want to have water. A few barrels, at least. We won't be crossing the Black Sands, but now and again it's hard to find good water in those mountains."

"I'll tell the others."

The Celestians were at dawn prayers, but when they emerged from the chapel behind Bassinos' house and began loading their own supplies, Asharre repeated Colison's advice. She did not include his mention of superstition.

"I don't see why we can't drink snowmelt," Heradion grumbled. "Not as if there's any shortage of it where we're headed."

That was true. The Irontooths were still swathed in winter white. Their slopes shone alabaster halfway down before hardening into flinty gray and vanishing into a mantle of deep green pines. Beautiful, but ominous. This early in the season, the passes were uncertain. A storm could mire them; an avalanche could bury them. They might die, if that happened, but it wouldn't be for lack of water.

She shrugged. "He said there were places where it was hard to find good water. Maybe the mines fouled it."

"The coal mines are on the other side of Carden Vale," Heradion pointed out, "and, anyway, I've never heard of a mine fouling snowfall. I don't want to be difficult, but water's heavy and we can carry only so much."

"If Colison advises it, we should do it," Evenna said. Her braid was down this morning. It swayed to the small of her back, blue-black and glossy over a red wool coat. "Bassinos says he knows these mountains better than anyone alive. We're not traveling with the man so we can ignore him."

"Fine." Heradion threw up his hands. "I can see you're determined to ride out like proper hayseeds, grass in your hair and all. I'll do what I can to oblige."

It took a second wagon to hold the barrels of water and bundles of fodder that Colison recommended, and hay was dearer at the end of winter than Asharre liked, but after highsun prayers they were ready to depart. Evenna drove one of the wagons, Heradion the other. They set out after Colison's men, their bullocks and wagons stretched in a rolling line.

The iron road ran alongside the Windhurst, weaving in and out of blue-tipped spruce and speckled birches. Crusts of half-melted snow sparkled between the trees, dwindling day by day. They passed isolated farmhouses and charcoal burners' cottages, but saw few people abroad. A rider in the blue and gold of Knight's Lake galloped by on a lathered mare, and they crossed paths with a group of pilgrims traveling south to the Dome of the Sun, but otherwise they were alone.

To fill the time, Falcien took to singing trail songs in a surprisingly clear tenor. Once Heradion tried to join him in an unsurprisingly terrible one, until Evenna shut him up by throwing an apple core at his head. After that he contented himself with teaching Asharre to drive their wagon.

"It isn't hard," he told her. "Calmest animals alive, these oxen. Just pretend they're big gray boulders and hold the reins relaxed, like so. It's a straight road here, you can hardly foul it up."

"We do not have animals like this in my clan," Asharre said through gritted teeth, holding the reins as if they were live snakes. The oxen plodded on, mercifully oblivious. Despite their fearsome horns, they did appear to be calm. Calmer than she was, anyway. "Goats, yes. Dogs. Sometimes a wolf. Nothing like this. Nothing so . . . big."

"If I didn't know better, I'd think you were afraid of them. Come now. You've been living in Calantyr for years. Surely you must be used to *oxen*."

"Seeing them. Not driving them."

"Well, then, you'll learn something new."

"We'll end up in the river," Asharre warned him, but to her everlasting amazement they did not.

In thanks, or perhaps revenge, she took to training with him by the campfires after the caravan stopped each night. Heradion was not as strong as she was, and he lacked her reach, but the Knights of the Sun had taught him well and he was a worthy opponent. Colison's guards lent them a pair of blunted practice blades. Though their balance and weight were nothing like Asharre's *caractan,* she could fight well enough with longswords to repay Heradion's driving lessons with bouquets of bruises.

After watching curiously the first night, Colison's men began to join them. Colison himself fought a few bouts. The merchant-captain used a quarterstaff rather than a sword, but he was no less deadly for lack of a blade. He was the only one, besides Heradion, who ever held his own against her.

"Are you sure you won't reconsider doing a Swordsday melee?" Heradion asked her one evening while they watched two caravan guards trade blows on a patch of muddy slush by the road. The slippery ground did nothing to help their footwork, and Asharre was not surprised when one of them lost his balance while backing away from the other. He splashed messily on his rump. The fallen man slapped the mud to signal his concession, and the victor raised his hands to cheers and catcalls.

Stupid to surrender there, she thought. The winner had hurried forward, careless in victory, even before his foe gave up. Easy to kick his feet out from under him and subdue him in the mud. Asharre shook her head disapprovingly, then glanced at Heradion. "What?"

"Melee. Swordsday. Remember? You could make a fortune in the contests. More to the point, *I* could make a fortune betting on you. They might not give away princesses anymore, but I'm a simple man. I'll settle for coin."

"*Sigrir* do not fight for sport. It would dishonor my training."

"Not even for me? What if I bat my eyelashes?"

Asharre snorted and watched the next fight. He'd have better luck convincing the Blessed to open a brothel. All she had left of her clan were her oaths and her scars, and she could no more part with one than the other.

The second fight was as pitiful as the first. Neither of the men fell into the mud, but that was the best she could say of them. Heradion chuckled at her expression. "You won't enter a Swordsday melee, but you're willing to match swords against the likes of these?"

"This is practice."

"Why wouldn't that be? You'd learn more than you do from these poor fellows."

Asharre thought about that as the last match ended and she retired to her bedroll. It was tempting. But she had never fought for glory or for money, and she was not inclined to make excuses to start. A *sigrir* fought for duty. There might be glory in it, and she could claim her share of plunder from the dead, but a *sigrir* drew her weapon only for the honor and protection of her clan.

Who was left to remember that, though? Oralia was dead, and these summerlanders knew nothing of a *sigrir's* rules or rites. The Skarlar would not care what she did; to them she was an exile and a traitor, unworthy of her clan name. If she tried to go back to Frosthold, her sisters would shun her and the rest of the Skarlar would kill her. She'd earned that for Surag's death, if not for her own betrayal.

No one knew the full weight of her oaths save herself. If Asharre wanted to be free of them, wanted to fight for glory or for profit, she could . . . but when she faced that thought, and considered the cost of her liberty, she wanted to cling to her oaths even more tightly. There was a kind of terror in the idea of giving up a name she had worn for so long.

Except she had no clan. When Oralia died, so did the heart of Asharre's oath. There *were* no other Frosthold Skarlar for her to protect, and without them, she could not be true *sigrir.* Yet she still had her skills and her scars, and she could no more change those than she could bring her sister back across the Last Bridge.

So what was she? *Who* was she? If she was still to have some place in the world—and, as Asharre lay under the stars amid the cracking shell of her grief, she realized that she *did* still want that, somehow—she would have to weld some new identity from the pieces of the old. But what?

Sleep stole over her before she found an answer.

The next morning Colison's guards rose groaning and joking over the bruises they'd given each other. One man had a broken finger, and another complained of sore ribs. Those two went to Evenna to have their hurts prayed over, while the others ladled bowls of oat porridge from the communal kettle to break their fast.

"Nobody ever comes to *me* for healing," Falcien grumbled.

"You're not as pretty." Heradion sniffed ostentatiously. "And your perfume leaves a great deal to be desired. What *is* that smell, anyway? Did you rub a wet dog all over yourself this morning?"

Asharre took her bowl and left them to their insults. She found Colison walking along the wagons and checking their cargoes. He stopped by a wagon loaded with covered wicker cages and lifted the oilcloth draped over one. Inside was a long, lithe beast, shaped like a stoat but larger. Colison dropped a dead mouse into its musky-smelling cage.

"What is that?" Asharre asked.

"Hmm? Oh." Colison dropped the oilcloth and moved to the next cage. It contained a similar creature, slightly darker. He fed it another mouse. "Ferrets. We're carrying five of them."

"For trade?"

"For safety."

"Safety?"

Colison rubbed a gloved hand over his bald head. "Friend of mine suggested them. Suppose I'll find out soon enough if he was just playing a bad joke. We'll reach the mountains today."

The day seemed to grow colder after that. Hour by hour, the road grew steeper under a sunless sky. Heradion took back the reins as the trees dwindled and rock walls closed in on either side. Silvery scales of ice clung to the road where the stones left it in shadow. They cracked under the oxen's hooves, and the rumbling wheels crushed them into tracks of melting powder. The wind shrilled constantly through the ravine, whipping at their clothes and hurling flurries of stinging snow from the mountainsides.

The next two days brought more of the same. "We'll go up another day, day and a half, before we come to

Spearbridge," Colison told them on the third afternoon. His cheeks were red with windburn, and he'd pulled a snug wool hat over his ears. "Once we cross the bridge, we'll come back down the other side, and then we'll be in Carden Vale. Call it four, five days. Almost there."

Asharre nodded, shivering under the yellow sheepskin she'd bundled atop her cloak. Somehow the Irontooths seemed to carry a fiercer chill than the winters of her homeland. Perhaps it was only the empty fortress that made it seem so. One of Duradh Mal's towers stood on a crag ahead, its windows black and hollow. A shattered iron lance, its pennon long gone, crowned the tower.

The bulk of the fortress was not in view. Colison said it stood on the other side of the mountain, overlooking Carden Vale, and that what they saw was merely one of several sentinel towers that guarded the approaches to Ang'duradh. Tunnels bored through the mountain connected Spearbridge Tower to the main fortress, allowing its soldiers to come and go without exposing themselves to freezing wind or spying eyes. Those same tunnels, he said, had carried Ang'duradh's doom to its towers.

It was easy to imagine baleful ghosts watching them from the tower, their mutterings mixed with the wind's howl. The story of Ang'duradh's doom was known even by the White Seas. Asharre had never listened closely— why did it matter how an army of summerlanders died centuries ago?—but now, riding beneath Duradh Mal's gaze, she wished that she had. Baozites were formidable soldiers, as fierce as wildbloods and far better disciplined. Even Ingvall's children paid grudging respect to the reavers' strength. Whatever could crush one of their strongholds, and do it so completely that not one soldier remained alive to tell the tale, was a power to be feared.

In six hundred years, it might have vanished. Then again, it might not. She spat to take the tang of fear from her tongue and turned from the tower back to the road.

"We'll get closer to it before we get farther from it," Colison said, not unsympathetic. "Spearbridge is as close as we'll come to the ruins. I won't lie. It takes some folk funny, that bridge, especially the first time. The old magic they used to build it . . . well, you'll see for yourself when we get there. It looks ruined worse than the rest, old Spearbridge, but it'll hold up under your feet. No problem with that. Problem's with the memories on it."

"Memories?" Heradion looked over, the reins looped around one wrist.

"Aye." Colison paced alongside their wagon, rolling a splinter between his teeth. "Memories. You'll notice we've been going through this ravine for a while. Widens up a bit ahead, but we'll be staying on a narrow path right up to Spearbridge. That's no accident. Road's made to meander more than it needs to, and to keep anyone on it nice and bunched together. Way back when, I'm guessing, the Baozites liked to have plenty of time to see who was coming, and to get rid of 'em easy if they weren't invited.

"Spearbridge, near as I can tell, was built with the same idea. But what this path does with rocks, it does with magic. Well, magic and a nasty long fall on each side.

"The bridge is made from things the Baozites took off dead folk. Weapons, shields, banner poles. All the things they lost. When you go across, you see their last memories—what happened right before they died. Mostly you see 'em getting killed by Baozites, and mostly it isn't pretty. You"—he tilted the splinter in his mouth so that it pointed at Asharre—"would probably see some wildbloods who raided a little too far south back before your grandfather's grandfather's day. Your friend might see some old Knights of the Sun whose crusade went sour on 'em. Me, I see a little of everybody, seeing as how my folks were wanderers before me. There's a few who don't see anything, or get to feeling happy as they go across. I got my theories about those. Seems to me they're the ones who aren't far from Baozites themselves. You see a man who doesn't wince on Spearbridge, you know he's not to be trusted.

"Anyway, the bridge won't cause you no harm. The oxen don't even notice. I've never lost a wagon on Spearbridge, though the memories always slow down the crossing something terrible. That was the point, back when there were soldiers in Spearbridge Tower to shoot down anyone they didn't care to see coming, but the tower's empty now and you don't have to fear no arrows. Just the memories, that's all."

"That sounds *wonderful*." Heradion said. A breeze ruffled his red-gold hair and left a dusting of snow crystals that melted as they rode. He ducked his head as the meltwater trickled down his neck, adjusting his scarf too late to keep it away. "Why didn't we take a barge to Carden Vale, again?"

"Bassinos said it was too early in the season," Asharre replied. "The ice on the river has not melted. He said traveling overland was safer."

"I'd rather deal with ice than dead men's memories."

"There's worse than ice on the river." Colison turned the splinter around in his mouth and began chewing on the other end. "People been vanishing off those barges. Whole crews. Someone else'll come along the river and find the barge drifting, or run up on the banks. Poles unbroken, dray horses unhurt, çargo seals untouched, but not a soul to be seen. No signs of fighting. Just . . . gone."

"Oh, now you're just trying to frighten us," Heradion complained. "Bassinos said it was peaceful all winter. Even the bandits are quiet."

"Worse things to be than frightened. Foolish, for one." Colison spat the splinter under the wagon wheels. "You ask me, the bandits are quiet only because they were the first to vanish, before whatever's out there started taking barge crews. But you're right, Bassinos doesn't know about it. Who'd want to carry him a story like that? 'I hear people are disappearing off the barges, reckon there's ghosts making off with 'em. Maybe it's the mad wind.' Carry him that tale, he's liable to think old Colison spent too long on the mountain and froze all his brains. Then it's no more caravans for me, and my Lalinda runs off with a spice merchant, and I'm left in an empty house eating watery porridge and wishing I'd kept my mouth shut." He chuckled. "No, Bassinos doesn't know. You need proof for a man like that. I don't have any. I'm only telling *you* this because you've already paid me. Once we're in Carden Vale, that's it for us. Onetime job lets a man speak more freely."

"If you like stories so much, let me tell *you* one," Heradion said, and went off on a meandering tale about a pair of children lost in the woods. Asharre stopped listening. She'd heard this one before. The only point to the story was how much time the teller could waste reciting it; she didn't think it ever came to a real ending. Heradion used it as revenge when someone else told an overly long-winded tale around the campfire. Last time he started, Evenna had thrown an apple core at him for that too.

She was beginning to wish she had an apple core of her own to hurl when Evenna came trotting toward their wagon with something cupped in her hands. Green leaves poked up from her fingers, and gravelly soil dribbled between them. Another plant.

The young Illuminer had been collecting odd herbs and bits of foliage since they'd left Cailan. Some of them she pressed in a book between sheets of papered glass, some she dug up and planted in buckets of sand, and others she simply sketched in a second book, discarding the plants after she had faithfully recorded their roots, flowers, and stems. Although spring had barely touched the mountains, Evenna had already amassed an impressive collection of specimens and drawings. Her own wagon had no more room to spare for her plants, so she had started putting them in Asharre's.

"What's this one?" Asharre asked, glad for a distraction from the pointless story. Colison looked over curiously. Seeing his audience lost, Heradion came to a disgruntled, merciful silence.

"A snowdrop. Where's my spare bucket?"

"You're out of spare buckets," Heradion informed her. "You've *been* out of spare buckets. Last time you had to borrow a mug from me. My sister made me that mug. When am I getting it back?"

"What? Oh, the one with the crooked sun on it that came out green? You said you were glad to get rid of it. Anyway, I need a bucket. Or another mug, if you have one."

"I don't. What's so special about this flower? Even I know it's a snowdrop."

"Look at the leaves. The roots." Evenna spread her fingers carefully, brushing dirt from the snowdrop's bulb.

It took a moment for Asharre to see what she meant. The leaves closest to the bell-shaped blossom looked like broad blades of grass, same as the snowdrops of Asharre's childhood. Those near the base, however, were wider and striped with thick reddish veins. They resembled flattened hands, their palms stretched open to the sky. The bulb was deformed too: instead of being a smooth, papery-skinned ball, it was knobbed and ridged so that it looked like a fist plunged into the earth. Its skin was blue-black and wet with rot, peeling off the bulb like the sloughed skin of a leper. The scent of decay clung to it.

"Oh, it's a *diseased* snowdrop," Heradion said.

"It's not diseased." Evenna closed her hands around the bulb. Asharre was strangely relieved to have it out of sight. "It's beggar's hand. And at the same time, it's not. It's a snowdrop that *turns into* beggar's hand. One plant changing into another. I've never seen anything like it."

"Where did you find that?" Colison had blanched beneath his windburnt ruddiness.

"Up ahead. The rock walls come down a little. There are a few things growing in the cracks where the stones have fallen." Evenna looked at him, suddenly doubtful. "Should I not keep this?"

"No. No, it doesn't matter. Safer in your hands than where it was, I don't doubt. Where you found it—was it a clearing? Were there rusting spears about the edge?"

Evenna shook her head. "The path didn't widen much. It's just that the walls fell a bit. I wouldn't call it a clearing. Would you like me to show you? It's not far."

"That won't be necessary." Colison cupped his hands around his mouth, calling to the wagons ahead. "Jassel! We've found beggar's hand! Spread the word!"

He let his hands fall and gave the three of them a curt nod, all efficiency once more. "Ladies. Sir. If you'll excuse me, I'd best be getting back to work. A caution: that water I had you bring? Drink that. Don't touch anything you see flowing hereabouts, and don't melt the snow. Don't let your animals crop whatever's growing. Keep them to the hay you carry, unless you feel like pulling these wagons yourselves."

With that, Colison trudged off to check the last of the wagons, leaving them bewildered.

"What was that about?" Heradion asked.

Evenna shrugged. She'd found a teakettle somewhere and was busily filling it with sand, half of which fell through her fingers as she trotted to keep up with the wagon. The snowdrop bounced on a square of sand-flecked burlap beside her. "Folklore's filled with warnings against beggar's hand. It's no more dangerous than ergot or devil's trumpet, really. Poisonous, but not magical. It looks unsightly and has an unfortunate name, so the superstitious think it marks the touch of Maol."

"His fear was more than superstition," Asharre said. "What does this plant do?"

"It causes delirium if ingested. Fevers. Some who have eaten it claimed to see demons cavorting in the air, or say they've heard imps cackling and ordering them to do mischief. The visions usually fade after a few hours. The patient stays weak for another day or two, and that's the end of it. A few people have died from eating entire bulbs, but the taste is foul enough to make that uncommon. You can't stomach that much of it accidentally." Evenna dug a hole in the sand and planted the snowdrop inside. She folded the burlap over it to protect the bulb against frost. "There we are. I'd better go see how Falcien is faring. It's my turn to take a hand at the reins."

"I don't suppose it'll be *your* turn soon," Heradion hinted to Asharre.

"As soon as you want to end up in the river." Asharre

watched Evenna climb back onto the wagon ahead of them. "I've never seen anyone so excited about a poisonous plant."

"You collect swords. No healthier having one of those in your stomach."

Asharre snorted, and the wagon rolled on.

That night they made camp in the clearing Colison had mentioned. It might have begun as a natural broadening of the mountain path, but the Baozites had smoothed and widened it to serve their needs.

A stone parapet ran along its outer rim. Tall iron spears jutted from its merlons. Most were broken, but a few stood intact, thrusting up at the air with barbed tips untouched by rust. Whatever protected the spearheads from time did not extend to their hafts; those that were not broken had been corroded to pockmarked red needles. Age-browned skulls hung from several of the spears, their mouths filled with windblown dirt and the red drool of rust.

The clearing inside the wall was more hospitable. There was enough dirt for grass and a few small trees to take root, though the trees were leafless and the grass was brown under a lacy shawl of frost. A shallow cave in the mountainside offered shelter from the wind. At one end of the cave, a rivulet of steaming water trickled from a cut in the mountain, feeding a small pool. Whiskers of ice silvered the stone on either side of the rivulet, but the water flowed free and the pool was clear.

Asharre stuck a finger in the water. It was uncomfortably hot, near boiling where it spilled from the rock. It did not smell of sulfur, as the hot springs near Smoke River did.

Colison, like the rest of his men, had been cutting away the dry grass before letting their oxen out of harness. When he saw her by the pool, he put down his short-handled sickle and hurried over. "Don't drink that!"

Asharre wiped her hand dry on her thigh. "Why? It doesn't smell fouled. This place was made for a camp."

"It was," Colison agreed. "I've been using this clearing as long as I've been coming to Carden Vale, but this past winter . . . I started hearing stories. Things changed. Men told me they'd heard the mad wind whistling around Spearbridge. Sober men, men I'd trust with my life. They said it wasn't the wind that carried madness, though, but the water. Plants too. Ones like your girl found, that'd turned to beggar's hand. I had it marked for nonsense . . . but I brought the ferrets to be sure."

"To be sure of what?"

He grimaced. "I don't know. That I'm a fool, maybe. Everything I've heard says the water's poisoned where plants turn to beggar's hand, so I suppose we'll give it a try and find out. Laugh at me if I'm wrong."

Asharre gave him a long look, but she gathered the others. Anything that smelled of magic was best seen by the Blessed. Colison met them by the cistern with a ferret cage in his hand. He set the animal down and fished a clay bowl out of his pocket. "I ought to apologize," he said as he dipped the bowl into the steaming pool. "I told you to bring water and hay, but I didn't tell you why. It wasn't just for fear of late snows. I'd heard troubling things about the water up here. Might make me look like a fool, but I thought . . . better to be safe. Just in case."

He opened the ferret's cage. The animal watched them with black, beady eyes. Moving slowly, so as not to frighten it, Colison put the dish inside and latched the door.

The ferret lapped at the water, tentatively at first, but it soon forgot its fear. Its small pink tongue flicked out faster and faster. Soon all the water was gone, and the ferret was licking the dry bowl. It combed its whiskers for every last drop, then licked at its paws for more.

"What's wrong with it?" Evenna whispered.

The ferret went from licking its paws to nipping them. Its sharp little teeth soon pierced the skin. Upon tasting blood, the animal flew into a frenzy. It thrashed and snapped in its cage, biting at its flanks and tearing at its belly. Loops of intestine caught around a kicking foot; its teeth scraped against bare ribs. A hind claw caught an artery in its neck and tore through. Blood sprayed the cage in rhythmic spurts, but the bleeding did not slow its rage; as the life ran from its neck, fury seemed to fill the animal's body instead. It shrieked, a high-pitched sound that held no pain—only hunger and what Asharre could almost swear was hate.

Within moments the animal was dead. It had ripped itself into a wet, twisted rag. Ashen faced, Asharre wiped some of its blood from her boot.

Colison covered the cage with a frayed piece of burlap. The corners touching the cage floor turned a slow, ugly red.

"Suppose it's true, then," the merchant-captain said. "There's madness in the water."

"Where did you hear this?" Heradion asked.

"There was a caravan last autumn that got caught in Yelanne's Pass for a few days. Not uncommon if you set out late in the year, and not too dangerous if you're ready for it and full winter hasn't set in. You might lose a few animals, but your caravan ought to get through. Horas Short-Ear captained that crew. I knew him; he wasn't one for stupid mistakes. He had them drinking snowmelt while they waited for the weather to turn. The buckets were sitting on the fire pits, frozen full of ice plugs, when the next crew found them.

"My cousin Torvud brought his caravan through the pass a week later. The storm had cleared by then. He found Short-Ear's people dead. All of them. There were some in the wagon beds who'd strangled themselves with knotted shirts, others who'd run into the snow to embrace the cold. The animals were no better. Oxen locked their horns into each other's ribs, dogs went wild on their masters . . . it was a bloody mess, Torvud said. So bloody, most of those who heard about it didn't believe it. Sounded like a wild tale of the mad wind. *I* didn't believe it, until now, and it was my own cousin who told me."

"You called a warning when I found the snowdrop," Evenna said. "Why?"

"Tainted plants mean tainted water," Colison replied. "Might be one causes the other, might not, but I was told you'll find them side by side. Seems that's true. That grass in the clearing? Looks fine from afar, but all its roots are little fisty bulbs, same as the flower you dug up on the road. It's beggar's hand. Let an ox graze on that, you might as well cut its throat with your own hands."

"Why would any animal eat so much?" Evenna asked, puzzled. "Beggar's hand tastes terrible."

"Does it?" Colison pushed up his hat to scratch his head. "That's not what I've heard. Torvud said animals that get a taste of it go as mad as that ferret did for water. They'll eat till there's none left, and fight each other bloody for the last bite."

"Sweet as wine, sweet as sin, sweet as death," Falcien recited. Asharre raised an eyebrow at him.

"*The Book of All Sins,*" he explained. "Ryanthe Auster-lan wrote it two hundred years ago. It was his life's work: an exploration of the world's dark faiths and the known magics of each. It doesn't make for pleasant reading, and much of what Blessed Austerlan wrote is cryptic or coded to keep the knowledge from being misused, but I spent a year studying it at the Dome.

"Blessed Austerlan tells of how Maolites succumb to the Mad God's touch. Most fall into sin gradually. The first taste of his power is 'sweet as wine,' intoxicating and liberating to those who've never had any power of their own. It causes a similar sickness after it passes, and it can be as addicting as wine to a vulnerable soul. The second is a reward for those who have become accustomed to doing evil in his name. 'Sweet as sin to a malicious heart.' The third comes when they've served their purpose and their mortal shells are completely broken. Then it is as 'sweet as death' . . . though what follows is unending horror for those who have given their souls to Maol."

"And that's why oxen will eat beggar's hand?" Heradion asked skeptically.

"That's why Maolites do," Falcien answered. "To them it is a sacred herb. They don't notice the bitterness, or don't care if they do. Most of the time, for most of us, the taste is unbearably foul, but when the Mad's God power is strong enough, he can make even the first taste sweet enough to addict."

"Ah. So Cousin Torvud's oxen ate beggar's hand because the Mad God's presence is so strong here that they didn't realize it tastes like warmed-over death served in an old boot."

"That's closer to what I meant," Falcien allowed with a small smile. "If there's something in the earth that turns harmless plants to his sacred herb, and something in the water that induces madness, it's clear that we must be dealing with some manifestation of Maol. No other deity is so heedlessly destructive. The bloodrage could fit Baoz, but as a rule, his reavers don't destroy *themselves*. Only the Mad God is that careless with the souls he's corrupted."

"Why?" Evenna asked. Her blue eyes were troubled. "Why now?"

"Something's risen in Carden Vale," Falcien suggested. "Blessed Austerlan wrote that Maol's influence can rise in only two places: in great cities, where his servants can hide among the teeming crowds, and in isolated hamlets, where they can seize the entire populace and kill those who resist too strongly. It might have begun with only one corrupted soul, but by now there are surely more. No single Blessed could draw enough power to poison an entire mountain."

"You're saying the entire town of Carden Vale has fallen under the Mad God's sway?" Heradion spluttered. "Then why, in the names of all gods living and forgotten, did the High Solaros send you here to serve your *annovair*?"

"He didn't know," Evenna said softly. "He couldn't have known. If Bassinos dismissed the rumors as wild stories, and no one recognized it for Maol's work until we came, how could the High Solaros have known what was needed? We're here now, though. Celestia guided us to this place for a purpose."

"That purpose was seeing the danger and going back to Cailan to tell the High Solaros. We've done the first part. We ought to get started on the second." Heradion crossed his arms. "I'm as brave as the next man, but I know my limits. I wouldn't try matching swords with Nhrin Wraithborn, and you've got no business matching spells with whoever could turn water into . . . *that*. That sort of thing calls for a company of Sun Knights. Not you. Not *us*."

"No." Falcien's dark eyes rested on the ferret's cage without seeming to see it. "I agree with Evenna. It's no accident that we're here. Our duty is to help the people of Carden

Vale. If we leave and tell the High Solaros to send Knights of the Sun, how can we be sure that the madness won't spread farther? Maybe I'm wrong about how far it's gone; maybe it started here, and the Mad God hasn't yet taken the town. Or maybe he has, and is only waiting for the river to thaw before laying siege to Balnamoine. It takes weeks to travel each way from Cailan. We can't afford the time. We have to act now, while whatever is poisoning the mountain is not as strong as it might become, and whatever souls it hasn't tainted might still be saved."

Heradion muttered something under his breath. He looked to Asharre for help. "How about you?"

"I think," Asharre said, "you should pray."

9

The Blessed prayed for guidance as Asharre had suggested, but it did little good. Falcien saw nothing but a wall of impenetrable black fog; Evenna's vision showed her a well of dark water in which human faces were upturned, fighting for air as the water rose higher. Both Illuminers' spells were cut short by crippling headaches that left them lying in the wagon beds, incapacitated and in agony, for a full day.

When they recovered, they agreed that it was Maol's presence that hobbled their magic. Neither had heard of such a thing occurring outside the great blight of Pafund Mal, where the Mad God's power was strongest in the world. And yet, even after that, neither of them wanted to turn back. The pull of history was too strong. They did not say it openly, but Asharre heard the awe of legends in their voices. Some of their determination to go forward was their training, and some was a true desire to help . . . but some of it, too, was that the Illuminers wanted to add their own names to the stories.

That evening, the three Celestians argued all through dinner about whether they should continue to Carden Vale. Asharre listened but said little. Privately she agreed with Heradion and thought it was a mistake to venture onward instead of alerting the Knights of the Sun. If Oralia had been among them, she would have said so. But the three of them had made it clear that Asharre's voice counted only for herself, and Evenna and Falcien were plainly determined to continue with or without her, so she said nothing.

If they accepted her acquiescence and let her come along, she could guard against their worst mistakes. If she protested too strongly, however, they might sneak off without her and get themselves killed. Better to stay quiet and keep her eyes open.

"I don't understand how they can be so cavalier about this," Heradion grumbled after the Blessed had retired to pray. "You saw that animal tear itself apart. That could have been any one of us. Am I wrong? Tell me I'm wrong. I would very much like to be wrong."

"You're wrong." Asharre returned his wounded expression with a wry look. "They're young."

"*I'm* young. I still know better."

"They are Blessed. Oralia was the same. She thought that whatever happened was the goddess' will, and that her faith could surmount any trial." Remembering her sister's absolute conviction made Asharre feel a little awed, but mostly tired. That faith had killed her in the end. "Of course they believe that whatever lies in Carden Vale is a test sent by their goddess. This is their *annovair,* their first task as full Blessed. For it to be something so profound is . . . an honor. In their heart of hearts, they will not believe failure is possible."

"Well, I do." Heradion scowled at a snapped bootlace as if the frayed leather was to blame for everything that had gone wrong during their journey. He yanked it out and threaded a new one into its place, jerking it harder than necessary through each loop. "What do *you* think?"

Asharre knotted her fingers together, feeling the calluses on both palms. "I think it is important to let them do this thing. Let us say that going to Carden Vale risks their lives. Maybe that is true, maybe not. But let us say it. So: if we stop them, we save their lives—and negate the purpose of those lives. They have trained for this. They are Blessed for this. If they cannot serve their goddess in the way they think necessary, what is the reason for their being?"

"They're my friends. You want to let them march into madness?"

"*Want* to? No. But I think it is necessary. Oralia was my sister, and she made the same choice." *And I would have stopped her if I could. If she had let me.* But Asharre had never had the chance, and in the long silence afterward she had come to understand, however much it hurt to admit, that Oralia had made . . . not the *right* choice, perhaps, but the only one that any of Celestia's Blessed could have.

"That was Sennos Mill, wasn't it? What happened there?"

Asharre glanced at him, saw nothing but honest curiosity on his face, and turned back to the fire. "She died."

"But you think she made the right choice in going?"

"I don't know. I know she had to try." They'd been in western Calantyr, a week's ride from Aluvair, when they'd received a desperate plea from Sennos Mill. A terrible sickness had taken the villagers there: a plague that dried their skin into brittle, scaly sheets that cracked apart and fell away, leaving their bodies raw and oozing. None of the infected survived longer than a few days, and the village herb woman was helpless to cure the disease. Their only hope was a Blessed.

Asharre had argued long and hard with her sister about Sennos Mill. The village lay in the no-man's-land between Calantyr and Ang'arta. It was not formally a part of either realm . . . but the soldiers of the Iron Fortress were known to ride through the region, and they did not take kindly to the presence of Celestia's Blessed that close to their borders. If something went wrong in Sennos Mill, they'd have no help from Calantyr; King Uthandyr would not risk an open conflict with the ironlords over one Illuminer who'd overstepped her bounds.

But Oralia refused to listen. She *had* to help the people of Sennos Mill, she said; there was only a chance of harm to herself, whereas the villagers were certain to die without her prayers. Even if she knew for a fact that the Baozites would be waiting to kill her, Oralia would have gone to pray for as many villagers as she could before that happened. That was what it meant to be Blessed; she could not refuse her healing.

Asharre disagreed. Vehemently. They agreed to sleep on it, and make no decision until the morning—but Oralia drugged her into slumber, and when the *sigrir* woke, she found her sister gone.

She rode after Oralia at once, but she pushed her horse too hard and it foundered, costing her three precious days. By the time she reached the village, it was too late.

Baozites had come to Sennos Mill, and they'd brought a Thorn. Her sister was defenseless. They'd slaughtered her and ridden back to Ang'arta, leaving Asharre with no enemy to take vengeance upon and no body to burn. The villagers had done that before she came.

The survivors told her that Oralia cured the plague before the Baozites fell on Sennos Mill. They wept, and thanked her, and said her sister had saved their lives. Perhaps that was true, and perhaps they only offered the words to salve her loss. Asharre would never know.

What she *did* know—and what she desperately wished she'd realized earlier—was that Oralia could no more have ignored her holy oaths than Asharre could have washed the scars from her face. And if she had accepted that, instead of trying to stand between a Blessed and her goddess, Oralia might not have drugged her. She might have been able to accompany her sister to Sennos Mill, and the tragedy might have been changed.

Maybe. Too late now; that song was sung. But in Evenna and Falcien she saw the same unswerving certainty, and this time she did not intend to repeat her mistake.

Heradion was waiting for the rest of her answer. Asharre shrugged at him and poked at the sputtering coals with a roasting stick left over from the evening's meal. The night was cold, and he did not need to hear her old griefs. "Their duty is to bring their Lady's magic where it is needed. Yours, and mine, is to protect them while they do it."

"If your hope was to reassure me," Heradion muttered, "you've failed miserably."

"Not reassure. Prepare."

"I'm not sure that does much good against Maolite madness, but I'll try." He tossed his own stick into the fire and left her.

The embers were fading. Asharre pulled her sheepskin closer, took out an oilstone, and honed her sword until it was too dark to see.

They got to Spearbridge at highsun the next day. Morning was colder than the night had been, and the wind's bite sharpened as the day drew on. The sky was the color of dirty snow, streaked with torn gray clouds. The bullocks' breath steamed and mist rolled from their shoulders as they hauled the wagons up the last turn in the road.

Then they were at the Gate of the Chasm, and Spearbridge lay before them.

The bridge measured twenty feet across and a thousand long. Stretched over a yawning rift in the mountains, it seemed thin as a wisp of spider's silk, at once barbarous and impossibly fragile. At either end the bridge was anchored by a gatehouse of black stone and rusting iron; between, it simply hung in the air.

Spearbridge was built all of twisted metal and sunbleached skeletons, woven together like threads in an unholy tapestry. Bent swords and dented shields tangled around enough bones to fill a hundred ossuaries. Most of those bones were human, but a few were too large, too heavy, to have come even from Ingvall's children. Some of the skulls had tusks and horns and curved red teeth as long as Asharre's forearm. She saw a six-fingered claw thrust into a rib cage, its talons bigger than scimitars. Amulets and holy relics from more faiths than Asharre could name lay broken and defiled among them, all fused together as if by some great blast of fire.

Gibbet cages creaked under the bridge. Several had snapped their chains and were lost to the chasm. Others held yellowed skulls worn smooth as beach pebbles by the tides of time. In one, Asharre saw the bristly bowl of an old bird's nest. Black feathers fluttered, trapped, on its twigs.

"Best if you get down from the wagon," Colison advised. He had wrapped a scarf about his face and pulled his hat low so that little more than his eyes showed. "I'll have Jassel or Gals drive it across. First-timers don't usually fare so well."

"I wouldn't like to fall off," Heradion agreed, climbing down.

"Not much chance of that. Truly. One foot in front of the other, that's all there is to it. The danger isn't in falling." Colison's eyes crinkled with a smile hidden by his scarf. "Reassuring, I know. But if I've survived it, so will you."

Slowly the wagons in front of them began to roll through the gatehouse and across the bridge. Their drivers hunched forward, jaws set and faces grim, as if they rode into battle. In a sense, Asharre supposed, they did.

Gals trudged over to take the reins that Heradion had left on the driver's bench. He was a small, sad-faced man with big ears and a lopsided gait from a broken leg that had healed badly. "Good luck," he called, as the bullocks pulled him away.

"Ready?" Heradion asked.

"No," Asharre answered, but she adjusted the *caractan* hanging across her back and followed him onto the bridge.

Blink.

She was running through the surf onto a rocky beach. Salty froth splashed around her sealskin boots. Her fellows charged up the beach around her, shouting challenges and war cries in the old tongue of Iskavir. A red bloom of fire crackled on the sea behind them: a dragonship burning. *Their* dragonship. Her bowsprit was a narwhal's horn, hung with five red hoops of ochre-stained ivory to signify the prizes she had taken. A well-blooded ship. Asharre felt a pang of angry grief that she should burn.

There was no time to mourn. Ahead were their enemies, half hidden by the smoke that blew from the burning ship. Ironlords. Twenty of them, gathered defensively with shieldmen guarding their archers. A woman, dressed in red and crowned in iron, stood chanting in the center of their knot. Asharre could see the glint of the soldiers' swords through the smoke, smell the rage that came off them like sweat stink. There was no fear in these men, though they were outnumbered and they faced Ingvall's children by the sea. No fear at all.

There was no fear in her either, and the wildbloods could match anyone for fury. She bit her tongue savagely. Hot blood filled her mouth. A red haze descended upon her and she heard herself scream, her own blood spilling across her chin. She wanted to bite these men, tear out their throats, taste their blood mingled with hers. The *caractan* in her hands felt light as a feather, sweet as a lover, an extension of her lust for death.

She barely felt the arrows when they came. She saw them, though. They filled her vision like black rain, and where they fell, men died. One slammed into her chest and another struck her thigh; she felt them dully, and would have kept running, but a third arrow plummeted from the sky and hit her in the face. It cracked through her nose and split her lip, pinning her tongue to her jaw. Blood gurgled out and she couldn't breathe, couldn't see. More arrows fell and she fell with them.

Her last thought, as she died, was regret that she had not been able to match swords with the soldiers, and wonder that ten archers could have filled the sky with so many shafts.

Blink.

Asharre touched her head groggily. It had seemed so vivid, so *real* . . . but no, she stood on Spearbridge, the wind snapping her cloak around her legs. Heradion stood frozen beside her. The young Celestian's face was white and drops of sweat trickled down his brow. He was not the only one so affected. Ahead of them, as many wagons were stopped as moving, and the people on foot between them were paralyzed between steps.

The line moved forward, but at a snail's crawl. Asharre did, too, dreading what she might see.

Blink.

Her name was Haruld, and she was fifteen. An important day: it marked the change from boy to man. At last she—*he*—would be allowed to join the raiders, to take a share of plunder and someday pay the bride-price for a wife. He wondered whether Kalle would wait until he could pay hers. Kalle was a pretty girl, her eyes blue as a morning sky; her bride-price would be high. But he was fifteen, and if he fought well, he might have it before he was twenty.

He looked anxiously ahead. They were very far south, almost to Delverness Wood, and he did not like being so far from the clan's lands. Ingris insisted that she could not find the herbs she needed anywhere else, though, and for all her youth she was the best healer in the hold, so he supposed it was worth the journey to get them.

Still, it was not like her to take so long to gather plants. "Ingris?"

There was no answer. He crept forward, quietly now, worried about what he might find. "Ingris?" He pushed past the trailing branches of a willow. The silver-green leaves parted with a shiver. What lay beyond them shattered him.

His sister was sprawled in the dirt among five men. There was blood on her mouth and her thighs. Her dress had been torn to the waist. Three of the men wore leather armor, travel stained and dulled to blend into the forest. A red fist marked their shoulderplates; the device meant nothing to him. The other two were half dressed. They talked casually, passing around a small wineskin.

He saw these things and he charged almost before he understood what they meant. There was no thought, only rage and desperate fear. All he had was a hunting knife, but he kept it sharp and none of them saw him coming. By the time they turned toward him, Haruld was across the clearing. He plunged the knife into the first man's side and jerked it out and punched the blade back into his stomach, shoving it in until his knuckles pressed into skin. The man hit back, battering at Haruld's head with his elbow, but his strength was already failing and the blows felt light as rain. Haruld tore his knife out and kicked the man down and he crumpled to the earth, weeping and cursing the pain.

The rest of them backed away, spreading out to circle him. Haruld didn't look down at his sister. He didn't dare look down. "Ingris, run," he urged, feinting at the men with his knife to keep them at bay.

He wasn't sure whether she heard him. She didn't move. One of the men—the other half-dressed one—lunged forward and Haruld slashed at him, laying open his right arm above the elbow. Too late he realized that it was a distraction, that the real threat came from behind. The armored men still had their weapons. He caught a blur of motion in his peripheral vision and a morningstar smashed into his hand, crushing his fingers and knocking the knife from his suddenly useless grip. Haruld darted to his left, trying to dodge the next blow, but another man seized his arm and the morningstar came in again, smashing his knee.

He dropped, howling. He saw, too late, that Ingris was already dead. Her eyes stared, sightless, at the sun. A wet brown leaf clung to her cheek. The man he'd slashed on the arm spat on him and stalked away, looking for something to bind his wound. The one he'd gutted was writhing in the grass and screaming louder than Haruld himself.

"Oh, shut up," the morningstar-wielder said, bringing the weapon down on his companion's head. It crunched and the screams stopped. Blood spattered Haruld's face, warm and sticky. He could taste the sour rust of it. "Bawling like a stuck pig."

"What about this one?" One of the men jerked a thumb at Haruld. "We could take him. Put him in the pits. He's big. Got the north blood."

"We could." The soldier with the morningstar prodded Haruld in the side with a boot. Haruld could only grunt and try to roll away. His crippled knee was an inferno of pain. "He can't walk, though, and I broke his fighting hand. Seems like more trouble than it's worth."

"What, then?"

They raped him. They raped him and they gelded him and when they finally let him die, answering his broken, begging prayers, they took their time about that too.

Blink.

Asharre came back to herself with bile curdling her tongue. She swallowed with difficulty. Everything she saw had happened long before her grandfather's grandfather was born. These people were long dead; she walked on their skulls and their ruined standards. There was nothing she could do for them . . . but knowing that did not make it easier.

Heradion had fallen two steps behind her. He trembled as a vision passed; she could only guess at what he saw. After he had recovered, he looked at her and managed a wan smile. "Lovely people, these Baozites."

"They're dead," Asharre said. She wasn't sure whether her own words were meant as reassurance or regret. "They're all dead."

She went on. She was old; she was young. She was a

man, a woman, sometimes a child. Once, she thought, she was a wolf. She died in fire, in water, under a hissing mantle of molten lead, beneath more swords than she could number. She died on sacrificial altars and in the throng of blood-soaked orgies. She died again and again in a cascade of years, but she went on.

Finally, exhausted, she came to the end. The gatehouse passed in a blur. Spearbridge Tower loomed above her, a monolith of black basalt. Lost in her cursed visions, she'd never noticed it. Had she been an enemy—had anyone been left to man that tower—its archers could have riddled her with impunity. If the gatehouse had been locked, she would have had nowhere to flee.

The road forked beyond the gatehouse. Around her, Colison's men changed places on the wagons, letting new drivers take a turn while the old ones stretched their legs. She saw Colison's hand in that. Switching tasks helped them shake free of what they'd seen. In a few hours, Asharre guessed, these men might be able to joke and laugh again. They'd been through it before. She wondered if the Celestians would recover as quickly—or, for that matter, whether she would. The depravities she'd witnessed seemed to cling to her skin like an oily film.

"We'll take the west road from here. Goes down the mountain. East road curves up toward the fortress. No reason we'd want to go that way. This is as close as we come to them." Colison studied her carefully, an unspoken empathy in his eyes. "You all right?"

Asharre nodded, not trusting herself to speak. He watched her for a moment longer, not quite believing her assurance, then left to get the rest of the caravan in order. Shortly after Colison had vanished into the bustle of wagons and bullocks, Heradion strode off the bridge. The red-haired youth was swinging his arms in a way she had seen drunk men do when they were shaking off the urge to hit something.

"Why?" Heradion asked, his voice full of angry disbelief. "Why make this thing? Why keep *those* memories trapped in time?"

Asharre glanced up at the battlements of Spearbridge Tower. "The arrows. You'd have been easy prey for the archers."

"It's more than that," Falcien said. Asharre had not heard him approach. There was an ashen cast to his light brown skin, and his eyes were reddened by recent tears, but the Illuminer's voice was steady. "It's a sacrament to their god. Each of those deaths was an act of worship—a gift of blood and conquest that pleased the Iron-Crowned enough to be remembered. As for why it's here, instead of some hidden temple . . . Spearbridge is a show of force: *see our strength, and tremble.* It would have been a powerful warning to anyone who thought of challenging Ang'duradh's power."

"Not that powerful," Heradion said. "Someone challenged them. And won."

Asharre chuckled bleakly. "And you want to challenge that. Madness."

Falcien touched the sunburst pendant that hung over his yellow cloak. "Faith. Not madness."

She shook her head but did not argue. They'd lingered long enough. Gals had turned their wagon so that it faced west on the split road past the gatehouse. Most of the others had already started moving. Asharre climbed onto the driver's bench, waiting for Heradion to join her. "Faith does not mean you'll win."

"No. It only means I must try." Falcien brushed his pendant again, reverently, and went to his own wagon.

The afternoon wore on, gray and gloomy. Asharre was startled that it was still the same day; after what she had endured, it felt as if weeks should have passed. Years, maybe. But the world remained indifferent to her turmoil, and although they had lost much of the day on Spearbridge, it was still light enough to travel.

The wagons rolled down the bare stone road. Snow dusted the basalt around them and fluttered in icy plumes whenever the wind turned. There was little to be seen of Ang'duradh, beyond an occasional glimpse of the Shardfield's obsidian glitter between the rocky heights, and Asharre was glad for that. She had seen enough of Baozite work for a lifetime.

Dusk fell swiftly. There was no sunset, no rich blue twilight, only a gradual lowering of the light from grayness into dark. The oxen laboring in their traces became bulky moving shadows, visible only as a curve of horn or the rise of an angled shoulder blade. The wagon drivers lit lanterns and hung them from short poles, throwing spills of yellow light down the mountain.

"We'll stop soon," Colison told them during one of his caravan checks. "There's another site on this side. Not much farther. We'll be able to set our tents out of the wind there, and Laedys keeps a wayhouse close by. No beds, but she might have hot broth for us, and we'll be able to get the latest news from the town. Laedys loves to gossip." He slapped one of the oxen affectionately and moved back up the line. "Remember not to drink the water till it's been tested, and don't let your animals browse. Don't know how far the poison's spread."

They plodded on in silence after he had gone. Then Heradion asked: "What did you see?"

She didn't have to ask what he meant. "Death." Asharre

had no desire to talk about it, but she knew the youth needed to, so she added the expected question. "You?"

"The same. A hundred different stories, a hundred different lives, but they all ended the same way. Death. Death and desecration. They never just killed when they could break their victims first." He fell quiet. The clop of the oxen's hooves was soothingly monotonous. "Why does anyone follow a faith like that?"

Asharre shrugged before she remembered he couldn't see it. "I don't know. Ask Evenna or Falcien. They study the soul."

"I will. I wanted to ask you too. Some say the Baozites aren't far from wildbloods."

"Maybe." She thought about the memories of fury that had filled her on Spearbridge—the bloodlust, the glory in violence. It had consumed everything else. She had seen echoes of that rage and terrible joy on the faces of her enemies in those visions. "They are not so different in battle. Who they are when they are not fighting—that is different. Wildbloods share the hearts of beasts, but they are Ingvall's children in their bones. That tension makes them what they are. Baozites do not have that. They are men always, and they are trained like beaten dogs. Beat a dog long enough, and the strong ones become vicious things, while the gentle ones die."

"How many wildbloods are left?"

"Not many." She kept her eyes on the road. Beyond the bobbing line of lanterns it was black as the trackless sea. "Few have the strength to live torn between two natures. There were never many, but there are fewer now. Some of those who might have become wildbloods choose to follow summerlander gods instead—more each year, the old ones say. In a generation, perhaps two, some think the wildbloods will be gone completely."

"Will you mourn them?"

"Others will. Not I." The lanterns had stopped ahead. Their bullocks chuffed in surprise as they nearly ran into the wagon before them. *Something must be blocking the road.* She passed the reins to Heradion. "Stay here. I'll find out what's happening."

Falcien joined her halfway, having left his own wagon in Evenna's hands. "Why have we stopped?"

"I don't know yet."

A small crowd had collected in front of the last wagon. Some of the drivers spoke in hushed voices; she could not catch the words, but fear ran through their murmurings. Their gathered lanterns made a shifting pool of light, and at its dappled edge was Colison.

Asharre pushed her way to the forefront. She was taller and broader in the shoulders than any of the drivers, and she muscled through the men with ease. Falcien followed, silent and sure-footed.

"What's happened?"

"I'm not sure." Colison's hand shook as he accepted a lantern from a wagon driver. It was a strange thing to see in a man who had crossed Spearbridge without blinking, and it filled Asharre with foreboding. "Come with me." He paused, glanced at Falcien, and nodded tersely. "You too. Might be we'll need your prayers."

The mountain wall curved inward as Colison led them along the road, tapping his staff on the stone with every step. Asharre heard water burbling. Bristly brown grass covered a clearing that mirrored the one on the other side of Spearbridge; above its dead carpet, leafless trees swayed in the night.

"This is the other campsite," Asharre said. A line of unshod hoofprints, like those of the ponies Colison used, crossed the ice-crusted snow before them. The prints vanished into the dark and came back. The pony had been walking when it left, but trotting when it returned. Something had alarmed the animal or its rider enough to hurry over treacherous footing.

"Aye." Colison shifted the lantern to his left hand and tucked his right into a pocket. "Jassel was riding ahead to scout the road. He came this far and turned back."

"Why?" Falcien asked.

"Said there'd been a killing." Colison trudged across the crunching snow. Asharre followed cautiously.

Halfway across the clearing, the lantern's light glittered off small panes of glass. A small cottage huddled against the mountainside. Snow-mounded firewood was stacked against its walls. A second woodpile, nearly as large as the house, stood to one side. It, too, was capped in untouched snow. A hickory pole thrust from the side of the cottage, holding a lamp with a steeply slanted metal cover. It was the hanging lamp's glass that reflected their light. The lamp itself was dark, and white dusted its bottom rim.

"No one's been here in a while," Falcien noted.

"Aye. Jassel said that too. Not many come this way in the winter   not that many come this way any other time of year—but he thought it peculiar that Laedys hadn't been using her wood. Worried something might've happened to her. She isn't a young woman. Then he found the dead man . . . here." Colison held the lantern steady as he rounded the woodpile.

It took Asharre a moment to make sense of what she saw. A thin coat of snow covered the corpse. It hid the man's face, mercifully, and softened some of what had been done to his body. But not much. There was not much anything could do to soften that.

Falcien murmured something that sounded like a prayer. The young Illuminer took a few steps back, his eyes wide and white in his dark face. She wondered if he might be sick. No shame in that. Asharre herself had been shocked when she saw the body; it was as if the worst memories of Spearbridge had become real before her eyes.

But Falcien wasn't retching. He was moving around Colison to get a closer look. The Illuminer had a stronger stomach than she'd thought. Asharre squatted in the snow beside him, curious for her own sake and also to see what he would notice. If these Celestians intended to investigate the strangeness in Carden Vale—and, now, a murder— they'd need sharp eyes.

"Well?" she prodded.

"A ritual killing," Falcien said, "but I don't know its purpose."

"What makes you say that?"

"They took his bones." The Celestian motioned to the dead man's nearest arm. It had been laid open in a straight line from wrist to elbow, and again from elbow to shoulder, like a slash in a lady's sleeve. His bones were gone. The corpse's hands and feet were intact, and his face was untouched but for the crossbow bolt that sprouted from his right eye like an obscene flower, but from his neck down to his boots, every bone longer than the palm of Asharre's hand was missing.

"You said 'they.' Why?"

Falcien gestured to several pairs of boot prints that dimpled the snow on the far side of the clearing. Even an untrained eye could see that they were old, partly filled by recent snowfalls, and that they had been made by a small group of men. Three to five, Asharre guessed. They'd come together in a group from Carden Vale, circled around the cottage, and gone straight to the corpse behind the wood-pile. Then they had gone back the way they'd come, leaving the body behind.

"You think that is why he was killed?" Asharre asked.

Falcien nodded.

"You are wrong." She took off a mitten and brushed the snow from the bolt in the dead man's eye. A pool of frozen blood shone black in the socket. "This killed him. Look at the fletchings. Green and black on a gray shaft." Asharre glanced at Colison, who nodded to confirm her guess.

"Gals gave Laedys a spare crossbow and some quarrels," the merchant-captain said. "A few years back, it was. He thought a woman living alone ought to have some way to protect herself, and a crossbow doesn't need so much strength as a bow."

"He was shot here, by the door." Asharre paced around the tracks to show the other two. Crimson spattered the solitary line of prints in a burst near the cottage door. More blood had fallen across the lone man's steps as he staggered to the woodpile, softening those marks, but it had frozen before the later group came to trample the red crusts it left in the snow.

Returning to the corpse, Asharre lifted a lifeless hand and showed them the blood on his palm, grooved by pale lines where the crossbow bolt's fletchings had wiped it away. "He staggered to the woodpile, pulled at the quarrel, and fell."

"No one could walk that far with a bolt in his eye," Falcien protested.

Asharre shrugged and put her mitten back on. It made no sense to her either, but the tracks showed what they showed. "This one did. He died here. Sometime later, the other men arrived. By the time they cut him open, he was already frozen through. Look." She moved her grip down to his wrist, holding the hacked flesh up to the lantern light. The knife marks looked almost shaggy where they'd torn through frozen muscle. Ice crystals shone in the corpse's flesh, visible even by the lantern's glow. "There is no blood underneath him except around his head, from the bolt. These wounds never bled. You see? He was ice when they did this."

"They took his bones but left his body?" Colison rubbed his mouth as if he'd bitten into something rotten. "Why? Could at least have had the decency to burn the man. No shortage of firewood about."

"I don't think decency was a pressing concern," Falcien said dryly.

"No. No, I suppose it wouldn't have been." Colison laughed, a little shakily, and adjusted his grip on the staff. "Well, we ought to do it. Man deserves at least that much. Whoever he was."

"A miner, I think," Asharre said. There was black dust trapped in the crow's-feet around the dead man's remaining eye, and more in the knuckles of the hand she'd lifted. His palm was callused by long hours of work with shovel or pick, and his hair was cropped short around his head. He'd shaved it not long before he died.

"He might have had family in Carden Vale. Someone who knows who he was, and perhaps why he came here. We shouldn't burn the body until his kin have had a chance to see him . . . and bid farewell, if they like." Falcien moved toward the cottage's door. "In the meantime, we may as well look at the house."

Colison balked. "It's empty. That firewood hasn't been touched in days. Weeks, might be. It's clear what happened here. Laedys caught the man prowling about, shot him, and was so frightened she went down to the village rather than stay out here alone. No need to go prying about her home while she's away."

"It isn't prying," the Illuminer said. "We're looking for anything that might explain who this man was, why he came, and what happened to him—both when he died and after. Laedys will probably be glad she didn't have to deal with it herself."

"Still don't like it," Colison grumbled, but he went.

There was no answer when Asharre knocked at the cottage's door, so she tried the handle. It was locked from the inside, but after three good kicks the door gave way.

Inside, the cottage was black and cold. Nothing moved. There was a stale smell to the air, and a whiff of the charnel house kept muted by the chill. Asharre stepped away from the splintered door and reached out a gloved hand. "Give me the lantern."

Colison hooked the metal handle over her fingers. Holding it high, Asharre went back in.

The place was a wreck. Broken dishes littered the floor. A brass mirror on one wall had been scratched and gouged until it became a maze of crazed, opaque lines. The wooden shutters that covered the cottage's two tiny windows rattled loose in the wind; lines of snow and broken glass shone white beneath each one. Cold ashes filled the hearth; scraps of charred paper lay among them.

As Asharre moved into the cottage, her lantern's light fell upon charcoal markings scribbled in loops all across the floor. They had the repetitive intensity of a madman's scrawl, though they were pictures rather than words. Most were meaningless to her, but some looked like the sunburst that Bassinos had put in the windows of his chapel: four rays over four, each one ending in a bulbed tip that made her think of grasping hands.

She went on. Countless sheets of paper fluttered on the far wall, rustling like a forest of dead leaves. Crabbed writing covered each sheet, some in charcoal and some in a reddish brown ink that looked uncomfortably like dried blood, but any curiosity about what they said was driven out of her mind by the corpse that crouched in the corner.

It was Laedys. Asharre had no doubt of that. The corpse was a small, gray-haired woman wrapped in a patchwork quilt that had yellowed and gone rancid with the sweat of bad dreams. At first Asharre thought she had simply died with her face in her hands, but then she saw the dark webs of blood spilled over the woman's wrists and realized that the first two fingers of each hand were sunk to the knuckles in her eyes. She had been dead long enough that the smell of slow decay crept through the cold air.

"Falcien!" she called. Her voice echoed strangely in the cottage, and for an instant she imagined that the papers nailed on the walls flapped in response. "Come here. I want you to look at this. Colison—better if you stay out. Laedys is dead, and it is not pleasant to see."

Glass cracked under Falcien's boots as he entered. The Illuminer stopped by Asharre's side, taking in the corpse and her scribbled surroundings with a quiet "Oh."

"What do these things mean?" Asharre asked.

"The markings on the floor are protective sigils, though none quite like I've seen before," he said, tracing one of the circular scrawls. "This one wards against the 'hunter in dreams'—one of Anvhad's servants, a creature that has not been seen in Ithelas since Rhaelyand fell. It isn't drawn correctly; these dots are misplaced. They should be here and here"—he tapped one of the sigils to indicate—"above the script, not below. Doing it in reverse changes the meaning. This one, the double spiral, is modified from an even more obscure sequence. It's at least six hundred years old. The original was intended to help its user find her way out again from god-granted visions, distilling truth from obscure symbolism and awakening her to reality when the spirit journey was finished. But it, too, is changed. The spiral's end faces in the wrong direction, west instead of east, and the doubled drawings cross lines too often. They should be kept clear of each another, and they aren't. Again, the alterations change the meaning, but I'd have to study them to determine exactly how."

"Do they have any power?"

"No. Well, I shouldn't say no. It's unlikely. The inscriptions have no power in themselves; all they do is channel the magic that a deity gives to one of her Blessed. Unless Laedys was secretly Blessed, these are just marks on the floor. Remarkable ones, though. I wonder how she knew so much of runecraft."

Asharre shrugged. "What about the writings on the walls?"

He hesitated, but plucked one off its bent metal pin and held it to the light. "This is written in bastardized Rhaellan. An older form, almost archaic, but that isn't uncommon in the mountains."

"What does it say?"

"'They are watching me. They are watching me. Eyes peeping in the glass, madness in the mountain's belly. The nightmare is waking, the old death is coming. This is my warning. Turn back: death comes from the mountain. It watches me in the glass and in the water and I cannot blind its eyes. Eyes everywhere.' It goes on like that." Falcien cleared his throat. "The others say similar things. Over and over again."

"But nothing that explains why she shot that man or clawed her fingers into her skull?"

"Not that I've seen so far. I'll have to take them to study, of course. I haven't read them all. But these writings suggest that she was trying to protect herself against something—watching eyes, evil dreams, the 'death from the mountain,' whatever that might mean. It doesn't appear she was successful."

Asharre rubbed the hilt of her *caractan*. The weapon was comforting, but not as much as she would have liked. "You still want to press on to Carden Vale?"

"We must. Whatever is happening here, it's killed at least two people already, and it will not be stopped by mortal means. I know we're young, and we must seem terribly green to you . . . but this is what we train for, what we live for: to meet the enemies that others cannot."

"That's what the Knights of the Sun train for," Asharre corrected him. "Not you." She'd seen Falcien handle a sword during their practice sessions. Once. A sick kitten would have bested him. For all his grace, the Illuminer had no idea how to fight.

"There isn't one Knight in a hundred who could have identified those runes. This is our battle. Whether you come with us or not, we have to fight it."

"I won't be coming," Colison said from the doorway, faceless in the dark. "Nor will my men. I don't know what's out there, but I've heard enough. We're going back. Any aid I can leave you, I will, but my first charge is my caravan, and that means we leave."

"Of course," Falcien said, lifting his head as if startled that the merchant-captain was still there. "We're grateful for all you've done."

"Least I could do." Colison turned away, hesitated, and added over his shoulder: "About the runes. I couldn't help hearing. I don't know what they are—don't care to come in and see them either, if it's all the same to you—but I know for a fact that Laedys was no scholar. She couldn't read or write a word, Bright Lady bless her. She'd save the letters her daughter sent so that I could read them to her when our caravan came through. And those were in Calant, not Rhaellan."

Falcien froze. Then he nodded, slowly, his lower lip pushed out slightly in a pensive frown. He took down the pinned pages, stacking them in the same order that they had hung on the walls. When they could no longer hear Colison's retreating steps, the Celestian glanced at Asharre. "Will you go with him?"

She shook her head. It wasn't even a question. She'd failed Oralia; she would not fail these Illuminers too. "Magic didn't cut the bones from that man outside. Knives did that. Knives in human hands. You need my sword. I'll stay."

10

Summer passed into autumn, and autumn's leaves turned red, without Corban selling a single black-fire quarrel. He hadn't even sent letters to any of the prospective buyers he'd considered. Every time he drew up a chair and opened his inkwell to begin, Corban found his mind locked stubbornly mute. He couldn't think of a simple salutation, let alone how to explain what he'd discovered without sounding like a liar or a madman.

In addition to being deadly as tools of war, the blackfire stones seemed to possess some healing magic. The scratches on Corban's hands, which had been inflamed and painful for days, were soothed almost immediately when he clasped a quarrel between them. They healed soon afterward, leaving scars like charcoaled bird tracks across the backs of his hands, but causing him no further pain.

A few days after the scratches had healed, Corban was plagued by sudden, blinding headaches. The quarrels were the only thing that could alleviate the pain, and they worked miraculously. After a few visits to his safehouse, the headaches were cured altogether. When he came down with a wracking cough the next week, he visited the apothecary's cellar once more—and that ailment, too, vanished.

Gethel hadn't mentioned that the blackfire stones could heal, but perhaps the scholar simply hadn't known. Anyway, why should it surprise him? The Sun Swords were said to be able to inflict vicious wounds and cure them with equal ease. It was only logical that another god's *perethil* could do the same.

Sometimes Corban caught himself wondering just which god had created the blackfire stone. It didn't matter, really—Gethel had cut the *perethil* free from their creator, whoever it was—but now and then he wondered, prodding at the question as he might have poked a sore tooth. What deity would release such savagery into human hands? *Why?*

Was it really wise to sell that?

That worry wasn't the only reason he hesitated to sell the quarrels, though. If that had been Corban's only concern, he would have shaken it off and sold all three crates the next day. He'd dealt in swords and arrows long enough for his conscience to have developed calluses over its calluses. Men would brutalize each other no matter what he did. If his new weapons frightened them enough to stop the bloodshed, well and good; if not, the sins were theirs, not his. He was only a seller of tools.

But this tool was different enough to terrify him. Not in itself, but because of what might befall him if the Celestians found it and took it as evidence that he'd been worshipping dark gods. The thought that someone might stumble upon his secret cache, and steal it or betray it to the Dome of the Sun, kept Corban awake half the night. He could hardly walk by a sausage-seller's cart without smelling his own pyre in the sizzle of smoke and roasting meat.

As the months went by, the idea of giving up the quarrels became increasingly repellent to him. For all those old reasons, yes . . . but also because they were the only things that brought him pleasure anymore.

Hidden in the apothecary's cellar, Corban could forget his fears and imagine the joys the blackfire quarrels would bring him: money, women, prestige at court. Once he let go of the bolts, the terror came rushing back, but *while* he held them he was soothed, and could relax into the pleasures of his imagination. He loved them as a miser loves gold: for their own beauty, and for the power they held, but above all for the limitless potential of what they might buy. They were the distillation of freedom, offering him infinite choices . . . as long as he never settled on one.

There was little danger of that. Enthralling as his imagined delights were, the reality of them had palled. No courtesan's perfumed caresses could be as tender as the ones he dreamed of in the seaside cellar. No wine could be so intoxicating. Money, once the measure of his victories, no longer interested Corban; he became so indifferent that he forgot meetings, neglected clients and suppliers, left cargoes to rot in ships' holds.

His clothes became shabby, his face gaunt under a beggar's beard. He barely noticed. His little orange cat, tired of waiting by an empty bowl, wandered off to hunt in the alleys. He was glad to be rid of the chore.

By the time autumn's last leaves flapped away on the winds of winter, Corban's once-thriving business had shriveled to nothing. He might have revived it, perhaps, if he cared . . . but he didn't. His world had narrowed to the apothecary's hovel, the secret cellar, and the crates that held the only thing under the Bright Lady's light that mattered to him.

And as he discarded the world, it discarded him. His

friends walked past him without recognizing, or *seeing*, his face. To them he was just a dirty pauper; he didn't warrant a single glance, let alone a second. The courtesans' palaces refused him, turning him away without so much as a glimpse of their sandalwood doors. Corban had money. He'd scarcely spent a penny since coming back to Cailan. But money alone had never been enough to buy the time of an Amrali-trained lady, and his once-polished manners had tarnished in the cellar.

None of it mattered. Their rejections only showed how little he'd lost. If his friends were that easily blinded by a little dirt, they were no true friends of his. If women who sold themselves for coin wanted to put on airs, let them; *he* knew what they were. Corban had better friends and sweeter comforts than anything they could offer.

He rarely left those comforts. The world outside his cellar was too cold, too bright. It stung his face and made his skull ache. Corban had grown sharp eyed in the dark: he could pick out the smallest details without a lantern, and the merest glimpse of the sun made his eyes water in pain. Another reason to stay below.

For weeks on end he kept vigil by the quarrels, crawling back into the city only when hunger forced him. Even that seldom happened. Corban had learned to pry off the sickly gray barnacles that clung to the pier's pilings. Sometimes he caught rats squealing in the dark. Not fine fare, but it was better than venturing up to the streets.

Once, as he was creeping back from an expedition to the city, Corban glimpsed his reflection in a sheet of pitted glass left over from one of the dead apothecary's experiments. He stared at it, unable to see himself in the bent gray man who gaped back.

The longer he stared, the more disquieted Corban became. It wasn't only that the face was wrong—although that surely couldn't be *his* face that was so worn and feverish—but that the eyes were.

They weren't his own eyes. Something else stared out at him from that makeshift mirror. Something that meant him harm.

Corban smashed the glass. He didn't think; he just balled up his fist and swung at those alien, reflected eyes. A white web shivered across the rippled surface; a few shards tinkled out of its center. Sucking on his bleeding knuckles, Corban hobbled away.

After that he avoided reflections. He kept a pocketful of rocks to throw at puddles, and he covered as many of the apothecary's monster jars as he could. Those he couldn't drape with scraps of stolen cloth, he hurried past, keeping his head down and eyes averted.

It helped, a little, but it couldn't give him peace of mind. Nothing but the quarrels could give him that.

The smell of smoke and sulfur, which had once repelled him, was now a reassurance: it told him that his secret treasure was still there, still safe. Sometimes Corban spent hours with his face buried in the packing straw, inhaling openmouthed so that when he left, he might take the scent of consolation with him.

In the increasingly rare moments that he slept, he curled around the blackfire crates, cradling them in the hollow of his body like a cat nursing kittens. His dreams were strange and garish, filled with impossible sensations. In them, Corban made love to headless women whose foggy bodies collapsed and dissolved under the force of his exertions. He drank black wine that filled his veins in place of blood, while his own blood poured out from slits in his wrists and filled the empty bottle.

Those were the ones he could recall. Most he could not. They were more alluring, more disturbing. Corban woke trembling and sweaty, glad to have escaped but yearning to return—to *remember*.

He never could.

Time flowed on, uncounted. Winter hardened its grip on the city, bringing long nights and gray, sunless days. Corban noticed the cold, vaguely, but he never considered leaving. The subterranean cellar was insulated enough for him; it wasn't comfortable, but it was safe, and that counted for much more.

If it had stayed safe, he might have whiled away the rest of his life there.

It did not. No human thieves violated his sanctuary . . . but late one night, as Corban lay in restless sleep, the rats did.

The sound of gnawing woke him. Rats and mice were as common in Cailan's underbelly as fleas on a mangy dog; while the noise was very close, Corban thought nothing of it until he rolled over, opened his eyes, and saw the wet brown backs of wharf rats scurrying in and out of his crates.

They were eating his blackfire stone.

He knew it immediately, furiously, scarcely stopping to question *why* rats would eat the foul-smelling stuff. They would and they were. The animals scattered and fled as he came at them, stamping and kicking, crushing them barehanded against the pier.

Some of the rats didn't run. Couldn't. They writhed on the pier, flopping like landed fish and shrilling piteously as the blackfire worked through their guts. Corban grabbed the nearest and dug his fingers into its throat, ripping the animal open. It was a thief—a cursed, sneaking thief—and he would have back what it had stolen. He tore away fur and flesh until he reached its stomach, the membrane pulsing hot around the meal that was killing it.

His meal.

With shaking hands he wiped blood and hair from the exposed stomach, ignoring the rat's dying squeals. He could just make out the inky slosh of dissolving blackfire stone inside. It was liquid; there'd be no stuffing it back into the quarrels.

He could still salvage it, though. He could.

Trembling, Corban pinched off one end of the rat's stomach and pulled it out. He fit the bloody end to his lips and pushed its contents out, filling his mouth with bitter bile.

What am I doing? he wondered for a cold, panicked instant, but the thought vanished before he swallowed. He was doing the only thing he *could* do: punishing the thief and reclaiming what was his.

The taste wasn't unpleasant. There was just the slightest tang of acrid smoke. Afterward he could not remember exactly how the blackfire bile tasted . . . only that he craved it, would have sold his soul for more. Desperate as a dreamflower addict, Corban reached for the next flailing rat, and the next.

And then, suddenly, there were no more. Corban blinked in confusion, looking around as though waking from a drugged dream. He wasn't sure, for a while, where he stood.

His hands were red to the wrist, striped with crimson smudges above that. He dimly remembered licking those spatters. Looking down, Corban saw six little bodies on the pier around him. They were stiff, doubled over around the holes he'd torn in each one's belly.

What have I done? Corban shivered. He wiped at his mouth, licked reflexively at the back of his hand, and then froze in horror at his own gesture.

What am I doing?

Retching, he grabbed the rats' bodies and threw them into the water. He washed the blood from the pier, scrubbing at it until what was left became indistinguishable from the old stains of the sea. With the worst of the grisliness out of sight, some of his terror began to subside. Corban spat into the water, trying to ignore the fact that nothing had come up in any of his heaves. Whatever he'd swallowed, it was still in there. Still in *him*.

He sat on his heels, digging his hands into his hair and rocking back and forth as if he could shake a solution free from his skull. Something had overwhelmed him. Something had made him commit a horror.

What?

He felt like a man who, having crossed an old and uncertain bridge, had looked back to see it swept away by a flood tide. He could remember taking the journey, even some of the individual steps . . . but when he tried to retrace the way he had come, he found it utterly impossible. A roaring chasm stood in its place, terrifying in its vastness.

Whatever had befallen him, salvation was beyond his own ability to find.

There was only one person he could trust. Only one man Corban knew wouldn't betray him to the Celestians, if only because his own sins were greater.

He hobbled out of the apothecary's cellar, squinting against the blaze of daylight and mumbling apologies to his quarrels for abandoning them. It was for a good cause, and only for a little while. A very little while.

Back in his long-neglected office, Corban blew dust from a sheaf of papers and selected a page less wrinkled than the rest. His ink had gone dry, but he spat in the well and scratched at it until he had stirred up enough to write a short message.

"Come," he wrote to Gethel. "Help me."

11

Carden Vale was a desolate town.

Viewed from a bend on the mountain road just past Laedys' cottage, the buildings and their mud-choked port seemed like ancient relics, forgotten for centuries, rather than places where people had lived and laughed and loved only a few short months ago. Asharre could not imagine, as she gazed down upon it, what it must have been like to call Carden Vale home.

All the Skarlar holds together would have fit easily inside its walls. In its glory days Carden Vale must have held thousands of souls; even now, with half its buildings collapsed and the others surrounded by weedy pines and silt instead of wheat fields and clean wharves, there was a certain ruined grandeur to its lines.

But the surviving core of the town was huddled within the shell of what it had been, and as Asharre stood and studied it, she could not shake the feeling that Carden Vale was under siege.

There were no enemies in sight, of course. There was

no one moving at all. It was the stillness that made it so eerie.

There should have been farmers out sowing their crops, women washing or drawing water from the river, children playing in the grassy market square. Asharre saw none of those things. There was only silence, as if all the lives in Carden Vale had ended when Ang'duradh fell, six hundred years ago.

"Admiring the view?" Heradion asked.

She shook her head and turned away from the steep drop at the roadside. The wind tugged at her cloak with icy fingers, and would have whipped her hair into her eyes if it had been longer. Another reason to be glad that *sigrir* wore theirs short. "Wondering what we will find when we arrive."

"Prayers, prayers, and more prayers." His blue-green eyes twinkled above the scarf he'd wrapped around his face. "Under the circumstances, however, I can't complain."

"No," Asharre agreed. Colison had wanted to give them another full wagon of supplies. It was only after both Falcien and Evenna insisted that his men needed them more—and demonstrated that they could purify the springs of Duradh Mal into safe water—that he'd begrudgingly settled for giving them a few extra water casks and bundles of fodder, taking Evenna's cartload of plants and drawings back south in return.

Wet snow sifted down as they came to the end of the mountain. The flakes beaded on Asharre's gray-green cloak and the bullocks' heads with melting droplets. By the time they reached the valley, the snow had shifted to rain, and all the world wore a silvery veil.

The fog was thicker on the vale's northeastern wall. It rose in serpentine blue coils, like the fragrant bundles of sweetsmoke burned at the Celestians' purification rituals. They had burned that incense at Oralia's formal funeral, too, though there was no body for the pyre at the Dome of the Sun. Asharre gazed at the swirling haze, remembering, while the misty rain gathered on her cloak and wept quicksilver.

"That's Devils' Ridge," Evenna said, following the direction of her stare. The Illuminer was walking between the wagons to stretch her legs. She wore no hood in the rain. Ringlets of glossy black hung around her ears where her hair had come loose of its haloed braid. "The stones are scalding all the way to the crest. In winter, when snow hits them, it's said to become a white wall of steam that rises high enough to hide the stars."

"What causes it?"

The younger woman shrugged, quirking her lips in a one-sided smile. "Some say the souls of all the Rosewayns' victims lie under those rocks, and that smoke is really their spirits trying to break free so they can cross the Last Bridge. Others say it's the souls of the Rosewayns themselves, burning in torment for the evil they did when they lived. I think it's just a vein of fire under the earth. Ang'duradh was built upon a volcano, if you believe the legends. The Baozites forged their swords in its heart and built the Shardfield from the stoneglass that the mountain flung out when roused."

Asharre held her palm up to the rain. "If the water carries madness, and the rocks turn it to steam, are we not in danger if the wind blows it our way?"

"I shouldn't think so. If that were true, the rain would already have doomed us." Evenna's smile turned wry. "Falcien spent more time studying theology than I did; I was more interested in herbs and healing. So the best I can offer is a guess. But I think the corruption has to be *swallowed* to take effect. The act of knowingly accepting it is important. Accidentally touching it, or breathing in vapor that fills the air, does nothing. The choices we make matter to the gods, even when the choices aren't quite what we think they are."

Asharre was still considering that when they came, at last, to the gates of Carden Vale. The town seemed even lonelier up close than it had from afar. A high wall curved around its southern side, but it was badly neglected. The crenels were clogged with mossy dirt, and the iron spears on the merlons were jagged, rust-gnawed stumps. Rain brought the night down early; it was full dark by the time they reached the gate.

It must have been a fearsome sight when Carden Vale was young. The southern wall was built of tree trunks, each one thicker than a fat man's waist and bound to the next by spiked iron bands. Crimson runes tattooed the metal between the spikes. There must have been some magic in their making, for the sigils shone like new-spilled blood after six hundred years.

Bronzed skulls leered atop the gates. Some were human, while others were strange and hideous. Serrated ridges crowned the brows of one; the next had five nose holes in an arc above a fang-filled grin. At first Asharre took the monstrous skulls for sculptures, but when they stopped before the gate, she saw that those, like the human ones, showed bone where the bronze had worn away.

"What sort of beasts are those?" Heradion wondered.

"*Ansurak*," Falcien answered. "Not beasts. Those were men, once. They gave themselves to one dark god or another, letting their bodies be shaped along with their souls, until they turned to monsters."

Asharre studied the skulls. There *was* something human about them. It was a faint and fleeting resemblance, but it was there, in the curve of an eye socket or the joint of a jawbone never made to hold fangs. She could believe that they had once been men.

"But why?" Evenna asked. "Why would anyone choose that?"

"Power. Punishment. The Baozites considered it both a blessing and a curse to become *ansurak*. For some, it is the culmination of a lifetime devoted to their god. For others, it is the price of disobedience—being transformed into a brute with no purpose but to fight and die on the field."

"And the other gods?"

Falcien shrugged, sending a cascade of droplets rippling down his cloak. "Maolites seldom choose it, though they suffer that fate more frequently than any other deity's servants. The madness of the Four-Armed Beggar finds expression in their flesh whether they will it or not. The Maimed Witches might mortify their bodies to honor Kliasta, or those maimings might be the marks of *ansurak*. We don't know enough about them to say. The Nightingale's faithful choose undeath rather than becoming *ansurak,* and we know too little of Anvhad's ways to say what his servants do."

Asharre frowned, puzzled. Even in the bones, she could see the strength that those creatures had possessed. "Why does your goddess not make *ansurak*?"

"She did, once. During the Godslayer's War." Falcien's eyes glinted in the depths of his rain-sodden hood. "After the slaughter on the Field of Sorrows, when the war was ended and Maghredan slain, we forswore the rituals that made them. *Ansurak* lose what makes them human. Ours lost the ability to understand weakness, to see sins and forgive. They became terrible in their righteousness. There was, as well, a danger in their pride. The Blessed already stand outside ordinary society; the *ansurak* of Celestia were feared and worshipped as gods. We did not want that. Our duty is to serve, not rule. Once we saw where that road would lead, we chose to walk away. The Bright Lady has no *ansurak*. The Blessed are enough."

"Enough to counter the others' monsters?"

"We've done well enough against them so far." The Illuminer shrugged again. "What good is a weapon if its use defeats the purpose of the fight?"

"What good is standing out here in the cold?" Heradion interrupted. "I'm wet and tired and hungry. As fascinating as these skulls are, I'm more concerned about my *own* soaked bones. I'd like to find a nice warm inn where I can put my feet up by the fire and maybe have a bit of roast mutton."

"You won't find it here," Asharre said, surprised he hadn't already realized that. "Look at the houses. The empty wharves. This rain has softened the road, but there were no tracks on it before ours. No one lives here."

"It looks like a plague town," Evenna agreed.

"Well, if no one lives here, there'll be no one to complain if I lay a fire in their hearth," Heradion said. "Staying cold and wet doesn't help anything."

Evenna wiped away a raindrop trickling down her cheek. "Should we leave the wagons outside?"

"Why?" Heradion asked.

"If they try to close us in . . ." The young Illuminer said no more, but no more was needed. Asharre thought of the bone-stripped corpse in the snow by Laedys' cottage. Whoever had done that might be in the town—might be all that was left of the town. The notion of being trapped inside Carden Vale's skull-mounted walls with such mad-men was not comforting.

If it came to fighting among the streets and empty buildings of an unfamiliar town, however, the odds would be against them with or without the wagons. And leaving their oxen outside the walls made them easy prey for wolves or feral dogs. She hadn't seen any of those beasts in the valley, but if they *were* here, they'd be hungry and bold enough to attack the wagons with all their other meals gone. "Better to bring them."

They found an inn near the gate. A sign over the door named it the Rosy Maiden. The specks of red glass in the common room's window, representing the five crimson jewels stolen from Baoz's crown in the age of myth before the Godslayer's War, suggested that once the place had borne a different, grimmer name.

Nonetheless, it was in good repair, and that was what mattered. The Rosy Maiden's stables were empty and the hearths cold, but there was firewood stacked under the eaves and water in the well. Heradion drew buckets for their animals and Falcien prayed to purify them, while Evenna went inside to build a fire and Asharre stalked around the inn's perimeter, checking for danger.

She saw none. There was no indication that anyone had been anywhere nearby for days. The kitchen garden was overrun with weeds, as were those of neighboring houses. The market square, which should have been littered with wilted cabbage and the feathers of unlucky chickens, was clean and bare. Even the town's cats were gone.

The emptiness added to her apprehension even as it deprived her of any solid cause. Defeated, she returned to the inn. The night passed quietly, and the next morning she went out again, ranging farther afield. Still she saw no one, apart from Falcien and Heradion on their own wanderings.

Many of the houses bore a peculiar sign carved or drawn in charcoal on their doors: a sunburst with four arms over four, identical to the ones she'd seen on Bassinos' chapel and Laedys' scribble-covered cottage. Its placement was random, as best she could tell; the marked houses didn't seem any more or less dilapidated than the others, and there was no pattern to where they stood. Both Evenna and Falcien recognized it from Balnamoine, and were disturbed to see it repeated in Carden Vale, but neither of them knew what, if anything, it *meant*. All they could say was that the suggestion of reaching arms and open palms, in this place, echoed the four grasping hands of Maol.

"It's eerie," Heradion said when they reunited in the Rosy Maiden's common room. Evenna had a fire going in the hearth and a kettle over the flames. The fire was a blessing: it banished the chill—the strange, senseless *fear*—that had settled into Asharre's bones.

Heradion took a cup of tea from the Illuminer gratefully. "There's no sign of fighting, no indication of pestilence or plague. The doors are locked, the curtains drawn, the doorsteps swept and tidy. It's as if everyone in town decided to go on holiday . . . and never came back."

"Not all of them left so peaceably," Falcien said. He paced moodily across the room, crossing before the fire every five steps. "I went to the gaol, wondering if I might find some record of violence or madness similar to what we saw in the mountains. If a man went bloodmad, as that ferret did, he should have hung and burned for his crimes."

"Did he?" Evenna asked, offering the other Illuminer a cup of tea.

Falcien held the cup without drinking as he continued his pacing. "*They* did. Near twenty of them. I'll spare you the recitation of their deeds. But they had a pattern: the killers extracted the victims' bones after every slaying; sometimes that was what caused the death. Cannibalism appears repeatedly in their crimes, and almost all of them attacked children in preference to other victims. They were mostly people with no history of violence, and many had become religious shortly before the killings. Several complained of bad dreams, and some wrote complicated rune circles or prayers in languages they had no way of knowing. Protective prayers," he finished. "Like Laedys'."

"How do you know so much about them?" Asharre asked. The few gaolers she'd known had been an uncouth, illiterate lot. They considered themselves put upon if they had to list their prisoners' names and crimes. Not one would have kept such detailed records.

"The town gaoler was one of the first to go mad. He murdered every prisoner in his charge. After his execution, the solaros took up his duties. He knew *something* inhuman was at work, if not what, and wrote down all he could about the killings as they happened. He was trying to puzzle out the *why* behind the slaughter, just as we are."

"Then we should go to the chapel," Evenna said. "If the solaros was struggling to piece together the mystery, he might have left something useful there. We'll go after dinner."

No one objected, although no one looked enthused by the prospect. Their meal was short and somber. Heradion tried a few jests, but stopped when the others refused to laugh. At sunset the two Illuminers prayed together, moving through the graceful sequence of the dusk ritual with fluid synchronicity. Asharre practiced the Sun Knights' prayer on her own; she had no use for the invocation, but her muscles needed the work.

When the prayer ended, Heradion strapped on his sword, Asharre swept her travel-stained cloak back over her shoulders, and the four of them went out to the chapel.

Carden Vale's chapel was neither large nor rich; the town had worshipped another god in its youth, and the Celestian chapel had been built well into its decline. Taller buildings surrounded the plain stone dome, but it was set to catch the light—if any had broken through the day's gloomy grayness—and it was favorably situated at a crossroads near the town's heart. No matter where they started, the convergence of the roads would have brought them to its doors.

Those doors were marred with gouges and blunt, splintered dents. The entablature was chipped; the windows nearby were broken. Those that remained whole were crudely daubed with the sunburst she'd seen on houses elsewhere: four arms over four, rendered in thick red strokes that strangled the light falling through. Rubble was piled knee high before the door, and some of it was stained with blood.

It unsettled her to see such brutal scars on this holy place. Other than the marks on their windows, the other buildings in Carden Vale were undamaged, but here the memory of rage hovered like a living spirit in the air. There had been hatred here, hatred as strong as if the long-dead Baozites had risen to find their ancient enemy's temple on their land.

"Who would do this?" Evenna asked softly, to silence. The young Illuminer stepped forward, picking her way carefully over masonry and fallen blocks. She laid her hands over the damaged wood, as if she could heal its wounds, then pushed inward gently. The door gave way with a shudder.

Inside, the devastation stopped abruptly. It was as if the invaders, having forced their way in, immediately lost interest. The only damage Asharre saw was a series of scrapes on the floor where some barricading object had been forced back by the hammered doors. The barricade itself, whatever it had been, was gone.

The rest of the small antechamber was undisturbed. It held pegs for cloaks and benches for aged worshippers to rest while they waited. An ever-flowing bowl, enchanted so that water flowed in equally from all sides of its rim and created the illusion of stillness in the center of perpetual motion, stood on a pedestal to one side. The bowl was a common symbol in Celestian temples; it invited visitors to wash the dirt from their hands and the weariness from their bodies, ritually purifying them before they proceeded into the sanctum. Straight ahead, a low arch, wide enough for two men to walk abreast, led to the main prayer hall. Rows of pews waited in dusty silence there.

"This place is desecrated," Evenna whispered as she led them in.

If it was, Asharre could not feel it. There was a coldness in the air, and a whiff of rot, but it was nothing compared to the ugliness she'd seen in Laedys' cottage.

The other Celestians, however, seemed to agree with Evenna. Even Heradion, never the most pious of souls, frowned and ran a thumb over his sword's pommel as he stepped across the threshold. He eyed the ever-flowing bowl as if he expected the water to turn to lye at any moment, and he kept close to the two Illuminers. Both of them made ritual obeisance at the bowl, dipping their fingers into the water and touching it to brow and heart, but neither Asharre nor Heradion did.

"There's no holiness here anymore," Heradion said

when the Illuminers looked at him. "No point in being purified for it."

"This temple is laid out in the traditional pattern," Evenna said, pointedly ignoring his comment. "Patients' rooms and healing garden to the east, to draw upon the dawn light. The solaros' private chambers to the west, where the long sun sets. The library, if he had one, will be to the west as well."

They went to the library first. A quiet air of loneliness hung over its cozy clutter. An overstuffed armchair, its once-red leather worn to a frayed pink, sat in the room's center with a round table at its elbow. Small, empty bottles dotted the floor at the chair's feet, along with a clay mug and a stack of well-thumbed books. Asharre leaned against the wall, crossing her arms. She understood the need to investigate, but nothing in this room seemed significant, and it felt ghoulish to pry into the details of someone else's life.

The others did not seem to share her compunctions. Heradion picked up a book resting beside the armchair. "*The Thousand Journeys of Shalai the Wise*," he read aloud. A loose button dangled from its pages, held by a knotted thread that served as a bookmark. He set it down and examined the next book. "*The Garden of Perfumed Delights*. I remember this one. Racy reading for a country solaros. Badly treated, though. Almost all the pages are torn out. Maybe he wanted to keep the good bits by his bedside?"

"Shouldn't need to tear a book apart for that. Why not just take the whole thing?" Evenna picked up the mug and held it to her nose. She paused, then sniffed again, frowning. "Dreamflowers? Was he having trouble sleeping?"

"*The Garden of Perfumed Delights* can be quite rousing," Heradion said. Evenna shot him an acid look, and they moved on.

A door on the far side of the library opened to the priest's private chambers. These rooms, too, had an air of comfortable, bookish poverty. More leatherbound volumes, and more tiny bottles, covered the lone table in the solaros' sitting room. They looked older, and grimmer, than the texts in the library. A plate and jug were pushed an arm's length from the table's only chair, allowing the books to be brought closer.

"A man who put writing above eating," Evenna observed.

"He'd have made a good Illuminer," Heradion agreed, leafing through the books. "Curious choices for dinner reading, though. *Eristhei on the Twelve Corruptions. A Codex of Curses. A Life of Halivair Rosewayn.* I rather preferred the books in the other room."

"So did he, I'm sure." Evenna lifted the *Codex* and riffled through it. Papers covered with hasty, smudged writing were tucked between its pages. Some were homemade rag papers, clumpy and matted. Others, Asharre realized, were the missing pages from *The Garden of Perfumed Delights* and the other torn books, their margins and the spaces between their lines filled with scribbles. The man must have been desperate for notepaper.

"This wasn't pleasure reading," Evenna said. "Look at these notes. Every page. He annotated *every page.* I can barely read this, the script's so small and shaky." She waved a hand at one of the empty bottles. "And do you smell that?"

Heradion sniffed at the greenish residue inside. "Burned cat hair?"

"Close. Tincture of vigil's friend. Burned cat hair would probably taste better. He must have been drinking it straight, or near enough to make no difference. It's a wonder he could keep his hands steady enough to write—

and no wonder he needed dreamflowers to sleep. Our so-laros was drugging himself for alertness and concentration, then drugging himself to sleep when he couldn't hold off exhaustion any longer." Evenna clicked her tongue disap-provingly. "A man could kill himself doing that."

"Seems a bit excessive just to take some notes," Hera-dion said.

"He was looking for a cure." Falcien glanced up from the book he held propped against one knee. "He knew there was some dark magic at work in Carden Vale. With the passes frozen and the river trade stopped, where could he hope to find answers except in his books? A shame his library wasn't equal to the task. The *Codex of Curses* is more fairy tale than fact, and while Eristhei collected the best information available in his time, much of what he wrote was badly distorted or untrue. But at least we know our solaros was working on the problem."

"We also know he failed," Heradion pointed out.

"But not why." Asharre stepped through the next door into the solaros' tiny bedchamber, leaving the others to their reading.

The blankets on the bed were knotted and untidy. Wrinkled starbursts showed where they'd been crumpled in sweaty fists. The stench of fear lingered on them, rank and bestial, and something else as well. Asharre had never smelled it before, but she knew at once what it was: bad dreams. Many nights of bad dreams.

A forest of burned-out candles sprouted from the bed-side table. More lay in a box at the table's feet. On top of the boxed candles was a book with dated entries. It looked like a diary, but Asharre couldn't begin to decipher the crabbed writing, so she carried it back to the Illuminers. "This was in his bedroom. Nothing else."

"I'll start work on it tomorrow," Falcien said, taking the diary and tucking it into his satchel. "We'll need more space to sort through all this, and I can't say I'm eager to try squinting my way through the man's handwriting by candlelight."

Evenna glanced at the windows. Azure twilight was rapidly fading to black. "Neither am I. The reading can wait until morning. Let's collect whatever else there is to find here and go back."

Each of them lit a candle from the solaros' stockpile, and Evenna led them to the chapel's east wing. The curved hallway ended in a door of goldenwood and dark windows: the entrance to the glassed gardens, where healing herbs could be cultivated when snow mounded the fields and the earth was frozen to icy rock.

The next door, Asharre guessed, would be the drying room, used for the preparation and storage of herbal medicines, bandages, and other tools of the healer's trade. Carden Vale might have had a real physician or two when the Baozites ruled Ang'duradh, but the poor town it had become had little to attract, or hold, such a man. Good doctors were nearly as rare as Blessed, and had no holy strictures preventing them from catering exclusively to the rich. The village solaros was probably the only healer in Carden Vale, whether or not he actually knew anything about the art.

Evenna bypassed the garden and the drying room to try the patients' rooms. The first two were unremarkable. Clean, airy, scented with a lingering hint of wintermint and wormwood. One had a wide, slanted table for women who preferred to give birth in a holy place, under the Bright Lady's gaze, rather than in their own homes.

The third room was a cell. It had been hastily built:

the floor stones had been pried up to drive iron bars into the earth, and only ash-smeared wood replaced them. The stones lay jumbled behind the door, caked with crumbling earth. The cell's bars were plainly scavenged from other places; though all of them looked sturdy, no two matched, and several had been crudely sawed off to fit. Decorative whorls swirled up and down one brass bar, dull between the bright toothmarks left by saws all along its length. The next bore a verdigrised lady's face in profile. The others, newer, showed no such artistry.

In the corner of the cell was a millstone with a chain looped through its center. The ends of the chain were linked to a man-size leather harness. Rawhide mitts dangled from the harness; rather than shackling the wearer's wrists, the restraints had been designed to immobilize his hands entirely. The mitts were frayed and spit stained, as if wild dogs had been at them.

There was nothing else in the cell. No dishes, no chamber pot, not so much as a blanket to ward off the cold. Its only adornment was a massive iron lock dangling from the door.

Papers covered in the same scratchy hand as the solaros' diary lay scattered across a rickety table facing the cell. Evenna set her lantern on the table and examined the pages.

"Anatomical diagrams," she said, holding one up.

It looked like a child's drawing of a half-remembered nightmare. The creature sketched on the page was impossible. Twisted limbs sprouted from its body at odd, useless angles; misshapen mouths broke through its skin like gaps in the seams of a rag doll. The solaros had drawn a stream of wavery black lines behind it, as if the creature left a trail of slime in its wake. Asharre couldn't imagine how it walked. She couldn't imagine how it *lived*. "What is that?"

"'Vordash of Knight's Lake,'" Evenna read. She looked up, doubtful. "A mercenary. The occupant of this cell, I believe."

"*Maelgloth*," Falcien said. "He was one of the Malformed. Not *ansurak*."

"What's the difference?" Asharre asked.

The olive-skinned Illuminer pointed to the drawing's jumbled limbs and drooling mouths. "Power and intent. *Maelgloth* are warped by the power of Maol coursing through their flesh, but they do not have the strength of *ansurak*. The transformation is just the last stage in their corruption; there is only enough magic in them to break their minds and turn their bodies into a misery, and they die soon afterward. This creature was not meant to live long. He was *maelgloth*."

Evenna squinted at the pages next to the grotesque drawing, rummaging through them until she came to some that were more text than pictures. "This Vordash came to the temple in early winter, complaining of inflamed scratches on his hands. Something he'd been working on for his employer . . . a visiting scholar? I can't quite make this part out. Later he was tormented by bad dreams. The solaros, treating him, worried that the dreams might be . . . contagious? Not sure about that bit either. He advised Vordash not to return to his company and to remain here for observation. Over time, the man's demeanor changed. He became violent, delusional. The solaros had him confined for his own safety while he sought a cure. The physical changes began while Vordash was confined. It's possible that the other killers in Carden Vale might have become something like this, if they hadn't been executed, but Vordash was the first to live that long."

Asharre wondered how the solaros had faced that horror. He'd been an old man, ready for retirement. A country priest lived a quiet life, dealing with farmers' mishaps and colicky babies. He might have seen the occasional broken arm or knifing among merchants' guards, but real magic, real *danger*, was something for tavern stories.

Until it wasn't.

How would he have dealt with it? How *could* he? A solaros in this backwater village, lacking Celestia's Blessing or any real knowledge of magic, would have been helpless before such a threat.

It seemed that he had tried, though. She admired the courage in that, even as she wondered why he had not gathered his people and fled. "What happened then?"

"The solaros built this cell." Evenna folded the papers and tucked them away. "He believed he could cure it, or treat it. In the end, however, he failed. Vordash died and was sent to the pyre. By then the priest was overwhelmed, so he sought a stronger cure."

"What?"

"He never says outright. 'A sword like a sliver of the blue dawn. A blade sharp enough to cut darkness from the soul.' He thought he could find it in Shadefell. That's all he wrote."

"Aurandane," Falcien breathed. Awe shone on his face. "Of course."

"Aurandane?" Asharre asked.

The Illuminer touched his sun medallion reverently. "The Sword of the Dawn. It was one of eight Sun Swords forged for the Godslayer's War, and among the strongest. It was lost when the Sun Knights razed Shadefell."

"I know that story," Heradion said. "Sir Galenar, who had the Sword of the Dawn, chased shadows away from his companions. Well, *they* thought he chased shadows. *He* swore there were monsters, and ran off to kill them while the other knights fought the Rosewayns and their servants. After the battle, they found him wandering around the servants' quarters, dazed but unhurt. Aurandane was nowhere to be found. He couldn't remember how he'd lost it—he couldn't remember much of anything, other than a voice singing to him—and the others couldn't find it. He died of fever outside Knight's Lake, a year to the day after his misadventure in Shadefell. Some say he died of embarrassment, really.

"I suppose the sword might still be in Shadefell," he added doubtfully. "I always assumed some scavenger dug it out and sold it ages ago, though. People are always trying to sell false relics on the streets of Cailan; why couldn't one of them have something real? The story's too well known, and the prize far too valuable, for it to have sat neglected all these years."

"This Aurandane could have turned *maelgloth* back to men?" Asharre asked.

"Perhaps," Falcien said, regarding the drawings doubtfully. "More likely it would kill them . . . but who can say where the Bright Lady's power ends? If it were truly to be found in Shadefell, it would have offered more hope than he had here."

Asharre took her candle and examined the cell more closely. How many days and nights had the solaros sat at that table, watching his monstrous charge and recording his hopes of a cure? *Could* such a thing be cured?

The cell held nothing to allay her doubts. What she had taken for saw marks in the brass bars were scrapes left by the gnawing of teeth harder and sharper than metal. The gray smudges on the wooden planks were not ash, as she'd thought, but the flaking residue of something that might have been the slime trails shown in the solaros' sketches. There seemed to be half-formed patterns in the peeling curls. Drawn, or accidental? She couldn't make out their meaning . . .

Asharre straightened, her teeth gritted. "The priest thought he could cure this?"

Evenna hesitated. "He had hopes."

"Hopes?" Heradion echoed. "Doesn't sound terribly optimistic to me."

"Before resorting to the 'blue-dawn' sword—Aurandane, I suppose—he wrote about trying to treat it with herbs. There is no herb I've seen or studied that could cure something like this. Nor does it seem he was successful, since he eventually gave up and chased Shadefell's legends instead." The slender woman shrugged. "But I'll admit to being curious about what he tried. We're here, so I suppose we might as well see what the drying room holds."

"Not the garden?" Asharre asked.

"No," Evenna said. "You saw what was growing on the mountainside. Whatever the plants in his garden were, they must have become beggar's hand by now. The drying room is more likely to be helpful."

Asharre glanced through the darkened glass as they walked back to the end of the hall. Clouds swathed the moon, letting only a hazy glow slip through, but it was enough to illumine the shape of the temple garden. Under the withered carpet of last year's herbs, the earth was roiled and hunched, its orderly rows heaved sideways and upward in frozen convulsions. Though nothing moved in the garden, Asharre could sense its suffering as clearly as if the earth had screamed aloud.

"This place *is* desecrated," she muttered, turning away.

"You sense it now?" Falcien nodded. "Yes. It feels . . .

stronger . . . here. The center of the taint is nearby. I think it is the cell where Vordash was held. Places can take on a residue of corruption from their inhabitants."

Asharre didn't think the corruption came from the cell. Her sense of it came from the garden, flowering over the dead earth like some rank black weed. But the Celestians had studied these things, and she had not, and it hardly mattered anyway. Whatever the source of the chapel's corruption, it didn't change their purpose in this place.

Falcien pulled on the door to the drying room. The door rattled but did not open. "It's stuck," he muttered, and pulled harder.

There was a sound like a bowstring snapping. The door jolted open and three blurred black shapes hurtled out. *Birds,* Asharre thought, and then: *no.* They were too fat to be birds, too ungainly to be airborne; they were as improbable in flight as bumblebees, but infinitely larger and deadlier in their sting.

They were crossbow bolts. The first one whipped a line of blood across Falcien's cheek and nicked his earlobe before clattering against the wall. The second thudded into his chest; the third hit his left thigh just below the groin. None pierced deeply, but the two that hit him lodged in his flesh.

Evenna started forward, a prayer on her lips and the glow of Celestia's power already flaring around her. Falcien stumbled away, thrusting out his arms as he retreated to the garden door. "Get back," he gasped. "Get *back!*"

Evenna's eyes widened as if she'd been slapped, but she stopped. "Why?"

They never heard an answer. Falcien's mouth worked in frantic silence for a tortured beat. Another. No sound escaped. Then the quarrels exploded into heat and grit and sulfurous black smoke, engulfing the end of the hall.

Asharre's nostrils filled with the choking stench of brimstone. Blinded, cursing, she groped along the temple wall. Her hand fell on someone's shoulder; she couldn't tell whose. Grabbing it desperately, she dragged the unresisting bulk with her as she staggered away from the smoke. Something wet and warm rolled underfoot; she tried not to think about what it might be.

The smoke ended at the antechamber. Asharre fell to her knees, gasping for air. She felt groggy, as if she'd taken a blow to the head after drinking too much. Her vision was blurred, her throat raw. Rancid oiliness filled her mouth.

It was Heradion she'd grabbed. He didn't appear to be hurt, but he was insensible, muttering incoherently and staring at the room with unfocused eyes.

Footsteps sounded behind her. Asharre scrambled out of the way, pulling Heradion with her. Evenna stumbled out of the hall, coughing, with Falcien draped like a bloody cloak around her shoulders. Gore and greasy soot smeared her clothes; cinders flecked her black hair.

Falcien was breathing. Asharre looked at him and just as quickly looked away. She had seen bodies mutilated in countless ways—many in her own life, more while crossing Spearbridge—but she had never seen a man so grievously broken and still breathing. Half his body had been blasted away. His left leg was gone entirely; a red hole swallowed his hip. The undersides of both arms were gone, leaving wings of flapping flesh over the exposed bones. His torso was ripped open, and in the wound his lungs showed wet and pink, studded with splinters of shattered bone. They moved, hideously, as he fought for breath.

"Let him die," Asharre rasped. Each word hurt coming out. She felt her throat, astonished. She had taken only one breath in the smoke.

"I can heal him," Evenna said. "If we can get him out of here—out of this desecration—" The young Illuminer coughed and spit, red flecked with black. "I can heal him."

It wasn't true, Asharre thought. It couldn't be true. Blood pulsed sluggishly from Falcien's hip. That wound should have gushed blood in a torrent; instead it leaked a slow black sludge. Magic poisoned his flesh. She did not think there was a spell in the world that could cure it.

Asharre closed her eyes and let her forehead rest against the floor's cool stone, waiting for the world to stop spinning. The foulness in her mouth was beginning to fade. Beside her, Heradion groaned and got back to his feet.

"We have to go," Asharre mumbled to the floor. "We have to get out of here."

Heradion leaned against the door frame like a drunk man, gazing into the darkness. At the sound of her voice, he turned toward the two women and his friend's ruined, breathing body. His face was grim.

"We can't," he said, and looked back to the night. A shivering howl splintered the stillness. Another took up the cry, closer. A pair of eyes, too large and radiantly white to be human, reflected the moonlight for an instant and was gone.

"We're not alone," Heradion said, unnecessarily, and reached with a shaking hand for his sword.

12

"Light," Asharre croaked. "We need light."

She pushed herself to her knees, then to her feet. Blood rushed to her head. The world swam before her eyes but she swallowed, counted two breaths, and stayed upright.

A third howl sounded. Beyond the flickering pinpoints of their candles, the splintered door opened to blackness. Clouds buried the moon, and the empty buildings around them thickened the shadows to velvet dark.

Evenna balked. "If I pray for light, I won't have enough strength to heal Falcien. He'll die."

"If you don't pray for light, we'll all die." Asharre drew her sword and stood in the doorway. Her head ached abominably; the *caractan* felt bulky and unfamiliar in her hands. What had that smoke done to her? "I can't fight blind."

"I'm not sure I can fight at all," Heradion said. The cords on his neck stood out, white and taut; between them his pulse fluttered visibly and far too fast. His face looked bloodless. "Feel like I might fall over if I tried."

Asharre grimaced. The doorway was a good defensive position, but holding it meant fighting shoulder to shoulder. If Heradion stumbled and fell in her way, he'd get them both killed. Safer if he stayed back. "How good are you with that bow?"

"I'm not. Rabbits and squirrels mock me with impunity. Monsters . . . I don't know what monsters might do." He placed a palm against the wall, steadying himself. "They *are* monsters, aren't they?"

"I don't know what they are," Asharre said. "We need *light.*"

There was a short silence, punctuated by the horror of Falcien's breathing. Then Evenna made a choked little sound and began to chant. The words were more sob than speech, but she finished the prayer. The candleflames stopped flickering and rose toward the temple ceiling like curving needles of golden glass. Strands of light spread from each elongated flame, arcing toward one another and joining the candles in a radiant web.

Bits of solid darkness wriggled in that web like inky eels trapped in a fisherman's net. Impossible—but there they were, burning between the strands of enchanted light. Asharre tried to ignore them. There were worse enemies in the night than shadow fish. She shifted her grip on the *caractan*'s hilt and waited.

"I really had hoped for a toothless dog," Heradion said.

She wondered whether fever had baked his wits. "What?"

His voice was frail, breathless, the words too quick. The smile he flashed her looked like a skull's. "If we were going to fight on the road. I'd hoped it would be an old toothless dog. Toss a stick and scare it away. Tell a braggart's story about it later. Never . . . never thought I'd *actually* have to fight monsters. Not for my first fight. Not ever, ideally, but . . . certainly not the first time out."

"Think of it as your goddess keeping you honest," Asharre suggested, hoping her reassurance sounded more convincing to him than it did to her. "Now you will have a true story to tell."

"Knew I'd be punished for my sins someday."

Asharre chuckled grudgingly and squinted into the dark. The holy light seemed to have intimidated whatever was out there, and she began to hope that perhaps they'd get out of the shrine without any more trouble . . . but then their foes shambled out of the night.

They were not human. But they had been. Asharre saw it in the mumblings of their mouths trying to form words, in their shuffling efforts to make contorted bodies walk upright. The horror of what they had become warred with the madness in their eyes. *They* remember. *They remember, and they hate us for being what they were.*

Because they were monsters now. *Maelgloth.* The things that came out of the darkness, snarling and slavering and cringing away from Evenna's prayer, were not like the *ansurak* whose bronzed skulls stood on the southern wall. The *ansurak* radiated power, even as clean-picked bones. These creatures were miserable, and terrifying in their torment.

One had a wild thicket of gnarled, yellowed teeth that sprouted through his lips and cheeks like a beard of bones. His teeth broke through the skin, curled across his face, and burrowed back into his flesh, caging his head in their tangled mesh. Every time the creature wailed, the skin tore between his teeth and added to the bib of blood that hung down his wrinkled chest.

The one to Asharre's left was even more grotesque. It scuttled on its belly, keeping close to the ground, like an enormous, soft-skinned cockroach. Its arms and legs had withered to lumps of bone rattling inside empty socks of skin. Its belly was covered with lesions, through which its intestines poured like a mass of fat, dirt-covered worms. It was on that writhing bed of worms that the creature moved, squirming back and forth between its hunger for prey and its fear of the light.

"Maol has taken them, poor creatures," Evenna said softly. "They cannot be helped."

More shapes moved behind them. They were too far back for Asharre to see clearly, and she was glad for that. What she *could* see was bad enough.

But they could be killed. She clung to that thought like a talisman. They could be killed.

"Come on, you bastards," she muttered. "Come and die."

The *maelgloth* with the mangled mouth cocked his head at her. His eyes were red and rheumy; what sentience was left in them drifted in and out of focus. Her words stirred something in them, though. The creature grabbed at his own lips, digging his fingers into the gaps between his teeth, and hit them frantically with the side of his other hand. The yellowed enamel cracked and broke. Shaking away the fragments, the creature moaned. "Save us. Help us. *Heal* us."

The one with the belly of worms took up the cry. Its mouth was a useless flap of skin hanging over a fleshless jaw; its voice came instead from the sucking holes that riddled its guts. They gasped in a slurred chorus: "Save us. Heal us."

"Evenna, don't," Asharre ordered, thrusting a hand out to hold the young Blessed back.

"I wasn't," the Illuminer said. "*Maelgloth* are too far gone. There's nothing I can do for them."

"Save us!" the first creature howled, flinging tooth shards from his cheeks with the force of his cry. When no answer came, he threw his head back and screamed.

That shriek was like nothing Asharre had heard before—inhuman, deafening, so shrill and despairing it set her bones vibrating and stopped the breath in her throat. It was the sound of a millstone crushing a condemned thief's hand, of an iron door clanging shut on a prisoner's last glimpse of light. If raw madness had a voice, it was in that scream.

Heradion gasped and Evenna cried out. Asharre slumped against the door frame, struggling to shake off the terror of that sound. As if the cry had been a trumpet calling the Maolite host to war, the gutted one doubled over. The worms in its belly churned. They grabbed at the ground and flattened out, and then all at once they *pushed*. The *maelgloth* sprang forward, its bare-boned jaw gaping open and its limbs flying wildly through the air.

Asharre saw the attack coming and braced herself for it, but the creature was quicker and wilier than she'd imagined. It landed just short of the rubble before the chapel doors, rearing back to flail at her with the dirt-crusted tentacles that writhed through the sores in its chest. Had she leaned forward to slash at it, she would have been dangerously overextended across the broken stones.

Instead she flicked her *caractan* out in a short arc, testing the creature's reaction. The *maelgloth* recoiled as the blade whipped past, wrapping its tentacles around its own body and pulling its torso back into an exaggerated curve. It hissed at her, filling the air with a stink like vomited meat, and in the wet black flesh of its throat she glimpsed more tentacles wriggling as they pulled themselves up through the *maelgloth*'s gut.

The other one was circling around to her left. Asharre kept him in the corner of her eye as she stepped carefully across the teetering stones. Halfway across, she feigned a stumble. The bloody-mouthed *maelgloth* lunged.

She was ready. Asharre brought the *caractan* around in a horizontal slash, swinging with a strength and speed that no summerlander could have matched. The *maelgloth* was monstrous, but he was no fighter; he was utterly surprised by the attack, and the blade crushed into his chest. His sternum cracked; ribs popped in a grisly staccato. Blood welled from the wound, dark and slow, as if it had already clotted in his veins.

The *maelgloth* reeled and stumbled, betrayed by the uneven footing and overbalanced by the weight of the teeth tangled around his head. Asharre seized the opportunity and hacked downward with a two-handed blow. Her weapon was a brutal thing, more cleaver than sword, but it held enough of an edge to take off his head. The *maelgloth*'s wail died in his throat, and he collapsed at the chapel door.

A frantic chittering sounded from the streets just out of Evenna's light. Asharre couldn't see what made the noise, but she could *hear* it, clacking chitin against stone.

She hoped the others could handle that, whatever it was; she couldn't. The tentacled *maelgloth* had scuttled closer. A pace away, it reared again. Its mouth gaped open so wide that its chin sank into the putrefying flesh of its chest. Its desiccated eyes rolled back in its head. The worm-like guts that she had glimpsed in its throat had pulled themselves into its mouth, where they pulsed like a mass of chewed tongues.

With a stuttering cough, the *maelgloth* vomited at her. Ropy bile spewed from the torn guts in its mouth, spattering over Asharre's chest and the side of her neck. She turned away too late to avoid the spray that came up across her face. It hit her like boiling oil; she heard her skin hissing as it seared. Acid stung her eyes, and she cried out, blinded.

Something sticky and wet took hold of her shoulder, wrapped around her arm, and yanked her forward. It, too, burned. Asharre felt skin and flesh bubbling, smelled the acrid stench of it. She could see nothing but throbbing red, like staring at the sun through closed lids, and wondered if her eyes were watching themselves dissolve.

"Help me," Asharre implored, then stopped, shocked by the sound of her own voice. The words were slurred, malformed. Her lips felt strange: loose and numb, as if they weren't connected as they should be. She shook her head dumbly, knowing it wouldn't help, unable to stop herself. A clot of acid-softened hair fell on her cheek and slid down, leaving a new trail of fire in its wake. "*Help me!*"

She heard Heradion's steps crunch over the rubble at the shrine's doors, followed by a sharp intake of breath. She didn't know whether it was because he saw her or something else. The insectlike chittering was close. Too close. Her skin crawled.

"Gods be good," Heradion swore, and plunged past her. Asharre felt the brush of air from his cloak. A sword cracked against a wooden shield; something that sounded far too much like a child screamed. She heard the scuff of the Celestian's boots as he was driven back, or drove some unseen foe forward. There'd be no help from him—not soon enough. Maybe never.

Something wet and warm was licking at her hand, pulling it in to be eaten. Asharre could barely feel it. She dropped the hilt of her *caractan* toward her left hand, praying to Celestia or the wildbloods' spirits or whoever else might listen that she would catch the weapon and be able to use it.

The hilt thudded into her palm. It was slick and sticky and her fingers sank into a pulp of her own digested flesh, but she had it. At once she struck left-handed at whatever had her right arm. She was too close to hit with any real force, but with luck the blow might drive the thing away long enough for her to kill it.

The *caractan* hit awkwardly, barely grazing her assailant, but the tentacled creature screeched as if she'd run it through. Asharre smelled hot iron and boiling bile, felt a gout of sticky steam. New heat washed over her scalded skin. She swung, and swung again, battering blindly while she had the strength to stand.

Abruptly the *caractan* sheared through empty air. Asharre staggered at the sudden lack of resistance. Her foot struck something on the ground and she nudged it cautiously. A tendril rolled away, clinging to the stones. Next to it was something heavier and softer, filled with rattling lumps: one of the *maelgloth*'s atrophied limbs.

It was dead. Her strength fled at the realization. She slumped to the ground, using her *caractan* as a crutch to control her fall.

The sounds of fighting carried on without her. Close, dangerously close, but they might have been on the other side of the world for all Asharre could do. She closed her eyes, or thought she did—there was no change in the red emptiness that filled her vision, and nothing she could feel through the burning bile—and let herself sob with the pain.

Footsteps approached. New ones, soft and tentative. Asharre gripped her sword. She doubted that she could lift the weapon, but she did not intend to die meekly.

"Don't move," a familiar voice whispered. Evenna. "Bright Lady have mercy, it's a wonder you're alive."

A hand lighted on her shoulder. She could *feel* it. A wonder. Soothing warmth flowed from that touch, and after it a flowering of new feeling: pain, then the bone-deep ache and buried itch of flesh knitting itself back into wholeness.

The crimson blindness receded. She could see the night again: skeletal weeds in a patch of starlight, the ivory glow of a spring moon through clouds. Bodies sprawled in the sea of blackness that lapped among the houses. She could not tell the hour, but it seemed darker than she remembered. After a moment, she realized why: the radiant web that Evenna had woven in the chapel was gone.

A ring of candles burned around the broken doors. Several had blown out, but enough remained to line the entrance in fiery orange tongues. The chapel's interior, and the town beyond the heap of rubble, were left entirely in shadow.

"The fighting is done." Evenna stood, clutching her hip and straightening like an old woman. "Heradion killed the last of the—the bone people. He is hurt, but he can walk and ride. So can you. We have to go. Now. The *maelgloth* that attacked us are dead, but who knows how many more there are. We'll be safer in the inn."

Asharre nodded. Standing taxed what little strength the Illuminer's prayer had restored, but after a few false starts she managed it. She waited out another rush of blood to her head—it seemed longer this time, worse, but perhaps that was just the toll of her wounds—then went back into the chapel to retrieve the records they'd fought so desperately to keep.

Heradion was already there. Blood crusted his red-gold

hair. He favored his left leg, leaning against the wall when he thought no one was looking. He'd stuffed the books and papers into sacks from the chapel pantry. Falcien's body lay in a corner, shrouded by an altar cloth.

"We can't leave him here," Evenna said. "This place is cursed. He deserves a pyre, but that will have to wait for morning. Until then we'd best take him back to the Rosy Maiden."

While the others took sacks of papers, Asharre hoisted the dead Illuminer over a shoulder. It was not penance, exactly, that she should be the one to carry him . . . but he might have lived if she had let Evenna pray over his wounds instead of calling light to illumine their battle.

Lived, and then died at the teeth of the maelgloth. She'd made the right choice in ordering Evenna to conjure light instead of healing Falcien. Sometimes one had to be sacrificed to save the rest; any wet-eared novice knew that. But the Illuminer's death was a grievous loss, and not only because he had been a friend.

Falcien was the best scholar among them. If anyone had a chance of deciphering the solaros' writings and finding the truth of Carden Vale's curse, it was him. Without his knowledge, their chances of learning what had happened here dropped precipitously.

Why did the maelgloth *choose that moment to attack?* Yes, they were vulnerable as they stumbled out of the smoke and confusion of the temple's trap . . . but they had been even more vulnerable when they split up to investigate Carden Vale separately. The *maelgloth* could have picked them off one by one as they wandered the unfamiliar streets. Why hadn't they?

Asharre picked at the question, finding no answer, as she collected two sacks of papers, wrapped a hand around

Falcien's shrouded legs, and led the battered survivors back to the Rosy Maiden.

The inn was eerily peaceful. There was not a whisper of sound save the echo of their own footsteps in the empty streets; even the clouds seemed to have stopped moving.

Asharre slowed, then stopped, a stone's throw from the inn. She couldn't *see* anything amiss. Nor could she smell it, not with the *maelgloth*'s bile clotted on her clothes and her own wounds barely healed. And yet . . . it was too quiet. They'd left the animals behind. The oxen should be lowing, the horses whisking their tails against the walls.

"Someone's been here," Asharre said. "The animals." She laid the dead man in a doorway, drew her *caractan,* and went to the Rosy Maiden's stables. Evenna followed, and her lantern showed blood on the straw.

The animals were dead. Only one survived, a gray mare trembling in a patch of sodden straw between two over-turned water troughs. The others had been torn open from throat to tail. The horses had kicked the walls and the oxen had rammed their horns against the wood in panicked attempts to break free, leaving bloody dents in their stalls. There was a dead *maelgloth* among them, a skinny child-size thing with enormous bony claws dragging down its wrists. A horse's kick had crushed its skull.

Evenna went to the mare, soothing the animal with murmurs and gentle gestures. There might have been a touch of magic in her words; Asharre had never seen a terrified horse calm so quickly. Soon the mare's agitated breathing steadied and it let Evenna stroke its nose, whickering into the Illuminer's hand.

"Why was that one spared?" Asharre asked.

The younger woman's lips were pressed to hold back something she didn't want to say. Her big eyes were even darker than usual, filled with . . . fear? Foreboding? Evenna stretched out a booted foot, shaking away manure and damp straw, and nudged a toe at the spill between the troughs.

It took Asharre a moment to see what she meant. The water had splashed into a peculiar pattern on the muddy floor. It resembled a snowflake . . . or a sunburst, eight rayed, with puddles at the end of each arm that mimicked the variant she'd seen scrawled on all those windows in the abandoned town. The image was lopsided and stretched to distortion, barely recognizable—but once she saw it, she could see nothing else.

That pattern couldn't be accidental. Asharre tried to work it out, imagining ways that the troughs could have fallen to create it. If they fell one after the other just *so*, splashing into each other, their contents diverted by the straw and manure piles on the stable floor, *maelgloth* and frightened animals tracking water to and fro in their struggles . . . was it possible that the sunburst had been created by chance?

She didn't think so. Judging by her shock and silence, neither did Evenna.

"But it worked," the *sigrir* said aloud. "It saved the horse."

"Maybe," Evenna said. She led the horse gingerly around the puddle, keeping her own steps clear of it. "Just as likely they left to attack us instead."

Asharre slid her sword back into its scabbard and followed the Celestian out of the blood-spattered stables. Under other circumstances, she might have tried to salvage some of the animals' meat, but she had no appetite for anything *maelgloth* had touched.

Inside, Heradion stirred up the fire, but it held little

warmth. None of them was in the mood for talking, or eating. Evenna tethered the surviving mare in the common room; she thought the animal would be safer inside.

Asharre was too tired to ask questions. She laid Falcien's body on a pallet by the door, then trudged up the stairs. She kept her *caractan* at hand and her boots on her feet, and was asleep almost before her head hit the pillow.

Sunlight roused her out of uneasy dreams. Asharre lay on the bed awhile longer, staring at the maze of cracks in the ceiling plaster. It took her a moment to recognize the weariness she felt. Not battle weariness; not wounds. Evenna had healed the gravest of her injuries, and what remained was no worse than she'd suffered a dozen times before.

It was fear that exhausted her: fear of the cursed town and its cursed inhabitants. Fear of losing Evenna and Heradion as she had lost Oralia and now Falcien. She had pledged to protect them—but how? This valley lay deep under Maol's shadow. She didn't understand it, and she didn't know how to defeat it. If it could *be* defeated.

Her own clan revered the spirits of the wild: ancient deities, remote and faceless, though sometimes they took the forms of snow-white beasts or showed their red eyes in storms. The gods of the White Seas could be cruel; they took tribute in blood and blessed their followers with fury. But they were not *evil*. The evil she'd seen in Carden Vale was something for which she had no answer.

Lying in bed wouldn't help her find one. Asharre threw back the blankets.

Downstairs Evenna was already awake. She'd set a kettle over the fire and sat upon a three-legged stool, gazing into a teacup. It did not seem that she had slept, although she had changed out of her filthy clothes into a tunic and breeches left by some forgetful guest. Her ink-black hair hung loose over her shoulders, trailing almost to the floor.

"Restless night?" Asharre took a knotted rag from its hook near the fire and wrapped it around the kettle's handle to pour herself a cup of tea. It was bitter, boiled down to dregs. Whitebriar tea, brewed to stave off weariness. Evenna had laced it with vigil's friend to intensify the effects. It tasted abysmal, but Asharre drank it anyway.

"No time to sleep," Evenna said. The shadows under the Illuminer's eyes were nearly as dark as her hair, but she managed a wisp of a smile. "Too much to be done."

"We'll need to make a pyre for Falcien. And one of you will have to go back."

"I know," Evenna said.

Asharre set her cup down in surprise. She'd expected an argument. "You do?"

"One of us will have to tell the temple what happened. If the rest of us don't return. There's a good chance of that. Something about this place . . . I could almost imagine that the town itself conspires against us. First we lose Falcien, then we lose all our animals—all but *one*, so we can send only a single rider back and have to split up again . . . it's convenient, isn't it? Too convenient. Something's toying with us. And yet, after all we've seen, and all we've lost, I still can't leave the people of Carden Vale."

"You think there are people left in Carden Vale?"

"Not in the town. I don't believe anyone's here anymore. But I think there might be some in Shadefell." Evenna brushed a hand over the papers stacked by her stool. "I spent the night reading the solaros' diaries. Falcien would have been able to glean more from them. He was the one who studied the fell gods. I did what I could, but . . . well, the last few entries are plain enough. The solaros took the survivors to Shadefell, hoping his scholar friend could protect them and, if he succeeded in his search for Aurandane, help him unlock the sword's magic. He wrote of the man as a wizard."

"Do you believe that?"

Evenna shook her head. "No. Not truly. I don't believe this Gethel was Blessed, so he couldn't have had any true magic . . . but a scholar might know enough to protect people. And if they did find Aurandane, he might know how to use it. Even if the sword isn't there, the survivors might have escaped Maol's corruption, or at least limited its effects, if they left this place. Maybe they delayed the madness. Maybe they outran it altogether."

"Then they'll be safe."

"For a while. Not forever. They'll need our help."

"Your help," Asharre corrected.

"I can't reach them alone. The *maelgloth* would tear me apart."

That was true. Oralia had sworn the same oaths when she became a full-fledged Illuminer: to serve the goddess faithfully, to help those in need without regard to pride or payment, and never to kill another person. That last oath probably didn't extend to *maelgloth,* who were no longer human, but since an Illuminer with a sword was as helpless as a cat in the saddle, that was small consolation.

And yet . . . "You did something to my sword. While I was blind. I could not see, but I felt it."

"Velaska's Fire."

"How?" Asharre's eyes widened. Velaska's Fire was a healing prayer—one not often used, because it was not often needed, but she had seen Oralia summon its red flame on occasion. Velaska's Fire surrounded a blade with cauterizing heat, enabling it to cut with less pain and helping its wounds heal faster. Incisions made with Velaska's Fire seldom infected; it could cut away flesh that had putrefied too badly to be saved, and what was left would be clean.

But it was *not* a battle spell.

Evenna's gaze dropped to her hands. She fidgeted with her clothes, plucking at the tunic's drawstrings. "At the Dome of the Sun, they taught us that Velaska's Fire originated with the Knights of the Sun, who used it to turn their swords into brands of holy flame. I'd never used the prayer to bless a sword before . . . but then I'd never faced *maelgloth* either. I don't think it broke my oaths. *I* caused no harm—and if they'd truly been living things, instead of cursed ones, your sword should have hurt them less, not more."

That sounded like sophistry to Asharre, but she wasn't the one who had to abide by Illuminer oaths. She only cared about one thing. "That was what killed the bile spitter?" It hadn't been *her* work, certainly. She knew her swing was bad when she made it. Her *caractan* couldn't have hurt it that badly unaided.

"Yes. The fire melted its flesh. Like water on salt."

"Then we have some chance of reaching Shadefell alive."

"A fair chance. Better than fair, if there are not too many *maelgloth* and the Bright Lady lends us her grace . . . and a few of my other guesses are correct." Evenna sighed. "I wish Falcien were still with us. I've been wishing that all night. I can't tell you how much *knowledge* was lost with that man. But be that as it may, we have a chance. Not a good one, I won't lie. One of us must go back. Someone has to tell the High Solaros the truth of Carden Vale."

"Heradion."

Evenna's blue eyes lingered on hers, weighing. "Why?"

"He's a better rider. I'm a better sword. If you're only taking one guardian, you should have the best, and he has a better chance of making it through the passes."

The Illuminer smiled at her hands. The expression was a little sad, Asharre thought. "I'll let you explain it to him, then. You had better reasons."

"Did I?"

"I was going to send him back just for the sake of a girl. One I'm not supposed to know about, at that." Evenna gestured to her sun medallion, letting her fingers fall before they brushed its gold. "Our road can be hard, but I think it's easier than his. You and I have no family, no obligations beyond the oaths we've sworn. It's no accident that so many of Celestia's Blessed come from the cloister children. We don't have any loyalties outside the temple. You've made equal sacrifices to dedicate yourself to your calling—or greater ones. You gave up a family, a homeland. Most of us never had that choice. Heradion, though . . . he has a family who loves him, a woman who hopes for his safe return. He tries to hide those ties, maybe so we won't doubt his devotion, but he has them."

"Good," Asharre said after a moment's reflection. "It will give him a reason to *want* to return to Cailan. Wanting helps, when the way is not easy."

"I get the uncomfortable feeling I'm being talked about." Heradion came down the stairs, rubbing his eyes. He'd washed the old blood from his hair, but new blood had seeped in and crusted overnight, and he continued to treat his left leg gingerly. Nonetheless, he looked alert, almost cheerful.

"You're going back to Cailan," Evenna told him. She stepped away from the stool and began emptying the pouches from her herb bag, counting her supplies and checking their condition with the precision of long practice. Oralia had done the same thing almost nightly on the road. Asharre looked away, remembering.

"Am I now." Heradion peeked into the kettle, then covered it again with a grimace. "No breakfast? That *is* a sin. Well, while I find something more solid than tea to eat, perhaps you can explain to me why I'd do that."

"Someone has to tell the High Solaros what we've found. That someone is you. You're the best rider among us, so you have the best odds of making it through the passes. Asharre and I will go to Shadefell and look for survivors from Carden Vale."

"If there are any," Heradion said doubtfully. He replaced the kettle of oversteeped tea with fresh water. "I don't mind the ride—really, there's nothing I'd love better than to bounce up a mountain on horseback while my arse slowly turns to a block of ice—but I must confess I'm not thrilled at the prospect of fighting *maelgloth* alone. My expertise with the sword awes all the ladies, but these monsters don't seem as easily impressed."

"You won't be fighting them," Evenna said, opening a tiny ceramic bottle and sniffing the tincture it held. "You'll be running. The *maelgloth* don't leave the town, and they don't come out by day." She exchanged an uneasy glance with Asharre. "They seem to be kept away by that variant sunburst we've been seeing too. Maybe. If they do come, you might try it. Anyway, if you leave soon, you'll be out of the Vale by nightfall."

"Well." Heradion gazed into the hearth, holding his palms toward the flames. "Nothing to hunt, no water but what I carry, monsters at my back, and madness in the mountains. Why, that's hardly any challenge at all. Are you *sure* you wouldn't like to cripple my horse first? Maybe tie my hands, give me a blindfold? Just to keep me from getting complacent, you understand."

"You'll go?"

"Of course I'll go." He looked up, grinned. "I could never refuse two beautiful ladies."

"I'm glad to hear it," Evenna said crisply. "Best go as soon as you've eaten. No sense wasting daylight."

They saw him off after a breakfast of boiled millet and honey. A night in the inn had calmed the gray mare enough to take a saddle, and the animal seemed glad to leave. Asharre stood in the cold, watching them, until they were out of sight behind greening trees and rocky walls. Then she went to help Evenna build Falcien's pyre.

A dule tree stood outside the crumbling walls north of Carden Vale. Under its rope-scarred branches, the earth was bare and blackened. Most towns had a communal burning ground, and this one was little different from the others Asharre had seen. A bark-roofed wall of firewood, spotted with small white mushrooms, ran alongside the pyre pit. Soot flecked the wood and sat between the logs like little drifts of black snow.

Asharre did most of the work, arranging the firewood in a cross-hatched pyramid. A proper Celestian pyre involved incense and prayers while laying the logs in ceremonial patterns, but Asharre didn't know the prayers or the patterns, and if she made any mistakes in her ignorance, Evenna did not correct them. The Illuminer hardly seemed to notice what was going on; she often fell into fugues or started at sounds Asharre didn't hear. The *sigrir* wondered how badly her companion was suffering for her sleepless night.

By midday the pyre was ready. They laid Falcien atop the logs, still shrouded in his altar cloth, and Evenna scattered handfuls of herbs and flowers over his body. Dried chamomile, for peaceful sleep. Dandelions, yellow and ubiquitous as sunlight. There were others whose names and significance Asharre did not recognize. After tossing the last sprigs over the logs, Evenna doused them with lamp oil and thrust a torch into the pyre's belly.

The fire was slow to start, but once it caught, it burned with a sudden red fury.

They watched it burn until sunset. Several times the wind turned, stinging Asharre's eyes with smoke and bringing a nauseating wash of decay from afar. The smell of Carden Vale's corruption, she thought. It stank of infected wounds and dead things rotting in mud, of sulfur and old urine and mold. But Evenna showed no reaction to the smell and never stepped back from the smoke, and Asharre's pride would let her do no less. She ignored it, at least outwardly, and refused to blink at the windblown ash.

After the first few times it was easy; by dusk she hardly noticed it at all. Weariness helped make her stoic. At sunset Evenna prayed by the smoldering remains of the pyre. After she finished, the two of them walked back to the Rosy Maiden to wait out the night.

The town closed bleak and empty around them. Even its ghosts seemed to have deserted it; Asharre could not imagine that the loneliest specter would linger inside the houses that leaned over weed-choked gardens and pitted streets. Shadows filled the broken windows, and the wind moaned across the clattering roofs in a haunting echo of the *maelgloth*'s cries. She gritted her teeth and willed herself not to hurry toward the inn.

It was a relief to shut the Rosy Maiden's doors against the dark. Asharre couldn't pretend that the inn was safe—not with Falcien's blood staining the commons and the stench of death seeping in from the stables—but it was better than facing the night and the creatures that hunted it.

The *sigrir* stayed up long past midnight, staring out the windows with a blanket around her shoulders. Sometimes she thought she saw misshapen figures darting through the streets, but they could not reach her and she did not fear them. Not as much as she dreaded the morning.

In the morning they went to Shadefell.

13

"She wants Ang'duradh," Malentir said. "She intends to reclaim it in her husband's name, for his glory and the triumph of Ang'arta. When our work is done, the Lord Commander will lead his armies here, and the Baozites will regain a foothold in a part of the world they lost six hundred years ago." The Thornlord folded his hands into his sleeves, regarding Bitharn and Kelland in turn. "I tell you this so that there will be no mistake about my goals or interests in this matter.

"My task, before my capture, was to learn the cause of Ang'duradh's fall and find a way to retake the fortress. I'd made substantial progress before events intervened. Thanks to your gracious intercession, I have the opportunity to finish my task and atone for my failure. I am in your debt." There was a hint of sarcasm in that, but only a hint, Kelland thought.

They sat in the common room of a farmer's house outside Carden Vale. Two Celestians and a Thornlord from Ang'arta, seated around a white oak table like old friends.

Hard to believe that the moment was real, but there they were.

There was no trace of the farmer or his family. Malentir had sworn that he had not killed them when he brought Kelland and Bitharn to the place. His sparrow spotted the house from afar, he said; its isolation, coupled with its relative proximity to the town, made it ideal for the three of them to use while they investigated Carden Vale.

Kelland couldn't argue with the second part of that, but he wondered about the first. It seemed an improbable stroke of luck that they should stumble upon an empty house precisely when and where it was needed. It was a rich house—incongruously rich, given the poverty of the town—and it hadn't been empty for long. Mice had barely touched the larders, and the footpaths leading back to town were in good repair. The farmer and his family might not be *dead,* but their disappearance certainly seemed convenient.

He'd ask Bitharn about it when they were alone. Her talent for tracking might uncover clues that his own eyes couldn't find. For now, that mystery had to wait. There was another that needed unraveling first.

"The Spider suggested to me that we might share some interest in Carden Vale," Kelland said. "She showed me a woman her servants had captured in Cailan. Her name was Jora." It was important to remind himself, and them, of that. Jora had been an ordinary woman, with a name and people who loved her, before evil blighted her soul. She deserved to be remembered that way.

"Jora was . . . poisoned," the knight continued. "I felt something in her, corrupting her heart and mind. A touch of evil. Inhuman. Divine." He avoided the word "Maolite"; if that was the enemy they faced, he wanted the Thorn to confirm it without prompting. "It terrified her. She mumbled things about a 'nightmare waking' and an 'old death,' and she claimed that she, or people she had been helping, were holding it back somehow. She said that they needed children to do it. 'Shapers,' she called them.

"The Spider said that Jora had been kidnapping children in Cailan and sending them back to this town. She suggested that our interests might align in Carden Vale. She did not tell me why. Now you say that the Spider's interest lies in reclaiming Duradh Mal. I fail to see how these things are related, or why it would be in my interest, or my temple's, to help you do that."

"It's the same thing, isn't it?" Bitharn turned toward the Thornlord. The morning light shone in her hair, turning it to a river of soft gold and amber. In profile, Kelland could see the faint lines that exhaustion had drawn on her face, but he thought she had never been more beautiful. Those lines were part of the price she'd paid for him. "Whatever took hold of Jora was the same thing that corrupted the boy I saw. It's the same power that prevents you from taking Duradh Mal."

"It is," Malentir said.

"What is it?" Kelland asked.

The Thornlord rose and paced across the room. His steps were soundless on the brightly colored rag rugs that covered the farmer's floor. "The last visitors to Ang'duradh were a band of monks known to history only as the Gray Brothers. The Baozites were never much for record keeping, and after six hundred years, you can imagine how little is left to mark the Brothers' passing. Calantyr was not yet founded, and the local lords were puffed-up bandits perched on piles of rocks. Few of them could read a word. I spent years trying to retrace the monks' steps, hoping to find some indication of who they were and how a handful of wandering pilgrims laid Ang'duradh low. I did not expect to find much.

"And yet, to my surprise, they *were* remembered. Wherever they'd passed, local folklore was full of dire tales: faceless, gray-cowled wraiths who stole wandering children, babies born as monsters, men and women who became ravening murderers after being bewitched by evil spells. Common stories all, but on the Gray Brothers' path they had unique details that echoed, however faintly, of truth. There was nothing directly useful to me in those stories . . . but much that corroborated my suspicions."

Bitharn's expression had sharpened, as it did when she was trying to puzzle out a confusing trail. She sat up a little straighter. "If the records held nothing, how could you know where they passed?"

"The records on the road held nothing," Malentir corrected her. "There is one account of the Gray Brothers that survives. Blessed Erinai of the Illuminers accompanied the expedition sent to Duradh Mal when the Celestians realized that the fortress had fallen. It is thanks to her journals that we know anything about the monks. Her writings are kept at the temple in Aluvair. I studied them at length."

"Wearing another face, I imagine," Kelland said.

The Thornlord smirked, but did not slow his pacing. "Several. I was there for some time. One would hardly have lasted long enough. In any case, through Blessed Erinai's writings I was able to trace much of the Gray Brothers' course north from what is now Calantyr into the Irontooths—and, ultimately, to Ang'duradh. Erinai believed, as I did, that the monks were corrupted by Maol. But this left a mystery, which neither she nor I was able to solve: how, if they were Maolites, were the Gray Brothers able to overwhelm the fortress?

"Servants of the Mad God seldom have much power. Few worship Maol of their own free will. Only the most degenerate are drawn to him, and fools of that sort make poor vessels for divinity. They destroy themselves before accomplishing anything worthwhile. Most Maolites—the unwilling ones—do not even have that. They are consumed by their god; they stagger about like fever victims, delirious and doomed, and the only danger they present is that they might spread their contagion before they die.

"Given the limited power possessed by most Maolites, it puzzled me that they were able to overwhelm Ang'duradh so completely. It is true that most Baozites have nothing of the god in them, just as the peasants who flock to your chapels are not touched by Celestia, but Maolites die like any other men, and Baozites are very good at killing. Even if the Gray Brothers possessed some real power, Baoz still had priestesses in that age, and they should have been able to deal with Maol's Blessed easily. They did not. They died.

"It was perplexing, but it could not be an immediate danger. Those who sealed the ruins, after all, had not suffered the same fate. When I was unable to learn anything more from indirect study, I opened the seals. Carefully, of course. Very carefully. I was better prepared than the Baozites who had been caught by surprise centuries ago, but I had no desire to be taken unawares by Duradh Mal."

"What seals?" Bitharn asked.

"Most of Duradh Mal was sealed by Celestia's Blessed soon after its fall," Kelland told her. "The Knights of the Sun and the Illuminers worked in tandem to craft those wards. After centuries of Baozite rule, the fortress was a locus of the ironlords' power. We destroyed what we could and sealed the rest to prevent innocents from stumbling inside . . . or people like the Thorns from trying to use it."

"You did," Malentir agreed. "To your credit, it was not easy to determine the pattern and unravel the weavings, and there were some moderately challenging traps hidden among them. But they were never meant to guard against *us*, and any wall can be broken, given time and the right tools."

"If you're so terribly clever, why don't you have Ang'duradh already?" Bitharn interrupted. Kelland was grateful for her retort; he was too unsettled to think of his own. What the Thornlord said was true: they *hadn't* considered that the Baozites might work in concert with another power to unravel the wards. The Spider had been sitting in her tower for the better part of a decade, weaving webs on Ang'arta's behalf, and they hadn't thought to change the seals on Duradh Mal. He never had, at least, and it seemed that the High Solaros hadn't either.

Who could have foreseen that the Baozites would want to revisit such a disastrous defeat, though? Or that they would find a way to reopen it? They fought *wars;* they weren't scholars of dead magic.

"I was not the only one interested in the ruins," Malentir said. "There was a fool from the Fourfold House visiting Aluvair at the same time that I was. He, too, was interested in Blessed Erinai's journals. His name was Gethel. A feeble old man, half dead by the looks of him. I considered him of no account. That might have been a mistake.

"Shortly after I unsealed Ang'duradh, something . . . escaped. I dealt with it, but your comrades came upon me unexpectedly while I did. That distraction resulted in my visit to Heaven's Needle, and I was away longer than I had intended.

"While I was detained, it appears, Gethel came to Carden Vale and blundered into the unsealed fortress."

The Thornlord paused. A troubled look flickered across his face, and he folded his arms, pressing his wrists over his elbows. "I believe that he stumbled upon whatever the Gray Brothers used to kill Ang'duradh, and may have loosed it into Carden Vale. I suspect, too, that Gethel might have caused, or encouraged, the distraction that led to my absence. If so, he manipulated your people as well. That is why my mistress said our interests aligned. We share an enemy in this. Whatever it was that Gethel released, we all want to stop it."

"If you hadn't broken the seals—" Kelland began.

"If, if." Malentir waved a hand dismissively. Barbed metal glinted in his sleeve. "Useless to wish for what might have been. If your fellows had not delayed me, I would have been able to stop him. But they did, and it is done. What matters is not what has happened, but what will.

"My mistress instructed that you should have time to decide your course. I will leave you to discuss that while I tend to other matters. Upon my return, we will begin our work or part ways, as you choose." He inclined his head, mockingly courteous, and left.

"I'm for leaving," Bitharn said as soon as the Thorn was gone. She leaned forward, frowning. "I don't trust him, I don't like him, and he's *said* he's after his own interests here. The only reason I dealt with the Thorns was to set you free. That's done. It's time for us to cut ourselves loose of their webs. Let him walk into Duradh Mal on his own."

"I can't." Kelland wanted to reach across the table for her hands. She was so *close*. A few inches. An arm's reach.

Easier if it had been a thousand leagues. He dropped his own hands into his lap, locking the fingers together. "I can't leave them to suffer, Bitharn. The people of Carden Vale, the children stolen from Cailan . . . you know my oaths. I realize the Thorns are taking advantage of that, but it doesn't change their need. I would be unworthy of Celestia's blessing if I turned my back on them."

"You wouldn't be turning your back on them. You'd be sending to Cailan for help." She searched his face. Her eyes were wide and luminous and frightened; his heart ached that he couldn't give her the answer she wanted. "We've been dancing to Ang'arta's tune every step of this sorry dance. I want an end to it. I *betrayed our temple* to have you free. Was that for nothing?"

"No," he said quietly. "But I have to stay. I'm sorry."

"It isn't *fair*. Your oaths bind you. Theirs don't. They'll always have the advantage." She pulled a hand away and dashed it across her eyes, not quite quickly enough to hide the welling tears. "I only just got you back."

"I know," Kelland said. "I'm grateful for that. I don't know if I will ever be able to say how much."

Bitharn let out a shaky breath. "Then why are you letting them drag you back into their schemes?"

"Because their schemes don't *matter*. Put them out of your mind. If it were only you and I here, what would the right course be?" He reached out tentatively to touch her wrist, willing her to understand and to forgive him. "The evil in Duradh Mal is clear. I don't want to help the Thorns any more than you do, but I can't leave people to suffer because I'm afraid trying to stop it might give Ang'arta some advantage."

She rubbed her eyes again, scowling. "They matter. They'll betray you again as soon as they have what they want, and what they want is bad enough on its own. If the Baozites had a foothold in these mountains—"

"Then what? Yes, they'll command the passes. Yes, they'll have the valley locked behind rings of iron, just as they did in Ang'duradh's day. But the world has changed since then. No one lives here, Bitharn, apart from the people in Carden Vale, and we are here to help them escape. Who will the Baozites dominate? The Jenje Plains have been desolate for centuries; the windlords' kingdoms are turned to dust and blown away. We stand to the south. Us, and Calantyr strong behind us. We can keep them safely contained in the mountains."

"You hope," Bitharn muttered.

Kelland smiled. He couldn't help it; her tone was exactly the one he'd heard so often when he'd embarked on some foolish scheme as a child, and, later, whenever he'd followed his heart rather than his head during their travels. It meant that she was resigned to his latest crusade . . . and would guard his back as he plunged into it. "All plans are founded on hope. The good ones are tempered with caution."

"No wonder I'm not convinced this is a good one."

She seldom was. That, too, made him smile. "Why not?"

"Maybe the Celestians can keep them behind the mountains—maybe. At what cost? What if you're wrong, and they fail? What happens to *us*, long before that's a concern?" Bitharn tucked a loose strand of amber gold hair behind an ear. "I don't like it. You can't trust the Thorns."

"I don't. It's one of the reasons I'm so glad to have you." He hadn't meant to say that—but, having begun, Kelland plunged onward. "I shouldn't have left you in Tarne Crossing." He'd relived that day a thousand times in the dungeons of Ang'arta. Cold winter light on his shield, the breath brittle as ice in his lungs, the crimson spatter of blood on the snow. The shard of doubt in his soul, more lethal than any blade. All Kelland had to do was close his eyes and the memories were there, vivid as the day he'd lived them.

"Kelland, I—"

He took her hand, silently cursing his earlier hesitation. Her fingers clasped his, holding on so tightly that he felt a heartbeat pulsing through them. Hers or his, he couldn't tell. "I need to say this. Please. I shouldn't have left you in Tarne Crossing. That morning, the only thing I could think of was the baker we'd found, and what the Thornlady had done to him. How badly he died. I couldn't let that happen to you. I thought, if I went out alone, I might win and I might lose, but either way you would be safe. It was . . . stupid, I *know* it was stupid, but I was so afraid.

"I failed because I tried to confront her alone, and because I was weakened by doubt." He drew a breath. "What I am trying to say, clumsily, is that I need you with me. You make me stronger. You guard against the dangers I don't see. I was a fool to forget that. By trying to keep you out of harm's way, I only weakened myself and forced you into dealing with the Thorns. I am sorry. So sorry. And so very grateful to you."

"Thank you," she whispered. Tears were falling freely down her face, but she did not wipe them away.

They sat in silence for a time. Kelland didn't know what she was thinking; he struggled with his own turmoil, trying to find the words to bring some order to the confusion he'd wrestled with since leaving Ang'arta.

"Before she let me go," he said at last, "the Spider told me that Bysshelios was right—that chastity is not a mandate from our goddess."

Bitharn's nose wrinkled immediately. She pulled away a little, green-flecked eyes narrowing. "Do you believe her?"

"I don't know," Kelland confessed. "But I don't think it matters." He'd spent a long while pondering it, and although he had never found a clear way out of the maze of those thoughts, he'd fumbled toward something like an answer.

Bysshelios, himself an Illuminer, had claimed that the Bright Lady was not as austere as the high priests claimed, and that her Blessed were permitted the joys of coupling. He had demonstrated this himself, publicly and graphically, several times; at the time the episodes had been well documented by scandalized witnesses. If their accounts were to be believed, he'd kept his powers afterward. Several of his adherents were Illuminers who had defected from the faith to join his schism. They, too, broke their oaths of chastity—and retained their divine gifts. For a time. As the years went by, Bysshelios granted himself ever-greater indulgences and privileges: he claimed that no wedding was sanctified in Celestia's eyes unless he had lain with the bride himself first, and that no healing could be given unless the patient, or someone on the patient's behalf, made a similar tithe to his faith. The tales of his abuses became so numerous and so vile that the Dome of the Sun could no longer overlook them, and finally the heresy had to be stamped out with sword and flame.

But he'd kept his magic to the end.

The histories taught at the Dome of the Sun argued that Bysshelios had not held *Celestia's* power, but had shifted allegiances to another god—perhaps Anvhad, whose ambit was treachery and deception—and received magic that mimicked the Bright Lady's in order to mislead the commonfolk and cause a bloody rift in their faith. Despite the Spider's claims, Kelland still believed that was true.

Perhaps it wasn't. Bysshelios might have kept Celestia's magic despite his sins. For Kelland, however, it didn't matter. He had sworn his oath. He was bound by it. The world was ever shifting and uncertain; the reasons he had been given might not be true. But temptation led to heresy, and he was a Knight of the Sun. He would keep his word.

"I cannot be more to you than I have been," he said to Bitharn, still holding her hand. "Not while I serve as a Sun Knight."

"But—"

"I can only ask you to wait." He searched her eyes, hoping she would understand, could give him even more after all she'd already done. "When my work is done, I'll step down from the order. Then—then we might have more."

Bitharn looked down, took her hand back, turned her own sun medallion over on its chain. Inhaled, a little unsteadily, trying to hide whatever she felt. "How long?"

"I don't know."

"A number. Give me a number, and I'll decide."

"Five years." He hesitated, shying away from the weight of that request. "It might be less. It won't be more."

"Five years." Bitharn nodded. "Fine. But if you ask for more than that . . ." She forced a tremulous laugh. "Well, then you had better *pray* the Thorns drag you back to their dungeons instead of leaving you to my mercy."

"Devoutly." He circled the table, gathering her in his arms so that he could press a kiss to the top of her head. Her hair smelled of pine and new leaves.

"Good," she mumbled. There was a silence. Kelland kept his face buried in her hair, hoping the moment might stretch into eternity. Hoping, against all rational thought, that it might lead to more.

It did not. Bitharn pulled away, gently but insistently. "I thought you'd be angry when you learned what I'd done. I thought you'd be furious. I betrayed our *temple,* Kelland. I had to. They wouldn't help. The High Solaros was sympathetic . . . but all he offered me was prayer and tears, and I'd had my fill of those on the ride to Cailan. He wouldn't *help*."

"He couldn't have." In the dungeons Kelland had had the luxury of infinite time to consider that problem. It was, he had concluded, impossible for the High Solaros, or any figure of authority in the temple, to negotiate for his release. Ransoming him from the Thorns would only have encouraged them to capture other Blessed. The wiser course was to turn their backs on him and show Ang'arta that they would not be manipulated so easily.

At the time, he had believed that meant he would languish in his cell until he died. He hadn't considered how bullheadedly stubborn Bitharn could be—or how brave.

"I know," she said. "I can't do it again. Please don't make me."

The simplicity of her plea cut him more deeply than anything else could have. She *would* do it again, if she had to. She would dismantle a mountain with her bare hands for his sake. And, knowing that, he knew with equal certainty that he could never put such a burden on her again.

"I won't," Kelland promised, for himself as much as for her. "Whatever else happens."

"I'd be more confident about that if we had some inkling of what we were facing." She dried her tears and stood, red eyed but resolute. "Something better than 'nightmares,' anyway."

That brought back something he'd puzzled over earlier. "What happened to the family in this house?"

"Did Malentir kill them, you mean?" Bitharn shook her head as she walked toward the house's larder. "I'd wondered that too. I don't think he did. The kitchen garden's gone to weeds, but there are a few rows of unpulled carrots and turnips. I found barrels of cider laid up in the cellar, none tapped, and dried apple pulp near the stables, none eaten. To me, that says these people left the house around the end of autumn. Maybe early winter. They didn't use any of their stores. That means they were gone before we left Heaven's Needle—so Malentir couldn't have killed them, nor could any of the other Thorns, unless their prophecies are a good deal more specific than we've been led to believe. Something else drove them out."

"What?"

"Maybe they noticed their neighbors were turning into monsters and rotting from the inside out." Bitharn raised a tawny eyebrow. "That would get *me* on the road right quick."

"Fair enough." Kelland followed her to the larder, looking over her shoulder as Bitharn rummaged through sacks of dried beans and barley. She twisted a bulb of garlic off one of the hanging ropes that crowded the ceiling, then dug up a fat yellow onion and a handful of long-whiskered carrots from a burlap-covered box in the corner.

"They left without taking their food," he observed from the doorway.

"Any of it, as far as I can tell. It's peculiar." She brushed past him, emptying her finds onto a table near the kitchen hearth. "This time of year, you'd be lucky to scrape together as much as a dandelion salad by foraging, and only a fool would trust to being able to buy all his meals along the road. So why did they leave all this behind? Let's say they abandon the servants to fend for themselves. That leaves the husband, the wife, and at least three children. Too many to support by scavenging. It's strange, too, that we've seen no sign of the servants. A house this wealthy surely had some. If they didn't go with the family, they should have stayed in the house to keep it safe from bandits."

"Or us," Kelland added.

"Or us." Bitharn picked up a paring knife and scraped off the carrots' whiskers. "If they *did* go with the household, then it's strange they left the pantry so well stocked, and stranger yet that they didn't take their valuables when they left. Nobody's rich enough to abandon their silver to thieves."

It was clear that Bitharn didn't want to revisit their earlier conversation. Kelland considered trying to help with the cooking, but that tenseness in her shoulders meant she wanted to be alone. "I'll see what I can find."

What he found was precious little. Bitharn was right; whoever had lived here, they'd left all their worldly treasures behind. The family silver lay untouched inside cedarwood drawers. A carafe of cut Amrali glass, worth more than most farmers could hope to earn in two years, stood on a side table between two dust-mantled goblets. The goblets were of hammered silver, edged in gold and set with tourmalines in blue and stormy sea green; they were better suited to a king's table than to this rustic house.

How had a farmer outside Carden Vale come to possess such treasures? Why hadn't he taken them when he fled? One of those cups would buy passage on a riverboat to Cailan. Two would get most captains to journey up the Windhurst to fetch them, even if there *was* some curse on the town.

Before Kelland could puzzle his way to an answer, he saw an even more perplexing artwork.

On the wall behind the carafe hung a towering painting in an ornate frame of mahogany and brass. The metal had been burnished to a golden sheen. At the top, the wavy rays of a Celestian sunburst formed a gilded crown; near the bottom, the frame's dark wood was carved into curling waves, their tips capped with mother-of-pearl. Cascades of sunbursts ran down either side of the frame. Their rays were flattened, spoonlike, on the ends.

The frame was so ornate that Kelland didn't immediately notice the picture it housed. The painting was surprisingly drab: a night sky rendered in simple sweeps of blue and black, with occasional slashes of silver to represent starlight or clouds. Silver and brass stars, fashioned of sharp-edged metal, had been punched through the painted canvas.

The knight recognized their pattern at once. The metal stars formed the Celestial Chorus. That constellation, the first to rise each night, crossed the sky and greeted the sun each morning. It was a popular pattern among the Knights of the Sun. To them, the Celestial Chorus represented virtuous men and women who kept faith alive through the world's dark hours. Every night the Celestial Chorus' stars burned bright, scattered and tiny though they were, and every morning the sun came to relieve them, restoring light and warmth to the world.

Outside their order, however, the Celestial Chorus was little known. The constellation was not nearly as infamous as the Spire Crown sacred to Kliasta, nor was it as useful as the Wayfinder's Star. It was an obscure symbol of a faith that had nothing else to do with the night, and it was vaguely unsettling to find it adorning a painting outside Carden Vale. The stars were slightly misaligned, their positions wrong in the sky and relative to each other, but if there was any astrologer's significance to the change, it escaped him.

"That's an odd frame," Bitharn said, wiping her hands dry on her shirt as she left the kitchen.

"It's a bit excessive," Kelland agreed.

"Not just that. Look here. There's blood on its edge."
She crouched next to him, tracing the edges of three blade-
like stars. They hung near the bottom, over the wooden
waves. Leaning closer, Kelland saw crusts of old brown
blood on the metal . . . and something else, too, tucked
behind the stars.

Bitharn saw it as well. Reaching to the back of the frame,
she teased out a small latch and tugged it. One by one the
bloodied stars split and parted. A jeweled handle emerged
from between them, offering itself to the Celestians.

It was made of some bright white metal, richer than
silver. White gold, perhaps, or platinum. Citrines sparkled
on the handle like fat drops of sunlight, alternating with
rings of moonstones that shone with a ghostly gray lus-
ter. A last ring of tiny, near-black rubies twinkled at its
base. The metal was scarred and misshapen beneath those
stones, as if the jewels had been moved and welded back
into place by a clumsy hand.

"I wonder what it does," Bitharn mused. "Maybe there's
a compartment hidden behind the painting."

Kelland hesitated. A premonition of dread tickled the
back of his neck. He couldn't say why, but he did not want
that handle turned. "Let's leave it."

She looked at him quizzically. "Aren't you curious to see
what it does?"

"No." He was being foolish, and knew it. There was no
reason for his fear. Still, Kelland could not shake the sense
that there was some hidden danger in the painting. It was
a subtle unease, like the jangling of warning bells from a
town on the horizon. No immediate threat, perhaps nothing that needed to concern him at all . . . and yet only a
fool would ignore it. "It's a curiosity, to be sure, but I don't
see how it helps us. I'll see what else I can find."

Upstairs he found most of the rooms neat and dis-used . . . save one, which had been boarded up at some point in the past and then, more recently, smashed open. The entrance to that room was concealed behind the back wall of a linen closet; Kelland would never have found it if someone else hadn't splintered the wooden paneling and strewn the linens and their sachets all across the hall.

Through the hole smashed into the closet, he saw a tiny, filthy bedroom. Books piled over the bed and slid down in yellow-leafed avalanches; loose papers buried the floor. Open inkwells sat on every flat surface, many with black-gummed quills slanted inside like arrows caught in dry corpses. Here and there metal twinkled: knives, paperweights, forks and knives left lying on plates that mice had long ago picked clean.

Holy signs too. There were dozens of amulets in the room. Sunbursts, nightingales, the Kliastan chain of thorns. Some of them were new; they dangled over the splintered closet entrance like the strands of a beaded curtain, chiming gently as Kelland ducked under them to enter. Inside, more rested atop stacks of paper or hung from nails on the walls. Three small windows overlooked the kitchen gardens on the far side of the room, and every one of their diamond-shaped panes had a sunburst etched crudely upon it by a shaking hand.

Dust lay thick on the bedroom's books and papers. At the center was a vanity that someone had been using as a desk, and the materials there seemed to have been more recently read. The dust was lighter on them.

Kelland brushed aside a leaf of wrinkled parchment to reveal the age-cracked tome beneath. *The Flame at Midnight,* it read, *Being a Study of Magic Without the Gods.* The gilt on the letters had peeled away, and there was a gash in one corner that let a few pages peep through.

The knight frowned. The title was vaguely familiar; if he'd paid more attention to his history lessons at the Dome of the Sun, he might have recognized it. At the time, though, those dry lectures about dead cults and competing theologies had been an unwanted interruption in his swordwork.

No use regretting it. He moved to the next book, a thin treatise bound in shabby red leather. *Volane on Enchantments.* Beside it, a six-legged dragon reared on the silvered cover of *Auberand and the Winter Queen,* a story he recalled from his childhood. It wasn't a long story, though, and the book that bore its title was hundreds of pages thick.

Kelland lifted the book and flipped it open. The pages were beautifully lettered, with gilt capitals and illuminations after each chapter, but someone had scribbled notations between each line. The scrawled notes were written in a tiny, crabbed hand, slanted sharply to the right as if the writer was in a rush to spill out the words. The book had been a work of art, but whoever had written on it had defaced it as thoroughly as if he'd taken a knife to the pages.

Kelland turned to the beginning, wondering what might have possessed someone to react so vehemently to a children's story. Before he could begin reading, however, a scream sounded from downstairs.

Bitharn.

He dropped the book and flew down the stairs, taking the steps two at a time. As he rounded the common room, he saw Bitharn standing by the kitchen hearth, white faced. Steaming barley and broth made a spattered arc on the floor by her feet. A wooden spoon hovered over the kettle, snared by a tendril of solid shadow.

"It's nothing," Bitharn said hurriedly. "I was startled, that's all. I'm not hurt. There's no danger."

"Untrue." Malentir stepped out of the pantry, seem-

ingly unruffled. Cool air and the scent of smoke clung to
him; he had just returned from whatever he'd been doing
outside. "You nearly died. You might have thanked me for
saving you, but I've learned not to expect gratitude."

"I was just tasting the stew."

"It would have been the last thing you tasted." The Thornlord made a small gesture, hidden within his sleeves, and the
spoon clattered to the floor. "Except, perhaps, for blood."

"Explain yourself," Kelland said sharply, a hand on his
sword hilt.

"Carden Vale is poisoned. Its water is lethal. I should
have realized that would happen once the seals were broken; all the water here is mingled with what runs down
from the mountains." Malentir glanced back at the pantry.
"I did not sense it in the food, so perhaps it has not yet poisoned the things growing in the valley, but it would be best
not to risk that. Do you know the purification prayer?"

"Yes," Kelland said. The purification prayer was one of the
Illuminers' most basic spells. Sometimes what commonfolk
called a plague was caused by bad water, or by eating food
that had spoiled without showing its rot. When the water
was purified, or the spoilage cleansed, the sickness ended.
For a healer tasked with the well-being of an entire town, a
prayer that could rid rivers of pestilence was invaluable.

That spell was slightly less important to the Knights of
the Sun, who focused on more martial pursuits. Still, anyone
who spent time traveling in the wilderness soon developed
a healthy appreciation for a spell that could keep mold from
blanketing rain-soaked food. A flux in the bowels could kill a
man just as quickly as a sword thrust, so all the Sun Knights
learned the purification prayer before they left the Dome.

"Use it," Malentir said. He pointed to the bubbling
stew pot. "Start with that."

There were a thousand questions Kelland wanted to ask, but he could see the Thorn was not about to give up his secrets. Rather than waste his breath, the knight walked to the steaming pot and prayed. The invocation was a simple one; he barely had time to feel his goddess' presence ignite in his soul before the magic flowed into the shape he needed and left him.

A finger-thin wisp, thickening rapidly, rose from the stew pot. Not steam: it was darker and fouler and it writhed like a living thing. As he released his spell, more black smoke belched from the soup. Its tendrils twisted and knotted around one another like a mass of serpents; he imagined that he could almost hear them, shrieking in shrill pain, just outside the range of sound.

The smoke hung there for another heartbeat, churning, and then it broke apart and blew away as if it had never been.

"Good," Malentir said smugly. "You can banish it."

"What *was* that?" Bitharn whispered, shaken.

"The doom of Ang'duradh. Of Carden Vale, too, I expect." The Thornlord retrieved the wooden spoon from the floor. "What killed one seems to have killed the other. The town is empty. If there are any survivors, I did not see them. I found some records in the riverport offices, and more in the town's last inn. Beyond that, there is almost nothing of note."

"*Almost* nothing?" Bitharn pressed.

"Yes," the Thornlord said. "I found no one living in Carden Vale, but I did find recent hoofprints. And a yellow cloak, bloody and torn, with a Celestian sunburst for its clasp. It seems your fellows in faith passed through not long ago. They are gone, now . . . but they left a warm pyre behind. So, as I said: almost nothing."

14

The tracks were too scuffed to follow. Someone had brushed them out, replacing disturbed rubble where they'd gone and flattening dead grass in false trails where they hadn't. Bitharn might have been able to pick out the true trail, given time, but the day was waning quickly and she had no wish to linger in Carden Vale after nightfall. Not after Kelland had identified some of the tracks as belonging to *maelgloth*.

There was no one *else* living in the town. All the shops and homes were shuttered, if not simply falling where they stood. Bitharn had peeked into a few of the abandoned buildings to see if anyone might be hiding inside.

In one home, she'd found the mummified bodies of three children, dressed in their Godsday best and lined up on a straw pallet. They should have rotted—Carden Vale wasn't cold or dry enough to preserve bodies, and it had rained almost every day since Bitharn arrived—but they hadn't. She could see their bones, strangely dark under thin-stretched skin, like sunken logs glimpsed in a frozen lake. Their lips peeled back from blackened gums in rictus smiles. There were no wounds on their bodies, but their clothes had wrinkled where they'd been dunked in water and left to dry. An empty basin, rimed white to the rim, rested nearby.

She'd found the mother slumped in the next room. The dead woman, as unnaturally preserved as her children, sat on the floor with her back to the wall. Rust red tracks ran in forked rivers from her wrists. The knife dangled from her fingers, caked to her palm by dried blood.

No struggle. No broken furniture. Just a mother and her three drowned babies, resting peacefully where they'd died.

After that Bitharn stopped going into the houses.

There weren't any bodies outside, but there weren't any signs of where they'd gone either. Bitharn scowled in frustration and straightened from her crouch. She raked her hands through her hair, tugging a few golden strands loose from her braid.

It was no use. If she'd had the eyes of a hawk and the nose of a bloodhound, she might have been able to find them, but she was only human and there was no hope for it. The sun was going down, and *maelgloth* would come out with the stars. Time to go. Hoping that Kelland had had better luck, she headed back to the inn.

The knight was sitting in the Rosy Maiden's common room, as he'd been since dawn prayers. Papers and books fanned over the table in front of him. Some were from the town's chapel, some from its gaol. All had been collected by the Celestians who had come to Carden Vale before them, and who had fled in such a hurry that they'd left their books behind.

Kelland had spent the day reading those pages, searching for something that might tell where the Celestians had gone or what had befallen the town, while Bitharn hunted for tracks and the Thornlord sifted through the memories of Carden Vale's dead.

Still annoyed, Bitharn thumped the door on her way in. Kelland looked up.

"I can't tell where they've gone," Bitharn said. "I picked up their tracks at the chapel. Didn't go inside, but I saw that they fought *maelgloth* on its doorstep. At least one of them was badly wounded or killed. Then they came back to this inn . . . but after that? I *think* they rode south, but there are signs pointing north as well. And east, and west, and every other direction under the sun. I can't be sure."

"South to safety," Kelland murmured. He stared out the inn's red-specked windows, thoughtful. Sunlight glinted off the white shells she had rebraided into his hair. The last vestiges of his spell-woven disguise had faded, leaving the knight wholly himself once again. Although she knew his appearance didn't change who he *was,* Bitharn was glad to have Kelland back in his own skin. Deception didn't suit him.

She thought he felt the same way, for he had chosen to dress in the formal white tabard of his order instead of the plain wool garments that had been packed with the rest of their supplies. Bitharn had noted, with some amusement, that Malentir eschewed the plain wool too; he kept to his ragged old robes, as if he needed to display the emblems of his own identity because the Sun Knight was wearing his.

With a sigh, she refocused on the matter at hand. "They might have gone south. Or north to the old coal mines, or east to Duradh Mal. It could be any of those. They were two or three days ahead of us. Time enough for a trail to fade, even if they hadn't hidden it. Did you find anything in the books?"

"Some. The gaoler's book is a chronicle of madness. The other writings tell the same story in bits and pieces. A sea of violence washed over this place, and when it receded, the town was gone. The Celestians retrieved this book and made a few notes, but I can't see that they got much more out of it than I did." He thumped shut the book he had been reading. A handful of papers scattered from between its pages, fluttering across the floor.

Bitharn gathered them up before they could fly farther. Cramped writing, more symbols than letters, covered the pages. "What are these?"

The knight leaned back in his chair and stretched his arms over his head, shaking out the stiffness. "Dreams. In the later days of the madness, many people had nightmares. The local solaros was among them. He tried to decipher what the visions might mean; as the whole town shared the same nightmares, he thought there must be some divine purpose to them. Some kind of warning, or guidance. Many dreamed of 'waking nightmares' and 'old death in the mountain.' The dreamers saw a darkness rising out of Duradh Mal. The priest believed the Bright Lady was trying to show them how to protect themselves against the evil that encroached on Carden Vale. Most of the scribblings are his attempts to remember the images he saw while sleeping. He thought they showed magical symbols that might ward off the taint."

"It doesn't work that way. Does it?"

"Not usually. There are stories about prophetic dreams, though, and some said they told the truth." Kelland rapped the book's cover with a brown knuckle. "Did these? Perhaps. The wardings, though—those would have been useless. Wards *channel* power, they don't create it. Runes without a god's blessing are nothing but pretty pictures. Eventually the solaros realized that and gave up. He took the survivors of Carden Vale north, looking for a sword or a man who he hoped might be able to save them. I'm not sure which it was—maybe both—but it's clear where he went. To Shadefell, and Gethel."

"Do you think the Illuminers went there too?"

"It's possible. Many of the pages that describe what the solaros intended, and where he went, are missing. The Illuminers might have taken them to guide them along the same path. I hope they had the sense to go south again . . . but if you didn't find their tracks, our best course may be toward Shadefell. If we're wrong, our mistake won't cause them any harm, and it might aid our investigation of what happened here. If we're right . . . well, if we're right, and not too late, we may be able to help them."

Bitharn nodded unhappily. She'd found some of the Celestians' letters and personal belongings among the baggage discarded with their dead animals in the Rosy Maiden's stables. From those effects, they'd learned that the High Solaros had sent Illuminers to Carden Vale, not Knights of the Sun. Newly ordained Illuminers, at that.

A scholar and an herbalist serving their *annovair* were ideally suited for a placid mountain village that needed closer ties to the Dome of the Sun. They were *not* well suited for surviving, much less containing, a plague of Maolite evil.

Bitharn wasn't sure that she and Kelland were prepared for that—she didn't count the Thornlord as an ally—but they wouldn't be helpless either. The entire purpose of Kelland's order was blending steel and prayer to deadly effect. She didn't have that, but she had her arrows, and if her confidence in them wasn't quite as steadfast as Kelland's faith in their goddess, it was close.

They had a chance. The Illuminers did not.

She hoped they realized that. One of them, perhaps more, had survived the fight with the monsters that Carden Vale's people had become. If they were wise, the young Illuminers would have seen the better part of valor and retreated.

If they were wise, she thought with a sigh, they wouldn't have been Blessed.

"I want to look more closely at the chapel," Bitharn said. "It felt . . . *wrong* . . . while I was there. Like something was inside. Watching. Waiting. Something hungry. It unnerved me."

Remembering made her shiver again. Staring into those calm, cool shadows, listening to the familiar gurgle of a temple's ever-flowing bowl, she had been seized with a sudden, inexplicable urge to run away and never look back. That part terrified her the most—that she should have been so afraid of a sanctuary of her own faith. "Something attacked the Celestians there, and I'd like to know why."

Kelland didn't question her. "Do you want to go now?"

"Yes," Bitharn said, although that was a lie. She would have preferred to go in the morning, with a full day of sunlight ahead. Better yet, she would have preferred never to see Carden Vale's chapel again. But if they wanted to unravel the mystery of what had befallen these people, they needed to look there.

And they needed to go soon, before the taint crept over them too. Not in the morning. Now.

"I'll get the Thorn," Kelland said, pushing away the books and striding toward the stables. Malentir had been there since dawn, weaving the spells that let him drain the secrets of the dead.

There were no human bodies in the stables, only the corpses of animals. Nevertheless, Bitharn did not follow, and Kelland did not ask her to. She couldn't look at the Thorn's handiwork without remembering Parnas and feeling a sick twist of guilt for his death. Yes, the man was a murderer; yes, he would have been hanged if not for the accident of his birth. But what had happened to him in Heaven's Needle was not justice.

Kelland knew that, and knew the guilt she felt over it. He tried to spare her the memories. For that Bitharn loved him, fiercely and a little sadly. *He shouldn't have to protect me from my sins.*

He couldn't, anyway. As long as they traveled with the Thorn, there would be new ones. Smaller ones, maybe. Perhaps they even did some good by keeping him controlled. But if they did, it was a small good, and she worried that it wasn't worth the corrosion of his company.

Drop a ladle of piss in a barrel of wine, and you've got a barrel of piss, a village solaros had once told her. *Drop a ladle of wine in a barrel of piss, and you've still got a barrel of piss.* Vulgar, but true: it was always easier to sully the pure than purify the sullied.

She was remembering that when the door swung open and the Thorn stepped through. He moved with easy, feline grace, untouched by the blight that blanketed the town. Blood stained the pads of his fingertips. Cold and clotted, almost black.

"You want to go to the chapel?" he asked. Kelland came in behind him, stone faced.

"Yes," Bitharn said.

He nodded. "I would have suggested the same. But we

should go to the pyre first. If my guess is correct, we will find the origin of the *maelgloth* written in ashes there. It may help us understand what we see in the chapel."

Bitharn glanced at Kelland, but the knight raised no objection, so she picked up her bow and inclined her head to the Thorn. "Show us."

He led them through the fading day. For a little while, in the golden hour, the loneliness of Carden Vale receded. Orange sunlight warmed the houses' walls and lent a firelit glitter to the town's few glass windows, creating the illusion that people still lived inside. But weeds filled their gardens and climbed over their doorsteps; spring storms had torn away shutters and let rain pour in unchecked, leaving rippled brown rings on the floors. No one was there to stop it, or care.

Once Bitharn noticed that, the illusion was broken, and the false warmth of the afternoon drained away. The town seemed lonelier afterward.

To distract herself, she studied the houses they passed. Many bore crudely daubed red marks on their doors and windows. There was no apparent pattern to which houses were marked, and she could not identify the sign. It resembled a crooked sunburst, or perhaps a compass rose, but all the arms curled off at odd angles instead of pointing to their directions. The ends of each ray were bulbous, like open hands extended to the air.

"What is that?" she asked Kelland.

"I don't know. I've wondered that too. It's not any Celestian sign I know. With the hands, it almost looks like a mark of Maol."

"It is," Malentir said without turning. "It is a mark of misbelief." He offered no more, and Bitharn did not press him, for they had come to the pyre.

It looked different by daylight. Last time Bitharn had

been so worried about Kelland that she had scarcely noticed her surroundings, and night had masked the town's ruin. Now the signs of neglect were all too clear. Moss and mushrooms grew on the wall of firewood nearby. A bird had begun building its nest in the arms of the dule tree, though it had abandoned the half-finished bowl of mud and straw to a slow, sodden collapse. Animals had tracked through the damp ash.

No, not animals. Bitharn approached cautiously, taking care not to disturb the prints. Kelland stopped beside her without needing a word. He knew when she had picked up a trail.

Two people had come this way within the last few days. A man and a woman, Bitharn guessed, judging by the length of their strides and the depth that their feet had sunk in the rain-softened ash. Cinder flecks lay atop some of the prints but had been pressed down into others. They'd built a large fire, watched while it burned, and walked back into town afterward.

No mystery there. One of the Celestians had died, and two others had built a pyre for their fallen companion. She felt a twist of shared, silent grief.

They were not the only visitors. Other tracks, newer, crossed over the Celestians'. No human made such tracks. No animal either. These creatures shuffled and staggered, dragging their limbs in laborious circles that moved sideways as much as forward.

There might have been as few as three of them or as many as half a dozen. Bitharn couldn't be sure; their trails tangled over each other like skeins in a knotted ball of yarn, and their individual gaits changed from step to step. They always moved like cripples, but the nature of the crippling was constantly in flux.

Maelgloth. Bitharn wondered what god could be so cruel as to break his followers and twist their bodies into something men would call Malformed. They couldn't even learn to use their mangled bodies before Maol's power broke them anew. She could hardly imagine their suffering.

The *maelgloth* had come to the pyre looking for something. Their fingers had raked long furrows in the ash; their footprints were deeper toward the toes, showing where they leaned forward eagerly as they dug. There were wider grooves, too, dotted with curling bits of dead skin. The marks put her in mind of pigs rooting through loam for acorns. Had the *maelgloth* snuffled through the cinders with their mouths? Had their lips peeled and torn as they did?

Their trails wove a dizzying web. The *maelgloth* had crossed and recrossed the pyre pit so many times that there was scarcely a finger's width of ground undisturbed. In places their feet had sunk deep in the ash, indicating that they'd stood still for some time. When they were finished they had trotted off together, heading north.

"Two of the Celestians burned a dead companion within the past three or four days," she told the others. "*Maelgloth* came after they left. They dug through the ashes, looking for . . . something."

"This?" Malentir bent, plucked something from the pit's edge, and tossed it at her.

Bitharn caught it reflexively. It was a splinter of charred bone. Tooth marks pocked its surface and had scraped away its marrow. More bone shards littered the ash. Not unusual, for a pyre pit, but all of them seemed to have been chewed.

She thought of the hunters who had chased down that crippled boy and devoured his dripping flesh. Dropping the fragment, Bitharn wiped her hand. "Why would they want bones?"

"*Maelgloth* are beyond any need for mortal sustenance, but their god's handiwork calls to them." The Thornlord smoothed the ends of his sleeves. It looked like an innocuous gesture, but Bitharn saw the cloth catch over the barbs of his bracelets as he pressed them down. Beads of blood seeped into the fabric. "If they came here to chew the Celestian's bones, it means that one succumbed to some degree of corruption. They were Blessed?"

Kelland answered. "Two were Illuminers. The rest were not."

"Most likely the dead one was not, then. It would take tremendous power to corrupt one of your Blessed into a state where *maelgloth* would be driven to gnaw his bones . . . and yet, until we know otherwise, it might be safest to assume that is what happened. Regardless, we did not come here to see whether *maelgloth* felt obliged to bid your dead companion farewell."

Malentir circled the pyre pit, stopping when he was within a pace of the stacked firewood. He gestured to the mushrooms that sprouted from ledges of windblown soil between the logs. "Dead man's feast. *Morduk ossain* is its proper name, but I would not expect you to know that. This was the beginning of the corruption's spread."

"That's *morduk ossain*?" Bitharn peered at the mushrooms with nauseated fascination. Dead man's feast was infamous among poisoners, herbalists, and anyone who foraged the woods for food. No one could work it. Only madmen tried. It killed scavengers that ate the corpses of its victims; it poisoned people who breathed the dust brushed from its caps. It was perfectly lethal, and perfectly useless.

It was also rarer than a Kliastan's mercy. Folklore claimed

that *morduk ossain* grew only on the bodies of victims who succumbed to the mushrooms' poison. Bitharn had never seen it herself. Most people destroyed it on sight. Over the years, it had vanished from the world, until it survived only on the borders of Pafund Mal and in other blighted places.

One of which, it seemed, was Carden Vale.

Bitharn held her breath as she studied the scrawny fungus. The mushrooms grew in nodding clusters. Their stalks were spindly white and shorter than her finger; the caps were blue as a corpse's lips. Fine white hairs cocooned the dirt where they clung.

She committed each detail to memory, and then she stepped away. "*Morduk ossain* couldn't have been the beginning. Anyone who ate it, anyone who touched it . . . they'd have died."

"Possibly," Malentir said. "It is not always lethal to Maolites. If its victims were under the Mad God's sway, the mushroom might not have killed them. Not instantly. The soil, however, is what I meant. The stories about *morduk ossain* are true: it grows only on the remains of poisoned bodies. But those bodies need not be those of its own victims. If Maol's power touched the corpse, *morduk ossain* can take root on it. We learned that in Pafund Mal. *Maelgloth* and rotworms grew bouquets of dead man's feast when they died, though it was us and not *morduk ossain* that killed them. So. What does that tell you?"

"The dirt it's growing on is . . . bodies? No. Ash from bodies." Bitharn frowned, working through it. "Ash blown away from the pyre when they burned. That means the executed criminals were corrupt enough for their ashes to sustain *morduk ossain* . . . which meant they were deep under Maol's thrall . . . but we already knew that from the things described in the gaoler's book. What difference does it make if *morduk ossain* grew on their ashes?"

"Think of who would have been here when they burned," Kelland said quietly. He turned a hand outward, encompassing the dandelion-spotted sward. "Remember how many people came to see justice being done when we rode through Langmyr? The bloodiest crimes, the most vile killers—those always drew the entire town. People wanted the reassurance of knowing those murderers were dead. Imagine how many would come to see the monsters of Carden Vale burn. All of them stood here, watching, while the ashes blew into their faces and the smoke blew into their lungs. That is how the corruption spread." He glanced at Malentir. "That is what you came to see."

"One of the things, yes," the Thornlord said. "I wanted to confirm my guess. I also wanted to know if the *maelgloth* were here recently . . . and, if they were, where they went when they left."

"North," Bitharn said. The hair she'd tugged from her braid tumbled into her eyes; she pushed it back impatiently. "They left in a pack. If they were human I'd think they were in a hurry, by the length of the strides, but maybe *maelgloth* always move like that."

"They do not." Malentir half-lidded his eyes for a moment. Wisps of darkness gathered around him, fluttering over his robes like wind-torn cobwebs. Bitharn gave him a questioning look, but the Thornlord ignored her. "Were they following the Celestians?"

She shrugged. "I don't think so, but I can't be sure. Once the pyre had finished burning, the Celestians went back to the inn. After that? Bright Lady only knows. I couldn't follow their trail. The *maelgloth* didn't hide theirs, though. Do you want me to track them?" Not that she wanted to. Something had the Thornlord uneasy enough to gather a shield of shadows around himself, and that put her on edge too.

To Bitharn's relief, Malentir shook his head. "It isn't important. What matters is that they left. With them gone, it might be safe enough to investigate the chapel."

The chapel hardly looked safe when they reached it, though. The doors were smashed wide open, as they'd been when Bitharn examined it hours earlier. Rubble cluttered the entrance, spotted with stringy ichor and blood new and old. There'd been bodies among them, earlier, but something had eaten them and licked at the blood spilled during that macabre feast. Swooped smears showed where tongues had lapped over the stones.

"Desecration," Kelland muttered, striding over the dirty stones into the chapel. His lips moved in a near-silent prayer that Bitharn knew well: godsight. It enabled the Sun Knight to read the patterns of divine magic and thus counter its attacks. While it lasted, he would be disoriented in the mortal world, but in this place it was invaluable.

As the knight prayed, Bitharn felt the malevolence she'd sensed earlier intensify around them. She couldn't see anything, but she *felt* it gathering like a bank of bruised clouds on the horizon, massing in preparation for the storm. The air thickened until she could scarcely breathe. An invisible hand pressed down on her, pushing her hair into a sweaty mat on the back of her neck.

A shimmer of gold settled over the knight's deep brown irises as his prayer came to a close. That much was ordinary . . . but as he spoke the last words, motes of blackness seemed to break away from his pupils. They swam amidst the gold like leaves caught in a whirlpool, spinning faster and faster, then expanding into streamers that widened until they eclipsed Kelland's eyes completely. Black sheeted his eyes from lid to lid.

"Kelland?" Bitharn whispered. There was no answer. The knight stared at her with black, blank eyes, his face vacant. His mouth fell open slightly; a rattling moan came out. Alarmed, Bitharn turned to the Thorn. "What's happening? What's wrong with him?"

"Take him out of here," Malentir ordered. "Quickly. Into the sun."

Fear gave Bitharn strength. She pulled one of Kelland's arms over her shoulders and wrapped her own arm around his back, guiding his unresisting steps across the rubble and back into the waning light. He was weeping, she realized, dismayed. Inky tears trickled across his skin, burning it like lye. One struck her shoulder and ate into the leather of her jerkin with a bubbling hiss.

Once outside, she guided the knight into a seated position on a rough-edged chunk of stone. Malentir grabbed his jaw and turned his face into the sun; Bitharn winced, but Kelland never blinked. More black tears ran down his cheeks, leaving blistered streaks across his face.

The Thorn hissed. He dug his fingers into the knight's face, murmuring an invocation to his Pale Maiden. Crescents of blood welled under his nails. Flecks of black grit emerged with it, and drop by drop the blood washed it away. Kelland's poisoned tears stopped as Malentir worked; his vacant expression twisted into a grimace of pain.

The bloodletting went on for an age—long enough to turn the knight's tabard into a butcher's apron, long enough for Bitharn to contemplate sending an arrow through the Thornlord's back to stop the torture—but she held off, shaking with anxious anger. As much as it hurt her to see

Kelland suffer, it was better than the terrible emptiness that had claimed him before.

Finally it ended. Malentir removed his hands and stepped back. There were no wounds on Kelland's face; the cuts and blisters were gone without a hint of swelling. Blood and black grit dripped across the golden sun on his tabard.

The knight jerked to his feet and yanked the dirty tabard off. He balled the cloth up and hurled it away, swearing and brushing his chest afterward. Malentir watched him with open amusement, Bitharn with equally open worry.

"What happened?" she asked.

"Maol," Kelland answered. The name sounded like a curse. He rubbed his cheeks where the tears had run. "The chapel is corrupt. I saw threads of poison swimming in the ever-flowing bowl; I saw it hanging in the air. It was so strong that it blinded me. I felt it . . . clinging to my eyes, trying to push its way in."

"Windows to the soul," Malentir said, visibly amused. Despite what Kelland had just endured, the Thorn seemed on the brink of laughter. "Do you want to go back in?"

"Yes." Kelland avoided any glance in the direction of his discarded clothing. "There's something in there that the Mad God does not want us to see. If he's trying to stop us, that's all the reason I need to go inside."

"After you," the Thornlord said.

"No," Bitharn said. "I'll take the lead. If we can't use Kelland's godsight, I have the best eyes." Without waiting for either Blessed to answer, she started back in.

There was more blood in the entry hall. Crinkled papers lay in drifts where the wind had pushed them against the walls. Some were trampled and stained with black grease; others were clean. Soot smudged the floor in a trail leading to the temple's east hall. Clots and streaks of ichor, and a few spatters of red-brown blood, dotted the largest smear.

"Something was dragged here, and died here," Bitharn murmured. "Or some*one*." She couldn't think of any reason the Celestians would have dragged the corpse of a *maelgloth* from the east hall to this room. More likely the marks had been made by their companion's body. If she was reading the signs right, he'd been the source of the ichor as well, somehow. Not a comfortable idea.

Only the ever-flowing bowl in the anteroom looked clean—and if what Kelland had seen was true, that was a font of corruption worse than the rest. Bitharn glanced at it uneasily.

"This place was a locus of contagion," Kelland said. "The water. The soil. Even the writing on those pages . . . the ink is soaked through with Maolite magic. What *happened* here?"

"My guess?" Malentir shrugged. "Maol did blindly what you or I would have done with purpose. He eliminated the only thing that could pose a threat to him. Perhaps he was drawn to your goddess' presence in the consecrated fountain; perhaps there was some other magic that it sensed. Regardless, once the temple was compromised, there would be no magic to oppose his and no moral authority to raise the people against him. A surprisingly sensible strategy for a madman."

Kelland's jaw set. "East. It was stronger that way." He took the lead from Bitharn, drawing his sword as he stepped forward.

Darkness cloaked the curving hallway. The only light came from windows in the rooms and the garden door at the end; there were no windows in the hall itself. Half-burned candles, rooted in their own wax, sprouted from the walls and floor like crooked mushrooms. The air smelled of stale smoke and rancid tallow. Ash and blood streaked the floor, unmistakable despite the gloom.

Like most provincial chapels, this one had rooms for patients who had traveled too far, or were too ill, to return to their homes the same day. One was fitted for birthing, another not, and the third one . . . the third one, Bitharn realized with deep dismay, was a cell.

Before she could ask Kelland what a prison was doing in a holy place, the knight walked past. He glanced at the cell, shook his head, and went on. "Not there. That wasn't what I saw—what I sensed. It was here." He stopped outside the drying room. The faint scent of dried herbs and liniments lingered there, barely perceptible through the newer smells of smoke and sulfur.

Charred starbursts stained the wall opposite the herb room's door. Cinder-flecked blood drew messy arcs on the floor around it. Two stubby lengths of blackened metal lay near bloodied dents in the wall, their ends blown outward like iron flowers. There might have been a third one with them; it was too dark for her to see.

A trap. Bitharn hurried forward, blanching. "Wait. Let me have a light."

"Light nothing here," Malentir snapped. "*Burn* nothing here. Remember the pyre. Madness spreads in the smoke."

"We don't need a candle for light," Kelland said. He spoke a short prayer, outwardly calm, but the tightness of his grip on his sun medallion told Bitharn that he hadn't fully recovered from the disaster of his godsight. She tensed, waiting to see if this prayer would end as badly.

It didn't. Golden radiance flared around the knight's sword. It steadied into a softer glow, shedding enough light to illumine the drying room and much of the hallway outside. The Thornlord bared his teeth and retreated as if the light pained him, leaving Bitharn to study what it revealed.

There *had* been a trap. The stubby bits of metal were crossbow quarrels. They were oddly formed, with open-work bulbs at the ends instead of sleek tips; they looked too heavy to fly. Strands of filigree were punched out from the center of each quarrel's head, blasted apart by an explosion from within. Kelland's light drew black smoke from a gummy residue on the metal. Bitharn stepped away, holding her breath.

The rest of the trap was easy to see. The snapped remnants of its trigger strings dangled from the drying room wall. There were three small hooks mounted inside the door. It would have been easy to loop the strings on before closing the door, or ease them off before opening it.

A trio of crossbows, propped on a crate and angled upward, pointed toward the door. All three had been triggered; none held a second shot. Smoke curled from them, dissolving in the knight's holy aura. More smoke billowed from the depths of the drying room as Kelland crossed the threshold, creating a shroud so thick that at first Bitharn couldn't see inside.

It cleared a moment later. She wished it hadn't.

The drying room was filled with bones. They bowed the shelves and dangled from the walls between ropes of knotted herbs. Many had been fashioned into tools: shoulder blades and hip bones served as shovels, affixed to the long bones of leg and arm by sinew wrappings. Other bones had been sharpened into picks and chisels. Some appeared to be knives. All were pitted and grooved by hard use, and all of them were human. Bitharn remembered the boy in the woods, trying to run on his cankered leg, and cringed. Were his bones among the trophies on the wall?

Black dirt caked the bone tools' edges. Like ice melting into steam, it softened and flowed and skirled away under the blaze of Kelland's light, leaving empty ridges behind.

The bones held Bitharn so transfixed that she almost failed to notice the other things in the room. The plants dangling from the ceiling and layered on drying racks were not the usual healer's collection. Bitharn was no herbalist, but she knew enough to recognize feverfew and comfrey, wintermint and blackroot. She would have expected to see those plants gathered here. Instead, the misshapen lumps of beggar's hand were the only ones kept in store.

At the back of the room was a cast-iron cauldron filled with chunks of rancid fat. Strips of skin clung to the pieces; one chunk, bigger than the rest, had been hacked from a human belly. Coarse black hair sprouted around its navel. Under the cauldron was a small pyre of splintered bone and black-stained wood, same as the logs by the dule tree. Next to it, a crusted candle mold waited to be filled.

A cluster of golden sun pendants, similar to the one Bitharn wore, hung above the cauldron on braided cords. The leather was gritty with clinging cinders; the rays of the suns were dull with soot.

"The priest," Malentir said, his voice soft with wonder. "Of course."

"No. No, he was going to help them. He took them to Shadefell in hopes of a cure. The others found proof of it . . . all those writings in the inn . . ." But Bitharn's words sounded hollow in her own ears, and Malentir merely raised an eyebrow at her protest.

The bones on the walls, the defiled sun symbols, the cauldron to render corpse fat into dead man's candles . . . all of it hidden behind a trap loaded with Maolite corruption. There was no accident, no innocent explanation.

Whether he knew what he was doing or was deluded into believing that he could save his people by some grisly "magic" in his rites, the solaros had acted to serve the Mad God's will in Carden Vale.

"He did not take them to Shadefell for a cure," the Thornlord murmured. "He took them to be sacrificed."

15

She dreamed of bones.

Asharre's sleep had been troubled since they'd come to Carden Vale. Her nights were full of wraiths and shadows. In her dreams, she ran from amorphous dangers that lurked behind the walls of unreal cities and hunted her through misty forests whose trees melted skyward into slumber and fog. She couldn't fight—she could never fight—only run. Most mornings she woke exhausted, but she had the small consolation of knowing her nightmares were just that, and over.

This dream was different.

She walked down a tunnel of blackness. Behind her it was an infinite coil, twisting endlessly through the bones of a mountain without ever reaching air. Ahead of her it led to the mountain's heart, hot and red and deadly. Asharre felt the heat pounding against her face, burning more fiercely with every step.

Bones surrounded her. There was no light, but somehow she saw them clearly. The earth was paved with knobs of spine and shoulder, interlaced with the filigree of finger bones. Skulls in stacks on the walls stared down, their secrets locked behind grinning teeth. The long bones of arms and legs came together in a steepled arch overhead. Fleshless hands dangled down among them, grasping weakly at her hair.

These were the dead of Carden Vale. Some had died during the town's recent troubles; others had perished centuries earlier. All were victims of the same ancient corruption. Asharre was sure of that, although she didn't know how she knew. Perhaps that was part of the dream.

They were the lucky ones. She knew that, too, with the unquestioning logic of dreams. These were the lucky ones, who died in the tunnels before coming to the mountain's red heart. They still had their bones, and something of their souls. Those less fortunate, who reached the end of the road, had neither. The fire consumed them completely.

Skeletal hands brushed Asharre's ears and tugged at her short-cropped hair. She walked faster, trying to escape them, even though each step brought her closer to burning.

The skulls' teeth rattled. A ghostly susurration blew through the bones: the voices of the dead, straining to speak across that final silence. *Wait,* they whispered, *wait. Do not run. It is a trap . . . a trap. Fear drives you to him.*

It did. The realization hit her so hard she stumbled. Sweat rolled from her chin and pattered onto the bone-tiled floor, steaming. By fleeing from the dead, she hurried toward her own doom—but these were the bones of people who had resisted, and had succeeded in keeping themselves from utter destruction. Fear was the Mad God's tool to keep her blind. Terror made her deaf to the secrets they might share.

They wanted to help her. They wanted to keep the evil in the mountain from claiming her too. She heard them struggling. The spirits of the dead fought against the magic that had killed them and held them trapped in this place; their voices were a babbling breeze. Asharre tried desperately to distill some meaning from the noise.

She saw the mountain's heart glowing ahead. A gust of wind, hotter than any forge's breath, came sighing down the tunnel. It ruffled her hair and dried the sweat on her brow. Asharre winced, bowing to its force. She knew that when she reached the source of that blistering heat, she would die. Worse than die: she would lose her soul. But she could not stop herself from walking toward it. She had slowed from a run, but her legs refused her frantic commands to *stop*.

"Help me," she cried to the dead. "*Help me!*"

Row upon row of hollow-eyed skulls stared back at her mutely. Their jaws creaked with their efforts to break free of their cursed silence. The hands hanging from the ceiling trembled; the finger bones laced into the floor shook. But all that escaped from them was an endless hiss, meaningless as the mutterings of the tide.

The glow did not brighten as she drew closer. It became hotter, crueler, *hungrier* . . . but never brighter. A sense of inexorable evil, nameless and older than time, pressed down on her. And still she could not stop.

"*Listen,*" one of the skulls exhaled. She didn't know which one spoke; it was already behind her, lost to the darkness, by the time it managed to force out the words. "*Listen,* and we will keep you from the Mad God's maw. Take my hand. *Take . . . it . . .* "

"Which hand?" Asharre asked, twisting her head back as her feet kept dragging her forward.

The skull made no answer. But all around her, the hands began rattling, clattering against the ceiling of bones and twitching their fingers through the suffocating air.

She reached up and seized the nearest. As their hands touched, living flesh against dead, dreamed bone, Asharre felt a shock of recognition. Memories flooded into her mind. Not hers—not of any life she could have imagined. They were older, starker, ripped from the edge of despair. They overwhelmed her. It was like standing on Spearbridge again, but the torrent of memories came faster, whirling in a blizzard of images she could not begin to comprehend. Horrors, but also glimpses of hope, and a circle of sigils drawn in flame. *Protection.*

Asharre faltered, but the skeletal hand would not let her fall. It dug its bony fingers into her palm, drawing blood. The jolt of pain slapped her back to her senses; the strength of the dead kept her standing. And the hand stopped her, finally, from going on.

"Thank you," she mumbled. Then the tunnel and its memories were breaking apart, spinning away into emptiness, and she was awake.

Blood pooled in her palm.

Asharre stared at it stupidly. Then she swore and threw back her blankets, keeping her hand cupped so the blood wouldn't spill out. She hobbled out of the Rosy Maiden and flung it into the street.

Four deep wounds punctured her right palm. Asharre ran her good hand through her hair, struggling to remember. The dream had already receded in her memory; she could barely recall what she had seen or felt in it, aside from a lingering disquiet.

There had been bones. She was sure of that much. There were bones, and they had . . . she had . . . reached for them, hoping for salvation. But the details melted away like frost on a spring morning. Her other nightmares had lingered long past waking; this one, the only one she *wanted* to remember, was already gone.

Asharre scowled and wrapped a strip of blanket around her hand, knotting it over the palm to stanch the bleeding. What dream left wounds? It was impossible. Yet the proof lay throbbing in her hand.

The injury made her clumsy, and by the time she finished making tea and porridge for breakfast, she was in a foul temper. Evenna was unusually late to rise, which worsened Asharre's mood. She wanted to be out of Carden Vale. But until Evenna woke, they could not go.

The sun crept steadily upward, and still Evenna did not come down. The Illuminer hadn't missed dawn prayers once during their travels, but it was halfway to highsun and she was still abed. Finally, her patience stretched to snapping, Asharre stalked upstairs and threw open the Celestian's door. "Wake up!"

Evenna mumbled and thrashed, but didn't stir. Scowling, the *sigrir* strode to the Celestian's bed. And, upon reaching it, stopped cold.

Sweat soaked Evenna's raven hair and plastered her shift to her body. Her legs were strangled in her sheets, swollen to an angry purple; as she flailed in the grip of her nightmares, the knots tightened even more. Heat radiated from her skin so intensely that Asharre, standing at her bedside, felt as if she was next to a furnace.

She should be dead with a fever that hot. Asharre had seen enough sickness during her travels with Oralia to know that. But Evenna was very much alive, if delirious. Her lips moved in a stream of mumbled gibberish, and she lashed her head from side to side, whipping the pillows with sweat-damp hair. Her fists yanked at the sheets as if she were trying to rip the cloth apart, or trying to rip herself free.

The violence of the Celestian's dreams was almost as disturbing as her fever. Asharre wasn't sure what the right treatment might be—her sister always relied on holy prayers for the most serious ailments—but she had to do *something*.

Lacking any other ideas, she took the most direct course. She retrieved a bucket of water and dumped it over Evenna's head. Only after the water splashed across the Illuminer's head and blankets did Asharre wonder: what was it, again, about the water? *Something* she was supposed to remember . . . some prayer, perhaps . . . but too late now.

The Illuminer jolted up, spluttering. She wiped straggling hair from her face and stared at Asharre, coughing up the water that had gotten into her nose. "What was that for?"

"You slept late. We should have been on the road hours ago."

"I . . . oh, my." Evenna pushed the sheets away. She gaped at her bruised legs in confusion, looked at the window and the lateness of the day, and winced. "I'm sorry. I didn't realize. I had . . . bad dreams."

"What dreams?"

"There was a forge, and it . . . it burned bones." Evenna touched her temple. "It was so vivid, but I can't remember anything else. Just the forge, roaring as it burned human bones. For some reason I thought it was important, desperately important, to pull them out before the fire consumed them. I was about to brave the flames to take them . . ." She rubbed her hands over the wrinkled sheets, then frowned at Asharre's bandaged palm. "What happened to you?"

"An accident." The *sigrir* opened and closed her hand to show that it wasn't seriously damaged. "You can look at it later if you like, but we have no time now. Get packed."

Evenna's fever faded with her dreams. Once she came downstairs, she seemed fine, apart from a slight stiffness to her step. An hour later they were on the road. Asharre's hand had stopped hurting by then, and the wounds didn't seem to impair her use of it, so she paid it no more mind. Evenna had her own troubles; she was just as happy not to let the Illuminer fuss over the wounds.

They picked their way through a broken section of the mossy palisade, following the tracks of the mule carts that had carried coal and ore down from the mountains for decades. No carts were on it now, and neither man nor beast watched them go.

Greening emptiness surrounded them. Young thistles dotted the pastures, opening needle-tipped leaves to the sun. The ditches and walls that guarded the town's northern side had eroded to gentle, grassy slopes.

It was a peaceful walk, and might have been a pleasant one if the silence hadn't been so oppressive. Not a single bird skimmed the clear blue of the valley's sky; not a deer slipped through its trees. Other than the two women, the only things moving in the world were the coils of smoke spiraling lazily over Devils' Ridge. Past them, the Shard-field glittered like the massed spear points of an army.

They didn't talk. Evenna, exhausted by her fevered dreams, walked with her head down and her footsteps dragging. Asharre simply didn't have much she felt like saying. Her thoughts wandered to Heradion: had he made it out of the mountains alive?

He was the clever one, escaping while he could. She should have done the same. She should have forced Evenna to leave. It was pure hubris to think she could protect the Illuminer in Shadefell; even if they found Aurandane, or convinced Gethel to help them, how could she guard against magic or creeping madness? Easier to cut down the sun with her sword.

But she'd promised to do her best by the Celestians, and she'd sworn to protect them as her own clan, so she was bound to do all she could.

Her injured hand throbbed suddenly. Asharre grunted, balling her hand into a fist and relaxing it until the pain went away. It didn't take long. Despite the depth of the gouges and her use of the injured hand, the bandages had yet to show any stain of blood. The wounds must not have been as severe as she'd thought. That was a relief. She couldn't protect anyone with her main hand maimed.

They reached the eaves of the forest on the north side of the valley by sunset. Evenna raised her hands in prayer to the dying sun while Asharre paced back and forth along their path, fists clenched at her sides.

She had to do more. The young Blessed was faultlessly devout, but that wouldn't protect her any more than it had Oralia or Falcien. The *sigrir* could not fail again. This was her last chance, the opportunity fate had given her to atone for the mistakes of her past. She needed to find *something* that could shield the Celestian.

But what? Long after Evenna's prayers ended, Asharre sat by their campfire, sharpening her sword and searching for an answer. The circling winds bore a breath of sulfur and smoke down from Devils' Ridge, and the scent followed Asharre into her dreams.

She stood beside Falcien's pyre, cinders stinging her eyes and the heat of the flames on her face. In the dream Evenna was not there. As Asharre watched the fire rise over the body, feeling renewed grief and shame at her failure, the dead man sat up on his burning bier.

"You have no time to mourn," he said. His voice was not as it had been in life; when he opened his mouth, she heard only the rush of flames and the crumbling crack of charred bone. Yet somehow those sounds held the meanings of words.

"Yes," Falcien said, chuckling at her surprise. Embers glowed at the back of his throat when he laughed. Part of his arm had burned through completely; she could see the dule tree through the gap between the bones. "There is meaning in the crackle of fire, the fall of leaves, the ripples of a lake. If you know how to read those things, the world holds no secrets. Here, with my help, you can understand them. Awake you cannot . . . yet. But you must learn to read them, quickly, if you are to survive. You don't have much time. If you haven't learned before you reach Shade-fell, you will die."

"Why?"

"Because you have no magic, and your companion's faith blinds her to other tools. Only by *seeing* the danger can you avoid it . . . or warn Evenna in time to fight it." He spread his hands wide, cupping an invisible bowl. Flames, fueled by his flesh, leaped up between Falcien's blackened fingers. The center smoothed into a wavering sheet, like a mirror of beaten bronze, while smaller tongues of fire danced about the edges.

In that strange mirror Asharre saw herself and her companions walking through the desecrated chapel of Carden Vale. This time she caught glimpses of meaning in the lay of the rubble at the chapel's door and the papers that skittered around their feet. It was like seeing the pages of a book in a language she had just learned to read—but the vision moved on before she could take any meaning from them. She wanted to stop the images and understand what the ruins were trying to say, but she had no power over the dream.

Asharre watched as Evenna and Falcien entered the chapel and dipped their hands into its ever-flowing bowl, touching wet fingertips to their brows and breasts in ritual obeisance. With the aid of the fiery mirror, she saw now that there were worms of corruption swimming in that bowl—tangled strands that looked like murky lakeweed and wrapped itself around their fingers when they touched the water. The black worms burrowed into their heads and hearts when the two Celestians made their gestures. Soon they were out of sight, vanished beneath skin.

"So you see," dead Falcien said, closing his hands and shattering the image, "we invited the corruption in without knowing. If we had been able to read the signs, if we had been able to *see* . . . I might have been spared. If you learn to find the patterns soon enough, Evenna might yet be. If you can follow them and find Aurandane."

"The solaros guessed rightly? It is in Shadefell?"

Falcien exhaled. A stream of sparks poured from his nose, burning his septum to a crumbling wall of cinders. "It is there. The sword is hidden behind shadows and snares; it is no accident that the Sun Knights of old could not find it. But it is there. With my help, you will be able to evade the traps that ring it and carry it out safely. I will lay a trail of scales for you to follow . . . like the Storm Queen's daughter finding her way back to the sea." His mouth twisted at the last words, making a smile that looked more like a grimace. The corners of his lips bubbled and burst.

"I do not know that story."

"No? It isn't important. Listen to me, and learn the signs. Knowledge will keep you out of Maol's traps."

"Unless this is the trap." But as soon as she said it, Asharre knew that was wrong. It was Falcien's appearance that was corrupted, not the man's message. The Mad God cast a shadow into her sleep, turning his victims into mockeries of themselves in an attempt to frighten her away from heeding their warnings. By that deception, Maol meant to steal the one weapon she might use against him.

"If this is a trap," Falcien said, his teeth cracking apart in the heat, "you would be right not to trust me. But I think you know the truth."

Asharre nodded hesitantly. A tiny voice of doubt piped at the back of her mind, but she crushed it ruthlessly. They needed this. "What must I do?"

"Listen. Only listen, and learn." Falcien extended his hand. Broiled flesh sloughed from the blackened bones. She took it, forcing herself to ignore the ugliness. His touch scorched through the bandages on her injured palm, but there was a sweetness to the pain, like the burn she felt after hard exercise. It was a pain that would make her stronger. Euphoria washed through her, drowning that tiny voice of doubt.

"Wake now," he said, "wake, and when you return to sleep, we will begin."

Asharre opened her eyes.

The last stars were setting through the western mountains. Sapphire and silver chased the snowy peaks opposite them. It was nearly dawn. The dream had lasted only a moment, yet the entire night had passed.

She clenched her hand under the bandage. It didn't hurt. Curious, Asharre unwrapped the knotted blanket.

The gouges from the first night had healed, after a fashion. Instead of the deep holes, there were only four swollen blisters, red and fat as grapes, where the wounds had been. Four new blisters dappled the skin between them, making a lopsided ring, like two diamonds laid crosswise atop each other.

Four over four. The thought was vaguely troubling. She'd seen a similar design before, somewhere . . . but it was of no consequence. She would have remembered if it were.

The blisters made it hard for her to close her hand, but there was no pain and she could use her fingers, albeit awkwardly. She rewrapped the bandage around her palm and went to check on Evenna.

The Illuminer was sleeping poorly again. Her teeth were bared in a rictus snarl; her hands were clenched into fists atop her blankets. She'd tossed and thrashed until her sweaty hair surrounded her like a halo of black snakes.

Asharre shook her roughly. "Wake up."

Evenna moaned. Her eyes fluttered open, stark white. Asharre shook her again, harder. The Illuminer sat up, immediately dropping her head into her hands. Her shoulders trembled as she gasped for breath; she dug her fingers into her tangled locks, pulling hard.

"Bad dreams?"

"Nightmares." Evenna shuddered, keeping her face buried between her arms. "I know . . . I *know* what we're doing is important. Lives depend on it. But oh, Bright Lady. I don't know if I can be strong enough."

"You are. *We* are. We have to be." *And we have more hope than you know,* Asharre wanted to add, but it was best not to speak of that until she was sure. Perhaps Falcien would not come back to her dreams; perhaps she had only imagined he'd help. She couldn't promise anything. Not yet. "What did you dream?"

"The forge again. It was burning bones, like before, but this time it held a tiny sun in its firepit. On the outside it was all white and gold glory, dazzling, but there was a black seed at its heart. I saw the people of Carden Vale cutting the bones from their own bodies, from their friends', from their *children* to feed that fire. They prayed while they did it. They believed that they were serving Celestia's will by their blasphemy. I saw it . . . and I knew it was true, even as the vision tried to use that truth to lead me astray." The Illuminer wound the chain of her sun medallion over her right hand and pulled it tight. Its links bit white lines into her fingers. "The corruption is trying to reach me as I sleep. It's trying to take me. It might succeed. If it does, if I should fail . . ."

"You won't," Asharre said, more brusquely than she meant to. "You have your goddess and your faith. You have me."

Evenna looked up and smiled weakly, pushing sweat-straggled hair from her face. "Faith is good, but a plan is better. Isn't that what you said? One must have a plan. This is mine. If I should fall, do one thing for me. Kill me. I can't allow myself to be corrupted. I can't . . . if the Mad God takes one of Celestia's Blessed . . . you mustn't allow it to happen, if I can't stop it myself."

"How will I know?"

"I don't know. But you must. Promise me."

Asharre shifted her weight uncomfortably, feeling the heft of the *caractan* press against her back. It felt wrong to give that oath, as if she tempted fate by uttering the words . . . but that was foolishness. They were dead anyway if they failed. Or worse. Maybe death *would* seem a blessing then. "I promise."

"Thank you." Evenna stood unsteadily. "I need to pray."

"Wait," Asharre said. "Do you know the story of the Storm Queen's daughter? The one with a trail of scales?"

The younger woman canted her head to the side. "Yes, why?"

Asharre shrugged uneasily. It had only been a passing mention in a dream . . . but it troubled her, somehow. "Tell me."

"It's a children's story." Evenna waited for a moment, but when Asharre did not seem dissuaded, she went on. "There was a prince who lived in a seaside castle and saw the Storm Queen's daughter singing amidst the waves at daybreak. She was beautiful, with hair and skin as white as sea foam and eyes that shone like pearls . . . but she was not human. From the waist down, her body was that of a silver fish, all covered in scales. Still, the prince fell in love and resolved that he would have her. He went to a sorcerer and begged for a boon that might bring the lady out of the sea.

"The sorcerer gave him a golden crown, and the prince laid that crown on the shore. At dawn the next day, the Storm Queen's daughter picked it up from the strand and lifted it to her head. When she put it on, the crown transformed into a golden net, and the prince ran down to claim her.

"She did not want to go with him, and she struggled and wailed, but the prince would not be deterred. He carried her off into the castle, intending to make her his bride. So that her mother could find her and save her—or, in some tellings, so that she'd be able to find her way back to the sea—the Storm Queen's daughter clawed off her own scales, one by one, and left them shining in a trail of blood to mark the way she had gone."

"The prince did not notice?" Asharre asked.

Evenna brushed the question away with a tired wave.

"It's a story. The prince never notices anything in stories. So the Storm Queen's daughter left her trail of scales. But a strange thing happened when she dropped the last one: she found human legs inside her fish's tail, and she forgot what it was to live in the sea. She had no more interest in returning to her cold life of stones and water; she wanted to stay with her prince.

"It was too late, though. The Storm Queen saw her daughter's blood and came to the castle in a fury. Crashing waves tore the castle down; lightning killed its soldiers. The Storm Queen drowned the prince herself, dragging him into the deeps, and brought her daughter back under the waves.

"But her daughter had become a princess, human in heart and body, and the sea was no longer her home. She drowned alongside her husband, and that is the story's end."

"A fine tale to tell children."

"Most folk stories are like that. They might have meant something else, originally . . . but they're for children now."

"Yes," Asharre said, wondering.

They were on the move again before the sun rose over the Shardfield. The day was gray and hazy, and the forest closed around them as the road climbed northeast along the mountain walls. Years of neglect had healed the scars left by soldiers and miners; as often as not the road vanished into undergrowth. Pine and spruce cloaked the slopes, leaving little to betray the fact that men had ever lived here.

Asharre wondered if they'd find anything more substantial than ghosts at Shadefell. It seemed impossible that the surviving townspeople of Carden Vale could have retreated into such isolation and left no signs of their presence. But they'd already come this far, and they had nowhere else to look.

That night she dreamed of Falcien again. The dead Celestian sat cross-legged on the embers of his pyre. Nothing was left of his flesh, and most of his bones had been consumed by the fire. Only the sunburst pendant fused to his sternum, a glob of gold and ash, told who he had been.

"You are traveling too fast," he warned her. Threads of burnt hair crumbled around his shoulders. "You will not have time to learn what you must before reaching Shade-fell. Better if you slowed; better yet if you turned back and retrieved the solaros' writings from the Rosy Maiden. If you had his work to build on, your studies would go much faster."

"We can't go back," Asharre said. "*Maelgloth* infest Carden Vale, and Evenna's getting weaker every day. Returning might help me, but it would hurt her, and her strength matters more than mine."

"Even if it means your life?"

"My life matters only as far as it shields hers. Help us find Aurandane. If we have the sword, we have a cure." *I hope.*

The dead man's jaw creaked into a grin. Most of his teeth had fallen out. "Yes. Yes, that is so. Its magic is still strong. Maol's creatures cannot touch the sword. It burns their flesh; it destroys their bodies. Only human hands can hold Aurandane. That is why the Mad God has not claimed it, all these many years, and has hidden it away instead . . . but the signs are there, for those who know how to find them."

"Tell me how to find it."

"Carden Vale's solaros followed the same path you walk

now. Trace his footsteps. His people lit the way to enlightenment, and he saw the sword, but he did not have the
strength to hold it. When you find his tracks, you will
know the path . . . but you must not falter, as he did. You
must not fail. Maol's creatures will try to stop you—but I
can show you the wards that will defeat them."

She set her jaw. "Show me."

He did, and she watched closely, but the dream lessons
proved nigh impossible. Asharre's strengths had never lain
in the scribe's arts, and that was all Falcien taught her. He
showed her protective runes and warding circles, arcane
sequences of numbers and invocations that could counter-
spell corruption. Asharre began to understand what Laedys
had been trying to capture in her lonely cottage, and why
the woman had worked so frantically to record each shape
and pattern before it evaporated with the dawn.

It was impossible to remember everything. There was
too much of it, coming too fast, and the dream's nature
worked against her. No sooner did a wheel of sigils appear on a page than her perspective shifted, or the page's
contents changed, or time stuttered and started again elsewhere, and she was stymied. The blisters on her injured
hand, which had hardly troubled her in waking life, here
made her as clumsy as if she were trying to write with a
plum wedged between each finger.

The only thing she was able to master was a simple sunburst, the ends of its rays flattened like hands . . . and there
was something that tugged at her memory about that too.
But the thought was gone as soon as it came, a little fish
glittering in a brief leap of light before it was pulled back
into the dark and drowning sea.

Falcien touched the back of her hand with the three
skeletal fingers left to him. Dawn softened the darkness

to the east. As it was in the dream, so it would be in the world.

"You must go," he said. "When you find the sword, let Evenna wield it. She is Blessed, and her faith is strong. Aurandane will be better in her hands than yours . . . but you are the one who must find it. Go, and do not falter."

The bed of embers had nearly gone out beneath him. Shadows swaddled the dule tree and filled the hollows between his bones. Asharre knew, somehow, that when the fire died completely and the darkness claimed Falcien, he would no longer be able to help her. Maol would swallow that spark of resistance, and she would be alone in the night.

"How do I keep the fire alive?" she asked.

He did not seem to think it was a strange question. "The price of that is too high."

"Tell me."

"Bones," he whispered, as the dream faded with the night. "The fire burns bones."

She woke. Around her the forest was blue-green and tranquil in the dawn. Evenna was still sleeping. Asharre traced the sunburst on the Celestian's brow, hoping she remembered its shape correctly, and was relieved to see Evenna's strained features relax. For a heartbeat she was tempted to carve the mark in with a knife, to make it permanent . . . but no, that was absurd. She shook the impulse away almost before realizing it was there.

Falcien's secrets worked. There was hope for them yet. Asharre let the girl sleep for another hour, until the morning was lively bright, then shook her awake.

"I've missed prayers," Evenna said as soon as her eyes opened. She looked around, confused as a child. "How did I miss the dawn?"

"You were sleeping. Peacefully, for the first time in a long while. I didn't want to wake you."

"Please don't let it happen again." Evenna hobbled to a patch of sunlight falling through the leaves. There was an ashen cast to her porcelain skin, and her body trembled visibly. She swept her hands skyward to begin the ritual, turning her face up to the morning. "I can't sleep through dawn prayer. It makes me weaker."

Asharre let her pray in peace, abashed. When she was finished, they went on. Late that afternoon, they came to Shadefell.

It was a grand folly: a collection of arches and interlocking courtyards that ringed a central tower like filigree around a jewel. Tiny windows peered out over ornamental bands of stone. Blind arcades adorned the front walls, converging on the great doors at the center. A circular emblem of carved stone, its details masked by dirt and moss, crowned the doorway's arch.

The Rosewayns must have spent a king's ransom to build it. Asharre tried to calculate the cost of bringing workmen and materials to this godsforsaken corner of the valley, floundered, and gave up. Even with the roads in good repair, they were days from Carden Vale, and that town was itself a speck on the backside of nowhere. Add in Duradh Mal's curse, and it was hard to see how the Rosewayns had managed to raise Shadefell at any price.

It was still harder to see why they'd bothered. Shadefell House defended nothing, controlled nothing. There were no passes nearby, no roads, no easy access to the river. The outer halls had no towers, no walls, only decorative battlements. Shadefell's sole defense was its remoteness.

"They'd be helpless if anyone attacked," Asharre said, marveling at the absurdity.

"It's a temple," Evenna said. "This is a perfect copy of a Vendathi temple. It was never meant to be defended."

"I do not know the Vendathi." She studied the buildings, looking for anything that might indicate they had living occupants. Not a smudge of smoke darkened the sky; what little she could see of the stables looked as dilapidated as the main house. The weeds between the courtyards' paving stones grew tall, untroubled by footsteps.

"They were a minor kingdom in Ardashir. The Vendathi believed that peace was the only true road to enlightenment, and they welcomed the world to it. They built all their palaces and temples without fortifications. This house is designed according to their precepts."

"Why? I thought the Rosewayns wanted to retake Ang'duradh. It's a long leap from coveting a Baozite fortress to emptying a treasury on an Ardasi peace temple."

"They lived in the shadow of Duradh Mal. Maybe they thought peace would protect them where walls and soldiers had come to ruin."

"Then they were wrong." Asharre pushed out of the brush. "There is nothing here. Perhaps the other side of the house will show more."

Evenna nodded. They followed the forest's hem, seeing nothing more than weeds and wildflowers and the brown veins of ivy wrapped around the courtyards' pillars.

The northern wing of the house swept out to the remnants of a kitchen garden. A tangle of blackberry vines spilled over the garden wall. The green spikes of new onions and feathery carrot shoots struggled for sunlight amidst the young pines and purple laceflower that had conquered the old beds. A doorway, partly blocked by fallen stone, led from the garden into the main house.

Asharre started toward the door, but Evenna pulled her back. "Wait."

She shrugged the younger woman's hand off impatiently. "What?"

"By the doorway. Look at the water."

A rill of inky water trickled out from a crack in the wall there. Where that thread of water flowed, nothing grew. A few yellowed weeds wilted at the edges of its reach, dying where they stood. Blooms of tiny mushrooms, blue as a corpse's kiss, sprouted from their remains. Otherwise, from the time the rivulet emerged from the house until it sank under the earth in a rippled fan of black sediment, the dirt was poisoned bare.

"*Morduk ossain,*" Evenna said. "Dead man's feast. The hand of Maol is here."

16

"I've found the missing Celestians," Malentir said. He brushed a finger along the underside of his dead sparrow's chin. The little bird sat motionless on his shoulder, as it had since returning from its flight. "One went south on horseback; my bird saw him retreating across Spearbridge. Two went north on foot. To Shadefell."

Bitharn winced. Kelland closed his eyes. "Which two?" the knight asked quietly.

"Two women. One bigger than most men, with runes scarred on her face and short white hair. She carried a sword heavier than yours."

"Asharre," Bitharn said. That description could be no one else. No wonder she'd thought the tracks by the pyre were a man's; the *sigrir*'s height and stride would confuse anyone who hadn't seen her in person.

"The other was younger, smaller," the Thornlord continued. "Black hair bound in a healer's halo. No weapons. She walked slowly; she might have been wounded."

Bitharn glanced at Kelland, who shrugged. "The lack of weapons confirms that she's an Illuminer, but it isn't much to go on. Jelian, maybe, or Evenna. I don't know the younger ones as well as I should. How far ahead were they?"

"Too far to catch easily," Malentir said, "and the auguries did not favor going to Shadefell immediately. Our chances are better if we go to Ang'duradh first."

"We'll be too late to help anyone then," Bitharn objected.

"If we *walk*, yes. That was never my intention. Gethel had a way of traveling by magic; he must have, else he could not have exploited my opening of the seals as he did. As soon as I was removed, he entered Duradh Mal. No one had time to see or stop him. He could not have acted so swiftly if he traveled by foot or horse . . . yet he had no magic of his own. Therefore he must have been using a *perethil*. This house once belonged to Renais Ruin-Hunter, and it is very likely that Gethel used his."

"That name doesn't mean anything to me," Bitharn said. She knew what a *perethil* was, of course, and she supposed some of those relics might have survived in Duradh Mal. The Baozites used *perethil* as engines of war, and the ruins had been sealed to scavengers for centuries, so any that Ang'duradh possessed should still be inside. But that didn't explain how Gethel could have used one *outside* Duradh Mal.

"You might have noticed that this house is wealthier than one would expect of a farmer in Carden Vale," Malentir said.

"Maybe," Bitharn said cautiously. She had, and she had also noticed that its treasures were decidedly old fashioned, more so than mere provincialism could explain. The silver had been lovingly polished so many times that its engravings of songbirds and rose-entwined wheels were worn down to suggestions, and it had still tarnished black after that. Two of the rugs appeared to be of genuine Khartoli make, woven from silk threads shot through with real gold and imported at staggering cost . . . but they were faded and worn, despite having been stored carefully and, probably, reserved for special occasions. Whatever the source of this family's wealth, it had come and gone long ago.

"Renais Ruin-Hunter, an ancestor several generations back, was the source of this family's wealth," Malentir said. "Within Carden Vale he was famous, or perhaps infamous, though the townspeople did their best to keep the rumors hushed. Renais found a secret way into Shadefell, where no one else dared go. He looted the Rosewayns' treasures for years, jealously guarding the means by which he found them. Those treasures made him a rich man . . . and, in the end, a mad one. His family walled him up in the house he built them—the same house where we now stand—and never went back to the ruins themselves. But death did not hide their family sin, or their secrets. I found them, and it seems that Gethel did too. He used Renais' *perethil* to enter Duradh Mal, and we will do the same."

"How did a farmer in Carden Vale get his hands on a *perethil*?" Bitharn asked.

"It was the Celestians'," Malentir said. "It was placed in Carden Vale's chapel when they first sealed Ang'duradh. If the seals failed, or some new danger came, they could use it to travel swiftly to the Dome of the Sun for help or to the wards on Duradh Mal to deal with it themselves. In the early years, Knights of the Sun stayed at the chapel, vigilant against any threat. But after centuries of peaceful silence, people . . . forgot. The Sun Knights stopped coming. A few Illuminers came—new ones serving their *annovair*. Then they, too, were needed elsewhere. Decades passed with no Blessed here, and the Dome sent less and less aid, and finally the village solaros sold off the chapel's treasures, one by one, to serve his people's needs. Food and medicine mattered more than brass and crystal. So Renais bought the *perethil*. He was the only one who knew what it was . . . and he only knew because it had come to him in dreams. Maol reached through sleep to instruct him. And he, fool that he was, chose to listen. When I found his bones and questioned his shade, he babbled incessantly about the lore he'd learned in dreams. Lies and traps, all of it, but they were all he could remember."

"Then it was already corrupted," Kelland said. "Maol was already trying to escape the seals on Duradh Mal."

"I do not believe the *perethil* was corrupt. Not at first. But over time, as Renais used it again and again to return to the Rosewayns' haunts, and altered its symbols to match the ones he saw in dreams, it changed. Once the path was opened to him by mortal hands, the Mad God was able to bend its magic himself and, eventually, turn it to his own uses." The Thornlord left the kitchen's waning light, stopping before the night-sky painting in the next room. He regarded its elaborate frame grimly. "The *perethil* made Renais such a monster his own family walled him up. It might have done worse to Gethel. But we must use it."

Kelland's mouth twisted. "Your spells would be safer."

Malentir stared at the knight. His eyes were flat and black as a snake's. At length he made a chill little smile. "I do not know whether to credit you with extreme cleverness or extreme foolishness, but in either case my answer is no."

"What?" Bitharn looked from one man to the other in bewilderment. "What is he talking about?"

"The Thorn could take us to Duradh Mal by traveling through shadows," Kelland answered, not breaking from their locked gazes. "He won't. Even though it would be safer than trusting to whatever corrupted magic Gethel used."

"Safer for *you*, and only until arrival," Malentir said, poisonously soft. "*I* would be left drained and defenseless . . . against whatever is in Duradh Mal, and against you. Forgive me if I am not inclined to make myself helpless for your benefit."

"Of course. If you'll forgive my reluctance to step into a blighted *perethil* based on no more than your storytelling."

"Your distrust is neither wise nor warranted. But certainly, if it will reassure you, test the thing for yourself. I will leave you to do it in private. By sundown I hope your fears will be assuaged. We can hardly hope to succeed in Ang'duradh if we stay at each others' throats the whole time."

"He has a point," the knight murmured after the Thorn had gone. "But I think I'll hold on to my distrust a little longer." He knelt before the painting, examining its dark canvas and metal stars more closely. The Celestial Chorus stared back at them, its silver-and-bronze stars reflecting fragments of their faces. Near the bottom of the painting's frame, the jeweled, misshapen white metal of its handle gleamed.

Kelland raised his voice in a clear tenor. The words were calm and sonorous, almost musical, and this time no foulness seized his spell. The golden haze of godsight filled his eyes.

Bitharn hung back, glancing over her shoulder for the Thornlord. A queasy, unsettled feeling collected in the pit of her stomach. There was no reason for it, really—Kelland's spell had succeeded, and a *painting* wasn't going to attack them, *perethil* or no—but she couldn't shake her unease. Something about the way those blackish rubies sat on the melted metal made her think of the old myths she'd read in the Dome's libraries: of *maelgloth* so corrupted that their blood fell to the earth like poisoned seeds, spawning monsters that leapt up vicious and full grown.

It was a story, only a story . . . but stories were like pearls, beautiful things accreted around a grain of ugly, gritty truth.

The knight sat staring at the painting for so long that Bitharn began to wonder whether its corruption had taken hold of him too. She was about to reach out and shake him when he exhaled a sigh and blinked the godsight away.

"What did you see?" Bitharn whispered.

"Poison," the Sun Knight replied. He pressed his hands to his knees and stood. "The *perethil* is tainted, as the Thornlord said. Maol's influence snakes through every thread of its magic. Once it was Celestian; from what I can discern by the shreds of its original spells, I imagine it allowed our dedicants to travel swiftly across any land in the Celestial Chorus' view. Now, however, it permits travel only to places desecrated by Maolite magic. More than that: it instills in its users a craving for such places. It makes them lust for the corruption that waits within. That lust is woven into its magic; we will not be able to avoid it if we use the *perethil*."

"Can we . . ." Bitharn swallowed. She wanted to hug her arms around herself—or, better, around him. Instead she touched the grip of her bow, taking what reassurance she could from wood and sinew. "How do I resist it?"

"Love. Focus on loves and needs stronger than its temptations." Kelland made no move to touch her, but his look held such intensity that it brought a flush of heat to her cheeks. "The *perethil* may be . . . hard for you. Are you certain you want to go through? We have to come back after Duradh Mal anyway, if we're to go to Shadefell. You might be safer staying here until we return."

Bitharn shook her head. She was touched that he wanted so badly to protect her, but irritated too. "Didn't you learn *anything* from your capture? Leaving me behind doesn't protect me and it surely doesn't protect you. It just makes us both weaker. You can't go alone. And what if you don't come back? How safe will I be then? The *water* here could kill me."

"I know. I just . . . I know." His shoulders sagged. "Forgive me."

"It'd be easier if you stopped doing so many things that needed forgiving." Bitharn brushed his cheek and stepped away. *He* could be as restrained as he wanted; *she* meant to cut that five-year promise as short as she could. If this was the last task Kelland ever did as a Sun Knight, she wouldn't weep. Bitharn shared his faith and had no wish to break him from it . . . but she'd almost lost him once, and that was quite enough.

Her gaze strayed back to the misaligned stars on the painting. "What do you suppose we'll find in there?"

"I don't know."

"Do you think the Thorn does?"

"Perhaps. I doubt he'd go in completely blind . . . but after six hundred years of isolation, and a misguided 'wizard' blundering around thinking he could unlock the secret of godless magic, who knows how much might have changed? Whatever was known about Ang'duradh before its fall may not be true today."

"Oh, good," Bitharn said. "I love surprises."

At sunset Kelland prayed and Bitharn joined him. Afterward they sat side by side, picking at a lentil stew with little appetite. Twilight passed with no sign of the Thornlord, and Bitharn bit her lip, wondering if they should look for the man. But Kelland didn't seem concerned, and she wasn't eager to go wandering through Carden Vale after dark.

Malentir returned to them as the first stars were winking awake. He was not alone. A skeleton in rotting rags shambled after him, dirt dribbling from its nostrils and green moss bearding one cheek. Leaf loam filled the crevices of its spine; mice had gnawed at its ribs. The left arm was missing altogether. But the right was intact, and it still had that hand.

"She will call the gate for us," the Thornlord said, ushering his macabre companion toward the star-hung painting. "If you studied the *perethil,* you will know that it is not safe for any of us to turn its handle. So I found another. Most of the old dead were burned, of course, and *maelgloth* are useless to me. Unfortunate, as there are quite a few to choose from tonight. This young lady was more troublesome to find, but she will be safer. As you can see, when she died there were still animals in the wood, so her bones should be free from corruption."

"Oh," Bitharn said faintly, settling back on her heels to watch.

Ivory mist coiled through the skeleton, snaking along its arms and legs like ghostly ivy around the limbs of a dead tree. Now and then Bitharn caught shapes in the mist— fingers, the curve of a shoulder, a wave of long hair swaying over the small of its back. Once, for an instant, she saw a misty face over the skull's mossy bone, and the agony on those translucent features was heartbreaking. That mist bound the girl's spirit to her bones, Bitharn was sure of it, and she was in torment.

"It won't be long," she murmured, hoping the words were true. She didn't know whether they were meant to reassure the spell-bound spirit or herself.

Malentir gestured to the jeweled handle protruding from the painting's frame. The skeleton walked toward it, foot bones clicking on the wooden floor, and grasped the lumpy metal in the claw of its remaining hand. Slowly, with mist rising and falling through its bones in a constant plume, the skeleton turned the handle. The bladed stars around it folded inward like the petals of sleeping flowers, cutting into the skeleton's fingers, but the turning never stopped.

Next to Bitharn, Kelland stiffened and bit back an oath. His eyes were gold with godsight again; she wondered what it revealed. As far as she could see, the cranking of the handle was uneventful until, abruptly, darkness poured from the top of the canvas, flooding the painting.

At first Bitharn thought her eyes were deceiving her. The painting was already rendered in deep grays and blues, and the room was dark; the wash of black was perceptible more as motion than color, and easily taken for imagination either way. But the paler smudges that represented silvery night clouds still shone distinctly in the gloom, and when the spreading blackness swallowed those, she knew it was real.

The stars moved. Sluggishly, unwillingly, as if they were being dragged into place by the inky tides that engulfed them. A low clicking sounded from them, jittery and uneven, as some of the stars rose and others sank, wheeling into new formations.

The sound and the stars stopped. The skeleton's hand jerked on the handle, slid off, and clattered against its hip. Malentir whispered a command, and the ivory mist swirled away in a thousand tiny ribbons, vanishing from view. As the mist dissipated, the bones collapsed into a lifeless heap.

Fresh gouges marred the bones on the skeleton's hand, inside and out. A film of greasy black coated the palm-side scratches. There was nothing on the handle that held an edge; it shouldn't have cut flesh, let alone scored deep into bone. Nothing on the silvery metal or its gemstones should have left that residue either.

"Best to burn her," Malentir said, his voice taut with distaste. "It would be safest for you to do that. Ordinary fire might be more dangerous than helpful."

Kelland glanced at the altered position of the Celestial Chorus on the painting. "If that's any indication, the gate won't open until after midnight. I suppose we have time enough for it. Bitharn, will you help?"

"What do you need?"

"Take some of the bones. Not the hand. I'll carry that."

She wiped the sweat from her palms. "Where do you want them?"

"The stableyard should be far enough. Let me go first. The *maelgloth* might be waiting."

The *maelgloth* were there, but dead. Bitharn's lantern threw back the gloom just enough for her to see the bodies lying broken in the road leading to their lonely farmhouse. It was hard to tell, as tortured as the creatures had been in life, but she thought they'd died in agony.

"The Thorn's work?" she asked.

Kelland nodded. "He couldn't use their bodies, but it seems he could use their pain."

"Is that—do we—" She exhaled. "Do we accept that?"

"Why not?" He looked back over his shoulder. The lantern washed his features in gold and turned the shells in his hair to fiery jewels. "Let evil feed on evil. We'll need the Thornlord's power in Duradh Mal. If he replenishes it by killing *maelgloth,* that's a small price to pay. I don't like it that he tortures anything, even these poor corrupted souls . . . but the world seldom gives us what we'd like. Considering where we are, and what we have to work with, this is the best we could hope for."

"And the girl whose corpse he stole?"

The knight was silent for a moment. Then he strode to the edge of the light, where the earth was beaten hard before the stables, and laid his burden down. "We'll give her what peace we can."

Bitharn added her bones to the pile. They made a small, sad heap. Kelland raised his hands to the sky, beginning a chant that drew from the traditional funeral rites and wove their words into the spell for sunfire.

At the end of his invocation, golden flame erupted from the bones. It consumed them in a soundless inferno: a pyre of sunlight, small but brilliant. Wisps of black smoke snaked from the gouged bones of the girl's hand, wriggling away from the sunfire like wraiths fleeing from the dawn, but the flames caught and destroyed each one.

Within moments nothing was left. Kelland let his hands fall and stared into the darkness, as if wishing he could summon sunfire to consume the bodies of the *maelgloth,* too, but shortly he shook himself and started back to the farmhouse. Bitharn fell in beside him, taking his hand on the way.

"Is it done?" Malentir asked when they returned.

"She's at peace." Kelland eyed the painting as the Celestians set about their final preparations. The stars outside were nearly in the position shown on the altered canvas. Less than an hour left. Bitharn checked the knives in her belt and boots for the thousandth time, then ran a finger over the stiff fletchings of the arrows in her quiver. In war, archers had boys who ran along their lines to replenish their arrows, but Bitharn didn't have that luxury. She had her hooded quiver and a second bag of oilcloth stiffened by wicker hoops, and that was all.

Malentir didn't even have that. The Thornlord wore a long knife, more ornament than weapon, sheathed at his hip. It was a single piece of carved ivory, its hilt worked into garlands of thorned vines. Other than that eccentric blade, which would surely shatter the first time it struck anything, he was unarmed. He wore no armor, either, and carried no shield.

Kelland had donned a hauberk of steel rings and a new surcoat of snowy white. A sun-marked shield was strapped to his left arm. He'd worn the same armor to confront the Thornlady in the winter wood, and Bitharn felt a tickle of dread at the sight of it. Foolishness, she told herself firmly, pure foolishness. He needed armor in the halls of Duradh Mal.

She herself wore hardened leather reinforced with chain between the gaps. Bitharn hadn't the strength to fight in full chain, and she'd never really learned to use a shield, but she knew better than to venture into battle unprotected. The Thorns were mad, all of them, for choosing to fight unarmored.

A star fell from the painting.

It struck the floor with a peal like the tolling of a funeral bell. While the sound was still shivering in the air, another star fell, then a third. As the echoes died and Bitharn's heart began to beat again, another chime ripped through the bruised stillness. Again and again the stars fell and sounded their unnatural tolls, each one sharper and more jangling than the last.

The final star did not fall. Around it, the painting's un-natural blackness rippled into fissures, peeling open the canvas—peeling open *reality*—in a web that took its lines from the points and angles of that last razor-sided star. Eight lines: a deformed sunburst. The embrace of Maol. It hung there, a ghastly wound in the world, edged in bleeding wisps of black. The rift was just large enough for a man to step through—but step through into *what*? All Bitharn saw within the gate was a wall of black and poisoned red, pulsing like an exposed heart through a mask of clotting blood.

"I'll go first," Kelland said, readying his shield. "Bitharn next. Malentir last. If the gate closes before you're through, Thorn, you can follow us through shadows."

Bitharn swallowed hard. "Go."

Kelland stepped into the well of tainted light. Tendrils of red and black clutched at his surcoat, pulling him in and closing around his back. Then he was gone. Gritting her teeth, Bitharn followed.

Darkness surrounded her. She could see nothing but a dim impression of red light, far away and flecked with black. The air was close, moist, uncomfortably warm. The bellows of heavy breathing sounded behind her, close enough to riffle the hairs on the back of her neck. Musk and smoky incense filled the air, underlaid with the stench of unwashed, rutting bodies—a strange smell, repulsive and intriguing at the same time.

Unseen hands wrapped around her. She couldn't tell whether they were attached to bodies or were simply parts of the darkness made manifest. They pressed against her lips, cupped her breasts, grabbed at her thighs and crept upward. She felt the bones jab through the fingers' soft, sloughing flesh, smelled decay and the reek of blackfire on them.

The hands terrified her, repelled her, and yet brought a pang of perverse arousal. Her breathing quickened; her skin seemed to become more sensitive to the corpse hands' caresses. She wanted to relax, to open herself to their rotting touches. *Why?* Her reaction frightened and disgusted her more than the hands did. Bitharn clenched her teeth against the intruding fingers, shook her head fiercely, and kicked the groping hands away.

Laughter filled the darkness, mad and meaningless and horribly *certain.* There was no sound to it; she felt the laughter directly in her mind. Invisible lips, cold and spongy with decay, brushed her brow. A tongue curled wetly over her breast, impeded by neither armor nor cloth. Then she stumbled forward into hard stone and stale air, infinitely cleaner than what she'd breathed in the *perethil's* gate. Bitharn spat the taste of corpse flesh from her mouth, wiped the sticky residue of corpse hands from her face, and breathed hard as she tried not to cry.

"It's all right," Kelland's voice said from the blackness beside her. He sounded shaken, but the knowledge that he was safely through did more to calm Bitharn than anything else could have. She clung to the familiar sound of his voice, using it to right her sense of reality after the *perethil's* assault. "We're through. It's over."

"It's not over." She croaked the words, harsh and half strangled. The taste of sulfur and rotting flesh poisoned every breath she took. Her skin crawled under her armor, and she cursed the fact that she couldn't change or bathe. "We have to go back. This had better be worth it. I can't see a thing. Where are we?"

New footsteps scuffed the stone behind her, lighter than Kelland's, softer than her own.

"We are in Duradh Mal," Malentir said.

17

The Thornlord's fingers brushed over Bitharn's eyelids, light and cold as falling snowflakes. When the chill shock of his magic passed, she could see.

It was not human sight. The world was black as a starless night, with only a fleeting silvery sheen across their surfaces to tell her where walls and ceiling stood. She felt as if she was standing in a blurred artist's sketch of Duradh Mal, not in the bowels of the actual stronghold. It dizzied her.

Her companions looked still stranger. All the living colors of their skin and clothes were gone. Instead they were a radiant white, brighter than mirrors held up to the sun. She could scarcely stand to look at them. Around them the world was better defined, as if the living shed light upon their surroundings.

There were subtle differences between the two men in this alien vision. Kelland was limned in ghostly golden flame; the sight spoke to her of danger. Malentir's aura had an ivory tinge, and he felt *cold,* as if whatever power had touched her resided in him. It was terrible, and commanding, and she fought away quailing.

"What have you done?" Bitharn whispered.

"You see the world as the *ghaole* do," Malentir answered. "They need no light, sense the living, and are able to recognize who is a threat—and who is their master."

"How long will it last?" Kelland's hand came to rest on his sunburst medallion, and by that Bitharn knew he liked this strange vision no better than she did.

"Until dawn. We have time, but that hardly means we should waste it. We are near the Gate of Despair, if my memories do not mislead me. North and east, the halls will take us back to the Shardfield or to the sentinel towers over Spearbridge. West will take us to the towers that watch over Carden Vale. South are the halls leading to the dungeons."

"Where do we need to go?" Bitharn asked.

It was Kelland who answered, pointing his sword down the hallway. "That way. Down to the heart of the mountain. I can feel it burning."

"Yes. The trail of Gethel's magic leads down." Malentir strode to the front and turned left when the corridors branched. "Through the Gate of Despair."

"Picturesque name," Bitharn muttered. "Why is it called that?"

"Because it leads to the dungeons." Kelland fell in behind the Thornlord, letting Bitharn guard their rear. "Every Baozite fortress has one. Ang'arta's is aptly named."

He would know. Bitharn suppressed a wince and followed.

The halls loomed black and empty around them. Two men could have ridden abreast down the halls of Ang'duradh, and once there would have been ten thousand soldiers to watch them go. Their trophies hung on the walls: banners from noble houses whose names no loremaster remembered, tapestries depicting nameless battles on forgotten fields. The skulls of a thousand heroes dangled overhead, speared upon their own weapons and worked into grisly chandeliers. Soft black dust covered everything.

"This will all have to be burned when the Baozites retake it," Kelland said as they walked, their steps echoing in the stillness. "Maol's presence permeates it all."

"Perhaps." Malentir did not look back. "Aedhras the Golden has little interest in anyone's victories but his own, so he might not weep to see all this burned. But if he wants it preserved, it will be . . . ghastly and tasteless as it is."

"You don't approve?"

"Whether I approve counts for nothing. My mistress adores the man; anything he desires, she will do, and I obey her commands."

"That can't be easy."

"Duty is never easy, knight. Hadn't you noticed?"

They went on in gloom and silence. Even if there was no trail Bitharn's eyes could follow, the Thornlord seemed to know his path. He led them down crooked stairs and pillared halls, stopping at last before an oaken door that towered twice Bitharn's height. An iron gargoyle snarled at its center. Rust hung a wavering beard from the gargoyle's chin, but the iron and wood had held strong through the centuries.

The lock had not. Fragments of it, ruptured by a tightly focused explosion, lay scattered across the floor. Two bodies sprawled among them: men in miners' clothes, with tool harnesses over their shoulders and water bags at their belts. They looked like they'd been savaged by a beast with a bear's height and a lion's claws. Fearsome teeth had torn out one's throat. Both bodies were desiccated, like those of the drowned children Bitharn had found in Carden Vale, their lips pulled back in yellowed grins.

Hunger knotted a fist in her belly at the sight of the bodies. Bitharn folded her arms, pressing on her stomach to quell the hunger and the nausea that came with it. It was just a part of whatever enchantment gave her the *ghaole*-sight, she told herself; it had nothing to do with her passage through the *perethil*. She wasn't sure that was much better, but at least that way she could hope the desire to feast on corpses would end when the Thornlord's spell did.

She forced herself to study the bodies dispassionately. The dead men had no defensive wounds, yet their tool harnesses were empty. Where had their weapons gone? Had their killer looted them? How, if it was a beast? Bitharn bent closer, trying to make sense of the scene.

She couldn't. The *ghaole*-sight defeated her. The flickering dance of silver light over black made it impossible for her to find the details that could tell the corpses' story.

A lantern had fallen near one man's outflung hand, leaving a greasy stain on the floor. Not all its oil had spilled, however; some gleamed in the dented reservoir. By its light, she'd be able to see what had killed these men, and maybe learn whether it was still in the fortress . . .

"*Burn nothing here,*" Malentir snarled, kicking the lantern away. It clanged against the wall. "I had hoped you were listening the first time I said that, but evidently you're a slow learner. Much slower and you'll be a dead one. Did you learn *nothing* at the pyre? Blackfire spreads its corruption through smoke. That lantern is a trap for curious fools like you."

"I only wanted to find out what killed them," Bitharn said lamely. She waved at her eyes. "I can't read the tracks like this."

"Then you should have asked. In theory we are working together. If you cannot trust me enough to ask something that simple, this alliance is doomed and I might as well slit my wrists now." Malentir exhaled audibly and ran a hand through his striped hair. "I did not give you *ghaole*-sight because I had nothing better to do with my time. There are other ways to learn what you wanted to know."

Ways that leave me dependent on what you tell me. Bitharn bit her tongue. Instead she said: "Fine. How did they die?"

He pointed at the gargoyle door with a wire-circleted hand. "This is the Gate of Despair. It was the last seal I left intact. Obviously Gethel found a way to open it."

"Celestian magic didn't kill these men," Bitharn said.

"Truly, your perceptiveness never ceases to amaze."

Nettled, Bitharn narrowed her eyes. "If sunfire didn't kill them, what did?"

"Where else have you seen your goddess' magic set awry?"

"Are you suggesting the seal was corrupted the same way the *perethil* was? Even if that's so—even if that's *possible*—how could it have done this? *Why* would it have done this? Why tear apart two men and not all of them?"

"Because these two still were men, and Gethel was not. I don't know whether he was that far gone before he came to Duradh Mal or if it was the magic lurking in these halls that finally claimed him. For the sake of my pride, I will hope for the latter; it would be altogether too embarrassing to think I overlooked a soul that tainted. Either way, Maol recognized him for what he was and spared him so that he might spread the Mad God's evil through the world. These two"—he nudged a corpse's lolling head with his boot—"were ordinary, and easily expendable to lay a trap for whoever might come later."

"That doesn't explain the claw marks. You don't think the ruptured seal did that."

"No," Malentir admitted.

"Then what caused those?"

"An ironclaw," Kelland suggested. "Taller than a man on its hind legs, claws like a lion's but longer. The marks match, and we know the Baozites bred them."

Bitharn balked. "This place was sealed for six hundred years. Nothing could live in here that long."

"Nevertheless, he is correct," Malentir said. "There was an ironclaw here. Hungry, bereft of its masters, it smelled bodies rotting in the dungeon and came down in search of food—or so I believe. For six hundred years it might have been trapped here, driven to madness and death and finally beyond death by Maol's power, and then it escaped."

"How do you know?" Bitharn asked.

"Because I killed it. I thought that ironclaw escaped because of something *I* had done; I tracked it to Vedurras in order to kill the thing before anyone else encountered it and realized I had opened the seals of Duradh Mal. When your Blessed found me in Vedurras, I assumed it was bad luck, that some villager had seen or been mauled by the beast and survived to seek the Sun Knights' help. Now, however, the pieces of the puzzle are sliding into place, and they show a different picture. I am beginning to think Gethel sent the ironclaw out to distract me, and that he told the Celestians how they could find me in a moment of weakness, after I'd exhausted myself killing the creature. Then—as he hoped, and as happened—the Sun Knights would be able to capture or kill me, removing me as an obstacle to his exploration of Duradh Mal. He played us both as pawns."

"Are you sure it was the same ironclaw?" Bitharn asked.

"Could it have been a different one that killed these men?"

"No, and yes. We will have to hope there was only the one." Malentir clasped his hands behind his back, examining the gargoyle door. Satisfied, he took hold of the ring dangling from the creature's teeth and dragged it open, ignoring the rusted screech of its hinges. Black dust fell from the open door in a rolling cloud of ghostly faces and grasping hands. The spectral figures reached for them, their fingers stretching longer than arms, and Kelland raised his shield to meet them. But when the dust settled to the ground, the shapes vanished, leaving the two Celestians to exchange a glance of misgiving.

"You saw them too?" Bitharn asked. She wasn't sure what answer she wanted. It was bad enough if she was imagining things. If they were real . . .

"I saw them," Kelland confirmed.

"And you will see worse ahead," Malentir said. "How long can you sustain your sunfire? As light, not as killing flame."

"It depends on how many things challenge it." Kelland lowered his sun-marked shield. "An hour, easily. Two, with some strain."

"Let us say we have an hour, then. Past this point we must travel within your aura. Maol's presence in this place is too strong for us to enter unprotected . . . unless you had some burning desire to become *maelgloth*."

"Thank you, but no." Kelland touched the wavy-rayed medallion at his chest, murmuring. Golden light unfurled around him, enveloping the three of them. The corpses on the floor steamed like blocks of ice brought up to the summer sun, and the dust that had poured from the opened door evaporated into rills of inky smoke.

Bitharn's *ghaole*-sight flickered violently in the sudden

light, flashing from silver and black to the daylit colors of true vision and back. She put a hand against the nearest wall, dizzied, until the Thornlord's spell finally surrendered to the sunfire and she saw with her own eyes again.

"Come." Malentir walked through the gargoyle door, taking care not to leave the Sun Knight's illumination. "We are wasting time."

Duradh Mal was no more welcoming in Kelland's sunlight than it had been in the silver dusk of *ghaole*-sight. The black dust seemed more sinister, rising in sinuous coils and vanishing as the knight walked past. Gaps and holes appeared in the walls. At first Bitharn thought the blocks might somehow have fallen out, but then she saw the corroded ends of bars in one hole's mouth and realized that they were the entrances to tiny, impossibly cramped cells. They were spaced unevenly across the halls so that no man could see any other's face, no matter how crowded the dungeon became.

"Was this where they kept you?" she whispered to Kelland. "Someplace like this in Ang'arta?"

The knight glanced back, his face strained, and said nothing.

Down a short flight of steps their surroundings became grimmer still. Dust-cloaked irons glinted in alcoves on every side. Vises and clamps rested on age-warped shelves above hammers and wedges for the precise breaking of bones. Next to those were racks of knives, their blades turned to moths' wings of rust, that had once been used to pry prisoners' fingernails from their hands and flay the living skin from their limbs. Bitharn walked past them quickly, not daring to meet Kelland's eyes.

Another bend in the hall took them to a cavernous chamber ringed by empty hearths. Every one had a pierced mantel carved with the Baozite crown, and every crown had five gaps bored through it so that the fires could shine through as red jewels when they burned. The room must have been an inferno when all were lit. Darkness filled them now, and not a single spider spun its web across the gaps.

Cylindrical pits, each fifteen feet deep and twenty across, riddled the floor. The bottoms and sides of the nearest pits were caked with some moist black substance, midway between dust and forest mold, that showed irregular gray lines where flat blades had scraped it away.

A susurration resonated through the dungeon as Bitharn came in. It could have been wind—almost—but the sound was too wet, too close to human words, to be the whisper of air through stone. Breathing, or sobbing: that was what she heard.

Bitharn peeked over the lip of the next pit and recoiled.

Blind faces peered back at her. They had no eyes; their sockets were packed with wet black dirt. Their hairless skin glistened, slimy and gray in Kelland's holy aura, more like frogs' skin than that of men. She could see scarred dimples on the tops of their heads, four over four, like the blisters on the miners who had killed that boy on Devils' Ridge. They cringed from the light, whimpering, even as they reached for their visitors with rag-muffled hands. Steel wire stitched each one's mouth shut, rusting around the holes punched into their bloodless lips.

They were packed in the pit like eels in a fishmonger's tub. She couldn't begin to count the bodies crushed against one another, the faces that stared at her in blind, near-mindless adoration. And it *was* adoration, or something very like it; Bitharn couldn't mistake the look on those gray, sightless faces. "What's *wrong* with them?"

"Feed us," the nearest creatures whispered, straining to speak through the wire that clamped their lips. Their scabrous arms shook; their upturned faces were taut with yearning. "Feed us. I serve—we serve—loyal, so loyal. *Feed us.*" Their moans rose and fell like the rush of phantom waves trapped in a seashell; the intensity changed, but the meaning never did. *"Feed us."*

"This is what the miners became. *Maelgloth.*" Malentir stooped near the pit's edge, his striped hair falling forward. The creatures whined and scrabbled away from him, crawling over one another in their haste to leave the Thornlord's presence.

"Why are they here? Why are they . . . like this?" Kelland turned to the Thorn. "Can you ask them?"

"Asking is one thing. Receiving an answer worth hearing is quite another. But I can try." Setting a hand flat on the floor, Malentir vaulted into the pit. The *maelgloth* recoiled, leaving an arm's reach of bare rock all around him. To Bitharn's surprise, the exposed floor was completely clean; there was no smeared dung or filth, nor any sign of the soft black mould that covered the other pits' walls.

Malentir strode toward the *maelgloth*, penning them back against the wall until they could retreat no farther. He drew the ivory knife at his hip and drove it into the nearest creature's chin, stabbing smoothly upward through the bottom of its jaw into its brain. The creature let out a squeal, made half a whistle by the wire stitching its lips, and writhed with the pale knife buried in its skull.

The Thornlord uttered a word, low and sibilant, and the *maelgloth*'s head collapsed, crumpling inward like a ball of paper crushed in an unseen fist. The body fell to the ground, and Malentir withdrew his blade. The ivory was clean.

"I didn't bring a rope," Bitharn called down.

"I wouldn't trust you to hold it," Malentir said. He sheathed the knife and stepped into the fringe of shadows past the reach of Kelland's light, forcing some of the *maelgloth* into the Celestian's glow. The black dirt packed into their eyes melted away under the sunfire's glare; they wailed shrilly and covered their faces with rag-mittened hands, sucking desperately at the smoke that leaked from their eyes.

Malentir was deaf to their shrieks. He pricked a finger on his knife, whispered an invocation to his cruel goddess, and vanished.

An instant later he stepped out of the shadows cloaking the nearest hearth. He came to the edge of the knight's sunfire and stopped there, drawing the ivory blade again. Pale mist spilled from its tip, forming a ghostly echo of the carved thorns that ringed the knife's hilt.

The mist spread and solidified into the figure of a hunched, sad-faced man. Blisters rose on his stubbled head and his posture was bent in agony, but no wire sealed his lips and his eyes were his own. A knotted vine of thorns, translucent as alabaster, cocooned him from foot to neck. A barbed ring from that vine wrapped around his face, just below the eyes, so that his lashes would brush it if he blinked. Droplets of foggy blood trickled from the shade's face as the thorns bit in.

"Who are you?" Malentir demanded.

"I can't . . . explain that to you." The ghost's face contorted. "You aren't ever the same person twice—people just call you that way. It's a useful pretending. But it's been . . . an age . . . since anyone called me." He groaned and rolled back his eyes. "You lose an old toy . . ."

"Never mind that," Malentir snapped. "How did you come to be here?"

"This mountain has a sickness. It is . . . a bodily sickness. You can see it, touch it. So you cut it out." He formed a blade with his hand and dragged it across his arm beneath the elbow. "Cutting the tumor was our task. A melted tumor makes tallow. Tallow makes a candle. Light the candle . . . that was the pure light. That would keep us safe."

"Clearly it didn't. Why?"

"We knew that the sickness . . . that it could be a trouble to us. You could not cut it the usual way. You could not cut it with metal. It has the same skin as flint—it sparks. So we cut it with bone. It cleaves well with bone—it is familiar, it recognizes its own. But even then . . ." The shade scratched anxiously at his arm, drawing beads of milky blood that vanished as soon as they fell. "Even then, the skin would flake and crumble into dust. And then you have it in your eyes, your mouth. So we caught the sickness, and once you have the sickness . . . you don't want anything else. You just want more. The master was wise. He closed our mouths to stop us."

"Of course." The Thornlord gave Bitharn and Kelland a flat look. "Is there any other gibberish you want from this wretch?"

"Why are their hands bound?" the knight asked.

Malentir turned to the shade. "Why are your hands bound?"

"He closed our mouths, but we still wanted. The sickness makes you eat. Its skin is sweet—and when you're sick enough you start to taste it in your bones." He held up his left hand. The tip of his ring finger was eaten away, exposing a worn and scratched nub of bone. The ghost thrust its fingers into its mouth, chewing furiously. The flesh peeled away from its fingers as it did so, leaving black-streaked bones to crunch between its spectral teeth.

"Finger bones *would* fit between those steel laces, wouldn't they. And I'm sure these wretches could tear other things to sufficiently small pieces, if they weren't restrained," Malentir mused. He glanced back at the Celestians. "Anything else?"

Bitharn shook her head. Kelland grimaced. "No."

"Good. Talking to Maolites is tiresome." Malentir gestured contemptuously at the shade. His thorn vine tightened, anchoring its barbs into unreal flesh, then wrenched away in ripping coils, tearing the shade into pieces. Howling, the apparition faded into the dungeon's gloom.

"Now what?" Bitharn asked. "That was useless."

"To the contrary," Malentir said. "That explained a great deal. A sample of the dirt they were collecting, I suspect, will explain still more." He peered into one of the cells wormed into the dungeon's walls. Unlike the others, it was not empty; a mass of coal-stained bones crammed its mouth. The Thorn drew out a human thigh bone, still affixed to half its pelvis by sinew wrapped around the ball of its hip. The pelvis had been chipped into a crude shovel, its edge worn down and coated with black grime.

"Tools to cut the darkness from the mountain." The Thorn scraped the shovel along a nearby pit, scratching loam onto the bone. "This, I presume, is what they collected for the master and what drove them to feast upon their own bones. The bowels of Duradh Mal are not the best place to study it, however, so with your permission I shall take this and devote more time to it elsewhere."

"That's it? You want to go now?" Bitharn blinked. "What about the *maelgloth*?"

"We have a sample of what they took from Duradh Mal." Malentir tapped the shovel's contents onto a small square of cloth, folded it neatly, and tucked the bundle into a silver-capped horn. "There is nothing more we can or should take from this place. All that remains is for the Sun Knight and myself to seal the ruins—a temporary measure, to be sure, but sufficient to keep Gethel and his pets from reentering until we can erect more permanent barriers—close off his *perethil,* and deal with him at Shadefell, now that we know he is not here.

"As for these wretches"—he flicked a hand at the *maelgloth*—"they will have to die. I need their pain, and they serve no other use."

Bitharn looked over the blind faces turned up toward the light. At the steel-bound lips, the slimy gray skin, the hands that had been tied to keep them from tearing each other, and themselves, apart. All around them, the savage majesty of the Baozite fortress closed in.

Evil for evil. *Let them all destroy each other.* She thought of the *perethil's* tainted gate, of the dead hands crawling over her flesh, and shuddered.

Kelland bowed his head, reluctance written on every line of his face. "As you will."

"Of course." Malentir drew his ivory dagger and dropped it into the center of the *maelgloth* pit. He did not go in again, but stood at the brink, praying for his Pale Maiden to bless the *maelgloth* with her gift.

She did. And the steel laced through the miners' lips did nothing to silence their screams.

18

"You are afraid," Gethel said when he came.

"Of course I'm afraid," Corban snapped, tugging his cloak straighter so that the scholar wouldn't see how thin he'd gotten, or realize how ragged he'd let his clothes become. The constant wind made it hard to keep the cloak in place, but this miserable lean-to was as far from his blackfire quarrels as Corban wanted to go, even if it meant their meeting had to be unpleasantly cold.

The two men huddled under a lattice of naked poles wedged into an alley near the apothecary's shop. Whoever had jammed the poles into the crumbling bricks on either side had meant for canvas to be draped over them to offer some shelter from the elements, but if such a tent had ever existed, it was long gone. The wind whistled with merry cruelty through its wooden bones.

It might have been better to meet Gethel in the apothecary's shop, which had a roof and four usable walls instead of a few thin poles rammed into a blocked-off alley . . . but Corban didn't want anyone to know where he hid. Even

Gethel, who had discovered the blackfire stone and sent it to him, couldn't be trusted that far.

Weeks had passed since he'd sent his message up the Windhurst River. Months, perhaps. Time had been slipping away from him ever faster, it seemed, since the night of the rats. It was past midwinter, he knew that much, but the exact date escaped him.

What did it matter, anyway? It was cold. There was snow. Gethel should have arrived eons ago, and in the meantime Corban had been going mad with fear.

He couldn't remember the last time he had slept. His dreams didn't leave, though; they just came to him awake. Corban was beginning to see things. Hear them. Voices whispered to him in the night, repeating unintelligible chants over and over until he began shouting back just to drown them out. Sometimes he saw pale shapes beckoning from the depths of the sea, or imagined that the cracks in the pier's boards were filled with oozing black liquid instead of empty air. Twice he had seen that liquid darkness flow and gather into pools. Once it had risen in an undulating pillar, defying gravity before his disbelieving eyes. He knew, somehow, that if he looked into that moving dark he would be able to read it like an oracle . . . and the truth he saw there would shatter what remained of his sanity.

Corban wasn't afraid. He was terrified. What was *happening* to him? He had never been devout, but he prayed to any god who might listen that Gethel would have an answer for what plagued him. And a cure.

"You are right to feel fear," the scholar whispered. Everything he said was a whisper. Corban thought it was a minor miracle that the man could talk at all. Gethel had looked unwell during their meeting at Carden Vale, but now he was a walking corpse. His eyes were a rheumy gray, covered with dirty cataracts; his skin hung loose as a scarecrow's rags. His nails had grown so long that they curled into his palms like mildewed corkscrews.

"Why? Tell me *why*." Corban hadn't told Gethel the full measure of his fears—hadn't told him much of anything, in truth—but, standing face-to-face with the man, he was suddenly sure he didn't need to. In the scholar's cloudy eyes he saw his own desperation mirrored.

"The harvesting of the stone was not simple," Gethel said. "We had to break seals, brave old evils . . . Duradh Mal was not abandoned, no. Not in the deeps where the blackfire stone lay. There we found horrors. Things without name. I was able to baffle and blind them with my spells, and we wrestled the blackfire stone from their lairs . . . but they pursued us, in their way. An old evil lives in the heart of that mountain. An old death. It is hungry, and it is not easily escaped."

"You told me you'd purified the blackfire stone," Corban said. "You said it was safe."

"And it is. It *was*." Gethel massaged the wrinkled skin under his eyes. "There have been . . . complications."

"What complications?"

"You saw my poor, late apprentice Belbas. He was the first, but there have been others. Many others. Duradh Mal is a sick place. A cursed one. Its sickness . . . clings to the things taken from it. I cleansed much of it . . . but some lingers. It seeps into the minds and souls of the weak, exploiting them, turning them against me."

"What of it?" Corban said impatiently. He'd had his fill of Gethel's delusions about spell-driven conspiracies in the man's letters, which made vague allusions to their schemes almost as often as they asked for money. Gethel had never bothered to specify what, exactly, he thought these faceless enemies were doing, much less how he intended to counter them—or what any of it had to do with Corban's problems.

"I had to learn to control them. To find and stop them. Some of the tainted souls were obvious. They fell into violent rages. Lashed out. Those I destroyed with the help of stronger and more loyal friends. But there were others who stayed hidden, trying to trap me in subtler snares. Thieves and spies . . . thieves and spies wearing masks of loyalty. The fire tells them true, but . . . I did not discover that at once. Some escaped me long enough to finish their schemes. One of those schemes may have replenished the sickness in the blackfire stone I purified. If that is so . . . their malice creates a many-pronged attack. Unreal voices, delirium . . . other things."

"What other things?"

Gethel's mouth opened, then closed. He shook his head, smiling the faint, wry smile of a man who knows he cannot be believed. "Monsters. They tempted men, and turned them into monsters. They corrupted whatever they could . . . even myself, briefly."

"But you can stop them?"

"I can," Gethel said. "I have." He fiddled with a little sun medallion stitched to the inside of his belt. He'd never worn any god's sign before—had prided himself on his freedom from their supposed superstitions—but Corban wasn't inclined to mock him about this one. If it worked, he'd wear a medallion of his own. A dozen of them. A hundred.

"How?"

"It is not easy," the scholar warned. "It will test your resolve. The schemes of the dark gods are ever thus: they test you cruelly, hoping that you will weaken and fail."

"I won't."

"There are two parts to it. First you must draw the poison into other vessels. It is a delicate balance. Transfer too much, and they succumb to the taint. Too little, and you put yourself at risk. It is one of the reasons I needed the shapers—they drew away the poison for me."

"You used children," Corban said. He felt slightly ill. He had sent some of those children to Carden Vale himself, promising that they'd find work on farms. At the time he'd reasoned that his claims were *essentially* true, since Gethel was staying in some farmer's house and they would be working for him . . . but he hadn't cared to look too deeply into what, precisely, Gethel was doing with them.

"They hold it better," Gethel said, "and recover faster." He rubbed a knuckle over the sunburst's pointed rays, pushing the soft gold down. He'd done it many times; the tips were flattened into bulbs, and his knuckles were callused. "It is for the greater good."

"I can't use children." There were still some lines Corban wouldn't cross. Couldn't. Or else he'd be as monstrous as any of the creatures in Duradh Mal.

"You must use *some* unsullied vessel. Or succumb yourself."

"I'll find something."

He must not have sounded convincing, for Gethel gave him a long look. "Try. Your soul depends on it."

"You said there were two parts to it. What's the second?" Corban asked. He didn't really want to know, didn't want to believe any of this nonsense . . . but something worse than hunger had driven him to eat those rats.

"Once you are purified, you must remain so. There are many ways to do it . . . as many paths to the sanctuary as there are gods beyond. But the easiest, I find . . . the most powerful . . . is to use the symbols of Celestia."

"I thought the Fourfold House didn't believe in gods."

Gethel scowled. His lower lip sagged wide, showing the stumps of his teeth. His teeth had been ordinary enough the last time Corban had seen him, but now they looked like lumps of sugar eaten away by dirty water. "Only fools would deny the gods' power. No . . . our grievance is that they demand the fealty of men, and dole out magic sparingly, giving just enough to enslave the people without curing all their ills. The gods use magic as an unworthy king uses gold: to pay their soldiers and keep the commonfolk cowed. The king does not create his gold, and the gods do not create their magic. We should not have to bow our heads to claim a power that is not truly theirs. But in times of war . . . even a free man may seek refuge behind the walls of a king's city . . . and even a wizard may choose to avail himself of the spells of faith."

"Fine. What do I do?"

"You must ward yourself in the symbols of faith. But not those the Dome of the Sun would give you. No. Those are . . . soft. Weak. They do not have the power to control the curse of Duradh Mal. You must go back to the *old* faith, the way it was when the Celestians first sealed that place and bound its darkness back. The signs were different then. Had greater strength. I will show you the correct signs, and how they can keep you safe."

"What if it doesn't work?" If he made some mistake, or forgot the instructions . . . "It takes weeks to send letters up the river."

"Longer. This has been a hard winter, and it grows harder by the day." Gethel untied the lumpy sack at his waist and held its mouth open. "But you need not depend on the river trade to reach me. Blackfire stone is not the only magic I have reclaimed from Duradh Mal."

Corban peered into the bag, then recoiled in revulsion. It was full of bones. All arm bones, all so small and light that they had to be children's. They were white as snow, almost translucent, save for a network of black veins that ran through the bone like the red flush of blood jade.

"Make a gate of them," Gethel said. Corban's horror didn't seem to touch his weary, implacable calm. "On your wall. I will show you. Then you will be able to pass through their hands to reach me, and I will be able to come to you as easily. Mountain snow or river ice will pose no obstacle."

I can't use children, Corban thought. Hadn't he just said that? Sworn it? But the words felt like a line he'd heard an actor recite in a half-forgotten play. These children were already dead. It wasn't his choice that killed them. If they *were* children. He was no expert in bones, and might be confusing bones taken from . . . lambs' ribs, or chickens, or *some* beast. It was possible. It could be.

Anyway, whatever they were, they were dead by no doing of his. Wasn't it a greater waste to discard their sacrifice?

Corban took the sack. "Thank you," he said.

Two nights later, he left the apothecary's cellar to hunt dogs.

Gethel said he needed innocents to draw off the contamination in the blackfire stone. To Corban, that meant either children or animals. The only adults he knew to be free from sin were Celestia's Blessed, and he had no intention of drawing their ire.

Children were out of the question. He hadn't the stomach for that. He hadn't the nerve either. Corban wasn't dealing with orphans in some mountain backwater. He was in the heart of Cailan, surrounded by guards and Sun

Knights. Any child he stole might have parents who would wail for justice if their sons or daughters went missing. One misstep and the wrath of court and temple would come down upon him.

Animals were easier. No one watched the city's feral dogs. Their lives were hard, desperate, short; they died in droves when the weather turned against them or sickness ran through their ranks. Packs fought one another for the best scavenging grounds. Street children tormented them for sport. No one would notice if a few more went missing. No one would care if they died. And the dogs themselves would never tell a soul.

Not only were they voiceless and unwanted, but he had no doubt that dogs had emotions. Minds. *Souls.* They would draw the curse from Corban, and by their innocence save him.

He caught his first dog near midnight.

She was a scrawny yellow brindle, not much bigger than a fox, with pricked-up ears and the gangly gait of an adolescent. One of her forelegs was bent stiff after a bad break; she hopped along on the other three, making her slower and easier to catch. At some point she had learned to trust humans, for after an initial wary sniff, she accepted the meat Corban tossed her way. With every piece he lured her closer, until the little dog was eating out of his hand.

Then he slipped a leather noose over her head, fed her one last piece of sausage, and led the unresisting dog down to the secret cellar.

AFTERWARD HE REMEMBERED ALMOST NOTHING OF THE ritual. The dog yipped once, at the beginning, but only once. There was blood, although not as much as he had expected. A knife. Drawings in charcoal and chalk: scrawled loops of runes and sigils, vital in the moment but meaningless when he looked at them again. Incantations that came into his mind word by word, and fled his memory as soon as each sound was spoken.

Corban didn't know where the chants came from, nor from where he drew inspiration for the scribbled runes. He'd never pretended to be Blessed. But there they were, burning bright and ephemeral in his mind, and vanishing like snuffed flames once used.

What he *did* remember—the only thing that lingered after the blood was cold and the chalk dust swept away— was the peacefulness that came over him when it was done.

It was as if a fever broke in his soul. The headaches, the delirium, the fog of weariness and pain that had clouded his thoughts and made every movement a trial—all of it vanished at the ritual's end.

Corban sucked in great gasps of air, unable to believe how *light* he felt. He leaped in the air, just for the joy of it, and laughed, unbelieving, when he landed. Nothing hurt. He was weaker, yes, and a little dizzy from long fasting, but the black miasma was gone and his head felt impossibly clear. He had forgotten how liberating it was to be whole.

Gethel was right. The curse of Duradh Mal *could* be controlled. Dazed by his discovery, Corban led the yellow dog off the pier. The animal followed unsteadily, breathing hard, her head down. Blood and black grit dripped from her flanks. He couldn't recall why the grit was there.

Opposite the ladder in his cellar, the apothecary had excavated a small cavern and lined it with brick, using it to store contraband. Corban had rigged a rope-and-board gate across its mouth. He pushed the animal in and closed the gate as she licked at the spiral wounds in her sides. As an afterthought he tossed in a dead fish he'd found floating on the water. Gethel had hinted that something dire would happen if he let his sacrifices die after drawing the poison from him, and Corban didn't care to find out whether he was right.

Gethel.

He needed the scholar's gate. Oh, it looked a horror . . . but Gethel had been right about the ritual, right about the blackfire stone, right about *everything*. And he was too far away, much too far. The gate would bring him closer, and all his wisdom with him.

Corban had left the bag of bones among the blackfire crates on the pier. He went back and hoisted it over his shoulder. It weighed almost nothing. The dog whined and scratched behind its makeshift gate as he passed, but the boards held it back.

Behind the ladder was a narrow space backed by a wall of crooked bricks. Corban could just fit inside if he bent and squeezed himself under the rusting rungs. The wall was patched and ugly, carelessly maintained by a dozen hands sealing rat holes and replacing lost bricks over the years. There wasn't an inch of it that didn't either bow or bulge . . . but it was straight enough to hold the gate of bones.

Fumbling in the cramped confines, Corban pulled an arm from the sack. He could scarcely see what he was doing; the angle was bad, and he hadn't room to turn his head. It was easy for his imagination to play tricks on him. The black veins laced through the small bones seemed to be shifting and spreading, responding to something in the wet dark. Inside the sack, the other bones clicked against one another, making a dry tick-rattle. It sounded almost purposeful, almost *alive* . . . and that unnerved Corban more than it should have.

He held the bony arm up to the wall, pushing it blindly against the scraggled bricks. Gods willing, it would catch in a cranny and stick.

It didn't. Instead the bony fingers spread wide and dug into the rotting mortar, anchoring themselves in the crevices they made. While Corban gaped at the skeletal hand hanging from the wall like some pale nightmarish spider, the next one scuttled out of the bag. It sprang onto the wall, climbing across the bricks until it was aligned with the first, fingers to shoulder ball.

Another arm followed, and then another. Faster than he could fathom, the bones tumbled out of the bag, and Corban stood slack mouthed at the outline of an archway drawn in animated bones before him. The sack dangled, deflated, in his hand. The space under the stairs was so tight that the knuckles of one skeletal hand brushed his nose.

He had done nothing. Almost nothing. Yet the gate stood whole before him.

Whole, but inert.

Gethel had told him this would happen. Seeing the gate, however, was entirely different from listening to the scholar describe it. *Seeing* the hands—the arms, the white clawlike fingers, all mere inches from his eyes, all possessed of something that wasn't life but moved like it—frightened him so badly that he would have fallen backward if the ladder hadn't held him up.

The dead hands waited on the crooked bricks, arms laced in a black-vined gate that reached higher than his head. Not a finger twitched, yet Corban stared at the bones with frozen, fascinated dread. *Run now, try to run, and they'll grab you. They'll pull you apart.*

Corban didn't run. Clumsily he drew the horn-handled

knife from his belt and slashed it across his palm, quickly, twice and twice again, before he could cringe from the expectation of pain.

The pain never came. The blade bit in clean and deep, drawing four lines of blood that crossed in the center and starred his palm with eight red rays, but it might have cut someone else's flesh for all Corban felt. His hand felt dull and dead, not his at all.

But it bled. He forced his numb fingers flat and pressed his wounded palm against the bricks at the center of the gate, following the scholar's instructions. Blood trickled along the channels in the rough mortar, spidering out to the sides as it fell.

One by one, like leaves turning toward the light, the skeletal hands at the periphery of the arch stretched their palms toward Corban's blood. As it passed through their fingers, the crimson stain flushed black—infinitely black, dizzyingly so, the light-swallowing emptiness of a void that knew nothing of warmth or sound or life.

The edges of the bricks adjoining the inky lines crumbled and trickled into the void. Then the bricks themselves did, faster and faster, breaking away in chunks that fell to grit and then to powder as they spun into the abyss and vanished. Soon there was nothing but gaping black inside the ring of bones. Corban, staring at it, felt the emptiness pulling him in. He had to avert his eyes and turn away before it swallowed him as well.

Gethel's magic had worked. He had a gate.

He thought of that infinite dark, and wondered: what *else* had a gate?

19

There were no mice in Shadefell's kitchens.

Sacks of flour and barley spilled across the floor, rounds of bread gone hard as granite piled the shelves, and ropes of onion and garlic dangled from the ceiling, their bulbs withered to gummy balls inside crackling paper husks. The kitchen's windows were broken and the garden door was cracked, inviting all the wild world to share in its bounty . . . yet not a roach skittered across the flagstones. The only animals in sight were the ones cut open on the counters.

Dogs and cats lay there, bound to the stone counters by dusty threads of dried blood. They had not been butchered, not properly; dirty fur clung to the bodies, crusted into wild tufts around the cuts. No one had cleaned them, and the meat was still there, dried to corrugated knobs of black leather. Only the bones were missing.

The animals were all small. Pets, Asharre guessed; none had the size to be a hunting hound or guard dog. Several had gray muzzles.

"Bones again," Evenna muttered as she came into the kitchen, arms clasped tightly over her chest. "Bones when I sleep, bones when I wake . . ."

"They were trying to fuel the fires." Asharre stroked a finger along one of the little bodies, tracing the gouges in its leg. It was strangely soothing. *His people lit the way to enlightenment.* Falcien had not lied: the solaros had followed this path before her. She pulled her hand back reluctantly. "These pets must have come from Carden Vale, so we know the townspeople reached the house. They cannot be much farther."

"Yes. Yes, that's true. Just . . . give me a moment, please." Evenna slumped against a counter, pressing the heel of her free hand into her eyes. "Maol's presence is so *strong* here. The temple in Carden Vale was nothing like this." She managed a wan smile, though she did not move her hand from her eyes. "I feel like . . . like I've eaten a bellyful of wormy plums, and I'm dressed head to toe in lead plate, and I've got to walk uphill in a hailstorm with the deadwinter wind trying to blow me straight across the Last Bridge."

Asharre swallowed the lump in her throat. She knew what Evenna meant. For days on the walk up to Shadefell her thoughts had been murky and obscure. Concentrating on anything was like trying to piece together a shattered vase without glue: she could fit together two pieces, sometimes three, but after that it fell apart into a meaningless jumble. Inside the house she felt a little clearer, but the Illuminer seemed worse. She tried to put a good face on it, though, forcing herself to sound as lightly casual as she could. "Is that all? Then it is almost nothing."

"Almost." Evenna's smile faltered. Her hand fell back to her side. In the broken light of Shadefell's kitchen, the marks of exhaustion were stark on her face. Weariness ringed her eyes in bruise purple and black; new lines etched the papery white of her skin. She looked a short step from death. "I'll manage. Let's go."

The *sigrir* hesitated. "We do not have to go now. In the morning you might be stronger—"

"How? Nothing will change." Evenna glanced around, shivering. "Nothing *can* change until we break the Mad God's hold on this place. Delaying only makes me weaker, and him stronger. We have to go on."

"As you say," Asharre agreed, quelling her unease. She pushed open the creaking door and led the way, her hand never far from her sword.

Shattered glass glittered in a wavy band along the threshold, following the door's sweep. Asharre stepped over it and into a high-ceilinged dining hall. A great oaken table ran from one end to the other, each of its legs carved with rearing serpents and the rose-braided wheels of the Rosewayns. Glimmers of gilt chased the serpents' scales and the roses' petals, though most of it had been chipped away so that it looked like an army of mice had been at the wood.

The last feast held in that hall had ended in carnage. Heavy blows had smashed the chandeliers into rib-caved skeletons of glass and metal; blood and dust dulled the fragments of crystal that clung to their rickety hoops. Not a chair stood upright at the table. Most were thrown back, as if their occupants had been suddenly roused; others had toppled over on splintered legs. The table looked like it had been washed in blood, and the walls were no cleaner.

More crusts of dried brown rimed the glasses and bowls on the table—but those, Asharre thought uneasily, did not look like accidental spatters. She lifted one and sniffed it, but the only smell was dust and mold.

Bones lay on a tarnished platter. Small ones. Child size. The other dishes were gone, but the looters hadn't dared disturb that roast to take its silver plate. She saw the delicate, dust-webbed fans of fingers locked behind the curve of a fire-browned spine, and swiftly averted her gaze.

"The last feast of the Rosewayns," Evenna whispered. "I thought that was just a story."

"No," Asharre said. She plucked a hair from a streak of dried blood on a chair back. It curled between her fingers, long and blond. "But it ended long before we came. All of this is ancient. It is none of our concern."

"Isn't it? It's all connected." Evenna dug her fingers into her tangled hair. Much of it had fallen out of her once-neat healer's halo, and it hung in a wild black shag around her shoulders. "What happened before, what's happening now . . . if only I could *think*."

Asharre studied a rose-marked cup with feigned intensity, trying to mask the wrench of pain she felt at her helplessness. They needed to find Aurandane. Once they had the sword, Evenna would be able to hold off the Maolite curse. She dropped the cup back to the table and searched the hall. The people here had come close. The dreams had told her so. She had only to follow their tracks.

The legless chairs and broken glass had been pushed aside in a trail that led from the kitchen to the two doors on the left. "This way. Someone came here."

"How can you tell? I can't see a thing."

How can you not? Asharre wanted to ask. It wasn't that dark. The hall's windows were buried inside and out in cobwebs and leaf litter, but enough light seeped in from the kitchens to pick out every detail. It had been harder to see under the glaring daylight outside.

Perhaps some enchantment was to blame. Maol's hold

on this place clearly crippled Evenna; it was no stretch to think it could blind her as well.

Asharre bit back her worry. They had to find something soon. She couldn't lead a blind woman through this hellhole. Leaving the hall's ghosts to their ruined feast, she turned to the nearest door.

It opened to a small room littered with broken furniture. The walls were gouged by sword swings, the marquetry floor scuffed and bloodied. Curling blossoms of char climbed toward the ceiling. A decapitated skeleton in a gold-trimmed doublet slumped by the far door, its long-haired skull cradled in its lap and an arrow in its ribs. The skull's teeth were filed to points, and Asharre felt its gaze following her as she walked past.

You will die here, the skull whispered, so quietly that only Asharre could hear. *Foolish to have come. Little breather, little bleeder. You will die here, little fool, and I will eat your bones. Eat, and live again. Yesss . . .* The words faded into whispery laughter, prickling the small hairs on Asharre's neck.

She drew her *caractan* and swung, smashing the skull where it lay. The yellowed bones of skull and spine cracked easily, pulverized between Asharre's steel and the sword-scarred wall. The skeleton toppled, and its whispery laughter died.

Evenna gawked at her, dropping the chair leg she'd picked up as a makeshift cudgel. She stooped and picked it up slowly, as if bending to the ground pained her. "Why did you do that?"

"I did not like how it looked at me." Asharre wiped bone dust from her blade and slid it away. Maybe she'd imagined the laughter; maybe she hadn't. Either way, it was gone.

She walked past the skeleton into a long gallery decorated with portraits on one side and dead trees in stone basins on the other. Tall, slender windows stood between each of the basins, letting in a dusty light. The fighting in Shadefell seemed to have stopped with the fanged defender in the last room, but the violence had not.

Every one of the Rosewayn portraits had been slashed and burned. Dark oils cracked as the canvas curled away from the rents in each painted face. Several had been torn out and trampled; those that remained hung askew, their features masked by dust and damage. Their eyes followed her, though, as the fanged skull's had before. Asharre refused to meet their stares, trying not to show the tension that knotted her shoulders and soured her stomach. The last thing she needed was for Evenna to think she was going mad. *Or to be going mad.*

"Oh." Evenna fingered one of the tattered portraits. "What is this?"

"What?"

"Someone's . . . fed the portraits. Or tried to." She turned one of the portraits toward Asharre. A grainy daub of blood smudged the face's lips, dripping thickly down the ripped canvas. It had been done after the picture was torn; both the painted and the bare sides of the canvas were soaked in the sludge.

You will die here. The portrait's blood-smeared lips did not move—of course they didn't; they couldn't—but Asharre heard the words clearly. She felt its gaze drill into her. *You will die here, and we will feast, we will feed, and we will live again.*

The other portraits took up the chant. *We will feast, we will feed.* Wisps of shadow stretched from the rips in their painted faces and the black blots of their mouths, reaching toward the living women in their midst. *We will live again.*

Asharre stumbled away, raising her sword defensively. She put her back to the wall, framing herself between two windows so that their weak spills of sunlight kept the hungry dark at bay.

Evenna had not moved. "What's the matter?" she asked, her eyes wide and white with fear. She clutched the cudgel like a talisman. "Why do you look like that?"

Asharre shook her head, unable to force any sound past the knot of terror in her throat. The shadows were taking on greater definition as they reached farther into the gallery. Some had grasping talons; others stretched into mouths, wide and thin and fringed with splintery obsidian teeth. They slithered toward the Illuminer, who stood blind and defenseless in their midst. The portrait in her hands was laughing, its voice a dissonant jangle of glee.

They aren't real, she told herself. *They* can't *be real. Pictures don't laugh. Shadows don't hunt. This is nothing but madness—some Maolite trap of the mind.* But she could not deny what her eyes were seeing, and she couldn't stand by as the fanged tendrils closed on Evenna. Cursing, Asharre attacked.

To her astonishment, her sword bit in. What it struck was not quite solid—but neither was it empty air. *Something* recoiled from the steel and shrieked, high and shrill as a glazier's saw on glass. More tendrils came at her as the wounded one flinched away. They snaked in from all sides, darting and flickering, trapping her in a vortex of swirling darkness.

Asharre fought desperately, her *caractan* a blur. Her sword cut through the shadows and left them thrashing on the floor. Yet there were always more, far more than she could stop. They bit at her legs, clawed at her sides, tore at her shoulders. Blood streamed from the wounds, spattering the floor as freely as her sweat.

The sight of it snapped Evenna out of her confusion. Clasping her sunburst medallion, she lifted the golden emblem into a shaft of sunlight and chanted. The incantation was familiar to Asharre—it was the same one she had used to make a dome of light in the *maelgloth*-besieged temple—but its results were not.

Instead of creating light, Evenna's prayer splintered it. The watery sunlight falling through the garden windows intensified to diamond whiteness, steadied, and burst into the shadows like a thicket of glowing lances. The creatures in the darkness shrieked and died as the holy fire stabbed their half-real bodies. And they *were* creatures, not just the claw-tipped tentacles or gnashing mouths that Asharre saw before the light struck them.

One fell at her feet, spasming. A sunbeam had burned a fist-size hole through its chest. The monstrosity had the size and shape of a man, though its head and hands were far too large and the skin over its skull was webbed like a frog's feet. Pustules raddled the spaces between its ribs, and its mouth was a wide, grinning gash that slashed from ear to ear.

Its entire body, and those of all the other shadow creatures that lay dead or dying around it, was made of wet black grit. Even as the women stared at them, the bodies dried out and dissipated into grains of black sand. Moments after Evenna's spell faded, nothing was left of their assailants. Only the scratches and bites on Asharre's body proved the attack had been real.

"You're hurt," Evenna said.

"Not badly." Asharre sheathed her sword and wiped

her palms. She tied strips of cloth around the worst of her scratches and banded her wrists so that blood would not spill over her hands. It took several tries; her hands were shaking badly. "These wounds are nothing. Save your spells."

It would have been better to wash the cuts, but they had no time for that. She wouldn't take blood poisoning in the next few hours. Asharre shouldered her pack again. "What did you do?"

"I don't know." Evenna fingered her medallion, glancing uneasily at the portraits. "That was how my goddess chose to answer my prayer. It was nothing I willed."

"Then trust to her wisdom," Asharre said. "Perhaps it was not oathbreaking. *Ghaole* do not live, and these things of dirt and shadow were deader than *ghaole*. If they were not alive, it was no sin to destroy them."

"What were they?"

The *sigrir* shrugged, feigning a nonchalance she didn't feel. "Dead."

"I suppose that's what matters." Evenna followed as Asharre resumed her exploration. The gallery ended in another debris-strewn room. A staircase spiraled into the musty gloom, its steps worn gray in the middle by decades' use. To the left was an archway of sea green stone carved into flowers and vines around rose-braided wheels.

The stairs seemed less dusty and more recently used, so Asharre went there. Ascending, she found a servants' hall. These rooms were cleaner than those below: their floors were swept, their windows washed, chamber pots and basins scavenged to suit their occupants' needs. But they were just as empty.

The smell of a goodwife's sachets, lavender and lemon balm, lingered in one. Another held a box of toys and a leash of red-and-blue leather, braided by a childish hand to fit one of the little dogs eviscerated in the kitchen. All were painfully tidy, with only the slight shabbiness of their furnishings to show that anyone had lived inside.

There was nothing in these rooms for her. Asharre knew that even before she opened the doors. They felt wrong: stale, empty, abandoned to dust and fruitless hopes of safety.

But what she sought was nearby. She was certain of it: Aurandane was close. The air was heavy with its presence. Magic crackled along her skin like the tingle of an impending storm on a hot, dry day. The fog that had swamped her thoughts for days was lifting, and in its place was a diamond clarity that Asharre had never felt before. This was the answer to their quest.

The sensation became stronger as she reached the end of the hall. She rested a hand flat on the last door. A faint breath of carrion came from the other side, but Asharre hardly noticed it. The sword was *here*. She felt its power thrumming through the thin gray wood. Trembling with anticipation, she pushed the door open.

The solaros lay rotting on a death-stained bed. His hands were folded atop his chest, the chain of a sun medallion woven through his waxy fingers. Unkempt stubble covered his cheeks; veins spidered green down the side of his neck, vanishing into the collar of his stiff yellow robes. The cold had slowed the body's decay, but his chest was puffed with foulness. Two small bottles of dark glass rested by the foot of his bed, both empty. The lip of one was stained with the final, fatal residue of its contents.

She did not see a sword. A wave of anger, hot and unexpected, rose in her chest and made her clench her blistered hand. Aurandane *was* here. Somewhere. It had to be.

A slip of paper rested under the solaros' medallion. Asharre had overlooked it in her haste and frustration, but Evenna worked it carefully from the man's fingers. The writing was larger and clumsier than that in the solaros' diary, and it stumbled rightward down the page as if his hand had grown heavier with every letter.

"All it says is 'Forgive me. Hope baited the snare,'" Evenna said. She put the note down and peered at the dead man's lips, then at the empty bottles by his bed. "He might have wanted to write something else, but the poison caught up with him first. Two bottles of dreamflower extract. I'm surprised he stayed conscious long enough to finish the second one."

"He had the sword," Asharre said. She threw open the trunk at the foot of his bed, but all it held was a heap of old clothes—moth eaten and crumbling, not even the priest's—and another handful of clinking, poison-filled bottles.

"Yet he stayed mad, and he died." Evenna rubbed her temples. Pain wrinkled her forehead. "What does it *mean*? The answer's there, right at my fingertips, but I can't think. He came to Shadefell. He found the sword. Then he . . . drank enough dreamflower extract to kill an ox, wrote a nonsensical note, and died? Why?"

"Because he was weak." Asharre gave up on the trunk and went back to the middle of the room. Evenna looked startled by her vehemence, but the *sigrir* pretended not to notice. To have hope, to have a *weapon,* and to choose death instead of a fight . . . that was pure, contemptible weakness. She would make no such mistake.

But why do we need a weapon when we came here for a cure?

She dismissed the question as soon as it came. Of course they needed a weapon. The attack in the gallery had proved that. This place was infested with monsters and demons, and Aurandane would defeat them. Then they could find a cure, if the sword itself was not one.

Standing in the center of the room, Asharre held her hands out at her sides and inhaled slowly, centering her thoughts as the dream-Falcien had taught her. It felt ridiculous, but he had sworn that it would work, and she had nothing else to try. The *sigrir* focused on her need, letting her consciousness flow outward, seeking, from that one command. *Find the sword.*

She opened her eyes. Her gaze drifted down from the bed and the corpse, past the clothes she had scattered on the floor, to the floorboards themselves. The cracks between the boards fascinated her. There was a secret significance to them, a purpose to the lattice of crooked black lines between the planks. As she watched, the darkness between them rippled and flowed out of the cracks, spreading into a slow spiral on the floor.

"What are you staring at?" Evenna asked.

Asharre did not answer. Her eyes stung with the strain of keeping them open so long, but she *had* to know what the shape would be, and blinking would ruin it all. She could not blink; she dared not speak. She had to hold the magic.

The wavering lines that had been floor cracks crept up the wall, pulling themselves along like climbing caterpillars. They stretched and dripped into a symbol Asharre knew: the sunburst Falcien had shown her, drawn in wet black shadow. Four over four. Their sign of salvation.

"It is in the wall," she said. The vision disappeared as soon as she moved, but Asharre had what she needed. She felt along the wall where she'd seen the sunburst, and when one of the boards wiggled loose, she pulled it out.

Aurandane waited in the space between the walls. A net of tattered strings cocooned the sword, and it was wrapped in an old yellow robe, but Asharre recognized the long, slim silhouette. She reached in, brushing aside the strings, and too late froze as the memory of Falcien's death flashed before her. Strings then, too, snapping and loosing black death.

But these were already broken, and they threw no quarrels at her. They had none to throw. As she peered into the hiding hole, Asharre saw that the strings were, indeed, part of a trap . . . but they were linked to sun medallions on bent-back sticks, not crossbows, and both sticks and strings were broken. Corroded. The sticks were dry and brittle, the strings brown and frayed, though they could only be a few days old if the solaros had set them. *More than time has touched them.*

Why should that surprise her, though? Magic had guided her to Aurandane; magic had cleared her path. She closed her hand around the steel and pulled it out, shaking off its wrappings.

Aurandane was a thing of beauty. It was heavier than she'd expected, more like her own *caractan* than the longswords that the Sun Knights favored. Hilt and scabbard were engraved with winding prayers in a tongue she did not know. The blade was steel edged with some brighter metal, white as new silver, and unmarked save for a thin fuller that ran along two-thirds of its length. A sky blue spinel, tiny as a teardrop, shone on its pommel. Hints of lavender and dusky rose twinkled in its facets, the color of the heavens at the first kiss of dawn.

"Take it," the *sigrir* said to Evenna, holding the sword flat on both hands.

The Illuminer recoiled. "Why me?"

"It is Celestia's creation. You are her servant. You should take it." *And I do not want it.* Her head ached miserably from whatever small, nameless spell she'd used to find Aurandane; the blisters on her palm throbbed as if filled with liquid fire. If that was the cost of magic, she wanted no more of it.

"It's a sword. You should use it."

"I have a sword. This one is consecrated to your Bright Lady. It is the weapon we came here to find, the key to banishing Carden Vale's curse. Will you take it or no?"

"I . . . I suppose I will," Evenna said. She lifted the sword hesitantly.

As soon as the blessed blade was taken from her grasp, the agony in Asharre's blistered palm subsided. She flexed her hand surreptitiously, trying to hide her relief. "Good. Then we have only to find the missing townspeople so that we can cure them. We know they are not here. Where would they have gone?"

"To pray," Evenna answered. "To the last, best sanctuary of our faith." The dark-haired woman gestured through the tiny windows to the shrine in the central courtyard.

There Shadefell's tower rose, its verdigrised spear point sharp above a ring of cloud white cherry trees. Celestian sunbursts glimmered in a gilded band around the tower's peak, bright despite the centuries. Paths of crushed marble, barely visible through the wild weeds, wound through the neglected gardens and converged on the tower like the strands of a ghostly web.

By the time the women reached the tower, dusk stained the cherry blossoms blue. A cool wind sighed through the bracken, raising gooseflesh on Asharre's arms.

The scratches inflicted by the gallery's dust creatures burned and swelled under their bandages, but she ignored the pain. Evenna had no magic to spare for her. The prayer in the gallery had drained her, and it seemed that carrying Aurandane was doing the same. Her abbreviated sunset prayer—shortened to two chanted lines, as it was for the Sun Knights on the battlefield—had relieved her weariness for a while, but she was visibly flagging as twilight fell. She used the sword like a walking stick, leaning heavily on the weapon.

But it will lend her strength. It must.

A spill of ash stained the earth on the lee side of the tower. Spring rains had washed the finer dust away, leaving a pebbled hill of charred bone fragments. Blue stalks of *morduk ossain,* half hidden in the gloaming, fringed the ash heap. They did not quite reach the walls, and Asharre let herself be reassured by that; perhaps the fact that Maol's weeds could not touch it meant Celestia still protected her sanctuary.

Whether she did or not, they were committed. Asharre sent a silent prayer to her sister's goddess and another to the old spirits of her clan. She looked back to see that Evenna was near. Then she pulled open the door, streaked with verdigris and rust, and stepped into the tower.

Black silence folded around her. It smelled of sulfur and the sour rust of old blood. Time and massive explosions had made a wreckage of the upper floors; beams and boards tumbled around her, filtering the moonshine into scattered fingers of silver light.

The stairs were a ruin of mangled iron and splintered wood, and the floors were more gaps than whole. A mouse couldn't have balanced on those teetering beams. Below, a pit yawned.

It was a rough thing, a pool of deeper darkness that had been blasted out of the earth rather than dug. She saw bits of metal embedded in its walls, a spiral of nailed boards leading into its depths, and nothing else: only the endless rift.

"Down," she told Evenna, moving back to the open door. The night's clean air tasted sweeter than wine. "They went down."

"It's pitch-black in there," the Illuminer said dubiously, peering into the ruins.

"Light a torch," Asharre suggested, though she felt a flicker of unease at her own words. A torch would signal to anyone down there, human or *maelgloth,* that they were coming.

But they could hardly walk blind into the depths, and the noise would ruin any attempt at stealth anyway. She shook away her doubts while Evenna fished out her lantern and struck a spark to it. Juggling the lantern with her awkwardly held sword, she followed Asharre back inside.

The lantern made it even clearer that no shovel had touched the pit. Asharre traced her fingertips over the ridged earth. Metal fragments studded the dirt. Steel was the most common, but she saw brass, melted tin, iron gone orange with rust. Most of the shards looked like shattered chain links, but not all. Some could have come from plate   or pots, or bent knives, or even chunks of statuary.

There were pieces of bone among them, too, none larger than her smallest finger. Here and there she saw dented fragments of plate with bits of bone lodged in the dents as if driven in by great explosive force. Gobbets of dried gore crusted over the metal.

Falcien. The realization made her drop her hand in horror. A death like his—if the victim was wearing plate mail, if he was wrapped in coiled chains—could have made those layered spatters on the walls. A hundred of them could have dug a gaping pit.

Would a hundred suffice? How many deaths would such an excavation take? Asharre couldn't imagine; she didn't want to. She looked away. Evenna was staring past her down the steps, her face drawn and sweat on her brow.

"This isn't a sanctuary," the younger woman whispered. "This is the heart of corruption. Bright Lady save me, it is so *strong*."

"Can you do it?" Asharre asked. "Do we go down?"

"Yes. I must." Evenna stepped forward. Black smoke hissed away from her lantern, surrounding them in a grainy mist. There was a pattern in its swirling dance . . . one she had seen before, Asharre thought.

"Wait," she said. Scraping a handful of dirt from the wall, the *sigrir* picked out the bits of bone and metal until only coarse earth was left. She spat into the dirt and mixed it with a finger to make a paste. The blisters on her bandaged hand broke open, soaking through the cloth and into the mud. Asharre ignored it. However unpleasant the mix, it was only a means to an end.

She dipped a finger in the paste and brought it to Evenna's brow. "Let me ward you."

The Celestian frowned but did not move away. "Where did you learn wardings?"

"From a friend. It should keep away the smoke—it will protect us against breathing in the poison." Hoping she remembered the sigils correctly, Asharre daubed the mud into a wavering circle, then added eight lines radiating outward and a dot at the end of each line. Four over four: Celestia's sunburst to keep her children safe. She painted the same onto her own forehead, unable to see the marks but confident that she had followed the shapes Falcien showed her in the dream. When the last stroke was in place, the mark seemed to melt and ripple, sinking into the Illuminer's skin. The mud turned an ugly shade of purple, then lightened gradually, through mottled green into the yellow of an old bruise and vanished. Evenna winced, but Asharre felt nothing. She rubbed a finger over her own forehead and felt only smooth skin. The dirt paste was gone.

And it worked. The murky smoke drifted away, buffeted by circling winds that never ruffled the ebon locks around Evenna's ears.

"There is no magic without the gods," Evenna murmured uneasily, eyeing the rippling haze. But she lifted her lantern, and they went down.

The steps were planks wedged into the pit's sides. Asharre picked her way down cautiously, switching her *caractan* from hand to hand as she circled the abyss. It was much deeper than she'd imagined; the vault seemed to bore into the mountain's heart. Soon the wooden webbing of the collapsed upper floors was lost to shadow, and the world shrank to the wavering sphere drawn by Evenna's lantern.

Farther down the creaking steps, the walls became smoother. No blood discolored them this far down; no metal glinted at their sides. Heat rose from the pit's depths, and with it the spoiled-egg reek of sulfur.

The blasted earth gave way to green-black stone, its mortarless pieces fitted so cunningly and the joins polished so smooth that the walls seemed to have been grown organically as a single whole, rather than being put together by mortal hands. It felt *old,* older than Shadefell, and in its way as inhumanly majestic as the soaring glass of Heaven's Needle.

She didn't belong here. No human belonged here. The

Rosewayns had been trespassers in their own day, digging into the nameless depths and putting up their flimsy stairs as if they, or anyone, could pretend to own this place.

They were fools if they'd believed it. This place belonged to an older power, a greater one. In its eyes human bodies were sacks of walking meat, held together by the thinnest puppet shells of skin, and as Asharre moved closer to its lair, she saw herself and Evenna the same way. Prey. *Food.*

But we have teeth. We can fight. This battle was won once. She prayed it could be again.

A crooked door waited at the end of the stairs. Behind it was a furnace red glow. Asharre knew that glow; she had seen it in her dreams.

The door's planks were baked into rattling unevenness. A wrist-thick chain coiled next to the door; a broken hasp dangled from the stone wall at its side. A sunburst in a spiral of delicate runes stood on the heat-warped wood. Vicious, black-edged scratches defaced the gilded carvings, but enough remained for the emblem to be identifiable.

The sight of it sent a stabbing pain through Asharre's head. Hot tears filled her eyes. She squeezed them shut, shaking her head dumbly. Beside her, the light swung and swam as Evenna's grip faltered on the lantern.

"Open it," the Celestian whispered, teetering on the sheathed sword. The words were half a sob. "Open it. Oh, Bright Lady, how was this *done* to you?"

Asharre clenched her teeth and took hold of the door's handle. It was like grabbing a fistful of coals. Her hands *burned,* though the pitted iron was no warmer than the hilt of her sword. She felt the sticky heat of fusing flesh, smelled her skin roasting. The pain was maddening but she jerked the door open then ripped her hands away, cursing Shadefell and her own weakness and whatever magic corrupted Celestia's symbol into something that caused such pain.

Beyond it was a charnel house. Bones, some whole but most burned black and small, piled up into ringed walls higher than the top of her head. The gaps between them glowed red as a setting sun.

An old, old man shuffled among the bones. He was tall but stooped so low that his chin nearly touched his chest, giving him a vulture's aspect. Loose robes hid his hands to the fingertips; loose skin fell in papery white folds around his throat, so voluminous that it seemed he wore a fleshy beard. He looked up slowly as they entered, and Asharre saw that his eyes were completely black. Liquid darkness filled them from corner to corner, trickling out in rivulets that he wiped away as he spoke.

"Visitors . . . ?" His head bobbed slightly. "Yes. Visitors. What brings you here?"

"Who are you?" Asharre edged through the doorway and into a space between the rings of bones, where she had room to use her sword. Ridiculous as she felt menacing such a frail old man, she did not lower her guard. Not against those eyes.

"I could ask the same of you." His smile was gentle under that empty, empty gaze. When he opened his mouth she saw that it was a glistening hollow. No teeth. A too-thin tongue, like a wet black worm. "I do not have many visitors anymore. Not for . . . a time." Puzzlement creased his brow and was gone. He wiped an inky tear from his eye and brought his finger to his lips, licking away the stain without seeming to notice it. "A time. Months? Years, maybe. Time . . . disappears down here. It flows differently. But I do not wish to be discourteous. Gethel, that was my name. Is my name."

"From Carden Vale?"

"Carden Vale? I . . . spent some time there, yes. Not long. My studies called me away."

"To this place?" Asharre flicked her sword's tip at the blackened bones.

Gethel ran a hand over a ridge of grubby spines. "Yes. It must look . . . macabre . . . to you. Terribly macabre. But there was a great mastery of magic here once. A great mastery. I came to learn. And so I did. So I did." Another black tear seeped down his wrinkled cheek, vanishing into the folds around his mouth. He licked that one away as well.

"And the people of Carden Vale?" Evenna followed Asharre into the sweltering room, her hands moving nervously across Aurandane's engraved hilt. "Why did they come? To learn the same arts?"

"To help." Gethel's smile widened as he canted his head toward Evenna. Asharre shifted her weight into a fighting stance, wondering if that smile was predatory. "They came to seek sanctuary, and to help me. They did, for a time . . . but the burden became too heavy for them, and they had to lay it down. Even the faithful. There were a few . . . there were a few who were not faithful. Monsters. Monsters, yes . . . but monsters can be hunted down, or held at bay. Controlled." His black eyes went up to Asharre. "Can they not?"

"Better," she said, keeping her eyes fixed on the man and willing Evenna to hear the command in her words. "They can be slain."

"No," the Illuminer said, slowly and softly, as if she were fighting her way out of a bad dream. "No, that isn't right."

"Kill him," Asharre snarled.

"No. That is . . . that's what he *wants*: to have the sword given to him by mortal hands. 'Hope baits the snare.' Oh, Bright Lady, it did. It did. And it almost took us." There was a clatter of metal against stone as Evenna hurled the sheathed blade away.

"Are you mad?" Asharre demanded. "Kill him!"

"Not mad," Gethel whispered. "But disappointing, yes. Disappointing. I had hoped . . . you might help. You have magic. I can sense it. I can taste it. But it seems you are . . . tainted. I can taste that too." He made a small movement of his hands. Evenna cried out and collapsed, her head thumping against a curved wall of bone. The sigils on her brow had reappeared, were smoking. Asharre rushed at the old man, *caractan* screaming through the air.

She wasn't fast enough. He repeated the gesture, stepping around a low wall with a speed she would never have believed possible. Pain split through Asharre's head like a shock of red lightning. She heard herself screaming, heard her *caractan* clatter on the floor, heard herself fall beside it.

The runes she'd painted on her forehead were scorching. Agony forked into her skull, hotter than a torturer's iron. *Why? They were to protect us,* she wondered, before a new pulse of pain drove all semblance of thought from her mind.

Gradually the agony abated into lesser beats. Tears dripped from her cheeks. Her hands clutched feebly at the floor's blistering stone.

Footsteps approached and stopped before her nose. It took an enormous effort to roll her eyes up to meet Gethel's blank, black gaze.

"It was a worthy try," he whispered, kneeling beside her. He took her hand gently. She couldn't resist. She could only stare as he unwrapped the dirt-crusted bandages to show the blisters broken there, four over four, weeping black liquid that turned to smoke as it dripped across her palm. "Brave, yes. Brave. But his touch is in you . . . and monsters must be controlled."

20

The last of the *maelgloth* rested its chin on the rim of the pit and died. A final shudder wracked its hairless body. Was it agony, Kelland wondered, or relief? The *maelgloth* wanted to die—had begged for it, once Malentir restored enough of their sanity for them to realize the horror they'd become—but the Thorn had taken his toll in pain before letting them cross the Last Bridge.

He'd forced them to contort their bodies into a ladder, locking arms and legs around the corpses of their fellows to build him a way out of the pit. Where their limbs stuck out at inconvenient angles, the Thornlord lopped them off and threaded them back into the grotesque scaffolding. The *maelgloth* endured that, too, without moving, though some could not help but chew on the nubs of exposed bone—others' and their own.

Kelland had watched as little of it as he could. He would have preferred to give the *maelgloth* a quick, merciful end. They were monsters, but not by choice, and they didn't deserve to suffer through the Thornlord's games.

But they needed his magic, and it was better to let Malentir prey on monsters than innocents. Wasn't it? Kelland fingered the wavy rays of his medallion, wondering if his acquiescence in the Thorn's cruelties was its own subtle corruption.

Would it be virtuous if I suffered a little more? That was an old heresy. Four hundred years ago the Colchennar had believed that ease itself was a sin, and that the righteous lived in ascetic suffering. Now and again a few fools revived Colchennar practices, wanting to show off their piety. The Blessed discouraged them—forcibly, if necessary—whenever they heard of a renewal, but the Colchennar heresy was a persistent one. People wanted to believe there was some holiness in fasting or mortification. It was easier, in many respects, than making the real choices that virtue required.

Like the choice that faced him now, between one evil and another. Kliasta or Maol? Cruelty or madness? What choice could he make that was not a mortal sin?

Use the tools you have, the High Solaros had taught them at the Dome. *Be careful of them, be conscious of them, but use them. Miracles are hard to work empty-handed.*

The Thornlord climbed from the pit. The ivory streaks in his hair shone gold in the knight's sunlight: the blood on his hands melted into drifting skeins of black vapor. A faint, sated smile lingered on his lips.

Kelland hoped the High Solaros' wisdom was greater than his own. "Is there anything else that must be done here?"

"The wards must be rewoven," Malentir said, "and it would be wise to slip in new traps for whoever might come to test them. The two of us cannot replace the old seals, but we shouldn't need to. Our wards need hold only long enough for the Lord Commander's soldiers to reclaim the ruins. Gethel's *maelgloth* are dead; he has no more allies in this place. Even simple wards will prevent him from returning to replenish his stores of blackfire stone. If we strike quickly, we should be able to trap and kill him before he realizes what happened and flees to Cailan."

Bitharn was standing at the pit's edge, looking at the ladder of broken bodies with mingled pity and disgust. "How could these wretches have brought Ang'duradh down?"

"They didn't." Malentir left the cavernous dungeon, ignoring the corpses in the pit, and turned his attention to the runes that glimmered around the shattered door. "*Maelgloth* would have been a minor inconvenience to Ang'duradh in its strength. The power that brought the fortress down was not theirs."

"Then what was it?" she asked.

Malentir touched the horn that held the dirt he'd scratched from the pit. "I will know soon. After we have left this place." He moved away, studying the runes farther from the door.

Kelland went to stand beside Bitharn after the Thorn had gone. He raised his sun medallion over the entwined corpses, bearing formal witness to their fate, and began the too-familiar Pyre Prayer to guide their souls across the Last Bridge. They deserved that much, whoever they had been.

Bitharn joined her voice to his. They had spoken this prayer over plague victims in chapels and murdered travelers by weedy roads; they had blessed the bodies of soldiers, servants, children. Never *maelgloth*, though. Never in a place like this.

As if sensing his unease, she reached over and took his hand. He squeezed her fingers, grateful for her strength and understanding. Grateful for the gift of love. She had been there, always, unfailing; she had braved Ang'arta's iron teeth and the poisoned gloom of Duradh Mal for him. And she was here, now, without his asking, offering solace and support and confidence when his own began to fail.

Bitharn bolstered his faith. She wasn't a threat, never had been. The only threat had been his own refusal to admit the truth. The lie was the sin. Not the love.

Lifting her hand along with his own, Kelland wove the invocation for sunfire into the Pyre Prayer.

Celestia's power suffused him, lighting his veins afire. The magic followed the shape of his words, accepting his guidance—but when it had taken that shape it swelled beyond him, overwhelming his control like a flood bursting from its dike. Golden flame descended upon the *maelgloth*'s bodies, devouring their gaunt gray limbs and gushing from their empty mouths. It melted the dirt from their eyes and turned their skulls to bowls of flame, then burned through those as well.

There was a glory in it—but a terror, too. The sunfire didn't stop when the corpses were gone. Kelland couldn't *make* it stop. He had no more control than if he'd been a pebble on a riverbed trying to rein back the waterfall at its end. The torrent of magic drove the knight to his knees. He wasn't praying anymore; he was gasping for air, incapable of thinking, let alone speaking, a word. Each breath felt like it was about to ignite in his lungs.

The pillar of fire soared higher, splitting apart as it leapt from the corpses' pit into the empty ones and scoured those with fiery whirlwinds. It filled the air with billowing sails of flame, white and yellow and red; it enveloped Kelland and Bitharn in a maelstrom of wind and fire, stranding them on an island of bare rock while holy fury roared around them.

The knight had never seen such a spellstorm, had never imagined that he might call one. Magic poured through him, raging through his bones, scorching every fiber of his body with blissful fever. It threatened to consume him. Mortal bodies were not meant to hold so much of the divine; mortal minds could not encompass such glory. Humans were fragile vessels. Filling them with such power was like pouring molten steel into a cut-glass vase: it could not help but destroy them.

But in that brief, incandescent moment between holding that fire and being destroyed by it, there was incomparable beauty. And power. So *much* power.

There was nothing he couldn't do with such magic, Kelland thought dizzily, intoxicated with divinity. Nothing. He looked to the doorway where the Thornlord had retreated to watch them from the shadows with flat black eyes. He could destroy Malentir as he had destroyed the bodies of the dead *maelgloth*. Easily. In this moment, with Celestia's strength coursing through him, he could purify all the foulness in the dungeons of Duradh Mal. Yes, he could destroy the Thorn, and . . .

. . . and what? Leave the people of Carden Vale to their fates? Let Maol's influence spread unchecked to Cailan, where thousands—*tens* of thousands, if men carried it like the plague as they fled aboard ships—might succumb? Abandon Bitharn to madness and death? *He* couldn't lead her safely out of Duradh Mal; unable to pass through shadows, he would have to walk through its blighted halls and whatever dangers still dwelled there.

No. He still needed Malentir. He couldn't kill the man yet. But the possibility was there, the *knowledge*. Before Kelland looked away their eyes met, and he saw that the

Thornlord knew it too. The day of reckoning might be postponed, but it would come.

Not yet. Kelland turned back to the dungeon, the magic still roaring in him.

The pits were scoured clean. Not a fingerprint of dirt remained in them. Sunfire darted up the walls in curlicues of white-gold flame, searing away the black mold that clung to the crevices between stones. It flashed across the ceiling and spun in the hoops of manacles; it splintered on the blades of ancient knives and danced through the tongues of crumbling whips.

Finally the last scrapings of black dirt were hunted down and burned, the last gasps of ebon smoke consumed. The Bright Lady's magic vanished as suddenly as it had come, stripping him of its strength. Kelland swooned forward. Bitharn grabbed his shoulders to steady him, pulling him back from the edge of the pit where the dead *maelgloth* had burned.

"Showy," Malentir said, stepping out of the doorway where he'd waited out the inferno. His hands were hidden in his sleeves, his face unrevealing. "But a waste. We have wards to replace and Maolites to kill. Or had you forgotten?"

Bitharn shot the Thorn an acid glare, keeping one hand protectively on the knight's shoulder. "We serve as the Bright Lady wills."

"Yes. I saw that. It was impressive. Impressively stupid, perhaps. There are other things he could, and should, have done before trying to purify all of Duradh Mal."

Was there a warning in those words? Kelland looked up at the Thorn and saw the cold certainty behind the man's impassive mask. The assurance was on the other side, now: Malentir could kill both of them as easily as Kelland could have destroyed the Thorn a moment earlier.

But he, too, held back. *Not yet.*

"It wasn't my choice," Kelland said, getting back to his feet. His throat was raw. Bitharn passed him a skin of tepid water, and he swallowed with some difficulty. It helped, a little. He stoppered the skin and handed it back. "The magic did what it wanted. I was the conduit, but I had no control."

"None?" The Thornlord raised an eyebrow.

"Very little."

"Curious. But, as I said, unwise. We must seal this place before we go, or else all we've accomplished here will have been the removal of a few *maelgloth* and one chamber's worth of blackfire dust. I have no doubt that Duradh Mal holds more. As we do not have time to burn it all, we must reweave the wards. If you still have the strength to manage that."

"I do." *Bright Lady willing, I do.* Kelland stooped to pick up his shield; he'd dropped it when the prayer surged out of his control. The floor swam under his feet and it took all his concentration not to sway with it, but he managed to hide the daze. From the Thorn, anyway. The crease between Bitharn's brows said he hadn't fooled her in the slightest. "Show me where."

"Come." The Thorn turned in a swirl of black-slashed robes, and the Celestians followed him. On the other side of the doorway, Malentir pointed to the walls.

There the runes that anchored the wards of Duradh Mal were faded and defiled, scratched away by the *maelgloth*'s hands. They'd attacked the sigils so ferociously that they'd left blood and broken nails smeared across the stone, but they hadn't been able to eradicate the markings altogether.

Pushing past the fog of his exhaustion, Kelland spoke a prayer for godsight so that he could read the magic more thoroughly. With its aid, he saw the runespells that clung to the walls in threads, flickering like tattered battle flags. Sullied, battered, but still proud.

The complexity of the interlocking wards astonished him. Guardian enchantments were more the domain of the Illuminers than the Sun Knights. True wards required weeks, sometimes years, of painstaking labor, every bit of it as precise as a master jeweler's craft. These were not the simple martial prayers that threw walls of sunfire across a battlefield or kept a campsite guarded overnight; these were designed to baffle and bind other Blessed, equally skilled in their own gods' arts.

He felt like a child who had just learned to whistle a note and was being asked to replace an entire cathedral choir. These spells were doubled into intricate, misleading braids; even with the aid of godsight Kelland wasn't sure what they did, much less how to repair them.

But Maolites were not clever foes, and he only had to hold them back for a little while. He brought his hand to the wall.

A subdued glow followed his touch. Kelland traced the shapes of the spells he knew, invoking light to blind, fire to burn, purity to destroy the bonds that held dead men in thrall. Fragments of the old magic flowed toward his inscriptions; they melded into the new markings, then spread outward, spinning their own complexities into a shining web he couldn't follow. The sigils hung white on the dusty stone, blazing for a heartbeat after his hand had passed, then fading to embers and silent black.

Malentir watched his work intently. "Interesting," he said when Kelland was finished. He offered no elaboration, but began adding his own sigils, drawing them with his ivory stiletto rather than his hand. Bone white runes joined the golden lattice, hiding among the Celestian spells like thorns nestled under luminous leaves. Those, too, dimmed until Kelland could scarcely distinguish them from the stone.

By the time the Thornlord finished, Kelland was shaking from the strain of holding the godsight for so long. Sweat dampened his braids and the padding under his mail. It was a sweet pain, less terrifying than the loosed rage of the sunfire; it was just enough to make him conscious of his mortal limits while inspiring him with the power of the divine. But he couldn't hold it forever. That was one of those mortal limits, inescapable as the clodding earth of his body: even a weak spell would burn through him if he held the magic too long.

Tingling needles stabbed his limbs. His head seemed weightless, wrapped in wool. He was very near collapse.

"Take us back to Carden Vale," he told the Thorn.

Malentir smirked. "You don't want to return through the *perethil*?"

"No." He didn't look at Bitharn. She'd be insulted by any suggestion that he was trying to spare her. Brave to the point of foolishness, she was . . . although he could hardly claim to be free from that flaw himself. "We'll have to use it to get to Shadefell, unless I'm mistaken." That was something the Sun Knights had guessed at after Thelyand Ford: the Thorns could walk through shadows, but only the ones they knew. Malentir had never laid eyes on Shadefell, had never learned how darkness draped its walls. They would have to go through the *perethil* to reach it.

"You are not."

"Then once more is enough. Take us back to the farmhouse."

"I suppose I will, since you ask so sweetly. Come."

Kelland released the last glimmerings of his spell, relieved to let go and yet bereft at the loss, as Malentir began his own. The darkness of Duradh Mal settled around them, black and vast and echoing with the reverberations of the Kliastan's prayers. In the darkness Bitharn pressed closer, resting her arm against his. Offering strength, not seeking it. A bulwark against the night.

"Thank you," he whispered, leaning in. He didn't know if she heard. A cold wind rose around them, snatching the words away. The Thorn's prayer was nearly complete.

The chill intensified, tightening its coils around them until Kelland thought his bones must crack, and slowly lessened its grip as blue starlight returned to their world.

They stood in Renais' abandoned farmhouse, facing the corrupted *perethil*. Its gate was gone. The fallen stars had returned to their places, somehow. Their metal edges gleamed, cutting the starlight to slivers on the black-washed canvas.

"Rest," the Thornlord said, moving smoothly to the door, "and pray, if you like. In the morning I will turn the *perethil*."

No sooner had he gone than Bitharn fumbled out her flint and lit a fire in the kitchen hearth. She filled a pan with water that Kelland had purified that morning and set it over the flames to warm. The task was so ordinary that it seemed almost absurd after what they'd lived through in Duradh Mal . . . but there was some solace in mundanity, and he could certainly understand why she'd want a bath.

By the time she'd found soap, a brush, and a basin to stand in, the water was bubbling. Bitharn wrapped a padded glove around the pan's handle, glanced at him, and wrinkled her nose. "I'm not sure which of us needs a bath most."

"There's enough water for us both."

"True. Only one basin, though. I found it, so I get it." She emptied the pan's hot water into a larger bucket half full of cold water, then poured some back into the pan for him. Kelland found a mouse-nibbled blanket to hang in the larder's doorway. Bitharn set the soap and brush under the curtain, then nudged him into the larder. "You get to wash with the carrots."

Kelland didn't argue. He went in, folded his clothes atop a sandy box of turnips and carrots, and sluiced away the filth of Duradh Mal while Bitharn did the same on the other side of the faded blue cloth.

His bath left the farmer's floor puddled with water, but neither of them cared. The night's chill covered them in gooseflesh, but neither of them cared about that either. It was enough to be free of the ugliness that Duradh Mal had wrapped around them like an invisible, leprous skin. Clammy clothes and a wet floor were a small price to pay.

Bitharn thrust a splint into the kitchen fire and lit one of the farmer's candles. Cupping its flame with her other hand to protect it from drafts, she started upstairs. Kelland followed closely, never more than a step away.

At her door she paused, holding the candle between them. "Stay with me tonight."

Kelland froze. Astonishment warred with exhaustion, leaving him momentarily mute. Love, desire, a thrill of apprehension so strong it verged on fear: all tangled up together, knotting in his throat. *What is the right choice?* "My oaths—"

Bitharn shook her head impatiently. "You are so *stupid* sometimes. I'm not asking that. It's only—" She stared at the candle, biting her lip. "I don't want to be alone. Not tonight. Not after what we've been through, and what we face tomorrow. Is it so hard to understand?"

"No," Kelland said, abashed.

There was only one bed in the room. Snuffing out the candle, Bitharn drew the farmer's blankets back and over them both. She curled with her back to him, the soles of her feet barely touching his legs. In moments she was asleep.

Sleep was slower to come for Kelland. Desire troubled him, but only a little; it was doubt that kept him awake.

He'd been wrong again. Too consumed by his own doubts and fears to consider hers. Too *thoughtless.* Lying beside her, with the moon trailing gossamer scarves overhead, Kelland felt a peacefulness settle over him that he had seldom experienced outside prayer.

He loved her. He needed her. She shared his devotion and strengthened it; and he was, once more, grateful for and humbled by that truth.

Why is that forbidden?

Was it forbidden?

Bysshelios kept his magic.

What did that *mean,* though? Had Bysshelios kept the faith, or betrayed it? He'd been a heretic, there was no question of that . . . but Kelland wasn't sure what the Byssheline Heresy meant for him. If anything.

He could ask the High Solaros when he returned to Cailan. If he lived to return. Here and now, he had more pressing concerns. Survival, and sanity.

Kelland brushed a stray lock of hair from Bitharn's neck and turned his face to the sky. He had to protect her in Shadefell. Against ironclaws, *maelgloth,* corruption, and madness . . . whatever was there, he had to keep her safe. That much, he knew to be clear and true.

That much, Kelland hoped as he slid into slumber, he could do.

At dawn they woke, prayed, and went downstairs to find the *perethil*'s stars wheeled into a new formation. A pair of skeletal hands, hacked off at the wrist and bound together by filthy string, dangled from the jeweled handle. The bones were stained with rings of rust: they'd come from a prisoner in Duradh Mal.

"He kept a souvenir," Bitharn observed dryly while making a porridge of oats and apples. "At least this one's small, so it should burn faster. That's thoughtful."

"You're in a grim humor today."

"Yesterday I was in Duradh Mal. Tonight I'll be in Shadefell. I think I'm allowed a little grimness." Yet she remained in a determinedly light mood, avoiding any mention of the *perethil* or their destination until the westering sun turned the horizon to a lake of flame. Then Bitharn's cheer dimmed, and she stole anxious glances at the painting's stars while she gathered their belongings and counted her arrows.

Kelland spent the time reading and rereading the papers the Illuminers had left behind, trying to retrace the steps of their desperate search. Aurandane. They'd gone in search of the Sword of the Dawn . . . but how had they intended to find it? And what would have happened if they did? He looked at the poisoned *perethil,* remembering the gouges its smooth metal had scarred on a skeleton's hand, and shivered.

Malentir returned at sundown. He held the black scrapings from the *maelgloth* pit gingerly in one hand, disdain etched on every line of his features. He dropped the little bundle onto a table and moved away.

"You could have left it outside," Bitharn said, eyeing the pile.

"That would have been unwise. Better to suffer its presence a little while longer and allow your holy companion to destroy it." The Thornlord dipped a cup into a barrel of clean water and drank. "I have learned all that can be gleaned safely from that. I have no more use for it, and it should be destroyed. It is not safe to keep."

"Why?" Bitharn asked, at the same moment that Kelland said, "What is it?"

"The second question answers the first, so I will speak to that one," Malentir said. He refilled the cup, watching its ripples until they stilled.

"The physicians of the Khamul Rhayat," he said, "believed that a spirit of corruption caused disease, and that it reproduced in various humors depending on the nature of the illness. The bottled breath of a fevered man could carry his ailment to others; the black blood lanced from a plague victim's buboes carried that sickness' spirit; the flooding from a rice-water sufferer's bowels, the same. Every disease had a corruptive spirit, driven to carry its affliction to a new host and dying if it did not find one. Transferring the spirit to a new victim did not cure the old one—indeed, this theory was of no use in *healing* anyone—so the Rhayati physicians eventually turned their attentions elsewhere.

"In the west you have your Blessed, and few know of the Khamul Rhayat. But I found an echo of their teachings here." He gestured at the cloth-wrapped ball. "That is blackfire dust. It is the cause of the madness and misery we have seen; it is what destroyed Ang'duradh. It is much like the Rhayati spirit of corruption—except that it does not carry any mortal sickness, but the Mad God's blight on the soul. And it is no mere humor expelled from a sufferer's body, but *that body entire*, condensed and consumed until all that is left is the essence of madness tied by threads of flesh and bone."

"I don't understand," Bitharn said.

"Think of how charcoal is made. One begins with a great pile of wood under sod. A slow fire burns through the heap—carefully, without too much air, so that it smolders without being allowed to break into flame. When it is finished, what is left is not truly wood, not anymore, but something closer to the combined essence of wood and fire. It has been transformed: it burns hotter, longer, with little smoke. There is less of it, but it has more power.

"Blackfire dust is like that, except it begins with human bodies and human souls instead of wood. Maol's power consumes them in a controlled burn, never bursting into its full fury. After death, its victims do not rot like the corpses of ordinary men, returning to earth and worms, but wither into the dust we saw in Duradh Mal. That dust is the essence of the Mad God's corruption in human flesh. Every speck of it is capable of spreading that blight. Breathe it as smoke, or let it touch one's blood, and it is more dangerous still.

"That is the curse of Duradh Mal. When Gethel broke the seals, the blackfire dust escaped. It seeped into the water and soaked into the earth, poisoning the valley. It may have spread faster when he brought the townspeople into those blighted halls, turning them into monsters. In Shadefell, I imagine, we will find more of that. The Rosewayns were not said to be numerous, but they held that place for many years, and I cannot imagine they did much to purify it while they were there. I've long thought they were called to that place and held there in thrall to Maol, rather than choosing it for the reasons they claimed."

"How do we shield against it?" Kelland asked.

"We stay within your light." Malentir's smile was grim. "A prospect I do not relish, but better by far than the alternative."

"What about Aurandane?" The knight put aside the last few pages he'd been reading. "The Illuminers believed they could find it, and that it could protect them."

"Then they were fools," the Thorn said indifferently. "The Sword of the Dawn is gone. Someone would have found it long before now otherwise—some knight of your order, or a scavenger like Renais. And if it is *not* gone, if it has lain in Shadefell all these years, then it is best left untouched. The curse on Renais' painting is nothing next to what Maol could do with a *perethil* as powerful as Aurandane."

"Why would this—Gethel, you said his name was?— why would he dig that up?" Bitharn asked, still staring at the little bundle of blackfire dust. "What could he *want* with it? Surely he didn't set out to unleash a Maolite plague in the world."

"It is unlikely that was his original intention. But we need not speculate. If he is in Shadefell, I will ask him."

"And you expect to get a sensible answer?"

"Yes." Malentir drained his second cup. "We are very good at interrogation."

"No torture," Kelland said.

"No," the Thornlord agreed. "Pain would be . . . inefficient, even if he can still feel it. There are better ways, and faster."

Unsure what to make of that, Kelland said nothing. He drew his sword, laid it across his lap, and meditated over the naked steel until the last light vanished from the sky. Bitharn busied herself making a kettle of tea no one wanted. As twilight gave way to luminous black, the knight found his eyes drawn to the *perethil*'s shifting, impossible stars.

Anxiety weighed heavy on him. Could any of Carden Vale's people still be alive? How? As *what*? He thought unwillingly of the *maelgloth* in their pit, their bodies decaying into blackfire dust even as they struggled to cram more of it into their mouths. If the townspeople were lucky, they'd be dead. If they weren't . . .

And the Illuminers? What would become of them if Maol's madness took root in their souls? If they found Aurandane, and it was—as Malentir had suggested—only a conduit of corruption?

Had the Illuminers known what they faced when they went to Shadefell? He didn't think so. If they had realized the danger, they wouldn't have rushed off to face it, undertrained and unprepared as they were. Only ignorance allowed them to be so brave . . . and ignorance in battle carried a terrible price.

During the Wars of the Five Fortresses, when Baoz's faithful marched against the armies of the rebel Maghredan, both Baozites and Maghredani had captured each other's Blessed and subjected them to unimaginable depravities, transforming them to blood-raged *ansurak* and unleashing them upon their former companions. They did the same to other deities' servants, when they could, and though the Blessed were stronger willed than other men, when they finally broke they became the most terrible monsters of all.

That was well over a thousand years ago. The tales of those wars were almost as fanciful as those about Moranne the Gatekeeper or Auberand and the Winter Queen—but they didn't have to be true to make Kelland worry. If Gethel *believed* they were true, and tried to enact those rites on the Illuminers, their suffering would be nearly as hellish as if they actually became *ansurak*.

And if they did . . . No one in living memory had faced *ansurak*, not in this part of the world. They were creatures of a bygone age, mythical as solarions or firebirds; they existed only as skulls on the walls of Ang'arta and drawings pressed between the pages of yellowed books in Craghail's libraries.

In the west, at least. In the east and the south, they had never completely vanished. Could Gethel have brought them back?

Kelland hoped he was wrong. But he couldn't *know*. He couldn't do much of anything besides wait, and brood, until the *perethil* opened.

An hour before midnight, its stars began to fall. As before, they tumbled of their own accord, and as before, each was accompanied by an unearthly peal. The sound was utter discord: some fell fast and erratic, stumbling into the last one's echoes, while others sang dolorous and slow. Each sounded longer and louder than the last, until the final star stood alone on the black, and the *perethil* tore a shivering rift into the world.

The Sun Knight stood. He straightened his surcoat, squared the sun medallion over his chest, and reached out to ensure that Bitharn was beside him.

She was there. He went in. The last thing he saw, as the *perethil* claimed him, was Bitharn raising her own sunburst to the dark and her lips moving in an echo of his prayer.

21

Black mist swathed Kelland as he entered the *perethil*, burying his boots and climbing up his legs. It did not blind him, as it had before. This time a murky, poisoned light filtered through the world, rising from the wet earth and falling from the shapeless heavens.

It illumined a never-world. Narsenghal. Shadows surrounded him, though there was nothing to cast them. They rose and fell like moon-pulled tides, and he was the moon that drew them. The gloom shaped itself into crude imitations of his form: faceless heads, lumpen legs, tenebrous arms that clung to their torsos only briefly and then fell back into the shadows, dissolving.

"What is this place?" Kelland muttered. He was the only solid thing in the world. There was no sign of Bitharn or the Thorn. The ember of his goddess' presence in his heart, constant even when he was not channeling her power, had gone out; he couldn't feel Celestia with him here. Around him the shadow faces mirrored his question with gaping, sagging mouths, fumbling through imitations of speech.

It is . . . yours. The answer came from all around him: it was the shadow faces who answered. They spoke in a varied susurration, each one articulating a word or a syllable before its voice dropped below a whisper or rose into a howl and another took up the thread of their thought. *We are yours. We are* you. *Your future, once you go to Shadefell. Your failure. Your fate.*

The shades' voices, initially as shapeless as their forms, sounded more like Kelland's with each word. Distorted, to be sure, always a half octave higher or lower or possessed of some inflection that the knight himself would never use . . . but recognizably, unmistakably, his. And although he knew it was part of the *perethil*'s snare, he couldn't help being unsettled by listening to a chorus of his own voice hissing at him, or by the constant cacophony of his own sighs and shrieks behind it. That alone was bad enough, but he could hear a hunger in their voices that unnerved him. The shades weren't content to imitate him; they wanted to *be* him, to steal his warm and living reality and wear it as their own.

Kelland didn't know whether that thought had been implanted in his head by some magic of the *perethil* or was recalled from some long-ago lesson at the Dome of the Sun, but he didn't doubt it was so. The desire in the shadow faces' writhing, and their frustration at the flaws in their mimicry, were too raw to be false.

He walked away, although he had nowhere to go in this swamp of shadows. The faceless shades followed, whispering and muttering at the knight's heels like a pack of ghostly dogs. Kelland ignored them. The first time through the *perethil,* the Mad God had assaulted him with raw filth and depraved lust. An obvious attack, and an ineffective one. This time, it seemed, the *perethil* was trying a different trick.

Do you think this only a trick? Wrong, wrong, the murmuring shadows said, and their cacophony took up the refrain, shrilling and sighing: *wrong, wrong.*

This is your fate. The fruit of your doubts. The Thorns never tested you, not really. They kept you, but they never tried to break you. The Spider wanted you whole. You would have been useless without your power. Yet still you doubted, even then, and that seed has flourished into fatal bloom.

You stand on the brink of heresy now. You know this to be true. Sleepless nights, doubt-filled days. You took the hand of evil, embraced the Thorn you should have slain. Blind fool, flailing fool—you flounder in love, pushing it away in your clumsiness, and you will fail her too. Fail . . . and fall . . . and join us here, forgotten.

I won't, he wanted to reply, but before he could say the words—before he had even finished forming the thought—he was stumbling out of the *perethil's* dreamscape and back into the world he knew. It was just as dark, just as filled with swaying shadows . . . but here they were cast by real things, and they danced only to the wind.

A tower loomed before him, circled by ruined halls. Its tarnished point thrust into the bellies of low-hanging clouds; its base was garlanded with drifts of snowy petals, silver-blue in the moonlight, that had fallen from the cherry trees behind him. Celestian sunbursts glinted at the tower's tip, but Kelland drew no comfort from them. All that emblem meant, in this place, was that her worshippers had failed before.

Bitharn stood beside him. Her face was bloodless and her hands white knuckled at her sides; she stared at the tower's door as if she read her death written in its rusty stains. Malentir waited a pace away, maddeningly serene.

"How do you stay so calm?" Bitharn asked the Thorn.

"How do you not?" He raked his striped hair behind his ears, looking past her to the tower's door. "We train for this. Don't you? Anything that an enemy might do to us, any torture they might inflict, we have already visited upon ourselves and survived. What men most fear is what they do not know, and there is precious little left unknown to us. Anyone who survives to leave the Tower of Thorns has already endured, or at least seen, every torture my mistress can devise. Anything Maol might attempt, next to that . . ." Malentir shrugged. "Anyone will break if tortured long enough. But it would take more than two walks through a *perethil*'s illusions to accomplish that."

"Might not for me," Bitharn muttered. She unhooded her quiver, glancing at Kelland. "Ready?"

He nodded, raising his sword. Holy flame limned the steel. Surrounded in its nimbus, Kelland led the way in.

Rubble littered the threshold. The ruins of the tower's upper floors, destroyed by some vast explosion, lay in rusting chaos around a gaping pit. Shards of bone and mangled metal studded the pit's walls. Wrinkled black ribbons flapped on them, and after an instant of blank incomprehension, Kelland realized that they were the remains of blood and flesh. Wooden planks hammered into the walls led downward in an uneven spiral.

The sense of evil that permeated the place was overwhelming. It pulsed in the air, suffocating; it wept from the walls like dungeon damp. Kelland's little light was fragile and distorted, and the pitiless deep pressed in from all sides. Kelland clenched his teeth and bowed his head, counting his breaths, until his will and the sacred flame steadied.

To his surprise, the Thornlord seemed even more affected. Malentir's eyes were closed. His throat trembled;

beads of sweat gathered at his temples. It took him longer to overcome the spiritual assault than it did the knight.

"I thought you trained for this," Kelland said.

"We do." Malentir laughed hollowly. He wiped his brow with the back of a wrist. The steel thorns of his bracelet left red scratches across his forehead. "Oh, we do. I was . . . made to remember it, that is all. The moment is past. Let us go."

Kelland started down the groaning stairs. Bitharn stayed close, her bowstave slung across her shoulders to free her hands. Malentir followed silently at their rear. The pit's walls grew smoother as they descended, shifting from metal-panged earth to glassy green-black stone. Occasionally the knight caught glimpses of pale faces trailing after them inside those stones, as if they were dark windows to some other place . . . Narsenghal, or an echo of it . . . but he steadfastly refused to glance their way. Whether he saw them because the *perethil* had planted the idea or because the faces were really there, there was nothing to be gained by staring at them.

The air became hotter and fouler as they descended. Kelland's holy light began to flicker at its periphery; curls of black smoke hissed away from his sword. A smoldering red glow signaled the pit's heart below the last twist of the stairs.

At the bottom of the steps was a crooked door propped open by a coil of chains. Flakes of broiled skin clung to the door's iron handle. Past it lay a labyrinth of bones. Dull crimson light seeped through the labyrinth's rings; it was momentarily obscured as a stooped old man shuffled out.

"Gethel," Malentir said. The name sounded like a curse. The old man lifted his head, turning slowly toward them. Kelland recoiled. The ancient scholar's eyes were solid black, like spheres of polished obsidian. Inky liquid dribbled from them.

"Yes," Gethel replied. His words were faintly slurred. The inside of his mouth glistened as black as his eyes. "Yes, I had that name."

The Thornlord made a small gesture, so quick that Kelland nearly missed it. His voice became sharper, more imperious, resonant with magic. The knight felt a breath of winter pass by him in the furnace pit. "What have you done here? Tell us everything."

Gethel flinched. Black tears crept down his cheeks. He licked them away with an ebon tongue, thin and long as a snake's. "Everything . . . ," he repeated, fixing his empty eyes on the Thorn. "Everything would take a long while to tell."

"You came here to study blackfire dust, did you not?"

"Yes."

"What did you learn?"

"It is . . . powerful. A great power." Gethel scratched the back of his head. The withered skin parted like wet paper, and a chunk of discolored bone fell from his skull. He brushed it away absently, revealing a bloodless hole filled with crumbling black grit. "Magic without the gods. I have the secret at last. At great cost . . . oh, great cost . . . but it is mine."

"Poor fool," Bitharn murmured. No one else seemed to hear her.

"What cost?" Malentir pressed.

"Devotion. Such devotion. So . . . *hard* for the weak-willed to accept. So many who should have helped me turned against me. They were envious. Greedy. Fearful. They were dealt with, yes, I dealt with them. Traitors. Monsters that hounded our heels. Dead things that lurked in the deeps. Many of my loyal helpers gave themselves to buy me time. But it was not in vain. Not in vain. I found the answers. I found the truth."

"And what of them?" interrupted Kelland. "What happened to your 'helpers'? Are any of them still alive?"

Gethel turned his blind black eyes onto the knight. His gaze was repellent; meeting it felt like being doused with filth. "Yes. Some few."

"Where are they?"

"In the workshop." He lifted a gnarled, long-nailed hand to the labyrinth of bones behind him. "The safest place. Consecrated. Monsters come here, too . . . but they can be dealt with when they do."

"What about the Celestians who came here before us?" Kelland asked. "Two women. Did you see them?"

"No. Only monsters came here. Only monsters."

"What are you *doing* with the blackfire stone?" Malentir broke in impatiently.

"It is . . . it can be a weapon. An ignoble use of magic, I know. But necessary to repay my patron. Without him I should never have had the opportunity . . . so I will send him the treasures he wanted, the weapons my shapers made . . . and when he has enough, when he is finished, I will turn my research to its true ends. Wisdom, and the betterment of the world."

Contempt hardened the Thorn's aristocratic features. "Who is this patron? What weapons did you make, and where did you send them?"

"I cannot tell you," Gethel whispered, shaking his head. Black grains spilled across his shoulders from the hole in his skull. He wet a wrinkled fingertip on his lips and dabbed them up, licking away the grit like a starving man savoring crumbs. "I swore an oath. I cannot give his name."

"Someone fell hard here," Bitharn murmured quietly to Kelland. She tilted one end of her bow unobtrusively toward the floor. "Broken glass. Herbs spilled on the ground. Not long ago."

He refrained from looking down himself, not wanting Gethel to realize what Bitharn had seen, but nodded to acknowledge her words. Locked on each other, neither Gethel nor the Thorn seemed to have heard her.

"I cannot say," the scholar moaned again.

"You can and you will." Malentir twisted one of his bracelets, pressing it viciously into his own flesh. "Who was it? What did you send him?"

Gethel whimpered, stumbling forward as if struck from behind. Murky tears funneled into the creases of his cheeks. "Corban. His name is Corban. I sent him quarrels. Hollow tipped, set with blackfire stone. The dust . . . becomes stone and reacts . . . unusually . . . to blood, once it's had a taste to whet its hunger. It was . . . what he wanted. Why he paid."

"Where is he?"

"Cailan," Gethel mumbled. "I sent the quarrels to Cailan."

"You truly were a fool." The Thorn dismissed his spell with a single sharp word. "There is nothing else of use to be had from this one. Kill him."

Bitharn already had an arrow set to her bow. Before the last word passed Malentir's lips, she pulled back and let it fly. The arrow whipped between the two Blessed and buried itself in Gethel's throat.

The old man crumpled onto the wall of bones behind him. He sighed as he slid down, and the sound was echoed by a whistling through the bloodless hole that the arrow had punched in his throat. The doubled sigh went on and on, endless and unbearable. Gethel's body had fallen out of sight behind the bones, but Kelland saw a plume of black dust fountaining above them. His prayer-granted light shrank back as the dust billowed toward them, and the sense of evil intensified in its reach.

Baffled and alarmed, the knight strode forward to see what was happening.

Gethel was collapsing. His skin was a wrinkled husk, like the shell of a rag doll with its stuffing torn out. Black smoke poured from his ears, his nostrils, the hole scratched in his skull. It spread out with astonishing speed, stretching sooty fingers from the corpse to the labyrinth around him. The smoke vanished into the crannies between the piled bones, and all around him Kelland heard the groan of walls tearing themselves up from their foundations, loud as the breaking of the world.

Birharn cried out in dismay. Kelland glanced back and saw that the smoke had reached past the labyrinth to the pit's blood-painted walls, high overhead. Wherever the cloud touched the walls, bone and metal fragments slid toward it like iron filings to a lodestone. Ropes of dried blood twisted up to join them, binding the shards of steel and bone into thrashing whips that cut off any retreat.

In front of him, the walls were pulling themselves apart with fleshless hands. The hands dug through the loose bones like five-legged ants, grasping pieces and fitting them together. From the rubble, skeletons rose. Some were so old that the bones of their limbs were brown and fractured; their skulls had no teeth, their feet no toes. Clouds of blackfire dust hung between their bones, forming ghostly replacements for missing ribs and jaws. Other skeletons were fresher, more intact; rags of skin clung to their shoulders and their joints squeaked over cartilage.

The stench of sulfur and decay choked the air as they rose from the wreckage of the walls.

Some of the skeletons showed grins full of filed teeth, and all had bones webbed with blackfire corruption, but they were human. Mostly.

The four creatures that loped out from the back of the labyrinth to join them were not. They walked on two legs, and they had the rough shape of men, but their skin fitted over them strangely: bulging in some places, sunk into wrinkled pits elsewhere. Shiny scar tissue filled their eye sockets, smooth as rippled water. Steel rings pierced their throats, dragging down the wattled skin. Their tongues were enormous, so thick and long that Kelland couldn't imagine how they fit inside the creatures' mouths. Each was raddled with a line of holes that whistled as the creatures flicked their monstrous tongues through the air.

The song they sang was strangely hypnotizing. Thin and discordant, it slipped under Kelland's armor, past the protection of his holy light; it vibrated along his skin, creating a physical sensation as real, and as hard to ignore, as centipedes crawling over his flesh. He could shut it out with an effort, but that was a distraction in itself, and in the tumult of battle it might well prove fatal.

"That's the monster that led the miners to the boy on Devils' Ridge. The one they ate," Bitharn whispered "There's more than one of those?"

"What are they?" Kelland asked.

"Mine," Malentir answered, shaking back his sleeves. His wrists were wet with blood. The bracelets drew it up along their thorns and diffused it between their points, surrounding his hands in crimson fog. "Destroy the lesser creatures."

"Don't look at me," Bitharn said. Her voice was steady,

but tension radiated through every word. "Bones don't bleed. My arrows won't help."

Only a scattering of small bones remained of the labyrinth's walls. The skeletons were crowded too closely for him to count, but Kelland guessed there might be twenty to one against them, and he could feel the Mad God's touch corroding his magic. Sunfire wouldn't work. Even if he could have destroyed them all with it, he wasn't eager to unleash that prayer here. It had raged out of control in Duradh Mal; he had no idea what it might do in this place. Magic became dangerously unpredictable, even deadly, when one god's power directly challenged another's. If he had no alternative, he might risk the inferno . . . but there were better choices.

"Steel Mirror." It was an untried spell, something the Sun Knights had developed in the wake of Thelyand Ford but never tested. They hadn't faced masses of the walking dead since that battle.

But it was the best weapon they had. Bitharn nodded, reaching back to her quiver, and her bow began its savage song. At such close range she could hardly miss. Each shaft lodged in a hollow rib cage, one after the other.

With the eyeless ones' discordant whistling in his ears, Kelland recited the unfamiliar words for Steel Mirror. The prayer drew from the one all Celestia's Blessed learned to keep themselves warm through northern winters. That one used fragments of glass to amplify the sun's heat just as ordinary mirrors amplified light, filling a sickhouse or a castle with goddess-granted heat. The variant was—if it worked, if he remembered its verses—more lethal.

Sunlight twinkled on the bodkin in the nearest skeleton's chest. It was the barest of glimmers, scarcely visible through the smoke, but it shone more brightly from the two flanking the first, and brighter still from the two flanking those. The light danced from arrowhead to arrowhead, gaining brilliance with every leap. Halfway through its course, it was strong enough that a blazing beam could be seen lancing from each skeleton to the next, and the steel bodkins burned inside each one as if their hearts were fallen stars.

The last skeleton burst apart in smoke and glowing cinders as the sunfire struck. Immediately the light retraced its path, still intensifying with each leap, and springing out to new ones as Bitharn continued to empty her quiver. The skeletons in its path crumbled into belching smoke, burning away too swiftly for a single dust mote to escape. As the last arrow-struck skeleton toppled into white-gold flame, the holy magic vanished. It was over before Bitharn had finished shooting.

Kelland blinked the stinging afterimages from his eyes. They'd destroyed a third of the skeletons. Perhaps half. But the rest kept coming, trampling through the dissolving smoke of their decimated companions, and now they were too close to risk a second prayer. Knots of dark smoke pulsed in the skeletons' chests; embers flared in their eyes. And Bitharn was nearly out of arrows.

Abruptly Kelland realized that the skeletons' march and their own breathing were the only sounds he could hear. The eyeless ones had fallen still and silent, their tongues clamped, bloody, between their teeth. Ivory mist climbed their limbs in ghostly vines, drawing out streaks of livid blackfire wherever they passed. Those dark streaks reacted violently to the incursion of Malentir's magic; the spell strands tumbled and spun around one another like the breaking of cloud and light at the end of a storm, each tearing at the other with no sign of which might prevail. The Thornlord was as motionless as his victims. Shadows cloaked the man, obscuring everything but the outline of his face and his long white hands. Utterly absorbed in his own arcane fight, he was oblivious to the danger marching toward them.

"Stay back," Kelland told Bitharn. He could hardly hear his own voice over the click of fleshless feet. Bitharn nodded and retreated toward the stairs, trying to stay out of the thrashing tentacles' reach.

If he'd had time, Kelland would have woven a trapfire wall to guard his back and give the others some protection . . . but there was no time. He'd barely chosen his position and raised his shield before they were upon him.

The skeletons raked at him with fleshless fingers, prying at his mail; they belched sulfur and fire, blinding him in a many-throated haze of smoke. Kelland bashed them away with his shield, trying to keep them from reaching Bitharn or circling around to attack him from behind.

One seized Kelland's blade, trying to wrench the weapon from his grasp even as its holy aura blasted the thing's fingers away. They died around him in waves, unable to withstand his goddess' fury, and yet they kept coming. He wondered if they *wanted* to die, as the *maelgloth* had, or if they simply had no minds left with which to comprehend their doom.

Or, he thought bleakly, as a malignant presence rose overwhelming in his soul, blotting out his own magic like a cloud over the sun, if they were only meant to delay.

The marching dead slowed and stopped. A great shadow rose above them. Where it fell, the light fled from the skeletons' eyes, the coiled smoke flowed up through their ribs to join it, and their bones clattered, empty, to the ground. The eyeless ones resisted an instant longer, but they, too, surrendered with spectral wails, their innards dissolving into fine black sand and pouring from their mouths. As it spilled across the floor, that sand melted into black mist and sifted upward into the shadow. Malentir gasped, staggered by the sudden dissolution of his spell.

Kelland lowered his sword, straining to see through the forest of paralyzed and failing skeletons. Sweat and smoke-stung tears blurred his sight. But he saw a shape rise from the shadows, and he felt its power roll over him like the tide.

The creature in the darkness wore Gethel's tattered skin as a cloak. Only that wrinkled fall of skin, and the glowing heat of its eyes, gave it any shape. It loomed over them, three times the height of a man, and its breath was a furnace blast. The cloak of skin burned where it touched that infernal body, leaving patches of bright, ash-edged lace smoldering across the dead man's hide. The bones of Gethel's skull could be glimpsed in its face, rising and receding like the spines of a reef in a wind-wracked sea, but nothing more was left of the man. Kelland *knew,* as he stood before that hellish presence, that the scholar's soul was gone, consumed by the deity he had unwittingly served.

Its appetite had not ended with Gethel. As the shadow creature gathered magic into itself, it destroyed more than the skeletons and long-tongued slaves. It drained the walls' thrashing tentacles into inert limpness; it drew the pit's unnatural gloom into its own body.

And in that hunger—in the sheer extremity of the power gathered against him—Kelland found an unexpected sliver of hope. With the Maolite magic pulled back, consumed to fuel the avatar before him, only ordinary darkness remained . . . and in it, the knight saw a gleam of steel amid the ancient bones on the floor.

Aurandane. He felt the echo of Celestia's magic reverberate in the fallen sword, muted and garbled but still as familiar as the return verse to a song he had begun. He sensed that his goddess' presence in her *perethil* was not whole—it felt sick, somehow, or wounded—but it was still, unmistakably, hers. Unlike the magic of the poisoned *perethil* that had taken them to Duradh Mal and Shadefell, the Sword of the Dawn was still sacred.

But it was too far away to do him any good.

Bitharn or Malentir might be able to reach Aurandane, but Kelland was on the wrong side of the pit. He'd have to pass the thing in Gethel's hide to reach it. The shadow's fiery eyes fixed on Kelland as if alerted by his thoughts, and he wondered if it knew he had seen Aurandane. If it did, they had no hope at all.

Submit, it thundered, in a soundless voice that crashed against the insides of Kelland's skull—the voice from the *perethil's* shadowland. His own, stolen and amplified and made monstrous. *Give in, and your death will be quick. Fight, and you will suffer.*

Kelland shook his head mutely. His throat was parched; his lungs felt blistered. The shells in his hair cracked from the heat. Celestia's presence was fragile as a candleflame in his soul, and it dimmed by the moment. "No. You cannot have this place."

Submit. You will die. She *will die.* The burning eyes lifted from him, and the suffocating intensity of its presence relented. Behind him, Bitharn screamed. The scream went on for an eternity, tearing at him, but he did not turn. He kept his face hard, despite the plummeting emptiness in his gut, and never lowered his guard. It was the hardest thing he'd done in his life.

A pity. The fiery eyes returned to him, and he heard cruel amusement in its thought. Bitharn's scream ended, cut off in a wet thud of flesh against stone. Something cracked viciously; he didn't know if it was her bow or her bones.

I will ask you once more. Only once. A gentle death. Or agony. I will make a puppet of her corpse. A whore for worms and maelgloth. They will make their own holes, burrowing into her flesh. Give in, and you may rejoin her just as swiftly.

Delay him, said a second voice in his thoughts, as direct as the shadow creature's but infinitely softer. *Delay him, and I will strike.*

He didn't know whether the new voice was a fragment of his desperate imagination or some new gambit of the Mad God's meant to distract him, but Kelland ignored it as he had the first booming threats. In his peripheral vision, Malentir got shakily back to his feet. The Thornlord's shielding shadows were gone. Blood streamed from his nose and mouth, shockingly bright against the pallor of his skin.

Listen to me, fool. I sense the sword, as you do. Malentir's black eyes were fixed on the knight's. There was no mistaking the source of that second voice now. *Distract the creature, and I will use it to strike him down.*

Will you? Kelland wondered. *Or will you flee through the shadows with the sword, and take it back to your mistress in her tower?* But what did it matter? He had no prayer of defeating the shadow creature on his own, and Bitharn was dead, or near it. Aurandane was their only hope. Aurandane, and Malentir.

The Thornlord wiped the blood from his mouth. It turned to vapor between his fingers, paling to the yellow of old bruises and then luminous ivory. He closed his eyes, breathing hard, and took a step to the side. Toward Aurandane.

Kelland thought of a winter wood, and of sunlight on snow. Of another Thorn, and another fight.

He had walked into death then, with so much less at stake. He could do it again.

Leading with his shield, the knight charged across the carpet of scattered bones toward the fire-eyed shadow. As he did, Kelland drew on the faltering flicker of Celestia's magic, struggling to gird and arm himself with faith in this place that blasted it away.

The thing in Gethel's skin coughed a guttural command as he came. The fallen skeletons' bones exploded. Jagged shards tore into Kelland, clanging off his shield and lacerating his flesh. Smaller fragments slashed across his face. He turned his head to the right, trying to protect his eyes, and saw Malentir dart toward the sword.

Almost there. Three steps. Two. Kelland had to hold the shadow creature's attention; he couldn't stop, couldn't fall. But he slowed, driven off balance by the shattering bones and dizzied by the sweat and blood that ran into his eyes. And as he stumbled in his blindness, the skin-robed shadow unhinged its jaw and exhaled a torrent of swirling murk.

It was not fire. It burned like fire, scorching Kelland's skin and covering his arms with drooping black blisters, but it reeked of corruption and it clung to him like mucus, dissolving his flesh and melting into it so that he could not tell where his own body ended and the Maolite filth began. The stench of his own putrefaction filled his nostrils. He could see *things* swimming in the blisters' bulges, half formed and hideous and growing larger by the moment.

He prayed. He gagged, and prayed, and ran, angling left to pull the shadow creature's attention away from Malentir. Celestia answered his call, filling his soul with radiance and purging the taint from his flesh. The burns healed, shedding great ashy flakes; the blisters burst, expelling their fetal monsters. They spattered on the ground, dying, as Kelland charged on.

The creature in the shadows was waiting. It raised a fist of solid darkness, Gethel's fingers dangling from its wrist in a smoldering bracelet, and when the knight came within reach it struck.

Kelland saw the blow coming and raised his shield over his head to deflect it. He slashed a counterstrike at the creature's arm, even as he dodged the incoming swing.

His shield caught the shadow giant's fist, and might have deflected it . . . but the steel groaned, corroding into rust faster than he could believe. The oak panel in the center crumbled into spongy splinters; the leather straps turned brittle and gray and cracked apart. Before Kelland recovered from the shock, the creature struck his arm through the decayed remnants of his shield.

The impact knocked him sideways. It was like getting hit by a giant's maul—and the physical blow was the least of it. His flesh rotted as quickly as the shield had. Creeping corruption purpled his arm, spreading outward from the point of impact. At its edges, feverish heat and the swollen tenderness of a sickened wound assailed him. At its center, he felt nothing at all. That flesh was dead, or beyond dead; sickly yellow bone poked out from its soft, stinking pulp. Kelland knew that if the fist had hit his chest, or his head, he would be a corpse already. Even with the blow partly deflected, he was dying fast.

But he had served his purpose. Malentir crept silently behind the hulking, faceless creature, and Aurandane was in his hands. Swift as a snake, the Thorn drove the steel into its side. He was holding it wrong, Kelland thought, dizzy and distant—like a spear, not a sword—but that did not seem to matter. The Sword of the Dawn plunged smoothly into unreal flesh, its blade sheathed in a nimbus of watery, tainted blue.

And the thing in the shadows was dying, melting, breaking apart. Sheets of darkness sloughed from its body. The scraps of skin and blackened bone that remained of Gethel crumbled into pale gray ash, translucent smoke, nothingness.

It didn't feel like victory. It didn't feel like anything.

Kelland couldn't breathe. Everything below his neck was a single pulse of pain. Malentir dropped the sword, and its blue blaze dimmed as it sank into the creature's failing ashes. It was a slower fade than usual, gentler, as if Celestia was loath to leave a place taken from her for so long. But it went black in the end.

Silence fell. The faraway gleam of starlight sifted through the wreckage of the tower, sending shafts of softer grayness into the bruised dark. Kelland could hear nothing but his own labored panting and the creak of chains. He couldn't hear Bitharn breathing.

Blindly the knight tried to push himself up, failed, fell. He was so weak. His magic was gone; the shadow creature's parting blow might have poisoned him, might have killed him, but there was nothing he could do to heal himself. He hadn't the strength to summon a fingerflame.

Someone stooped over him. His fingers caught on soft cloth, a warm limb. The Thorn staggered slightly and pushed him away. "Be still."

A wintry chill washed through the knight as Malentir prayed over him—but it was a cleansing chill. The fever in his chest subsided; the throbbing of his arm became almost bearable. The numbness of near death receded, leaving him wracked with pain. "Bitharn," he mumbled when the constriction in his chest relaxed enough for him to speak. "Where is she? Is she alive?"

Malentir's eyes shone milky white. He straightened, surveying the pit. "Ah. It is not pretty, knight. Be glad you cannot see."

Fear seized Kelland's throat with icy fingers. He grabbed at the Thornlord's sleeve again, cutting his hand on the man's barbed bracelets. "Is she alive? Help her. *Heal her.*"

"Be still, I said." Malentir jerked away, hobbling through the dark. "You do no one any good by stumbling around like a halfwit. She is alive, and I will not let her die."

"Thank you," Kelland breathed, collapsing onto the rubble.

The Thornlord stooped and began another spell. Ivory ghost-light swam around him, illumining Bitharn's broken body for the heartbeat it took the glow to seep beneath her skin. Even before the woman stirred, Malentir left her and turned his unearthly gaze to Kelland. "This is not kindness. It is a debt. You owe me a life . . . and you will soon have the chance to repay it. Aurandane was poisoned."

22

Bitharn opened her eyes to a constellation of pain. Every muscle in her body ached. Her bones ground against one another and popped at the slightest movement, as if they'd all been forced out of alignment and hadn't quite slid into their proper places. Blood and sweat soaked her clothing. Her lips were crusted with something that tasted of copper and salt—*blood, of course it's blood*—and her teeth wiggled loosely when she poked them with her tongue. She still had them, though. That was something.

She still had her sight too. It was so dark that she wasn't sure of it for a moment, but she could make out a smoldering glow behind the walls of bone, and when she touched her lids she could feel the eyes moving underneath. She breathed a sigh of relief. Blindness was one of her great terrors. What good was an archer who couldn't see to shoot?

Her fingers slid downward and brushed against her cheeks. She felt the tracks of something too sticky to be tears, too thick to be blood.

Eyes. Bitharn jerked her hands away, flinching. No. *No.* She could see. Those couldn't be her eyes dripping down her cheeks.

Unless they were healed. Was that possible? Maybe. She didn't remember exactly what the thing in Gethel's skin had done to her. She didn't want to. The flashes that she did have were enough. It had soaked her in a cocoon of slime that forced its way into her mouth, her nose, every seam in her skin. She'd drowned in it, had swallowed it, had begun to *welcome* its foulness, just as she'd lusted after the corpse caresses in the *perethil.* That was the worst part, the *wanting . . .*

Stop it. Stop. It's over.

Bitharn fumbled for her bow. It was miraculously unbroken, although she doubted that she had the strength to draw it. Not that it mattered. Her arrows were gone; the last three had tumbled out and broken when that shadow thing threw her against the wall.

"You're . . . well?" Kelland asked hesitantly, offering a hand. His shield was gone. The sleeve of his shield arm was soaked with blood and what looked like, but wasn't, pine tar. Malentir must have prayed over him, too, for the arm itself seemed whole inside that ruined sleeve, but smaller cuts still bled on his chest and shoulders. It was hard to see the extent of his wounds in the gloom; blood didn't stand out clearly on his dark skin. But he looked as battered as she felt.

The whole place looked battered. A pale, soft mass, studded with dull steel rings, lay crumpled to her right: the skins of the eyeless hunters. Nothing else was left of them. Around the pit's perimeter, a ring of bone debris and metal bits had collected—the remains of the skeletal army, Bitharn supposed. Many of the wooden planks had been ripped out of the walls and smashed into flinders by the tentacles' flailing, or perhaps by the thing in Gethel's skin. Whoever had destroyed them, there'd be no getting back up those stairs. The only way out, unless Malentir felt like carrying them through the shadows, was through a low-ceilinged doorway at the back of the pit. Through the Rosewayns' old dungeon.

Despite the destruction, and the fact that the loss of the stairs left them trapped, the room felt safer than it had while the labyrinth of bones still stood. The suffocating malevolence had lessened . . . but, Bitharn realized with exhausted dismay, not gone. It lingered like a bad smell, stronger toward that doorway. *We've won a battle, not the war.* The thought was unbearably exhausting.

She nodded wearily to Kelland, using her bow to push herself up rather than taking his hand. He'd turned his back on her to fight. *He had to. We'd be dead or worse if he hadn't.* That was true, and took away some of the sting, but it had still been a shock to open her eyes and see the Thorn standing over her, ghostly eyed and pitiless, instead of Kelland.

She'd needed him. It wasn't fair, and she wasn't proud to admit it, but Bitharn was hurt he hadn't been there. "I'm alive. Not sure I'd say 'well.' Kliasta's healing seems a little less than thorough."

"I do not have strength to spare on your comfort," Malentir said icily, picking his way through the rubble to the mouth of the tunnel. He moved stiffly, as if crippled by some hurt under his robes, and held the Sword of the Dawn as a walking stick to steady his steps. "You will live, and you will be unmarked. Anything more than that would be wasted. This way, your suffering repays some fraction of what I spent to restore you. If you had any sense you would be grateful for that. Neither of you is in any condition to fight, and we dare not use Aurandane again. Not while it is tainted. I am the only one with any strength left, and I do not expect we've seen the last of Maol's monsters."

"Well, it's a good thing we've got you to rely on," Bitharn muttered, shouldering her bow. Her lantern had been destroyed when she hit the wall, but Kelland's had survived the fight. She lit it and took the lead.

Past the shattered labyrinth was a small tunnel dug crookedly into the earth. Iron-grated cells gaped along both sides and in pits pocking the floor. Each held sprawled corpses, sometimes two or three to a cell. All wore the rough homespun of farmers or miners. Men and women alike had shaved heads, each one crowned with four blisters over four. Bitharn thought some of them might have been in the party that killed and ate the boy on Devils' Ridge, but the corpses looked so much alike that she couldn't be sure.

None had any wounds she could see, but they were dead just the same. "How?" she wondered aloud.

"Soul-drained," Malentir answered. He spared barely a glance for the dead, striding past their cells toward the tunnel's end. "For the Mad God to bring so much of his presence into the world, he needed power. He took it by consuming their souls . . . whatever was left of them. If his need was great enough that he devoured these wretches, this may be easier than I had thought."

The smell of sulfur grew stronger as Bitharn followed the Thorn. There were other smells too: stale urine, unwashed bodies, rotting food. Something had lived down here. Something other than the miners, she hoped.

The flicker of her lantern light sent phantoms dancing along the tunnel walls. The same phantoms that had haunted the smooth walls of the pit as they descended,

Bitharn thought. They'd banished those, but the apparitions lingered here. A premonition of evil prickled at the back of her neck. She eyed the corpses in their cells, touching the hilt of her knife as she hurried past. It was such a small weapon, so close to useless, and it was all she had left.

Beyond the cells was another open archway, smooth and glossy black, as everything was down here. Runes were carved around it in a ring. They weren't in any language Bitharn knew, and they seemed to swim and shift when she looked at them, so after the first glance she kept her eyes away. Maol's magic might have lost its hosts, but it still lurked in this blood-soaked earth.

The room beyond the archway was dominated by a dais of black-flecked granite. On it sat a great tangled table that looked like a charred bramble bush or some undersea creature petrified in obsidian. Spikes and chains wrapped around the table in chaotic patterns, too unevenly spaced to be restraints. A cloak of dust coated the table and masked the faces of the onyx gargoyles that squatted at its base.

Kelland drew a sun sign over his chest. "The Rosewayns' altar."

"Once. It served another purpose more recently." Malentir approached the altar, his black eyes lit with macabre curiosity. The Thorn hooked a finger around the chains, following their course, and bent one of the table's twisted arms up for closer examination. The arms were jointed and eerily flexible; the piece of obsidian moved almost like a human limb. "There is blood on this one, and less dust. Gethel modified it to suit his needs. Here and here. But why—aah. Of course."

"What?" Bitharn peered at the chains from the doorway, unwilling to set foot in that room.

"The price of his godless magic." The Thorn raised the

table's arm higher so they could see it. A cuff was crudely affixed to the stone. It was made to bind a human's arm to the table's, and it had a slight backward angle that would force a captive's hand into the shallow cup behind it.

That cup was too small to hold an adult's hand. Bitharn recoiled. "He was sacrificing children?"

"Using. Not sacrificing. It would have done him no good if they died too quickly." The Thorn moved out of the lantern's reach, vanishing into the darkness on the far side of the altar. "His knives are here. Knives, and the blackfire dust his creatures brought up from Duradh Mal. This is where his shapers bled, awakening the spirit in the dust so that it could be formed into weapons."

Bitharn glanced at Kelland. When the knight stayed silent, she looked back to the Thorn. "Shapers?"

"Come and see. There is no more danger in the altar than anywhere else in this accursed place."

Reluctantly she entered the altar chamber, clutching her lantern. Whispery hisses surrounded her as she crossed the threshold. Tiny faces—the hungry, bloodless reflections of creatures not there—swam up from the obsidian table's depths to gape at her. The gargoyles at the altar's feet gurgled quiet laughter, and their breath left a clammy whiff of decay in the air. The sounds, and the sensations, died when Kelland walked in. He'd drawn into his exhausted reserves to call forth a fingerflame of holy light, and its radiance seemed to quell whatever restless phantoms lingered.

Bitharn took small comfort in that. Whether her perceptions were madness or truth, they were brought by the hand of Maol. And there was another doorway on the other side of the chamber, so they still had farther to go.

Three bone knives hung from hooks on the far side of

the altar. Two boxes of coarse black grit rested under them, and a third was filled with lumpy pebbles the size of quail eggs. The pebbles had ridges that reminded Bitharn of her dismal attempts to make piecrusts as a child. She'd never been able to work the dough well; she always squeezed it too hard, breaking it into chunky crumbs that showed the lines of her fingers.

"This was the shapers' work? Pressing blackfire dust into balls with their hands?"

"With their hands and their blood, on the Mad God's altar. Yes." Malentir looked more haggard than he had in the labyrinth; the veins stood blue on the backs of his hands, and the shadows under his eyes had spread until his face looked like a skull's. But his voice did not quaver. "Bone and blood awaken its magic. That was one of the reasons his creatures used tools of bone in Duradh Mal, and that is what he did here. He cut the children's hands and had them pack the dust between their bleeding palms, and so the stones were made. Gethel might not have understood the power he tapped, but *something* guided him toward the proper rites."

Kelland had been peering through the archway past the altar while they spoke. "Something's alive in there. Something human," he said abruptly, striding from the chamber.

Bitharn hurried after him, gripping her knife. A kernel of anger had begun to burn through her fog of fear and fatigue, but that nascent rage froze as she came to the doorway. Sniffling sobs drifted through it, and the woeful familiarity of the sound chilled her bones.

A child's suffering had been used to bait them into a trap once before, outside Tarne Crossing. There would be no rescue if they fell victim to one here. Maol, unlike the Thorns, had no reason to show them mercy.

Cautiously Bitharn crept forward. Kelland's shoulder

blocked some of her view, but she saw a short hall of black stone that ended in another archway. This one, however, was not empty as the previous doorways had been. Obsidian carvings wrapped around its frame in a serpentine tangle. Each of its black tendrils was an arm, and each one ended in a bony hand that reached toward them, its claw-tipped fingers outstretched. No door of wood or stone barred the entrance, but the air crackled with malign power, as palpable as that of the curtain of sunlight that held prisoners in Heaven's Needle.

On the other side, something moved.

"Thorn!" Kelland shouted. "Remove this ward."

Malentir came down slowly, tapping Aurandane before him like an old, blind man with his cane. He brushed past Bitharn in a swirl of tattered robes and unsettling fragrance; he had reapplied the scent of amber and almonds to ward off Shadefell's stenches.

"Are you certain that is what you want?" he asked. "They are tainted, these creatures. Dangerous."

"They're *human*. I can save them. Remove the ward."

The Thornlord did not move at once. "Some of them," he said, studying the flow of the obsidian carvings around the doorway, "will have to die. I can unravel this spell, if that is what you want. It is crude, and much of its strength died with Gethel. But if I do that, I will not have the strength to take us all from this place. I certainly will not be able to carry all the survivors along my Lady's path. Not without their bloodprice. Are you willing to pay that?"

Kelland's jaw clenched. The tiny flame hovering over his hand flared white. But he nodded.

Malentir drew his ivory stiletto and went to the tangle of hands. "Then move back. I cannot work with you holding that flame so close." The Sun Knight retreated, his light dimming with distance, and the Thorn stabbed at the archway's outstretched palms. He pierced each one precisely in the center, striking clean through their hands as if the obsidian were living flesh. The hands clenched into fists, grasping futilely at the ivory blade, and dissolved into black sand.

White cores of bone stood revealed as they crumbled, like the ephemeral skeletons of burning leaves; then those, too, broke apart. Bitharn had a glimpse of the monstrosity that lay around the doorway: a spell-forged creation of dismembered arms, grasping for the last memory of life left to them . . . but, mercifully, the vision dissipated as its bones did. She closed her eyes to forget.

"It is clear," the Thornlord said, stepping aside. He closed his eyes, tilting his head back and struggling to breathe. "Go."

Bitharn did, dreading what she might find. Near the entrance she saw dried human feces and well-gnawed bones. She took another step, pushing the darkness away.

Half a hundred eyes stared back at her. Children, gray and gaunt, huddled in the lightless room. Most were bald, and all were naked or near it, clad in rags as filthy as their skin. The whites of their eyes were muddy yellow, their pupils wide and black, their teeth eroded to gray mush . . . but they were human.

All their hands were scarred. Wounds crisscrossed their palms, raw red lines scored over half-healed ones in a palimpsest of pain. Dark grit was embedded in the cuts, and Bitharn could see the children's bones, black under their pallid flesh.

Some warbled softly to themselves in singsong cant. One scrawny boy cradled his bent head in the crook of his elbow, swinging it back and forth. A girl had peeled the lips off all around her mouth, leaving her teeth exposed in a monstrous grin. She picked at the remains, but the torn gray flesh didn't bleed. Most of the children just stared at Bitharn, glassy-eyed and apathetic.

At the wavering shore between light and shadow, a woman's boot stuck out. Brass nails glinted in the sole. The heads were worn from long walking, but a sunburst showed on each one. Bitharn's breath stopped. Cobblers in Cailan used those nails, promising the faithful that such boots would help them "walk in the Lady's light" and keep them in good fortune.

"Oh, no," Bitharn whispered.

She'd found Evenna and Asharre. They were alive. Alive, and not *maelgloth* . . . but that was the best she could say for them. Biting her cheek to keep from crying, Bitharn raised her lantern over them.

Evenna's beauty was gone. She'd raked the lower half of her face to rags. It looked like a horrid Festelle mask, all curls of twisted leather around a seeping pit of a mouth. Above her cheekbones, her face was untouched except for a sooty smudge on her brow. A mote of blood dotted the tip of her nose.

The Illuminer's hands lay motionless in her lap. Her nails were caked with blood and pink strips of skin. She'd done this to herself . . . and now she sat serenely uncaring, her attention fixed on empty space. Bitharn turned away, unable to bear the sight.

Asharre wasn't maimed, but there was such a terrible despair in her eyes that it was almost easier to look at Evenna. Although the *sigrir* was head and shoulders taller than the black-haired Illuminer, she slumped so low against the wall that they seemed to be of equal height. Behind its wall of ritual scars, her face was dully hopeless. Grease and cinders caked her short ice blonde hair. Her brow, too, was stained with dried mud, and there was a ring of wilted blisters under that. Four over four, Bitharn saw with a chill.

"I betrayed them," Asharre mumbled. The words had the sound of rote repetition, their meanings long worn away. Cottony blackness coated her tongue. More stained the palms of her hands and the pads of her fingers, creeping up her wrists like a fungus. "I failed. I betrayed them."

"It wasn't your doing," Bitharn said. "Gethel and his blackfire dust corrupted these people, not you."

"It was my failure." Asharre turned her face to the wall and raised a black-stained palm to thrust their intrusions away. "Maol knew I was the weak one. He knew. Leave me to my failure. *Leave me.*"

"We do need deaths," Malentir said, toying with his ivory knife and looking over the huddled figures with evident amusement. Neither the filth nor the misery of the children in the pit seemed to touch him; if anything, he seemed stronger in the presence of their pain. His own weariness receded as he stood there, watching.

"Not hers," Kelland said.

"Then whose, knight? Please choose quickly. Gethel is dead, and we have found your so-precious victims, so our work is finished in this place. I have no wish to linger. Maol's presence is still strong here, and the taint I took from Aurandane spreads deeper by the moment. Wait long enough, and we may well rebuild that labyrinth with our own bones, for all our 'victory' in battle."

"How many deaths do you need?" Bitharn asked.

"For us? One. For all these poor useless souls . . ." He gave the room's hollow-eyed occupants a considering look. "There is likely to be some interference with my prayer to keep us from escaping, and I am weaker than I was. So let us say five. These creatures are dull minded, and their ability to feel pain is lessened, but five should suffice."

Bitharn nodded. She pointed out four of the unmoving ones and the girl with the torn lips, quickly, before Kelland could do or say anything. The Sun Knight couldn't choose some and condemn others—not without committing a grievous sin—but *she* could. And they had no other way out.

Better for some to die than all of them. She chose the children because in the cold, hard part of her soul that could consider such things, she thought they might be too deep under Maol's sway to save. The graylings were already half monster, whereas Evenna and Asharre were still themselves . . . and if Kelland could clear their minds, and if the Thorn *did* plot some betrayal before they returned to the Dome of the Sun, the Illuminer and the *sigrir* would make better allies than unarmed children.

So Bitharn told herself, knowing that there was no right answer and that, in truth, she was trying to convince herself only because she had to believe *something* to endure the Thorn's choice. She hoped death would be a release rather than a torment for the empty-faced children, and she hoped Celestia would forgive her.

The Thorn took the nearest child's chin in one hand, turning the boy's face up to his gently. It looked like the prelude to a kiss . . . but as Malentir smiled, he raised the ivory dagger. Bitharn averted her eyes.

One of the children whimpered, but the rest succumbed in silence, and the others sat like statues around them as they died. Bitharn didn't look at Kelland until it was over. Instead she fixed her thoughts on Evenna and Asharre, and on the children who would survive because the others did not. *It had to be done.*

"Gather them," Malentir said.

The children didn't resist as Bitharn shepherded them into the middle of the room. They shuffled along uncomprehendingly, stumbling to stops when she let go of their wrists. Some had to be lifted bodily, and she was shocked by how light they were; they felt like hollow husks. Kelland worked beside her, helping Asharre and Evenna toward the others, but Bitharn couldn't meet his eyes. It was a surprise, and a welcome one, when he clasped her shoulder in passing.

Malentir began his prayer as soon as the children were gathered. The shadows swelled and swayed to the rhythm of his words; frost sharpened in the air. An icy rime spread across her lantern, killing its light with a crystalline snap. At first the darkness held back from the white burn of Kelland's fingerflame, but at a gesture from the Thornlord, the knight closed his hand and let the flame die. Utter blackness engulfed them.

Bitharn felt the magic solidify around her in a cage cold as winter iron. It clamped around her, vise tight, so frigid that her skin would surely freeze and tear away if she moved. The sensation built to overwhelming pain, forcing a gasp from her in the blackness, but she never heard the sound. Tears trickled down her cheeks and froze to tinkling ice. The agony intensified, driving her to the edge of breaking—

—and yet the cage of pain was almost comforting compared to what she sensed beyond it. A chittering malevolence lurked there. Vast and manifold, it pressed against the weave of the Thornlord's spell, searching for a way in. She wasn't sure if it was many minds or a single one fragmented beyond recognition, but its hate for them was absolute.

With a sudden sense of alarm Bitharn realized that

something was clawing at the spell cage from the *inside,* trying to weaken its strands enough to admit the screeching madness. Unseen claws scratched around her, shrill as the scraping of steel on steel.

"No," Bitharn whispered. The chill in the dark became a bone-cracking freeze. If she had plunged naked into the White Seas she could not have been colder. The claws stopped—were frozen, she knew somehow, were dead— and the madness outside receded as it was left in the distance, howling.

Bit by bit, the icy dark thawed. Land and air separated. The scents of earth and spring sap filtered in. Woodsmoke touched the air, which was warm enough to move once more. Wispy clouds limned the branches of an ancient oak and silhouetted the thatch of a low-roofed cottage. A forest spread around them.

Over the wood, the spire of Heaven's Needle shone gold. They were twenty leagues north and west of the Dome, Bitharn guessed. Perhaps a little more. That put them in Lord Gildorath's land. A wise choice for a Thorn: Gildorath's commonfolk were well accustomed to closing their eyes and ears to uncomfortable things.

The lonely cottage, however, seemed deserted. Brambles had begun to reclaim the path that threaded through the forest toward it. There was no one to see them arrive—or what might happen to them after. Bitharn bit her lip and turned as Kelland struck a spark to her lantern, shining it over their charges.

A third of the children were dead. Ice glittered on their eyes. Their heads were crushed like the shells of boiled eggs, fissured and dimpled but intact. Evenna and Asharre were still breathing, though the blood in Evenna's hair had frozen into tangled black icicles.

Malentir looked over them with weary annoyance. He staggered away from the huddled group, dusted pine needles and loam from a boulder on the other side of the cottage's clearing, and sat. "They tried to bring the Mad God with them. Had they succeeded, we would be dead, or worse. It was necessary to stop them."

"I know," Bitharn said. "I felt it."

"Are we safe?" Kelland asked.

The Thornlord shrugged. He closed his eyes and tilted his head back tiredly. In the moonlight his face was very white, with an unhealthy bloom of blue at his lips and temples. "More than we were, less than we should be. These children are Maol's creatures, and they carry his taint. As do I, and as does Aurandane. Sooner or later, if it is not burned out, he will be able to reach through the creatures he has corrupted. I will wait to see whether you can restore them. If not, I will destroy them before returning to my mistress' side."

"You're leaving us?" For some reason the thought startled Bitharn. It shouldn't have been a surprise, and she should have been glad to see him go . . . but she wasn't.

He isn't even an ally. Not truly. The soldiers of Cailan had a saying for that: "The enemy of my enemy makes good arrow bait." Accurate, if unsavory; a shared enmity could be useful, but only a fool put any trust in it.

But the Thorn had saved them. He hadn't betrayed them.

Malentir cocked his head at her. She was uncomfortably sure he could read her thoughts. "For a time. It is possible, even probable, that I will return. Corban is here, or was, and he poses a greater threat than Gethel did. Gethel was a deluded fool who had no idea what he invited, and he was isolated. Corban knows, or knew, and chose to tamper with it anyway. And he is in Cailan. Where there are enough people—enough *victims*—to infect all Ithelas with the Mad God's plague."

"We will be glad to have your aid," Kelland said. Bitharn's eyebrows went up; she agreed with him, but she hadn't expected the knight to accept so quickly. Malentir saw her surprise and smiled, though he said nothing until Kelland left to pray over the rescued children. As the Sun Knight began an invocation to Celestia, Bitharn took a seat on a mushroom-spotted log near the Thorn. She didn't especially want his company, but there was nowhere else to sit except in the dirt.

"You were hoping he'd refuse?" Malentir asked.

"No. Just surprised he accepted so quickly. It's the right choice."

"Is it?"

"Of course it is." She tossed her braid behind a shoulder impatiently. "You saved our lives in Shadefell. You could have killed us or left us to die after taking the Sword of the Dawn, but you didn't."

"Ah. That convinces you of my good nature?"

"No. But we'd be stupid to ignore it."

"Good." The corners of his mouth twitched up in a cadaverous smile. In the few moments since their arrival in the clearing, the hollows of Malentir's cheeks had sunk visibly. The bones rose above them sharp as knife blades. "It was need that drove me, not kindness. Need is . . . stronger."

"Aurandane's taint?"

"That is a part of it." His hand crept toward the sword, which leaned against the boulder near his foot, the tiny jewel on its pommel twinkling. "I knew there was . . . some trap to it . . . but I thought it might have been drained like the other slaves and snares. I was wrong."

"It's killing you."

"Perhaps." The Thornlord's eyes were glassy with fever, but he laughed raspily. "I hope so. The alternative would be worse. But if I am only dying . . . your knight owes me a life."

"The Spider held him in Ang'arta for a full winter. He doesn't owe you anything."

"That is her debt, not mine. Your knight understands that. He is an honorable man . . . and a sensible one." Malentir lapsed into silence for a time, watching the radiance of Kelland's prayer wash over the undersides of the budding branches and turn the clearing's grass into a white-capped sea. Malentir's face looked like a *ghaole*'s, all dead white skin stretched over bone. "And you need me," he added, his voice soft as the whisper of wind over ashes, "and need is stronger than kindness."

Bitharn didn't answer. She looked away through the trees, where the light of Celestian magic was bright enough to sting her eyes. The children moaned and squirmed in the rotting leaves, trying to escape its embrace, but none of them had the strength to get up and run. Evenna thrashed wildly in the white light; Asharre sat stolid as stone, pink-tinged tears trickling down her chin. Blackfire dust whirled around them, pulled from their bodies into the light, where it burned in shimmers of colorless flame. The grayness receded from their bodies, and the emptiness cleared from their eyes as the dust blazed away.

The power of faith allowed Kelland to purify them. The price of faith meant he had to. Despite his exhaustion he could no more refuse the children's need than he could stop breathing. Bitharn was privately, grimly glad that not all of them had survived the passage. It might have killed him to heal more.

Would it kill him to heal the Thorn? Now, or later? If Kelland waited until after sunrise, his magic would be stronger, but he would also risk the possibility that the Mad God might kill his victims rather than let the knight reclaim them. It wasn't a chance worth taking for the innocents. Was it worth taking for the Thorn? *Need is stronger than kindness.* Did they need Malentir so badly?

That choice was not hers to make. She'd spared him from sin in the bowels of Shadefell; she couldn't do it again here. Brooding, she watched the prayer go on, and kept the Thorn in the corner of her eye.

Finally the last of the blackfire dust burned off. Bitharn was surprised that the sky was still dark; it seemed that it should be dawn, if not the next day's dusk. The children's moans died out as the light receded, leaving them in the cool spring night.

Kelland emerged from the tree shadows, his white surcoat stained with filth yet aglow with starlight. His eyes met Malentir's, then Bitharn's. Weariness weighted his shoulders and made every step a stumble. Nevertheless, the knight knelt wordlessly beside the Thorn, and the light of holy prayer sprang up around him again. The jewel on Aurandane's hilt winked in the colorless flame. Bitharn thought she saw a glimmer of shadow in its dawn blue depths, and the reflection of a face that was not there. Burning eyes, a burning soul.

It lasted just an instant, but she stared at the stone until the magic died.

23

"Close enough?" the wagon driver asked. His donkey brayed at an approaching oxcart on the road that circled the Dome of the Sun. Ahead the luminous glass of Heaven's Needle was a spear of brighter fire against the sunset.

"Yes, thank you," Bitharn said. Yellow-robed Illuminers were hurrying toward them while acolytes ran to fetch healers' bags and tell others of their arrival. Carts hauling the sick and injured were a common sight at the Dome of the Sun, and the temple's servants were well versed in their response.

They were home. Home, and as safe as they could be anywhere in this world. The relief of it was overwhelming.

Bitharn climbed down from the wagon bench, balancing Aurandane awkwardly in one hand. She'd thought it best to disguise the Sword of the Dawn by carrying it in Kelland's scabbard rather than its own, but it was too long for that sheath. A scarf wrapped loosely around the hilt concealed the poor fit, but it made the sword clumsy to handle. She'd be glad to get rid of it, for that small reason as well as the large ones.

Once on the ground, she tried to offer the driver a coin, but the gnarled old farmer pushed her silver shield away.

"No need for that. It's honor enough to serve." The farmer cleared his throat and straightened his battered hat, trying to look more respectable as the Illuminers approached. He'd been terrified when he first saw the burden he was asked to carry—all those children lying amid the frozen graylings, Evenna with her torn face, Kelland delirious and covered in black blood—but the long ride had calmed him enough to recognize, and take some pride in, the importance of his part. "I can't guess what you went through, but I'm glad to have been able to help. The Burnt Knight, cursed children . . . You keep your shield. The story's payment enough for me." He chuckled in disbelief, shaking his head at the strangeness of the world. "Glad just to serve."

The Illuminers had arrived. Bitharn helped them move the children and Celestians from the farmer's wagon bed onto the canvas-covered boards that the acolytes brought out from the temple. The carrying boards had restraints for patients at risk of hurting themselves or others, and Bitharn made sure every one was fastened before she let the Illuminers haul them back to the healing rooms. Malentir had said the corruption was cleansed from them, and she knew he couldn't lie . . . but he could have been mistaken. Even if he wasn't, there was no telling how the children would react when they came back to their senses. If they did. Passage through the *perethil* had nearly been enough to derange *her,* and she had only walked through it twice. Being mired in the Mad God's power for days might have destroyed their minds altogether.

They'd made it to the Dome of the Sun, though, and if they could be healed, they would be. There was no better place for it in Ithelas. She watched the acolytes carry the boards into the temple, then turned back to the farmer. "Thank you," she said again.

"Welcome. Most welcome. Bright Lady's blessing." He patted her shoulder, climbing back onto the wagon. Ordinarily the gesture might have annoyed her, but right then Bitharn was grateful for the farmer's clumsy reassurance. He meant well, and she would never have gotten her charges back to Cailan without him.

After Kelland healed him, Malentir had shadow-walked back to Cailan or Ang'arta or wherever it was he went, effectively leaving Bitharn alone in the forest. The Thorn hadn't taken Aurandane with him, but the sword was no help; if anything, it added to her apprehension. Kelland had nearly killed himself with the strain of purging black-fire corruption from so many souls. Asharre, Evenna, and the children were delirious or comatose. Bitharn had been terrified to turn her back on them for a moment, much less abandon them for hours while she looked for help, but she hadn't had any choice.

Near dawn, she'd finally stumbled across the trail of poachers dragging a deer through the forest. They'd been clumsy—and would have been hanged for it if Lord Gildorath's huntsmen had found the tracks instead of Bitharn—but in her exhaustion, it was only because of that clumsiness that she'd been able to follow the trampled trail back to their village. There she'd hammered on doors and begged for help until the sleepy, frightened villagers followed her back to the wounded. This turnip cart had been a godsend.

Bitharn waved farewell to the retreating cart with all the

politeness she could muster, then hurried after the retreating Illuminers.

There was little she could do to help, but they let her into the healing rooms. She gave an abbreviated account of their experiences in Shadefell to the lead Illuminer, a woman who dispatched acolytes and fellow Blessed alike with the same efficient, steely calm. After answering the woman's questions and handing the Sword of the Dawn off to a Sun Knight, Bitharn retired to a chair in the corner of the healing hall and surrendered to her fatigue.

No sooner had she closed her eyes than a beige-robed acolyte was shaking her awake. "The High Solaros wishes to see you," the boy said. "Sir Kelland and the *sigrir* Asharre have already been called to his study."

Sunlight warmed her face through a nearby window. It was late morning, almost midday. She'd slept through the night and the next day's dawn prayers. One of the Blessed must have woven a small prayer over her while she slept; her teeth didn't feel loose anymore, and her bruises had faded to yellow-green rosettes.

Somehow, she managed to feel wretched despite the healing. Her limbs were stiff and sore after a night spent sleeping in the chair, and her mouth tasted like it had been packed with dirty wound lint. She was surprised she couldn't hear her back creaking when she stood. "How long do I have?"

"He expects you momentarily. The others are waiting."

"Let me wash." A quick scrub of her teeth, followed by a rinse of cold whitebriar tea, had her feeling almost human; a splash of water on her face helped too. She longed for a bath, and for a good long stretch, but those would have to wait. The acolyte waited politely, and then she followed him to the High Solaros' study.

Kelland and Asharre sat in the library outside. Neither spoke. The knight gazed pensively at his sun medallion, winding its golden chain around his brown knuckles. The scarred *sigrir* stared at a bookshelf, seeming hardly more aware of her surroundings than she'd been in the pit below Shadefell. Her shoulders were slumped, her face slack. The healing of her physical wounds didn't seem to have touched her despair; if anything, she looked worse.

Bitharn hesitated, wanting to say something, but the acolyte was watching, and although he did not interrupt she could sense his impatience. She raised a hand in greeting instead, and just caught Kelland inclining his head in return before she was ushered through the door into the High Solaros's study.

Over the years, she had probably visited the High Solaros' inner sanctum ten or fifteen times—not often, spread over the course of a decade and more, but enough to think of the place as eternal. There was always a hint of sweetness to the air: cedar and sandalwood from the costly carvings, roses from the gardens in summer and mint when the weather turned cool, fragrant candles in winter when the gardens were sleeping. But though the seasons might turn, and the scents change to match them, the study itself never did. It was a timeless sanctuary, warm and filled with light. Wide, clear windows invited in the sun, adding their own colored-glass sparkles of ruby and gold to its natural brilliance. The High Solaros' collection of books and maps lent the room a whiff of leather and parchment, but far from being musty or unpleasant, to Bitharn it smelled purely of knowledge.

Unlike his study, however, the High Solaros was subject to age. She was quietly shocked to see how much older he looked. Thierras d'Amalthier had never been young in

Bitharn's memory, and every year saw more snow in his hair and more lines on his face, but she had seldom seen him as weary as he was today. In his private chambers, he wore simple yellow robes with only muted gold embroidery about the hem to signify that he was not an ordinary Illuminer, yet even that small reminder of his office seemed to weigh heavy on the man. "Light's blessing upon you. Please, sit."

"Thank you, Eminence." Bitharn leaned on the armrest to lower herself into the chair. Her legs were still wobbly.

The High Solaros sat opposite her, steepling his fingers over the map of Ithelas that covered his desk under glass. "I understand you were recently in Carden Vale."

That surprised her. She'd expected him to ask about the Thorn's escape first. Surely he had to know that she'd helped Malentir flee Heaven's Needle. "I was, Eminence."

"How did you come to be there?"

So it was about the Thornlord after all. Inwardly Bitharn quailed. But she told him everything, from Kelland's capture outside Tarne Crossing to her bargain with the Spider and betrayal of Versiel. There was no point in hiding it; he would have heard about Malentir's presence in Shadefell from the others, and it was better for him to know the whole truth. At least then he might understand *why* she'd betrayed the faith.

"Do you regret freeing him?" Thierras asked at the end of her tale.

"I regret that it was the best of the choices I had. But I don't think I made the wrong choice, if that's what you're asking. I'd do it again if I had to. I'd do it a thousand times over."

The High Solaros nodded, not in agreement, but as if he had expected no other answer. "Sir Kelland was not the first they took. The Thorns have been trying for some time to capture one of our Blessed. I suspected it when the first reports came back from Thelyand Ford; I was sure of it when I learned of Oralia's death. But I did not know *why* until now."

"They want Duradh Mal. And they need a Blessed to purify it."

"So it seems." The High Solaros' gaze settled back upon her.

Bitharn braced herself against his disappointment. "Will I be censured?"

"No. Your guilt is penance enough. We'll let the public story stand. The Thorn tricked you and escaped; as far as anyone outside this room needs to know, you were an unwilling captive. As it happens, your disobedience may be the only reason Evenna and Asharre came back to us alive. The goddess works in strange ways . . . here, it seems, by making a tool of love."

Bitharn stared at her fingertips. She felt the burn of a blush in her cheeks and wished desperately, hopelessly, that she could be anywhere else in the world.

"We've . . . we've talked about that," she mumbled at last, when the silence became too oppressive to bear. "We've found our answer." It wasn't the one she wanted, and she wasn't sure it was right, but what she *wanted* had already caused enough shame.

"Have you?" Thierras rang a small bronze bell on his desk. A moment later the door opened. The acolyte stood at the threshold, questioning.

"Bring in Sir Kelland, please," the High Solaros said.

Bitharn knotted her hands together and tried to quell the hammering in her heart. She hadn't expected this. Admitting her complicity in the Thornlord's escape had been infinitely easier. She'd been ready for that. She had wrestled through sleepless nights with what she would say, had prepared herself for the buckling weight of the admission. But this . . . this was a surprise, and she was in no condition to deal with surprises.

The acolyte returned with Kelland and a silver tray of pastries, some sweet, others savory. A teapot and a trio of porcelain cups sat in the center of the tray. He laid the platter on the desk, waited for the High Solaros' nod of dismissal, and left discreetly. Bitharn took a sugared roll, more to occupy her hands than because she was hungry. She hadn't eaten in two days, apart from a handful of mushrooms and sausages on the turnip cart, but anxiety strangled her appetite.

Thierras rubbed a thumb over the heavy gold ring of his office. "When we spoke earlier, you asked whether the Spider lied about Celestia's proscription of physical love."

"I asked whether that love was a sin," Kelland said. Bitharn's breath caught. She nearly dropped the sweet roll she'd been picking apart. He had *asked* that?

"Yes. And I said—"

"—that oaths are simple, but questions of sin are not. Which was not an answer."

"It was the best one I could give at that time." The High Solaros sighed. He didn't seem offended by Kelland's lack of deference; his tone carried only a weight of regret, and perhaps of worry. "Now I see things more clearly."

Again he fell silent. Bitharn picked the raisins from her roll, showering her lap with flakes of pastry. It was a waste, but she couldn't have swallowed a bite if it was the last food she'd get all day.

Thierras tapped a jagged black line cut across the map:

the Irontooths, a long line reaching north across Carden Vale. The town wasn't marked on the High Solaros' map, but Ang'duradh was. It had its proper name there; the map was very old. "You asked about Bysshelios too. His heresy."

"Yes," Kelland said. "He broke his oaths, but he kept his magic."

"For a time. He lost it in the end, when his sins became excessive . . . but you are correct: Bysshelios kept Celestia's Blessing after he took women to his bed."

"Then the oath of celibacy is a lie."

"No." The High Solaros seemed to be looking *through* them more than *at* them, Bitharn thought; he had the air of a man remembering old conversations and weighing past words as much as choosing what he wanted to tell them in the here and now. It made her afraid. What was it that he was treading so gingerly around?

"The oath," Thierras said, "is founded on the belief that, in this matter, it is best to have a clear rule rather than allowing our Blessed to flounder into a treacherous and complicated sea.

"Love, itself, is not a sin in the Bright Lady's eyes. But it can still tempt people—even good people, even careful ones—into others. Whatever the singers claim, love is not a cure for all the world's ills; too often, it is their cause. Most of Celestia's Blessed are young, and have enough difficulty meeting the demands of the faith without being distracted by the confusion and temptations of carnal love. For them, the oath is a safeguard."

"A safeguard against what?" Bitharn asked blankly. She wasn't sure she understood. "You just said love isn't a sin."

"In the abstract, that is true," the High Solaros said. "But we live, and serve, in an imperfect world. The two of you are lucky—luckier, or wiser, than you know. You love each other, and that love strengthens the faith you share.

"But what if it were otherwise? What if one of you followed the Shadow-Tongued, or the wild spirits of the White Seas, or denied the gods altogether? What if you didn't want to spend your life on the road, following someone else's holy quests, and tried to pull Kelland away from his duties instead? What if he failed to appreciate your devotion, souring it into hate? And those are only the things that might go wrong *after* you two loved each other. Often love is not reciprocated, or is forbidden. Blessed have fallen in love with people already married, or too high- or low-born, or who owe fealty to lords in other lands. Longing turns to bitterness, jealousy to spite—and those *are* sins, or lead to them, and destroy a gift that is already too rare. It is easier, and safer, if we remove the temptation. The oath of chastity draws a clear line. It provides certainty where otherwise there would be none."

"What becomes of us if we cross that line?" Kelland asked quietly.

"You become Bysshelios," the High Solaros replied. "Or you stay as you are. In the eyes of the world, it must be one or the other. As to what *your* truth is, in your own hearts . . . that is for you to find. You've refused the easy answer; the hard one will have to be your own."

Bitharn brushed away the crumbs on her legs, grappling for sense amid the welter of her emotions. "What would you have us do?"

"Try not to tear the faith apart," the High Solaros answered dryly. He made it sound a joke, but it was still sharp enough to make Bitharn squirm. "The oath remains a safeguard for the other Blessed, and I will not have you weaken it. I trust you are unlikely to reawaken the Bysshelline Heresy, or we would not be having this audience . . . but if you openly forsake one oath, you forsake them all."

Openly. What did that mean? Was the High Solaros giving his blessing for them to do otherwise in secret? Or was he only saying that he didn't want to know?

"There's still Duradh Mal," Kelland said. It was an abrupt change of subject, but Bitharn wasn't surprised by that. He wasn't ready to confront the possibilities that the High Solaros had opened for them. Neither was she. Not yet. They'd deal with that later, together.

"Maolites on one side, Baozites on the other." Thierras traced the painted mountains on his map, stopping his finger on the black dot that marked the cursed fortress. "You still want to help them reclaim it?"

"Yes. That map shows why. The same mountains that made Ang'duradh impregnable can keep its soldiers penned up just as easily. It will be years, maybe decades, before the fortress hosts a fighting force again. In that time we can be prepared to confront them."

"At a considerable cost in blood."

"We accept that possibility when we choose to serve. The people of Carden Vale did not, and the price they paid was worse."

"You're certain of that?"

"Yes," Bitharn answered. What she'd seen with her own eyes and read in the gaoler's book proved that much. She'd only read a few pages of that grisly chronicle before pushing the book aside, sickened, but one would have been enough. Death in battle, even death at the hands of Baozites, was one thing. Madness and monstrosity was entirely another. Nothing the Baozites did could compare to the horrors that Maol's victims inflicted on their families and themselves.

Kelland nodded. He rested a hand atop hers and went on. "If we leave Duradh Mal as it is, sooner or later someone like Gethel will release its corruption again. We were lucky this time; we were able to catch the madness before it spread beyond the mountains. Even so it destroyed Carden Vale and threatens Cailan. We should expect worse if it happens again. Next time we may not realize the seals are broken until all Calantyr succumbs."

"Ah. So you want to do this because the Baozites are easier to watch?"

"Easier to watch, and less dangerous. Baozites are soldiers. Maol is a plague."

"I wish I shared your certainty," the High Solaros said. "There is something they want in Ang'duradh that goes beyond the fortress itself. I'm certain of that."

"Aurandane?" Bitharn asked. But as soon as the name passed her lips, she knew that was wrong. Malentir had left the sword with them, even though he could have taken it before or after Gethel's death.

"Perhaps," Thierras said, although clearly he thought it as unlikely as she did. "In the last few years, Baozite soldiers have made inquiries with scholars, libraries, and book dealers from Aluvair to Seawatch, buying or copying anything that purports to deal with Ang'duradh and its fall. They've been discreet about it, relatively speaking, but a rough-spoken soldier interested in that historical era is an unusual buyer of books."

"They can't have been that concerned with secrecy," Kelland said, "or they would have used the Thorns, and we would never have known who they were."

Thierras shook his head. "The Thorns were otherwise occupied. They were hunting our Blessed. You were not the first one they attacked. You were only the first to have been taken."

"Why?" Bitharn asked, at the same time Kelland said: "Who?"

"Isleyn Silverlock, though he escaped their trap. Oralia of the White Seas, who died rather than let herself be taken. Riulan of Knight's Lake, Tanarroc Hillwalker. There were others. They've been been trying since the Battle of Thelyand Ford." Thierras turned to Bitharn. "Your question is not as easily answered. I thought, initially, that they wanted to interrogate our Blessed, or perhaps sacrifice them. Some spells are more powerful when written in holy blood. But Kelland was neither questioned nor tortured, and now I wonder if all along their goal was the reclamation of Duradh Mal. If my understanding is correct, the attacks began around the time Malentir realized that Maol was behind the fortress' fall."

"What if it was?" Kelland asked. "If retaking Ang'duradh is truly what they want, they'll keep hunting our Blessed until they have one. Better if we cooperate— and go in with our eyes open. Working beside them in Duradh Mal will let us learn the strength and shape of their magic before it's directed at us. The chance is too valuable to waste."

"You assume they'll let you come back alive to report anything," Thierras said.

"The Thorn could have killed us in Shadefell. Instead he saved our lives."

Thierras shrugged, filling his cup with tepid tea. "Because he needed you. You told me yourself; he was dying when you left that place. Only your prayers spared him from Maol's claim."

"He'll need us in Duradh Mal as well," Kelland said. "You taught me to use the tools I have. This is an opportunity. We can watch the Thorn, learn from him, find weaknesses we'd never see otherwise. I've already seen at least one. There's a hidden cell near the south docks. An albino girl named Brielle guards it."

"It isn't much."

"It's more than we knew before. Now that we know they have a foothold in Cailan, we can watch it, and see who else goes there, or seize the girl and question her. I expect she is an acolyte, at best; I doubt the Spider would have shown me anyone truly valuable. But it's a beginning. In Duradh Mal we're likely to learn much more."

The High Solaros glanced wryly at Bitharn. "Did he give you this speech as well?"

"Something like it," she admitted.

"Well, if you couldn't talk him out of it, I won't expect to do better." He turned to Kelland. "You were held in Ang'arta; you know the beast's nature. If you are still determined that this is the best course, so be it. Go to Duradh Mal. Help the Baozites reclaim their fortress. Learn what you can, and come back to report it."

"I'll see that he does," Bitharn said, and the two of them saw themselves out.

Instead of going to the training hall, as Bitharn had expected, Kelland took the spiral paths to the gardens. New green softened the rosebushes' gnarled stems. Nodding white snowdrops and purple-tipped spikes of crocus flourished on their rich black beds, stretching toward the afternoon sun.

Bitharn closed her eyes and turned her face to the sky. It felt so warm here, so *clean*. She understood why the flowers gloried in it. "I'm going with you to Duradh Mal."

"It won't be pretty," Kelland warned.

"Oh, I know. You never take me anywhere pretty."

"This is."

"It is," she admitted, opening her eyes. "But we'll have to leave it soon."

"We might, yes." He took her hand again, folding her fingers into his, and pressed their clasped hands over his heart. "But we're here now."

24

"*Shurr.*" The word was harsh and mangled, but Asharre recognized her name. She had been dreading, and hoping for, this moment since she woke to find herself in the Dome of the Sun's healing halls. Apart from a short debriefing in Thierras' study the day after her arrival, she'd spent all her waking moments sitting by Evenna's bed. After attending to the worst of her wounds, the Celestians had moved Evenna to a solitary room where she could recuperate without being disturbed by the clamor of the main healing halls.

There Asharre had gone every morning, waiting for the Illuminer to awaken. Waiting to find out how badly she had failed. Sometimes Bitharn sat with her, but mostly she waited alone.

Yellow curtains and white-oak cabinets gave the sickroom a sunny air, although the morning was cool and misty. A black-and-white cat dozed on the windowsill. Paintings of orchids and saffron crocuses adorned the walls. It was all almost cheerful . . . as long as Asharre ignored the woman on the bed.

Swallowing her guilt, she made herself look at Evenna. "Yes?"

The Illuminer was staring at her fiercely. From the nose down, her face was gone, torn away by her own nails. Scars covered the lower halves of her cheeks, healed smooth and shiny around the stretched-thin holes. Every word took a tremendous effort to force past her ruined lips, and Asharre could barely recognize the sounds. "Not . . . your fault."

"I led you into Shadefell. Into the Mad God's snare."

Evenna shook her head. Her eyes were clear and luminous, still beautiful. "*Our* choice to enter Carden Vale. We knew . . . better than you . . . what limits were. My pride . . . pushed us on after Falcien died."

"I should have stopped you. I failed to do that and I failed to protect you."

"You kept . . . me alive." Evenna touched the rippled scars on her chin, glossy as pink obsidian. "*I am not my face.* You told me this. Taught me. Loss of vanity is . . . nothing. Less than nothing. I live. I serve. Because of you. Not . . . a small gift."

"It should have been more. I'm sorry," Asharre whispered.

"No. Be sorry if you stop." The Illuminer pushed herself against the pillows, sitting up higher. Her blue eyes blazed. "*Then* . . . would be a waste. Wasted on pity. Did not go to Shadefell to surrender. Or so you could. Go. Go to High Solaros. Help them. Fight. Shadefell did not end it."

Tears stung Asharre's eyes. She couldn't let them fall. Not in front of Evenna. "Forgive me," she said, stumbling from the sickroom.

She hurried out, chin lifted, and strode from the healing halls without troubling to see where she was going. Away, that was all that mattered.

When she realized that she had turned toward the eternal gardens, Asharre hesitated. She had avoided that part of the temple, and the memories that lived there, since Oralia's loss . . . but she heard no grief in the gentle rustling of maple and flowering elm, and the trilled songs of unseen birds spoke of renewal rather than mourning. The morning's mist had given way to sunshine, and the beauty of the place was a balm on her soul after Shadefell's desolation.

She walked past the formal gardens with their rings of crocuses and snowdrops, past the rose vines that would blaze white and gold in summer but showed only serrated green now. The silvery laughter of the fountains drew her, and the medicinal fragrance of healers' herbs.

The herb gardens were, as they had always been, the wildest and sweetest place in the Dome. Some small magic kept them green year-round. Although the season was still young, the herb gardens were in full bloom. Pebbled silver leaves of sage spread over tiny-flowered carpets of thyme; lacy stems of yarrow and needle spikes of rosemary reached to the sun together, exuding a tangled spice. In the shade of the linden trees that swayed along the paths, wintermint and wormwood grew.

Asharre brushed her fingertips through their leaves as she passed, bruising them to bring out their scent. Worm wood and wintermint: the two most sacred healer's herbs, Celestia's gift to her mortal children. They grew in shade as easily as sun, so that they could be planted and used where the Bright Lady's light did not reach.

Her sister had always carried wintermint and wormwood. Wintermint to soothe pain and mask unpleasant flavors; wormwood for its healing properties and its bitterness, which so many took to mean that the medicine was as powerful as its taste. Adding wintermint or wormwood to change a potion's flavor was a small trick, but Oralia had always said that half the healer's art was inspiring confidence. The patient's belief healed as much as the Illuminer's did.

She'd loved these plants, as she had loved the people they healed. That love drove her skill. Oralia hadn't always won her battles. Sometimes the wound was too grievous, the disease too advanced, an old body too frail. Sometimes she lost. But she never turned back from a fight, even if victory was measured only in lessening pain and fear at the end.

Asharre walked slowly through the garden, breathing its bittersweet perfume, and then she straightened her back and squared her shoulders and went in search of Thierras.

He was not in his study. The acolyte dusting the windowsills said that the High Solaros had gone down to the practice halls, and it was there that Asharre found him.

Thierras stood with his elbows on a goldenwood balustrade, watching knights-in-training spar in pairs on the scuffed, chalk-ringed floor below him. The clack of wooden swords against weighted shields resonated in the practice hall, along with the novices' chanting.

All those sweating young men praying as they hacked and parried made a peculiar sight, although Asharre understood the purpose of the exercise immediately. The Knights of the Sun had to build their lungs along with their muscles so that they did not lose their breath chanting in battle, and they had to be able to meld those prayers into their fighting without distraction.

"What do you think?" the High Solaros asked.

Asharre looked over the pairs. They were getting sloppy as they tired. A few slowed their footwork in time to the pauses between chanted lines, which made them predictable and therefore easy targets. And they were all too evenly matched: each youth faced off against one of comparable size and strength, which no doubt made for fairer sparring but was poor preparation for fights against bigger men or smaller ones.

There were fewer than fifty of them. Most were striplings, thirteen or fourteen years old. They were so young, and so few, to carry the weight of the Bright Lady's duty across Ithelas.

She shrugged. "They work hard."

"The look on your face suggests you could say more than that," Thierras prodded.

"Why? I am not their teacher."

"You could be. I think you'd make a good one. We lost our master of arms recently, and though Sir Gardain has done well, he does not have the breadth of experience that you would bring to the post."

Asharre rubbed a thumb over a scarred cheek. She *could* train the Celestian knights. It would repay her debt to the temple for sheltering her after Oralia's death, and it would, in its way, honor Surag's teachings by passing them on to the young. The old warrior might not have been pleased to see his lessons given to summerlanders . . . but he was dead, and she thought he might have approved of the Sun Knights' code, if not of the knights themselves.

Yes. That was all true. But.

"I am honored that you would trust me with such a duty," she said, "but there is something I must do first."

"What?"

"I failed in Carden Vale. Because of my mistakes, Falcien died and Evenna was maimed. But our loss, and your Sun Knight's victory, did not end that threat. The fight continues here. I wish to rejoin it before I retire to teach your novices. I cannot leave the field with only defeat behind me."

On the practice floor, a bull-necked man in a leather jerkin walked down the line of knights-in-training, bellowing for them to stop their sparring and form up into groups. Wearily the youths obeyed, pairing up and resuming their drills, now in sets of two against two. They were still too evenly matched, though. Thierras watched them fight for a while before he looked back to Asharre. "Is it pride?"

"Maybe. A part of it," Asharre admitted. "If I claim to be a warrior, yet every battle I fight ends in a loss . . . my claim becomes meaningless, does it not? What right have I to teach anyone anything?"

"If you believe that you're a fool, and I have never thought you a fool," the High Solaros said. There was a sharpness to his voice she had not heard before. "If anyone is to blame for what happened in Carden Vale, it is I. It was our practice, not long ago, to ask the Bright Lady for guidance before sending anyone on an *annovair*. No matter how safe it seemed, we prayed for her insight first. Had I done that, I would have known that Carden Vale needed a full company of Sun Knights and Illuminers, not the two barely sworn Blessed I sent."

"Why didn't you?"

"Carden Vale had been peaceful for so long . . ." Thierras turned the gold ring over on his finger, hiding its sacred sun and bringing it back around again. "I made the mistake of assuming it would stay quiet. There has been a great deal of turmoil in the world these past years. Dark omens, grim portents. More such signs than I have ever seen, and many we don't understand. We don't have enough magic to unravel them all. Not nearly enough. We can watch over a few people and places of great import, but that comes at the cost of ignoring other duties. Falcien and Evenna's *annovair* was among the things I chose to ignore. The mistake, and the failure, was mine."

Asharre stared at him. That mistake, weighed against hers, was nothing. He had failed to see the warnings from the Dome of the Sun, but *she* had seen them on the road, in the ferret's bloodlust and Laedys' frozen death, and had let her charges traipse blithely past them. "You could not know."

"I could have known. I chose to be blind. Because of that, you were set on a road harder and darker than you had any reason to expect. Unprepared, unarmed against the curse of Duradh Mal, you managed to keep two of your three companions alive."

"Did I?" Asharre interrupted. "Has Heradion returned?"

"Not yet," Thierras admitted, "but our prayers have found him safe on the road. He's reached Balnamoine, and there are no further dangers on his path. It is no lie to say you sent him back to us. Even if you choose not to accept credit for that, you saved Evenna's life."

"The Burnt Knight did that, not I." Even the *Thorn* had played a greater role in rescuing Evenna than Asharre had. The knowledge galled her, but she could not deny it. All she had done was lead them into defeat.

"You kept her alive long enough for him to find her. That was no small achievement, *sigrir*. You have nothing to prove. We know what you're worth."

"What I know is that twice I was charged with protecting your Celestians, and twice I failed. What I know is that you gave me a task, and that task remains undone. We escaped the corruption in Carden Vale; we did not end it. Cailan faces a greater danger than that valley ever did. Yet you speak of taking me from the battle and putting me here, training puppies while wolves run wild."

"The puppies do need training," Thierras said mildly. "In any event, purifying Carden Vale is beyond you."

"Corban isn't."

The High Solaros raised an eyebrow. "What do you know about Corban?"

"Little enough, and less I trust," Asharre admitted. Most of what she had learned had come through Bitharn. They had discussed Corban a few times while sitting in Evenna's sickroom, waiting for the Illuminer to awaken. Asharre had told the other woman about what she had seen in poisoned dreams and waking delirium; neither knew if there was any truth to what those visions had showed. But the simplest part of it, she thought—the bedrock on which all the distortions rested—was clear. "He was the one who set Gethel on that path and brought ruin to Carden Vale. And he is here, somewhere in Cailan, with more of the Maolite poison."

Thierras turned back to the sparring trainees. He said nothing more until their bull-necked teacher bellowed them off the floor, each boy carrying his wooden sword and shield in arms gone limp with weariness. Only then, as they filed from the practice hall, did any of them look up to where the High Solaros watched.

"They don't fight to impress me," he said as the last of them departed. "They fight because they are Called to that duty. Whether I am here or not makes no matter. They would fight with the same dedication either way. The same pride." He walked down the eastern stairs, motioning for her to follow. "So. You wish to join the hunt for Corban."

"Yes. He is a man, or was. If he can die, I can kill him."

"Are you certain? Gethel was much more—or less—than human. Corban may be worse. Not only is he likely to be dangerous in himself, but to confront him you will have to accept unsavory allies. Sir Kelland has insisted that the Thorn Malentir is necessary to his cause." The High Solaros' stare was piercing. "The Thorns killed your sister. Can you fight alongside one to kill Corban?"

She didn't know. "If I must."

"Come, then." Thierras led her across the practice hall and down the long corridor that went to the Dome's armory. Chalk dust shimmered in stripes of sunlight. The trainees' sparring left the prickly scent of sweat.

Asharre knew the armory well, but she was unfamiliar with the path Thierras took. He opened the door to a storage room piled with dented helms, gap-riddled chain mail, and breastplates punched through by lances or bolts. Stepping past the damaged armor, he pulled a sword from a jumble of weapons awaiting repair.

She knew that sword: the hilt engraved with prayers, the shining silver edge, the jewel on the pommel that held all the delicate promise of the dawn.

The High Solaros turned back toward her, the blade laid flat across his hands in an unsettling echo of her offering it to Evenna that final, fatal afternoon in Shadefell.

"No." Asharre recoiled.

"Take it," he said. The gentleness with which he had always treated her was gone. Now he was the High Solaros, not Thierras; the full force of his personality and the weight of his office bore down on her. Asharre felt her resolve weakening. But not her fear.

"No," she said again. She couldn't look away from the sword. The gleam of its rose-edged blue jewel seemed pitiless as a serpent's eye. It hypnotized her. "That blade is a trap. It betrayed us. It nearly killed Evenna."

"*Maol* nearly killed you. The sword was blameless. The Mad God wove his snares over Aurandane, but he never touched it through living hands. Evenna cast it aside in time, as did the solaros before her. We have purified and reconsecrated it: Celestia's power, and *only* Celestia's power, lives in the Sword of the Dawn.

"You do not have the luxury of revulsion. In Shadefell and in Carden Vale, our enemies caught you unprepared. Corban must not. Neither must Malentir. Sir Kelland might trust the Thorn, but I don't.

"I fear that dark times lie ahead for our faith. Sir Kelland and Bitharn are two of our best; we cannot afford to lose them. Or you. You need Aurandane. Take it, or pass the duty to one who can."

She held out her hand.

The touch of its hilt was a shock. It felt exactly as she remembered. She had thought—had *wanted* to think—that the scattered fragments of memory she kept from Carden Vale were all wrong, twisted and distorted by the Mad God's hand. But Aurandane slid into her hands as if it had been forged just for her.

"Keep them safe, *sigrir*," the High Solaros said. "Bring them back to me."

Asharre slid it into the place of her *caractan*, grimly proud that her hands were steady. "I will."

THIERRAS TOLD HER WHAT HE KNEW about the sword's history. It wasn't much. The eight Sun Swords had been forged early in the Godslayer's War, once the Celestians realized that the bloodshed might go on for decades. During those years Celestia's Blessed died in great numbers, far too quickly to be replaced, and the survival of the faith itself was in jeopardy. The Sun Swords were forged to fill that desperate need. Each of the eight blades was dedicated to one of the holy hours—dawn, dusk, the solstice's Midnight Sun—and each of them held every power Celestia granted to her mortal children. Healing, sunfire, the Light of Truth: the Sun Swords commanded all those prayers, as did any hand that held them.

Little else was clear in the written histories. Some of the confusion was deliberate, the High Solaros explained; the Illuminers had hesitated to write too plainly, fearing their enemies might use that information against them. Instead they cloaked their meanings in metaphors, or wrote allegories instead of plain fact. At the time, the conventions they used had been widely known . . . but in the centuries since, many of the allegorical meanings changed, or were forgotten altogether. Thus, while Thierras could tell her that the ancient chroniclers described Aurandane "banishing shadows from the battlefield," he could not tell her what that *meant*.

Nor could he tell her how to awaken the magic in the sword, or make it do what she commanded. None of the Sun Swords had been used in living memory. All he could tell her, in the end, was that Aurandane would shape itself to fit its wielder's hand, and shape its spells to meet its wielder's need.

It wasn't much, and it felt like less with the knowledge that she'd soon be facing one of Maol's servants again, this time with a Thorn as a dubious ally at her side.

In the days that followed, Asharre tested Aurandane herself. She went to the Sun Knights' sparring rooms, alone, and tried to coax magic from the sword.

Nothing came. There was *some* enchantment in Aurandane; that was clear. Even if Asharre had known nothing at all about the sword, she would have sensed that. The Sword of the Dawn moved light as a dream in her hands, and its edge was keen enough to split the notes of a song. With it she could slice through a falling feather or, just as easily, a fired brick.

But she could do nothing else. She couldn't summon sunfire, or light a dark room, or heal the small cut she opened on her arm as a test. The blade might as well have been plain metal. *Good* metal, stronger and sharper than steel, but metal just the same. Any other power it held remained out of her reach.

She tried to remember what Oralia had told her about magic: that the power was ever present in her soul, constant as sunlight, shapeless as water. That it had to be given meaning by word and movement, but could be felt even when formless.

Asharre felt nothing like that from Aurandane. Any power it held slumbered in her grasp, and nothing she did would wake it.

She sought out the Burnt Knight next.

Asharre didn't know Sir Kelland well. She knew *of* him, of course—just as he doubtlessly knew of her, another oddity in a temple that seemed to collect them—but she had never worked with either the Burnt Knight or his companion Bitharn before. They had spent most of the past few years riding circuit in the west, just as she had traveled with Oralia, and their roads had not crossed until Carden Vale.

She met them in the gardens, on a morning very like the one that had driven her to find Thierras. Bitharn was wandering under the lindens, idly stroking the trees' low branches as she passed beneath them. She was dressed like an acolyte in soft beige lamb's wool, but she still carried her bow.

Sir Kelland, the Burnt Knight, sat on a tree-shaded bench, watching. He seemed thinner than Asharre recalled. Thinner, and older, with the first strands of silver showing in his braids and new pain lurking in his dark brown eyes. He'd been captured at the end of autumn, she remembered; he would have spent the entire winter imprisoned in Ang'arta. That would be enough to age anyone, let alone a Sun Knight.

Both of them were a good ten years younger than Asharre herself, but they had none of the dewy innocence that her last charges had shared. Young they might be, but these two had been hard tested, and they had endured.

Bitharn came over as Asharre approached. She sat next to Kelland on the bench, shifting her bow out of the way and looking up at the *sigrir*. "You're to help us deal with Corban."

"If you will have me, yes."

"We're not inclined to turn down help." Bitharn tried for a wry smile and didn't quite reach it. "*Any* help."

"So I have heard." There was no harm in bluntness, she judged. Not with these two. "Do you trust the Thorn that much?"

"It is . . . not precisely trust." Kelland said. "Soon after we returned to the Dome, I prayed for guidance. Celestia answered my prayer with a vision. In it, I saw the Irontooths, and Carden Vale between them. The valley was green and peaceful, but mountains that enclosed it were made of black bones. In the first vision—if we let Malentir lead us to Corban and again to Duradh Mal—a blue dawn broke over those mountains. The black bones melted away like mist, leaving slopes of clean stone.

"In the second vision—if we led the charge against Corban and into Duradh Mal on our own, without the Thorn—the dawn rose red like fire, and those black mountains *burned*. Their bones burst into flame under the sun.

Smoke poured into the valley and the river glowed like a volcano's spew. In time the smoke blew away, and the river turned back to clear water, but the carnage before that . . ." His left hand lifted, reaching unconsciously across his thigh toward Bitharn. "I took those signs to mean that the Baozites would go to war with us for Ang'duradh, even at the risk of freeing the Maolite magic contained inside. They want it that badly.

"They've been trying to capture a Blessed for a while. For Duradh Mal, I think. Some escaped. Some died. If I help them, I will be the last.

"I might be wrong about that. But even if I am, the vision was clear that the better course was to let Malentir lead the way. He has means and magics that we do not. We can't even *find* Corban. Any prayer that tries to locate him just returns a vision of churning black and cripples its sender with headaches. Evenna said it's the same thing that happened to them in the mountains above Carden Vale. Maol is shielding his servant from us . . . but Malentir might find a way through."

"I walked across Spearbridge," Asharre said. "I have seen what the Baozites are, with or without their pet Thorns."

A breeze stirred through the lindens and died. In the silence, a squirrel chattered. Then Kelland spoke, his voice quiet and measured. "I'm not blind to that. They held me in that hole for so long . . . I know what they are. But tell me true, *sigrir*: if an outsider looked on your people, would they seem any kinder?"

Asharre thought of defeated warriors staked out on the ice, of dragonships with their sacrificial tails. Of a solaros with a face of pulped meat. "No."

"Then you understand the choice we made. The Baozites are men. Perhaps not *good* men, but men all the same.

Even the Thorns are, after a fashion. 'One cannot be too choosy with allies, if one expects to have any.' Inaglione wrote that."

"But bad allies are worse than none,'" Bitharn said. "Inaglione wrote that too. We all know the Thorns will be our enemies tomorrow. I just hope we can trust them today."

"Thierras did not send me unprepared for treachery." Asharre drew Aurandane, holding the blade out to the sun. The engravings on its hilt were black rivers in the yellow light, repeating prayers in runes she could not read. The spinel on its pommel shone bluer than the sky.

"The Sword of the Dawn." Kelland raised his gaze from the inscribed steel to the *sigrir*'s face. "That is a powerful weapon."

"It is a sharp one." Asharre slid the sword back. "If it has any other powers beyond its edge, I do not know how to call them. Do you?"

"No," Kelland admitted. "Aurandane saved our lives in Shadefell, but it did so in Malentir's hands. As soon as we returned to the Dome, the Illuminers took it to the High Solaros. I was told they purified it, but I was not a part of that ritual. There's nothing I can tell you. I'm sorry."

Asharre nodded, disappointed but unsurprised. "Then I will hope the legends tell true."

25

The magic was failing.

Corban didn't know when or how the change had come. But it *had* come. His protections, his wardings, even the ritual that had lifted the creeping curse from him and sunk it into his captured dogs . . . and other things, in the end; there had been other things too . . . all of them were failing fast.

Failing, and leaving him to . . . to *what?*

The memories were all in pieces. Shards of colored glass thrown into black water, shapes in fog and shadow. He couldn't tell, anymore, what was real and what imagined. Often he thought that the things he imagined *became* real, as if the dead things floating in the apothecary's jars would see because he thought they could, or the herbs hanging from the rafters would change shape to match his visions.

Maybe none of it was real. Maybe it all was. How was he to know? The memories spun and slipped through his fingers and shattered. Nothing he did could keep them intact.

He'd used dogs, for a while.

Wild barks, wild howls. The grief and rage of dogs. His doing. He'd thrown so many dogs into the fire to keep his own skin from burning. It had worked, in the beginning; he'd been free, blessedly *free,* whole and healthy and strong.

Then . . . that strength had gone. He remembered that. He'd sought out other dogs to renew it, so many that he couldn't keep them penned in the secret cellar . . . but letting them run loose had proved no problem. Not after the ritual.

He'd used them up, one by one. Small dogs and big ones, scrawny curs and soft-footed lapdogs. He'd marked them all with spiraled dirt and sent them to the fire. And they had given him strength . . . but each dog granted a weaker reprieve, and the pain hurt worse every time it came back.

In the end . . . Corban ground the heels of his hands into his eyes. What *had* he done in the end?

Men. He'd hunted men. The dogs stopped helping, and the agony had driven him to desperation, and so he had . . . stolen men, yes, drunks and dreamflower addicts, anyone ale-blind enough to accept his pretense of friendship. Not innocents, but they'd do. Corban had led them to his secret cellar, down to the sighing sea, and he had fed them to the flames.

Three times. The memory hit like a blue bolt of lightning: for an instant everything was illuminated, and then it was gone and he was blind again, dazed with the after image of sight. Corban covered his eyes with his hands, weeping. The tears trickled dark through his fingers, stained by . . . what? Charcoal? Blood? He shook the dirty tears away.

Three times he'd led drunks back to his cellar. Three,

out of all the drunks he'd accosted in Cailan's alleys . . . and only two had done him any good.

The first one was rotting somewhere nearby. The stink of him drifted in and out of Corban's awareness, ephemeral as the impish laughter he sometimes heard or the swirling dance of specters at the corners of his eyes. He held his breath when the smell came.

Careless, so careless. Corban hadn't bothered to tie the man before beginning his circles of charcoal and chalk. Hadn't even thought to search for weapons. He'd just assumed, stupidly, that the man's ale stupor would be restraint enough.

It hadn't been, of course.

The dogs gathered in silent, staring circles whenever Corban began a new ritual. They assembled for the drunk as they had gathered for each other. The man woke in a ring of their green-glowing eyes.

Perhaps it was the dogs that unnerved him, or perhaps he saw something in those scribbled runes that told him what lay ahead. Whatever it was, the drunk had an escape hidden in the top of his boot, and he used it.

By the time Corban finished drawing the sigils and went to fetch his guest, the corpse was already cooling. Runnels of blood ran from his wrists to the sea.

Corban left the body there. He thought the dogs would eat it, but they never did. It was still sprawled on the pier, fat with gas, when he brought the next man down.

The second time he made no mistakes.

He remembered it with a hurting kind of bliss, as a starving man might remember the last grand feast of his life. The moments after the end of that ritual had been so sweetly free from pain. It was better than the respite the first dog had given him, if only because his suffering had been so much worse. For those few hours, Corban believed that he'd broken the curse's hold on him, that having made the ultimate sacrifice of another human being, he was truly, gloriously free.

But it was, again, a lie.

Too soon, the pain crept back, reclaiming his body inch by inch. The old gray scars on his hands throbbed. His teeth ached; his eyes felt swollen, too big for their sockets. Maddening prickles ran up and down his legs, jabbing him out of sleep.

Corban knew then that there would be no escape. Not through dogs, not through men. Not for him. Even the path his first victim had taken was closed to him. He'd tried.

So he had sought a third drunk. One last sacrifice.

And it was working, in a small and limited way. The tide of confusion that smothered his mind was . . . not gone, but receded. Enough that he could piece together these scattered memories, at least. Enough that he could think, and act. Barely. The fiend that tormented him had relaxed its grip just slightly, allowing him enough sanity to carry out the rite.

Corban no longer doubted that the fiend existed. He didn't know *what* it was—god, curse, or malevolent shade—and he didn't know why it was torturing him, but he knew that it was there, goading him with pain and luring him with promises of relief. Pulling him into perdition.

Gethel was wrong. No saboteur had laid a curse on the blackfire stone, and there was no way to purify it. The blackfire stone *was* the curse.

Gaping holes riddled his memory, yet Corban could still look back and see scattered events, stepping-stones on his path to damnation. The smoke he'd breathed in Carden

Vale, the scratches he'd taken from the packing straw, the rats . . . each one dragging him a little deeper, each one eroding the foundations of his life until he had nothing left to stand on and was flailing, drowning, spinning into the void . . .

He'd tried to stop it. He *had*. But Corban was only human, and whatever plagued him was not.

Stopping it was beyond him. It had probably been beyond the man he was; it was certainly beyond what he'd become. He could try to slow it, though.

He had to do it now. Before the tide came rushing back. This was the best, perhaps the last chance he'd have; any respite Corban might earn by giving up another damned soul would be feebler and more fleeting than this one. The magic would answer—whatever god or demon had accepted his gifts was bound by the laws of sacrifice, and had to answer his prayers if he paid in blood—but it might come too weak or misshapen to do him any good.

The drunk was mumbling. Confused. He didn't yet realize where he was, or why. Soon enough, he would.

Corban picked up his knife, gathered his worn lumps of charcoal and chalk, and began.

WHEN IT WAS OVER HE WALKED toward the ladder, splashing through the foul-smelling effluvium of his long stay in the cellar. The dogs watched him with incurious eyes. They had their own ritual to attend. Surrounding the bloodied drunk in a circle as united in purpose as it was disparate in appearance, the dogs waited for him to stir. At the first sign of his awakening, they closed in, lapping his wounds clean like so many mothers washing birth fluids from a monstrous, two-legged puppy.

Corban hurried past them. He'd seen the dogs' rite once before, and it had disturbed him profoundly—not only for its ugly parody of birth, but because of the animals' unnatural unity. The intelligence that guided them was not their own. A single will shone in their eyes, and it terrified him. He had put it there.

But it was, for the moment, distracted . . . and that gave Corban his chance.

The gate of bones stood silent behind the cellar's ladder: a hanging pit framed in a wreath of stark white hands. Its very stillness frightened him. No sheet of polished stone was ever so lifeless. Onyx or obsidian misted with the viewer's breath, shifted its reflections as the world around it moved. Even the vastness of a starless night was less implacable than the darkness of that gate, for the sky was graced with clouds and moon and the awareness, however remote, that under it living things walked and sang and bled.

The gate admitted no such possibilities. Corban's mind tottered under the finality of its gaze.

It was from this place that the doom of Duradh Mal had come. He'd been a fool to give it a window from which to escape—but, he thought, that window could be closed.

Corban grabbed one of the fleshless arms. A sucking cold brushed across his fingers: an unreal wind pulling him into the abyss. Quickly, before his sanity and courage could desert him, he yanked the bones off the wall.

The arm came free in a tumble of cracking mortar. The yawning void of the gate vanished like a pricked bubble, leaving a ragged hole in the wall. Dirt on the other side. Just dirt. Before Corban could catch his breath in relief, something struck him from behind, growling furiously as it knocked him to the ground.

Dogs. The dogs were on him. Snapping fangs, heavy

paws, a flurry of rank-smelling fur. A dewclaw gouged his cheek as a mastiff trampled his face. One butterfly-eared lapdog locked its teeth into his foot, ripping through his rotted boot and biting off his toes.

But they were too late. The gate was broken, the arms stripped of whatever magic had let them latch onto the wall. Reduced to inert bone again, they were falling off the bricks like empty cicada shells toppling from tree trunks.

He'd won. The gate was gone. It was gone . . . and the demon that rode him remained. Corban closed his eyes, laughing and weeping, as the dogs tore into him.

26

On the night that Bitharn came for her, a storm rolled in from the sea, smothering the moon and casting the city into rain-drowned gloom. By midnight it had not lifted. Asharre lay on her pallet and looked out to a city that shivered under a sky cold and wet and grim. Even Heaven's Needle seemed pallid under those leaden clouds.

She hadn't slept. A peculiar alertness had suffused her since sundown. The *sigrir* felt every current in the air, every thread in the rough wool blankets pressed against her skin. It was the same acute awareness, at once attuned to her immediate surroundings and strangely remote from her own body, that came over her before battle. Her heartbeat was a steady drum, calling her to a dance that was about to begin.

It did not surprise Asharre when Bitharn knocked. She had been expecting the signal, or something like it, for hours; even before opening the door, she knew Bitharn had come to summon her to the hunt. The *sigrir* rose, swept on her cloak and swordbelt, and stepped outside. She carried Aurandane, not her own *caractan*. Her weapon was an old familiar friend, but it would not serve tonight.

"The Thorn has found Corban," Bitharn said, slightly breathless. Under her hood, her cheeks were flushed from cold and exertion. Her rain-sodden cloak dripped a puddled circle around her feet.

"Where?" Asharre asked.

"Near the docks. He wouldn't tell us more than that. We're to meet him in the Illuminers' safehouse on the Street of Little Flowers. Kelland should already be there."

Asharre nodded, raised her hood, and followed the younger woman from the temple into the storm.

Outside the sweeping dark fell upon them, whipping them into silence with lashes of wind and rain. Asharre pulled her cloak tight, huddling against the deluge and narrowing her focus to Bitharn's boots splashing across the cobblestones two steps ahead.

The city was empty in the storm. Half-blinded by the sleeting drops, with her only companion a faceless wraith ahead, it was all too easy for Asharre to imagine that she was back in Carden Vale—or, worse, walking through a vision of what Cailan might become if they failed.

The streets would run red first, though. And the conflagration that would consume the city before it settled into the silence of ashes was a horror Asharre did not want to imagine. She closed her mind's eye to it, concentrating instead on the weight of the rain on her cloak, the slippery cobblestones underfoot, the wail of wind over stone-tiled roofs.

It was almost a surprise when they came to the safehouse. The Street of Little Flowers, named for the cheap brothels that lined it, was one of the rowdiest parts of

Cailan. Sailors and dockworkers stumbled through it at all hours, drunk or on their way there, while bawds called enticements and footpads stalked them in the alleys. Tonight, however, that endless game of chaser-and-chased had been pushed indoors. The glow of firelight through the brothels' rain-drummed windows, accompanied by snatches of rowdy song, suggested that the merriment continued there—but the street itself was desolate.

The safehouse, which ordinarily stood out like a maiden aunt at a drunken revel, was just another house shuttered against the storm tonight. Curlicued ironwork barred its windows, and salt-poisoned rosevines clung feebly to the trellis over its door, suggesting a certain gentility, or at least an attempt at it, in an environment utterly unforgiving of such graces.

The door opened to a musty-smelling sitting room carpeted in drifts of cat fur. Scented candles dotted the tables and alcoves between the windows, adding a layer of cloying sweetness to the stuffy air and giving just enough light to outline the two people who sat waiting for them inside: Kelland, trying without success to pick cat hairs off his trousers, and a sleek-haired older lady who knitted deftly in the near-dark. A fat dowager cat sprawled in the woman's lap, twitching its ears to the click of her needles without opening an eye. Another sat on the back of her chair, and a third paced sinuously around Kelland's boots, weaving its body through an endless double loop.

"Homey." Bitharn swatted at a puff of cat hair on a chair, then made a face when it stuck to her wet hand.

"Don't get too comfortable," Kelland said. "We aren't staying long. As soon as Asharre is disguised, we'll go to meet the Thorn."

Bitharn looked up, surprised. "I thought we were meeting him here."

"Good. You were meant to . . . as was Malentir. In truth, it was a bit of hair-splitting. *We*, meaning the three of us, are meeting here. We'll meet him near the brothel across the way."

Bitharn's nose wrinkled. "Coisette's? That place is a snake pit."

"Hardly fair to the snakes. But yes, it's a den of degenerates and dreamflower addicts—and, as it happens, our upstairs windows have an excellent view of its doors. I can think of worse ways for a Thorn to occupy his time than trying to ferret out which of Coisette's patrons are secretly Celestians.

"Whether or not he chooses to spy on Coisette's guests, however, he won't know where the real safehouse is. And," Kelland added, as the old woman put away her knitting and removed a case of tiny bottles and brushes buried in her yarn basket, "we won't have to rely on him to disguise us tonight. I expect he'll want us to wear the faces of the dead, and while I can see the wisdom in hiding ourselves from Corban as long as possible, I *don't* see any reason we should resort to bloodmagic to do it. Our disguises will be simpler things. Hooded cloaks for the two of us. A little more for Asharre."

He gave the *sigrir* an apologetic shrug. "No other woman in Cailan looks like you. I don't know that Corban truly has any sentries guarding his lair—if he did, I'd like to think we would have found them—but there's no reason to chance being spotted early."

The old woman set her case on a stool near Asharre and clicked it open. The *sigrir* looked into it curiously. She'd heard a little about the sisters who lived here from Oralia.

In their younger years, both sisters had practiced on the Avenue of Camellias, where they'd learned the arts of paint and powder from an Amrali-trained courtesan. They could turn a toothless drab into a beauty, or a handsome youth into a wart-covered fright. As Oralia told it, when they were finished with a man, his own dog might not recognize its master.

After surveying Asharre with a critical eye, the woman clicked her tongue, nodded, and reached into the case. "You'll make an easy man," she said. "A big full beard to cover some of those scars on your face, an old case of pox to explain away the rest . . . yes, you're an easy one. Hold still." She dabbed a strong-smelling glue on Asharre's face, covering each daub with a pinch of coarse reddish hair.

"You don't need better light?" Asharre asked.

"Hush. No talking, unless you want your new face put on crooked. There, now . . ." She chuckled softly as she worked. "Weak light suits these old eyes well enough. It lets me see you as the man I'll make you, not as whoever you are . . . and you'll not be wearing this face to one of Lord Gildorath's galas, will you? The eyes that see you will have no better light than this. It's the outlines that need to be strong tonight, not the details."

Asharre had her doubts about that, but she held her tongue. After finishing the beard, the old woman mixed a thick putty and applied it to the *sigrir*'s brow and upper cheeks, filling in some of the scarred runes while emphasizing the ridges of others. When she finished, Kelland stood, pulling his cloak's hood over the white shells in his hair. Gloves covered his dark hands, and the sun-marked hilt of his sword was wrapped in nondescript leather.

Bitharn had watched Asharre's transformation curiously, but waved off any suggestion that she should wear the same. "Paint never suited me," the girl said, wrapping her damp cloak around her shoulders. She checked the watertight case that held her bowstrings, fastened an oilcloth cap over her quiver, and led the way out of the safehouse.

The storm's fury had not abated during the hours they'd spent inside. Cascading water foamed across the cobblestones, running so strong in places that it threatened to sweep Asharre's feet from under her. She trudged through it stolidly, splashing across the street until she reached the brothel's door.

Inside Coisette's, all was eye-watering smoke and oniony fish stew and the raucous, desperate laughter of the damned. Drunk bawds swayed on the laps of drunker patrons, and although the dingy torchlight made Asharre a convincing man, it could not hide the exhaustion under those painted smiles. The *sigrir* sat at the periphery of a dice game, halfheartedly losing money, until a persistent tap at the window put an end to her purse's slow bleed.

It was a sparrow. A little brown sparrow, eyes glossy with rainwater and death.

She had to remember to breathe. The sight of the bird had stunned her with remorse, resentment, rage—all the things knotted around her old grief. All the things she couldn't afford to show, couldn't afford to *feel*.

Asharre inhaled. Exhaled, striving for control.

"That is a truly unfortunate beard," Malentir said a moment later, sliding into an empty chair at the dice game. He wore another face, but Asharre knew it was the Thorn; his black eyes were too cold to be human, and the other men at the table muttered and moved away from him, troubled by the new arrival without quite knowing why.

"We thought it best to surprise our host." The dice cup had come around to her again. Asharre gave it a shake and tossed the dice, watching them tumble with suddenly intense interest. The spinning pips meant nothing to her, but they were safer to look at than the Thorn.

"Oh, I agree," Malentir said. He lifted a hand. Silver and glass gleamed in his sleeve: three tiny bottles tethered to his wire bracelet by delicate silver chains. "I would have offered a solution, but I see the knight found his own. It *was* his suggestion, wasn't it?"

"Yes." And the purpose of that disguise, Asharre realized, was less to deceive Corban than to send a message to the Thorn: the Celestians refused to depend on his magic, or accede to his methods. He had, clearly, taken in their meaning at a glance.

The other players were drifting away, too unsettled by Malentir's presence to keep their minds on the dice. Kelland and Bitharn took the chairs they vacated.

"Have you learned more?" the knight asked quietly. His words were nearly inaudible in the clamor that filled Coisette's. Asharre pulled her own chair closer and passed the dice cup to Bitharn.

"Nothing worthwhile. Corban has at least one victim's corpse lying in his lair. The restless shade led me to him. It was, regrettably, of little use beyond that; less is left of that poor soul's mind than those of the *maelgloth* penned in Duradh Mal. I know where Corban hides, but little else."

"That'll have to be enough, then," Bitharn said, plucking at her cloak with a sigh. She checked her lantern, ensuring its flame was steady before she started toward the door. "Pity it couldn't be closer. I'm exceedingly tired of getting wet."

Once more they ventured into the storm. Curtains of black rain billowed over the narrow roofs and blotted out the moon. The streets were rain-dimpled rivers, foaming white where they came down steep inclines.

Through this Asharre trudged with her hood pulled low and dripping past her chin. Bitharn and Kelland were blurs in the rain beside her, Malentir another ahead. None spoke. The storm drowned speech as surely as light, and they made their way in silence broken only by the hammering hiss of rain and the far-off boom of thunder over the sea.

The Thorn led them nearly to the water's edge. In the harbor, past the last ragged fringe of buildings, ships curled tight against the driving rain and bobbed on swirling waves. Slick-backed rats scurried through the alleys, quarreling over choice morsels. Corban's house squatted in one of those alleys, but no rats ran down that way.

The hovel's door, taken off its hinges, sagged against its entrance. Bird droppings caked the step in front of it. Rather than forming a dumpy ridge like every other such pile Asharre had seen, those droppings rose into vaguely familiar, spindly-stalked shapes.

"Mushrooms," Bitharn said. "They're making the shapes of the mushrooms we saw in Carden Vale. *Morduk ossain.*"

Malentir's hood dipped in a nod. "That is not Corban's doing, but his god's. It gives me hope . . . and fills me with fear. The Mad God is not fool enough to let *morduk ossain* bloom on the Dome of the Sun's doorstep, but no Maolite could mistake this sign. There is a locus of Maol's power inside, it tells them: enter, and be sanctified. But does that signal mean that Corban has given himself completely to Maol, or that his god seeks new vessels to replace a failed one?"

Kelland moved past him without answering. He grabbed the door in gloved hands and pulled, shattering the unnatural sculptures on the stoop. For an instant something seemed to squirm inside the cracked shells of bird dung—as if larval *things*, neither worms nor mush-rooms but blind pale squirmers somewhere between the two, gestated inside. Then the door swept across them, knocking them apart, and they dissolved into the rain.

Bundles of herbs dangled from the rafters of Corban's hovel. They hung swollen and strangled in their strings, dripping slow brown slime. No longer were they feverfew or chamomile, wintermint or tansy; while a few moldy leaves on the outside of each bundle still retained their original shape, their hearts had all bulged into the con-torted knots of beggar's hand.

Fat glass jars squatted under the bundled herbs and dry-ing racks, and in them dead things swam. Kelland's light skittered over dissolving arms and shriveled tails, toothless mouths filled with brine and sleeves of decaying flesh that hung loose from soft soaked bone.

The stench of rotting, fermented fish that emanated from the jars was incredible. Several of their lids were askew. Wrinkled fingers clutched at their rims, stilled in the act of climbing out. The creatures' bodies, malformed and plump with brine, swayed gently in their jars; their fingers, exposed to unforgiving air, were dried and cracking on the glass.

"What stopped them?" Bitharn wondered. She walked over to one—a curled white thing with stubbed teeth and a single round eye over its upturned snout—and leaned over, using her belt knife to poke at its paws.

It didn't move, but something else did. Asharre glimpsed something, or *things*, slinking predatory and swift through the hovel's shadows. A familiar, wild rankness came from them. Something like . . .

"Dogs," Asharre realized aloud, a heartbeat before they came.

The dogs poured like rats from the walls, charging in a snarling, yapping horde. She couldn't fathom where they'd come from; the hovel was far too small for them to have hidden as the Celestians entered. Yet they rushed in, a dozen or more of them, as real as she was. Some were big and muscular, with the wedge-shaped heads and slab shoulders of dockside maulers. Others were gaunt and mangy: feral scavengers from the streets. One, barely bigger than Asharre's boot, had the silky fur and butterfly ears of a highborn lady's pet, but it growled as ferociously as the scarred mastiff beside it.

Not one of the dogs was whole. The fur along their flanks was shaved in winding curves, and in those patterns their skin was cross-hatched with thin black cuts. Around those cuts their flesh was hideously bubbled, glistening like hard black roe. Their eyes were wet black marbles, and their front paws were stretched to grotesque fingers, each knuckled with two joints unlike any true dog's toe. Several dogs had gaping, gnawed wounds, dealt by their own teeth or others'. The little lady's lapdog had the worst of these; its bones bulged out from a rip that laid it open from tail to shoulder. That wound should have killed it, but the dog wasn't even slowed.

"Back to back," Kelland shouted. A terrier ducked a low swing and snapped at his legs. He brought a boot down on its head, crushing the animal's skull, and kicked the struggling body away. "Back to back!"

Malentir shook back his sleeves, staying where he was. Asharre and Kelland backed toward one another, closing defensively in front of Bitharn. The girl retreated out the open door, setting an arrow to her bow once she had room enough to draw.

The beasts were on them. Brave or stupid, the Thorn

was on his own. Asharre drew Aurandane. She had no time to hesitate, no time to doubt. The beasts were on her, and she attacked. Uncertain as she was of Celestia, the *sigrir* had perfect faith in her own skill.

As if in answer to that faith, pale blue radiance blazed up from the steel. It eclipsed the smoky light of Bitharn's lantern with its brilliance. The dogs drew back, snarling soundlessly. Smoke trickled out between their teeth and wept from their lifeless eyes. Then their hesitation snapped, and the animals leaped.

Asharre met them with Aurandane. Her sword caught the mastiff under its jaw and sheared cleanly through its skull, spraying blood and motes of sticky blackness that hissed and burned as they flew. The headless body staggered on a few steps, stumbling over moldy leaves and broken glass. She hit it again and sent the corpse careening into a drying frame. It collapsed in a shower of cracking wood. Asharre dashed scarlet spray from her brow—thicker and colder than it should have been, closer to wine-jelly than blood—and squared to meet the next.

An unnatural chill spread through the air. Frost crackled across the sodden floor, spreading quick as wildfire. The dogs' paws froze to the ground, and although many fought free, they left behind claws and entire toes when they pulled loose. In the corner of her eye, Asharre saw the Thorn raise his cupped hands higher.

Pale mist spilled from his fingers. The mist slowed some dogs, killed others. Their skulls fractured, burst open by ice swelling the flesh inside their bones. Frost-flowers of sickly yellow and dead gray blossomed from their eyes and nostrils; their jaws creaked open as frozen bile pushed its way out.

Bitharn chose her targets from the dogs that didn't die.

She shot cleanly between the *sigrir* and the knight, but the confusion of their bodies hurt her aim; the gray goose shafts still flew true, each one burying itself in a furry throat or chest, but they came slower and fewer than Asharre liked.

"Hold them," Kelland rasped. "I need time."

Bait them, you mean. She couldn't hold them back herself. Asharre jerked her head in a nod and bulled forward, pulling the throng away from the knight.

The little lapdog seized the opportunity. It sank its teeth into Asharre's ankle, its entire body whipping from side to side as it worried at her flesh. Blood filled her boot. Two of the mastiffs lunged at her; Asharre slashed one deep across the chest and sidestepped the other. It charged past her, its claws scrabbling on ice. The wounded one stumbled, knocked off-stride by her blow. Blood soaked the short black fur on its chest. She'd heard its breastbone crack at Aurandane's impact, knew the force behind the swing . . . but the dog was not dead, hardly even seemed slowed. Blackfire had the animal deep in its grasp, and it did not let go lightly.

Asharre closed on the injured dog. It sprang, and the shining sword smashed into its jaws. She heard the rattle of the dog's teeth striking the wall, heard Kelland's voice lift in prayer. The dog's raspy growls, labored and wet, sounded much louder than the Celestian's chant. Blood and froth drooled from its ruined mouth. Its heart, a withered black thing, throbbed in the mangled hollow of its chest. And still it did not die.

Golden light blossomed around her, joining the dawn-pale blue of Aurandane's glow. Kelland's prayer, she realized, as the light rose to fill the hovel. Asharre felt only welcome warmth as the aura closed around her, but the dogs burst into flame. The little one locked onto her ankle whined, its teeth still buried in cloth and muscle, and looked up at the *sigrir* with what she would have sworn was sudden awareness, and sudden horror.

The fur fell from its face like dust blown in the wind; the black lumps of its eyes dissolved, leaving empty holes in a bare-fleshed skull. Sinew and muscle cracked like sun-baked clay and fell away in smoldering showers. The bones stood naked an instant longer; then they, too, crumbled in a wash of heatless flame.

The others fell more quickly, although not as completely. Their insides melted away, leaving their empty skins collapsed on the apothecary's floor. Above them, the hanging knots of beggar's hand erupted into colorless flame; below, the Thorn's spell-summoned ice hissed into steam. As fire and ice and cursed unlife all sputtered out, Kelland let his prayer go.

Once the immediate danger faded, the pain of Asharre's injured ankle flooded back in. She sucked in a breath, shifted her weight off the bad foot, and clutched Aurandane's hilt tighter. The Sword of the Dawn had the power to heal her wound. The magic was there, locked in its steel . . . but it had vanished as soon as the last of the dogs fell, and she didn't know how to call it back. Useless.

Instead she used the sword's tip to prod the wrinkled dogskin. "What were they?"

"An attempt at making servants," Malentir replied. He didn't appear to have been wounded, although his spell-woven guise had eroded visibly after Kelland's prayer. The ivory pallor of his own skin showed through the fading tan of his false face, and his tunic and trousers seemed baggier, reverting toward the loose flow of robes. "*Maelgloth,* most likely. Perhaps *ansurak.* Whichever it was, the attempt was not entirely successful. They were unevenly transformed—that is why the skins are left of some, and nothing of the rest—but I don't know why. Nor do I know why the Mad God channeled his power into dogs rather than men. Ordinarily his servants take humans when they can. It is a promising sign, however. His dominion here is incomplete."

"Let me see your foot," Kelland said. He knelt beside Asharre, examining her ankle, while Bitharn and the Thorn sifted through the wreckage of the hovel to find Corban's hiding-hole. Warmth flowed from the knight's hands as he prayed, washing the pain away.

Asharre bit the inside of her lip. If only she could *use* the sword the High Solaros had given her, she wouldn't have to be a burden on the Blessed. Instead all she could do was nod gratefully to the knight as he finished.

"Found it," Bitharn called, pushing a mold-stiffened rug away from the other side of the hovel. A small trapdoor sat in the floor underneath. She reached for the ring in its center, but Malentir waved her away.

"I will look first," he said.

Bitharn shot him a sour look, but she stepped aside without comment.

The Thorn ignored her, sweeping his hands a few inches over the trapdoor. After tracing its outline twice, he nodded to himself and pulled the door up by its ring. He drew out a sparrow's carcass from a hidden pocket in his robes, whispering over the stiff curled body. The bird opened its wings and straightened its head with a tiny crack of cartilage, then plummeted through the open door. Malentir settled back on his heels, waiting. Twice he murmured inaudibly to himself, but he never spoke to them.

The others exchanged a glance. Then Kelland shrugged and sat crosslegged in a corner, lapsing into meditative prayer. Bitharn wandered among the dogskins, retrieving what arrows she could. She was sliding the last of them into her quiver when Malentir finally stirred.

"Our quarry awaits," he said.

27

Kelland approached the open trapdoor cautiously. "What did you see?"

"The ladder goes to a small cellar," Malentir answered. "Part of it is closed off with boards and rope. There is a dog behind the boards, but I do not believe it can escape. A short tunnel leads to a smuggler's pier. There is a warding at its threshold; I did not send my bird onto the pier."

"Anything dangerous?"

"Nothing insurmountable."

The knight's lips thinned in annoyance at the Thorn's reply, but he nodded. "I'll take the lead. Asharre, after me. Bitharn follows. Malentir has the rear. No one goes past this warding until we've both examined it." Sheathing his sword, Kelland took hold of the ladder's top rung and swung down. Asharre waited at the top, holding the lantern high. Once he reached the floor, she passed it to the knight. He set the lantern on the ground nearby and moved deeper into the tunnel.

Asharre followed. The descent was cramped, and her body blocked most of the light, so she felt her way along the ladder half-blind. Flakes of rust broke off on her palms. The metal rungs creaked and swayed under her weight. She did her best to ignore that, as she did the sweat that trickled slowly from her temples to her chin.

Halfway down, Asharre glimpsed something in the cracked brick wall behind the ladder's rungs. Some shape, some ghostly outline, barely visible in the shifting gloom. It looked like a scratched-out circle—the silhouette of a doorway, maybe—marked by peculiar, uneven holes in the bricks. For the merest instant, she saw the spectral image of a ring of bones hanging on the wall, arm locked around arm in a grisly wreath . . . and as soon as she realized it, Asharre closed her eyes, shaking her head in refusal.

That trap had caught her in Carden Vale. The illusion of meaning was just a snare, one of Maol's infinite tricks to lure the unwary into his grasp. She wouldn't fall into it again.

No sooner did the thought come to her than the rungs under each of her feet gave way with an oddly wet noise, closer to the ripping of flesh than the pang of snapping metal. The ladder's sides ran through her hands like a rope of sawblades, tearing her palms. Asharre hit the ground hard. Pain shivered up her legs and back. Trembling, she tested her footing and felt a flash of surprise that she had not broken a leg.

The twang of a crossbow—no, two—sounded behind her. It was a sound out of nightmare: the same sound that she'd heard before Falcien fell. Panic blanketed her mind.

Snatching up the lantern, Asharre ran to Kelland's aid. He was on the ground, gasping, two black bolts protruding from his chest. Past him, the lantern's light revealed two crossbowmen sprawled outside the low-ceilinged entrance to the smuggler's pier.

They were already dead. Rivers of black blood spilled from their noses and ears. Ice crystals glittered on their skin. Their chests, carved with ashen spirals and runes, drew no breaths; their hands, elongated and bulb-knuckled like the toes of the deformed dogs' paws, lay limp on the stocks of their weapons. The only wounds on the bodies were those that marked their transformation from men into *maelgloth*, but the Thorn had never needed blades to kill. Asharre was not surprised to look back and see him alighting at the bottom of the ladder. He approached the fallen knight and crouched, examining his injuries.

Kelland scarcely seemed aware of the Thorn. His shell-tipped braids snaked across the floor; his dark lips moved as he mumbled something she couldn't hear. The bolts jutted obscenely from his body.

Quickly, mercilessly, Malentir pulled them free and tossed them aside. Kelland's torso jerked convulsively; Asharre flinched, watching.

"Help him," Malentir ordered.

"How? I'm no Blessed."

"You have the *sword*. I pulled the quarrels from him before they could explode, but their poison is killing him. Use the sword to burn it out, or the knight will die."

Asharre licked her lips uncertainly. She nodded, holding Aurandane out like an awkward dowsing rod as she approached to examine the knight's injuries.

The first bolt had hit him low and to the side, scratching the ribs. It might have struck a lung; she couldn't tell. If it hadn't, he might survive. Many men took fever and died after a deep puncture like that, but she'd seen a few recover, with care.

There was no surviving the other. The stink of it told her it was a gut shot even before she looked down to confirm it. Asharre grimaced. That might have been an accident, or else very good aim. If the taint took him, he'd stagger on, half alive and utterly mad, like those wretched dogs. If not . . . it was a cruel death for an enemy.

Black grit stained the wounds. Asharre touched it, cringing inwardly. The blood was cold, the grit burning hot, as if it drained life's warmth to fuel its own inner fires. It dissolved in the blood on her finger, just as it dissolved in the knight's body. She could see the blackfire taint seeping into his flesh, trickling through torn muscle and opened veins.

Could she heal that? Asharre clutched Aurandane's hilt, blind with fear and ignorance. She'd called flame from it before, but now the Sword of the Dawn sat inert as ordinary steel in her hands.

She held her breath, willing herself to touch that power again. To shape it. *Something* tugged at her soul, like the strains of distant music or the far-off crash of the sea. It called to her, and it struck a quivering chord of terror in her heart. *Divinity*.

Asharre pulled back from it, even as she longed to follow its numinous song. She couldn't relax her hard-won control, couldn't trust that siren melody, without seeing dream-Falcien on his bier and her own hand tracing corrupt sigils on Evenna's brow.

Was it truly Celestia's presence she felt, or did Maol's touch still linger in the steel? If Aurandane *was* pure, did she trust the Bright Lady to save her Blessed when the goddess had failed Oralia and Evenna and herself? *How?* She did not know the shape of spells. She could kill, but healing was another art entirely.

Kelland was dying. There was no time. *Decide!*

She shoved the sword at Malentir. The Thorn had drawn upon Aurandane's magic once before. He knew how to channel its power—and he could do so again quickly, and surely, enough to save Kelland. *She* could not.

"Heal him," Asharre said, choking on her helplessness.

Malentir asked no questions. He took the Sword of the Dawn and slid it into the larger, deadlier wound. Blood gurgled around the blade, weakening with the knight's pulse. But Aurandane began to shine, blue and white, its steel becoming translucent as crystal. Spectral flames pulsed in Kelland's flesh, casting a scarlet radiance up through his skin; the buried sword burned like the deep heart of the earth.

With surprising gentleness, Malentir pulled the sword away and gave it back to Asharre. The blade came up bloody, spattering crimson drops across the floor . . . but it was clean blood, and warm. The blackfire dust was gone from both wounds. But the holes remained, pooled dark with blood that spilled over his body every time Kelland drew a breath.

Those wounds would kill him, blackfire stone or no, if he was not brought to the Blessed soon. Asharre returned to the ladder and looked up. Bitharn was staring down, her face white and stiff with fear. "What's happened?" she whispered.

"Kelland is badly hurt," Asharre said. "He will die if he does not get to the Dome soon. Can you take him there?"

Bitharn nodded fiercely. Her eyes were glassy with unshed tears, but the white shock was fading rapidly. "Yes. I will."

Asharre took hold of the knight by the shoulders and dragged him to the ladder, then hoisted him bodily up the rungs. Blood spattered across her face as she boosted him above her head. He grunted once, and made a small strangled gasp when she pushed him up, but never said a word. Bitharn caught him under the arms and, with Asharre's help, pulled the knight out of the cellar. The *sigrir* stood by the ladder, watching, until Kelland's red-stained boot soles slid out of sight. Then she scrubbed the blood from her face with a sleeve and walked away.

Had the Thorn known the crossbowmen were waiting? She couldn't read those flat black eyes . . . but a prickle of suspicion crawled up her back, and it grew stronger when she brushed past him to examine the rest of the tunnel.

"He'll live?" Malentir asked.

"If Bitharn reaches the temple in time."

"Then he'll live. The second coming of Maghredan would not stop that girl."

Asharre wondered if it was disappointment or relief she heard in his voice. Or neither. Perhaps he hadn't betrayed them at all . . . but she looked at the dead crossbowmen, and thought of corpse-hands moving on puppet strings of mist and magic, and felt that prickling distrust sharpen into a sting.

There was nothing to do but go on, though. Whether or not Malentir had manipulated the crossbowmen's ambush to isolate her—and she might have imagined that; why would the Thorn eliminate his strongest ally before they'd even reached Corban?—it was too late to turn back. They had the Maolite cornered. He'd surely flee if they let him, and Asharre had no intention of letting that happen.

Partway to the secret pier, a makeshift barrier of boards and ropes clogged part of the tunnel wall. Dog hair feathered the gaps between the boards; the smell of feces and wet hound was overpowering. A few cracked bones with blackfire stains in their marrow-gaps littered the floor nearby.

Asharre glanced over her shoulder at the Thorn. "This is where you saw the dog?"

"Yes."

"There is only one inside?"

"Yes."

She nodded, pulling away loops of rope and loosening the boards. Through the widening gaps, she saw a limping yellow brindle cringe from her. The dog bore cruel black spirals similar to those on the dogs they'd fought in the apothecary, but its cuts didn't seem as deep, and they didn't cover as much of the animal's flanks. Although its eyes were clouded with a murky haze, they weren't completely black, as the others' had been. Asharre guessed that this dog had been one of Corban's early victims. Perhaps he hadn't mastered the magic he used to transform the others, or perhaps his connection to Maol had been weaker in the beginning. Whatever the cause, it was clear to her that this yellow brindle was not as corrupted as the others.

"What are you doing?" Malentir asked.

Asharre broke a section of the barrier free and pushed it to the side. The dog flattened its ears and pulled its lips back to show sharp, black-veined teeth, but it did not attack as she approached. "A test."

"Of what?"

"Faith." She advanced into the tiny cavern, holding Aurandane slanted defensively as she closed the dog into a corner. The brindle's hackles rose, but it backed away.

When she was close enough to touch the dog, Asharre stopped. She concentrated on Aurandane, seeking the faint, luminous melody she'd sensed from it when Kelland fell. After a moment she felt it, or heard it, or simply *knew*, instinctively, that it was there. The magic was at once enveloping and elusive; trying to control it was like walking into a bank of sea-mist and grabbing at it with her hands.

She didn't try. Steeling herself against all her instincts and training, Asharre simply opened herself to the magic, allowing it to flow through her in whatever shape it chose. It took all her discipline to let go . . . but that, she thought, must be the essence of faith.

Surrender was anathema to her, and trust in Celestia only slightly less so, but Asharre forced herself to embrace both.

Aurandane flared into flame. Blue and blush and silvery-pale, all the colors of the dawn. Light washed over the dog. The cataracts melted from its eyes in smoky tears. The spirals in its sides wept black fog, leaving clean bone and muscle.

The dog sank onto its side. It was still hurt—dying, maybe, with the artificial sustenance of its blackfire corrosion stripped away—but the eyes that stared up at Asharre were a clear soft brown, and the yellow brindled tail wagged weakly against the ground.

She redoubled her efforts, trying to heal the newly cleansed wounds. The half-heard song swelled into a thundering assault, and suddenly she understood what Oralia meant when she had spoken of being overwhelmed by Celestia's power. It was like standing in a waterfall: she couldn't see, couldn't breathe through the pounding torrent.

Staggered, she pulled away, closing her mind to the sword's song. The light went out like a snuffed candleflame. Asharre retreated from the cavern and, by the infinitely weaker glow of her lantern, replaced the boards she'd removed. She left them leaning against the wall; she wanted the dog to be able to escape when it felt well enough to walk. It might, eventually. In the last glimpse she'd had before the magic died, its wounds had been a healthy pink.

Malentir watched her back away from the cavern. Around him the shadows stirred like living things, pulling close to his body. "Are you satisfied with your test?"

She shrugged off his question. "Where is Corban?"

"This way. The entrance was warded." He pointed to the wall above the low-ceilinged hole that led to the smuggler's pier. The bricks around it were cross-hatched with scratches. Asharre swept her lantern over them. Some of the marks had blood and black dirt embedded in the gouges, but the rest were only scratches. The clean ones were newer.

She lowered the lantern. "Was? The wardspell is gone now?"

"It was gone before we came." The Thornlord traced two fingertips over the scratches without touching them. "Corban defaced the sigils himself. It seems Maol's yoke does not sit easy on his shoulders."

"Good," Asharre said, stepping through.

On the other side was a subterranean dock. A short wooden pier stretched over black water, with the sigil-marked hole at one end and two mooring bollards at the other. Loose ropes trailed from the bollards into the water. Dusty crates, stamped with the mountain-over-river of Carden Vale, were stacked at the pier's far end. Her lantern's light scattered in wide yellow ripples around the pilings, shining over barnacle-speckled wood and empty water. No boats.

Smudged rings of chalk and charcoal stained the pier. Rusty brown dappled the boards, and tufts of dog hair fluttered from splinters. A human corpse lay near those blood-spatters, reeking of rot. The body wasn't marked with black spirals, however, and it appeared to be purely dead, so she walked by. Nothing else moved until Asharre was halfway down the pier.

"That is far enough. Any closer, and I shoot." The voice was rusty and frail; it was a voice that barely remembered the shape of words.

Asharre slowed, setting the lantern down carefully, but she did not stop. No one who called out warnings after she'd killed his dogs, stepped over the corpses of his curse-bound guards, and seen his Maolite wardings was likely to shoot her for walking down a pier. She'd declared herself an enemy and had shown herself to be a dangerous one. If, after all that, the speaker hadn't shot her on sight, she had little to fear from his threat.

Corban—it had to be Corban—was a scrawny man crouched behind the crates at the pier's end. His arm trembled as he pointed a crossbow, one-handed, in her direction; the bulbous quarrel swung drunkenly through the air. A pebble of blackfire stone rattled inside its filigreed head.

"Put it down," Asharre said. She didn't expect him to obey; she just wanted him to hesitate long enough for her to close on him. Yet, to her surprise, Corban lowered his weapon shakily.

"I never wanted this," he said. A dry sob wracked the man's body. "You must believe me. I wanted . . . I wanted . . . I was greedy. I confess. But *this* was never supposed to happen. Not this. Gods save me, I've suffered for my sins. Haven't I suffered enough? *This is not what I wanted.*"

There was something wrong with him, Asharre thought. Not his mind; despite his obvious thralldom, he seemed surprisingly lucid. But there was something amiss with his body. The shadows it cast were all wrong. She took another cautious step, reaching for Aurandane's magic as she did so. It was easier this time, almost natural. Blue flame sprang up around the blade, allowing her to see more clearly.

It wasn't the shadows that were wrong. It was his flesh. Asharre stopped, staring at Corban in disbelief.

Half his body, in bits and pieces, was . . . missing. Erased. His right arm was gone below the elbow. Two-thirds of his face had been cut away: one remaining eye stared out over the twin slits of his nostrils and a split, frayed bottom lip. There was no upper lip. Chunks of his thighs were missing in a spiral of carved flesh around the bone; what was left was white, wrinkled, and bloodless as a cellared turnip.

Darkness filled the gaps. It was thick, tenebrous, pulsing with something disconcertingly like life. It wrapped around his exposed bones and sent oozing tendrils under his skin. When he moved, it seemed to Asharre, it was the darkness that moved first, manipulating Corban's body on its tentacles like a mutilated puppet of meat and bone.

"The Mad God has taken you," she whispered.

"No. *No.* There is a demon. A voice in the stone. He has not taken me . . . but he tries. He *tries.* I hear him. He whispers . . . offers me power. Offers me peace. Such dreams. Such threats." Corban shook his head vehemently, nearly dropping his crossbow. Flecks of something—hair? flesh? corruption?—flew from his scalp, struck the water, and vanished. "Always he whispers. And hurts me, hurts me so I will obey. He drives me like a beaten ox . . . and gods help me, gods forgive me, I have run before those blows. I have sinned."

"Is that why you cut yourself?" Asharre kept her voice calm, her movements slow. The man's condition repulsed and frightened her, but she had a duty to end this. She took another step toward him.

"I cut the traitor flesh. The . . . the hand that touched blackfire stone, the tongue that tasted it. The eye that saw it and wanted more. I wanted it so badly." His skinny shoulders jerked with another sob. "I couldn't stop the wanting . . . so I mortified the sin. To punish myself. To show *him*. I wouldn't give in. I wouldn't succumb. After all his tricks, all his traps . . . no more."

Another moment, and she would be in striking distance. She needed him distracted just a little longer. "Why did you do it?"

"Because I believed it was possible to separate the gods' power from their purpose." A laugh caught, choking, in his throat. "I *believed* that. Such . . . such a fool. Such a greedy fool."

She was close enough that Aurandane's blue light fell across Corban. He recoiled from it, but not quickly enough to avoid a swift blaze of magic across the darkness that engulfed him. Some of the cloudiness seemed to leave him; something like sanity crept back in. Corban looked to his missing hand—the hand that was made up of shadows woven around dead white bone—and his features contorted in sudden loathing. He jerked his wrist upward, flapping it from side to side as if he could shake away the corruption like water from his skin.

He threw back his head and howled through his torn lips, a sound of raw and absolute anguish that made Asharre flinch back. Not for long, though; she recovered swiftly and closed the remaining distance.

Corban didn't seem to care. He got to his feet, panting with the effort, and hurled the loaded crossbow away. The weapon flew past Asharre and clattered on the far side of the pier, near the tunnel that led back to the smuggler's den.

"I can't hold off the whispers for long," Corban wheezed. He pressed the heel of his good hand to his chin, digging the fingers into his flesh. The hand climbed up his face like a giant, spasming spider, dimpling his cheeks and brow. He stared at her wildly through the gaps between his fingers. "I have tried everything to keep them at bay. *Everything*. I cannot do it. He will not let me go. The men you killed, the dogs . . . they were not my guards. They were my jailors. *He* keeps me here. Captive. Isolated. He wants to pry the knowledge out of my skull—to make me finish my original plan, to make me sell madness and death to fools. Pain didn't break me, so he gave me awareness instead . . . let me remember, let me dwell on all the evils I've done. And when I can bear it no longer, when the weight of the guilt destroys me, I will beg him for oblivion . . . and he will have my mind. It will happen. He will win. Save me, lady. *Stop* me. You have a sword. Use it. *Use it*."

"Gladly," Asharre said, and thrust Aurandane into Corban's heart.

He died quietly. She had expected something more—a crack of thunder, a flash of sunfire, *something*—but there was none of that. Corban made a little grunt and doubled over onto the blade, clutching it like salvation. A muted blue glow shone from the hollow of his body where the sword went in; the darkness that permeated his flesh swirled like a windspout as it was drawn into the light and destroyed. In moments it was gone.

Asharre stepped away, withdrawing her sword. She nudged the corpse with a boot. It shifted limply, well and truly dead. Barely a third of Corban's original body remained on his bones.

She turned back to the tunnel, lowering the Celestian blade, and froze before taking a step.

"Drop your sword," Malentir said. The slack-mouthed corpse stood next to him, Corban's crossbow in its hands. The Thorn's puppet held the weapon perfectly steady, its deadly quarrel leveled at her.

She curled her lip, refusing to show her fear. "I knew you were a traitor."

"A traitor would have to be a member of your faith, no? I've never made any pretense of that. Now drop the sword, please, lest I be forced to kill you."

She thought of other dead men with other crossbows. Other Maolites used to keep blood off Malentir's hands, so he could claim without lying that he had not murdered his companions. "As you killed Kelland?"

"He won't die. I need him alive. You, however, I do *not* need, and as you still cling to your weapon . . ." He shrugged, and the corpse's hands twitched.

The quarrel took her just below the left breast. There was a punch of pain as it sank in, but that was immediately swallowed by stranger and more frightening sensations.

Her flesh was melting and re-forming around the quarrel, losing whatever made her human and becoming something else, something alien and malign. Bubbles formed just below her skin, bulging and deflating it violently as they rose and popped. Feverish heat spread from her wound, yet her own blood was cold on her hands. The black grit that flecked it was burning hot, just as it had been in Kelland's wounds.

It all happened in an eyeblink, maybe two . . . and the horror of it, Asharre realized with a sudden snap of panic, was meant to distract her from the horror that would come. She dropped Aurandane and grabbed desperately at the quarrel, fumbling to pull it out before its blackfire stone exploded.

The quarrel's ungainly design saved her. The blackfire bolt hadn't dug in deeply. On the second tug it came loose. She tossed it onto the pier, where it bounced once and rolled off the planks, tumbling into the sea. A muted thunderclap sounded from the black depths, shaking the pier on its pilings . . . and Asharre fell to her knees, gasping in agony.

She was alive, but the poison was still in her. Hot tears ran down her cheeks. Clenching her teeth against terror and spasming pain, Asharre reached for the fallen sword.

Malentir stepped in front of her, nudging her hand away with his boot. Unhurriedly he stooped and picked up the Sword of the Dawn himself. "I will take that, thank you."

"Why?" Asharre croaked. Aurandane blazed into life as soon as the Thorn lifted it, and the sword's blue-dawn glow made her eyes water anew. She raised a hand feebly to block it from her sight. "Why do you need the sword?"

He paused, tilting his head at her, and then shrugged and turned away. "I owe you no answers."

Asharre grunted, hunching her back in a half-feigned shudder. Her pain was real—but it was rapidly subsiding into the familiar pain of an ordinary wound. Whether Malentir willed it or no, the Sword of the Dawn was burning out the venom in her veins, just as it had freed Corban from his bonds of madness and slain the corrupted dogs. *The gods' power cannot be separated from their purpose.* That truth had doomed Corban, but it might save her.

The shadows that surrounded Malentir were weakening in the sword's light as well. They fluttered wildly around him, trapped and burning. The sight gave her hope, and desperation gave her strength. If he realized his spell was failing, or saw that she was feigning her weakness, or decided to kill her cleanly rather than prolonging her misery for his own magic . . .

She lunged forward, throwing herself against Malentir's ankles. Against any half-decent swordsman it would have been suicide, but the Thorn was no better trained than the Illuminers had been, and she took him unawares. He tumbled onto the pier, stripped of his grace for once, and Aurandane skittered across the boards.

Malentir scrabbled after the sword, trying to seize the weapon and get back to his feet at the same time. Asharre gave him no chance to do either. She punched him, again and again, swinging anything she could reach. The tattered remnants of his shadowshield stopped her first strikes, but they grew thinner with each blow, and soon her fists thudded into unresisting cloth and flesh. The exertion tore her own wound wider, but Asharre ignored its sting.

Finally she sat back on her heels, breathing hard. The Thorn lay crumpled on the planks, his own breaths a weak echo of hers.

She stepped over him, collecting the sword. Warmth flowed into her, restoring her strength and sealing the gash in her chest. Malentir lifted his head, looking at her with bruised, exhausted eyes.

"Vengeance?" he asked.

"Justice," she said.

"Justice." He laughed, weakly and without mirth. "For whom? Not the Celestians. They will not thank you for this."

"No." She had nothing to gain by telling him, not really . . . but she wanted him to know the truth before he died. "For my sister. Oralia. You killed her at Sennos Mill."

"I had no part in it. I was in the tower, did you forget?"

"Your *kind* killed her."

"She killed herself."

Asharre pressed Aurandane's point to the soft skin of his throat, drawing a bead of blood. "What do you know of it?"

"What we all know." He did not seem discomfited by the steel at his neck; he closed his eyes and leaned into its cold, cutting kiss. "We wanted her alive, as we wanted the Burnt Knight alive. He chose to aid us. Your sister chose otherwise."

"Why?"

"For Duradh Mal. Why else? The evil that holds it is ancient, and rooted very deep . . . and beyond our power to burn out. We needed one of Celestia's chosen. More than one, perhaps." He inhaled again, shuddering at the effort. A slow red line seeped from his throat where it pressed against the sword's edge. "If some misfortune befalls the Burnt Knight in Duradh Mal—and that is very likely; it is a cursed place, and he is too brave for his own good—we will take another of the Bright Lady's Blessed. And another, when that one fails. We will steal them and burn them like candles, and when one is exhausted or ends herself as your sister did, we will discard her and find another to light the halls of Ang'duradh. But *you* have a piece of the sun. Give us that, and we will have no further need of Celestia's mortal candles."

Lies, Asharre thought, but she remembered Kelland's words too well to believe that.

They've been trying to capture a Blessed for a while. For Duradh Mal, I think. If I help them, I will be the last.

She looked at the blue-flamed steel in her hand. Weighed it, and thought of the horror that twisted Bitharn's face when she saw the Burnt Knight gasping near death, of her own blind grief when the headman of Sennos Mill told her of Oralia's end. She thought of the novice Sun Knights in the Dome's practice halls—so few, so young, so determined to stand against all the world's evils—and wondered how many of them might die in the cursed depths of Duradh Mal, and how many more might be scarred by those deaths.

Was it surrendering to give up the sword?

Yes, Asharre decided, but that was not all it was.

Let them take the poisoned bait. Let them have Carden Vale with its madness and its ghosts. *They use us*, Kelland had said. *Why can't we use them?*

Bring them back to me, the High Solaros had told her.

She withdrew the sword from the Thorn's neck.

Quickly, before Malentir could try some new treachery, Asharre stepped on each of his outflung hands, crushing the fingers underfoot. She would have cut his hands off, but she did not know if the sword could heal that. He made a small, hissing cry, recoiling violently, but she kicked him back down.

"Swear to me that if I give you Aurandane, you will not take the Burnt Knight into Duradh Mal and you will not capture any other of Celestia's faithful to use as your pawns," she said. "Swear it on behalf of all Ang'arta."

Malentir licked his blood-flecked lips. His eyes shone black as onyx in the sword's unearthly light. Asharre watched him closely, ready to slit the Thorn's throat at the first sign of betrayal, but the man only nodded, his mouth drawn tight with pain. "Very well. I will swear to it. Give us Aurandane, and we will release the Burnt Knight from his oath to purify Ang'duradh. We will take no more of the Bright Lady's servants, Blessed or not."

"Good." She struck each of his ankles hard with the flat of her sword, kicking his feet sideways at the same time.

Again the Thorn screamed; again Asharre ignored him. He'd need the pain to walk the shadows back to Ang'arta, and *she* needed the time to make good her escape. She was no Celestian, and his oath did nothing to protect her.

She thrust Aurandane between the slats of the crates at the other end of the pier. Inky smoke poured from the boxes of blackfire stone as the sword's magic began to consume them.

Asharre did not wait to see the end of it. She strode away, past the writhing Thorn and into the narrow tunnel that led back up to Cailan, and from there to the sweetness of the open sky.

EPILOGUE

"Have you seen Asharre?" Heradion asked.

Bitharn looked up from her book, resting a finger on the pages to mark her place. With her other hand she shaded her eyes against the late morning light.

She sat on a sun-warmed bench in the temple gardens. Lacy flowers sighed on the trees around her, shedding petals across the bench and surrounding paths. Heradion's cloak wore a dusting of white and yellow petals too; he'd been walking through the gardens for a while.

He looked , healthy. A little thinner, a little tired, but whole and well. Bitharn smiled. "When did you get back?"

"Yesterday. As soon as I arrived they hauled me up to the High Solaros and then it was questions, questions, questions all night long. Being interrogated by that man is more terrifying than anything I saw in Carden Vale. They finally let me go around midnight, but I was too exhausted to do anything but collapse. I thought a walk around the gardens this morning would help me recover, and so it has. Anyway, have you seen Asharre?"

"She went by a while ago," Bitharn said, pointing to the path that led to the herb gardens. "Walking her little yellow brindle. Why?"

"Oh, I was just hoping to tell her about all the blood-curdling adventures I had on my way back from Carden Vale."

Bitharn raised her eyebrows, using polite disbelief to conceal a little tingle of alarm. Had one of the monsters of Carden Vale escaped? "That dramatic, were they?"

"No." He stretched his arms over his head, grinning broadly. "No, they were not. In fact, I didn't have a single one. No bandits, no *maelgloth*, not so much as a thieving raccoon in my camp. The worst part was being forced to eat my own cooking on the road, and past Balnamoine, I didn't even have *that* bit of misery anymore. It was . . ." He lowered his arms. The grin subsided into a vastly contented smile. ". . . boring. Gloriously boring."

"Gloriously?"

"Indeed." Heradion paused. "Did you say Asharre was with a dog? I thought pets were forbidden in the temple."

"They are. Generally. But when the groundskeepers tried to tell Asharre that, she said if the High Solaros wanted her to train his puppies, he was going to have to tolerate hers. No one's said a word against it since."

"Wise of them. *I* wouldn't want to cross her over a dog."

"Especially not that dog," Bitharn murmured.

Heradion gave her a questioning look, but when she didn't immediately elaborate, he shrugged and turned toward the path she had indicated. "Well, I'll try to catch her. If you see her before I do, tell Asharre I'm looking for her.

I'd like to thank her for keeping me alive long enough to get so wonderfully bored on the way home."

"I will," Bitharn said, amused.

"And thank you, too. For keeping *her* alive."

She glanced up, smiled, and returned to her book.

Hours passed in welcome stillness. Clean air, warm sun, the sweetness of spring flowers . . . it was a world apart from the bleakness of Duradh Mal, and its verdant lushness banished the shadows from her soul. Bitharn had spent most of her days in the temple gardens since finishing their work with Corban, luxuriating in the sunny calm.

She hadn't seen much of Kelland in recent days. He seemed preoccupied, sometimes secretive; she wondered about that, and worried, but had decided not to press him on it. They had each endured their troubles over the past winter, and she hadn't felt much inclination to talk about hers, either.

All wounds healed in time. Maybe his just needed a little more.

She could hardly fault him for that. Bitharn still remembered the retreat from Corban's den vividly: the limp weight of the knight dragging at her side, the storm pounding her head and heels as she raced death back to the temple. The Illuminers had kept Kelland in the healing rooms for weeks after her return. It was a miracle that he'd lived, they said, and a greater one that he'd sustained no lasting damage.

At least she had the consolation that he'd be spared any further strain in Duradh Mal. Neither she nor Kelland had seen Malentir since leaving him with Asharre that awful night. The *sigrir* had returned, with that skinny yellow dog and without the Sword of the Dawn, but the Thorn had not.

Asharre never said what she had done there, but Bitharn

knew. She read the answer in the High Solaros' silence over Aurandane's loss and Malentir's failure to return. Either Asharre had killed the Thornlord, or she had given him the Sword of the Dawn. Whichever it was, it had ended any chance of alliance.

And Bitharn was relieved. She had no desire to see the Thorn again; she dreaded the prospect of walking back into Duradh Mal. The memories unnerved her as much as the danger did. Guilt, terror, grief . . . there was no escaping those ghosts in the mountains. Not for her. If the blight of Ang'duradh could be cured without her, and without Kelland, she was all too happy to stand aside.

Bitharn closed her book, brushed stray flower petals from her clothes, and started back toward the Dome. After a few steps she stopped. A quiet thrill of nervousness went through her; her palms went damp at her sides. Kelland was approaching.

He had something small in his hands. A box. It was flat and rectangular, made of some reddish wood polished to a satin sheen. A goldsmith's mark was incised on its top. She didn't recognize the house; it wasn't the one that made most of the temple's sun medallions.

The expression on his face startled her. He looked frightened but determined, as he often did before marching into battle. His back was stiff, his shoulders squared; he cradled the box so gingerly that she wondered if it held live coals.

"Oh, did you buy me a ring?" Bitharn asked. She meant it as a joke, hoping to lighten his tension, but Kelland started as if she'd dropped an icicle down his back.

"I can't give you a ring," he said gravely. "I want to, and I will, but . . . not yet. That must wait until I'm ready to step down from the order. Until then . . . I'd like you to wear this." He offered her the box.

Feeling oddly hesitant, she folded her hands behind her back. "What is it?"

"Open it." The trepidation was still in him, but his lips twitched too, as if he wanted to smile and didn't quite dare. "It's not a snake, I promise."

"I was thinking hot coals," she said, lifting the box's lid.

Gold twinkled on a bed of velvet inside. Two sun medallions nestled next to one another, separated by thin golden pins that affixed them to the velvet. They were similar to the one Bitharn wore, but more finely wrought, and each of them had a chip of diamond throwing fire at its heart.

She looked from the jewelry to Kelland, astonished. "What is this?"

"A gift," he said, pressing his hands over hers on the box. They trembled, although he no longer seemed afraid. "I read about it when I was researching Bysshelios . . . and the history of my oath. In Pelos, near the end of the Ardasi Flowering, it was the custom for newly married couples to exchange sun signs at weddings. They gave each other medallions that were made of gold, as ours are today, but were also set with a diamond to symbolize their love: a part of this mortal earth, but a beautiful one—and a prism through which the full splendor of the light could be seen."

"It's lovely," Bitharn breathed.

Kelland exhaled, relaxing visibly at her approval. He unpinned one of the medallions and held its glimmering chain over her head. "Will you wear it?"

"Yes." She tilted her face up, mirroring his smile. Happiness swelled in her. As he settled the delicate chain carefully around her neck, Bitharn leaned forward, surprising him with a kiss. "Yes, I will."

ACKNOWLEDGMENTS

This was a hard book to write. I have quite a few people to thank for the fact that it ever got done, rather than ending unceremoniously as a never-finished manuscript buried in an unmarked . . . um . . . trunk. I owe debts of gratitude to:

Jennifer Heddle and Marlene Stringer, for their encouragement, clear-eyed honesty, and (especially!) willingness to crack the whip when this thing got mired too long in the bogs of despair.

Victoria Mathews, who saved me from at least seven face-plants in print.

Dan Andress, Nathan Andress, Ian Hardy, David Montgomery, and Cliff Moore: the valiant team of early readers, who generously gave of their time and brainspace to read half-finished drafts on short notice and comment thoughtfully on same.

Hugh Burns, for being extraordinarily understanding when deadlines crashed into deadlines.

Peter, for being calm, patient, and quick to distract me with zombie cowboys on flaming horses when mere rationality wasn't going to do the trick.

And my dog, Pongu.